Praise for

P.C. CAST

**Multiple *New York Times* bestselling author
of the House of Night series!**

"A mythic world of humor and verve."
—*Publishers Weekly* on *Goddess by Mistake*

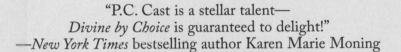

"P.C. Cast is a stellar talent—
Divine by Choice is guaranteed to delight!"
—*New York Times* bestselling author Karen Marie Moning

"P.C. Cast has created a wonderful and rich mythology
for *Elphame's Choice*."
—*SF Site*

"[A] true master of her craft."
—*New York Times* bestselling author Gena Showalter

P.C. CAST

Elphame's
Choice

**HARLEQUIN®
TEEN**

HARLEQUIN®
TEEN

ISBN-13: 978-0-373-21015-2

First edition December 2004

ELPHAME'S CHOICE

Recycling programs for this product may not exist in your area.

www.HarlequinTEEN.com

Printed in U.S.A.

To my amazing daughter, Kristin Frances,
the perfect blending of two and the inspiration for Elphame.

ACKNOWLEDGMENTS

As always, I thank my agent and friend,
Meredith Bernstein. In this particular case
you deserve The Big Thank You!

I am so appreciative of my editor, Mary-Theresa Hussey.
Thank you, M-T, for keeping me on track
during the complex task of world building.

Thank you to my father, Dick Cast, for his
invaluable information about wolves (it's turned out
to be a good thing that you're a member of a pack!)
and about flora and fauna in general.

I appreciate my sister-in-law, Carol Cast, RN, BSN,
for detailed info pertaining to horrid wounds and dead bodies.
Any bodily fluid errors are mine and mine alone.

And I would like to express a soul-felt thank-you to
my fabulous fans who fell in love with Partholon years ago
and kept/keep asking for more and more and more....
I truly appreciate you all so very much!

PARTHOLON

Symbol	Legend
Bridge	Bridge
Castle	Castle
Conifera	Conifera
Escape Route	Escape Route
Forest	Forest
Invasion Route	Invasion Route
Marsh	Marsh
Rivers & Sea	Rivers & Sea
Temple	Temple
Village	Village

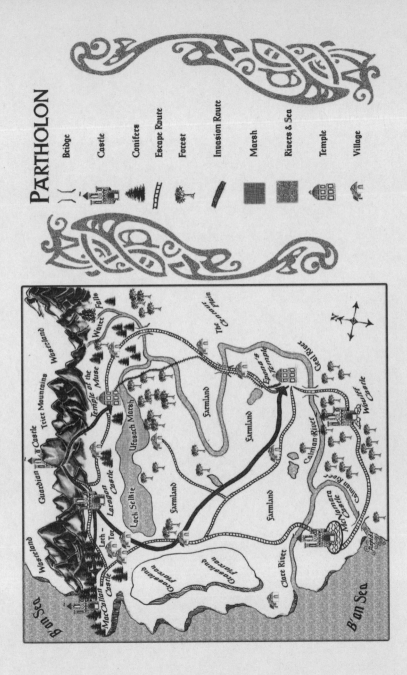

Prologue

THAT DAY HAD started with deceptive normalcy.

The dawn offering to Epona had been particularly moving. The Goddess had filled Etain so completely that afterward she carried the glow of Her presence throughout the morning, and for once she was allowed some time alone—temporarily freed from the duties of Goddess Incarnate.

The contractions began as a vague sense of unease. She couldn't find a comfortable place on her well-cushioned chaise longue. She snapped with uncharacteristic impatience at the enthusiastic servant who checked to make sure her mistress didn't need a refill of hot water. Not even the thought of a long soak in the mineral springs bathing pool seemed appealing.

Etain hoped a stroll through her magnificent flower garden would ease what she thought was just a little difficulty digesting the strawberries from lunch. The walk appeared to be helping—until she paused to sniff a brilliant crimson blossom and her water broke violently all over the Goddess Incarnate's silk-lined slippers.

Normalcy had also been broken.

"Isn't that always the way of it?" She grimaced and clenched her teeth as another wave of pain blanketed her body. Bending at the waist she leaned heavily against the woman whose arm was linked through her own.

"Sssh, Etain." Fiona spoke soothingly in her light, melodic brogue. "Donna speak, my friend. Just concentrate on your breathing."

Etain jerked her head in a sharp imitation of nodding agreement and tried to match her panting gasps to Fiona's calm, deep breaths. The contraction peaked and receded.

A flurry of activity ensued. The Goddess Incarnate's clothes were changed by her bevy of attendants, who then began notifying the Wise Women who lived in the villages closest to Epona's Temple. Wrapping her arm around Fiona's waist, and using her sturdy presence from which to draw strength, Etain continued her stroll through the temple gardens. The Chosen One's friend and advisor had assured her that walking would aid in the child's birth.

As the day crawled methodically past, the image of Etain's oasis of tranquility dissipated, but the residue of Epona's morning possession calmed her—as always, Epona's Chosen drew upon the familiar thread that bound her to the Goddess and found strength and comfort.

Fiona smiled encouragement and the two women turned around, heading back toward the floor-to-ceiling windows that led from Etain's bedchamber to her private garden. Gauzy curtains the color of liquid gold fluttered from within the open leaded-glass panes that served as door and windows. The Goddess Incarnate breathed deeply, trying to steady the racing

of her heart and ready herself for the inevitable next contraction.

"I think that really is the worst part." As always, she spoke
her mind aloud to Fiona.

"What?" She looked thoughtfully at her friend and mistress.

"The inevitability of what's happening. I can't stop it. I can't
pause it. I can't really affect it at all. The truth is that I'd like
to say, 'This has been interesting, but I'm ready for it to cease
now. I want to bathe, eat a lovely meal and get a good night's
rest. We'll just begin from here tomorrow, shall we?'" Fiona's
expression of polite curiosity changed to bubbling laughter.

"That would be nice."

"Nice?" She grimaced in a very ungoddess-like manner. "It
would be wonderful."

Etain took another deep breath, appreciating the intoxicating
sweetness of the voraciously blooming lilacs that framed that part
of the walk. The path curved to the left and the lilacs gave way
to a profusion of violet-colored roses, which were in full bloom.
The delicate drapes billowed from the entryway, and fluttered
like the wings of giant butterflies over the tips of the roses. They
paused a few feet from the bedchamber that had housed Partholon's Beloved of Epona for countless generations. The breeze
carried the enchanting sound of women singing praises.

"We are the flow of water
The ebb and tide
The rush of knowing
All truth inside"

The words were woven together in a harmony of pitch; the
underlying beat was hypnotic. It beckoned to Epona's Chosen
and soothed her frayed nerves. Slowly, her swollen body relaxed
as she was filled with the women's greeting song.

"We are the sound of growing
A Goddess root
Stretched strong and knowing
An endless shoot"

The words propelled Etain forward so that she eagerly entered her bedchamber. The Wise Women filled the room. At the Goddess Incarnate's appearance, the tempo of the song increased. Spinning gracefully they seemed to float around the room until Etain and Fiona formed the center of their joyous circle.

"We are the soul of woman
A wondrous gift
Both rich and knowing
In praise we lift!"

With the word *lift* the women raised their arms to the domed ceiling and spun, humming the melody together. The silky clothing they wore drifted around their bodies like falling leaves, framing them in shimmering rays of changing light. All of the women were smiling, as if they were taking part in an event filled with such wonder that it was impossible to contain within them, and the happiness came spilling out of their bodies. As Fiona helped her mistress settle back into the cushions of the chaise longue they could clearly see formless glitter outlining each dancer like spiritual halos.

"Magic," Etain whispered.

"Of course," Fiona responded in her no-nonsense tone. "Would ye expect less at the birth of a goddess?"

"Of course not." But the truth was that although Etain had been Epona's Chosen for almost a decade, she still found it easy to be awed by the power of her Goddess.

The song ended and the dancers stepped gracefully out of

their circle. Some of them approached Etain, each with a smile and a kind word.

"Epona has richly blessed you, Chosen One."

"This is a great day for the Goddess, Epona's Beloved."

Seen separately they lost a little of their magic and once more became what they were—simple human women who were there to support and encourage the birth of a much-awaited child. They ranged in age and beauty, but they were of a single mind.

The next contraction started high on Etain's abdomen. She felt herself tense. The pain peaked. The contraction caught her, trembling through her body. It was a wave in which she was drowning.

A young woman cradled Etain's shoulders with her hands. "Do not fight it, Goddess." Her voice whispered softly into the laboring woman's ear. "It is not a battle to be won. Think of it instead as the wind."

Another woman's voice spoke earnestly when she paused. "Let it fill you, Chosen One."

Yet another woman added, "Yes, fly with it, my Lady."

"And breathe with me, Etain." Fiona's reassuring face swam back into view. The Goddess Incarnate struggled to slow her breathing as she was swept into the vortex of the contraction.

After a series of endless moments the pain flowed temporarily away. A cool, damp cloth wiped the sweat from Etain's forehead. Fiona held a goblet of clear, icy water to her friend's parched lips.

"Let me check the progress, my Lady."

Etain opened her eyes to peer up into the calm aquamarine gaze of the Healer. She was a stoutly built, middle-aged blonde who carried with her the unmistakably confident air of a woman who knew her job intimately and performed it well. The Chosen One nodded and obediently raised her knees. She was wearing only a cream-colored cotton chemise so fine it felt like it had been spun from clouds. The Healer pushed it up around Etain's nonexistent waist. Her touch was gentle and thorough.

"It goes well, Beloved of the Goddess." She smiled encouragingly and patted her thigh before rearranging Etain's clothing.

"How much longer?" she asked wearily.

The Healer met the Goddess Incarnate's gaze, understanding her impatience. "Only the Goddess can tell you that for sure, my Lady, but I do not think it will be too much longer before you will greet your daughter."

Etain smiled and nodded at her before the Healer faded back into the group of women, whom she ordered about with a voice made of velvet steel. Fiona bent to stroke an escaping curl from her friend's damp face.

"He's not going to be here in time, is he?" Etain couldn't stop the tremor in her voice.

"Of course he will," Fiona said firmly.

"I should have never insisted he go. What was I thinking?"

Fiona tried unsuccessfully to stifle her laughter as she answered. "Let me see…. Ah, yes! I think I remember what you said. Something about if he didn't get out from under your feet and stop asking how you were feeling every moment you were going to flay the skin from him." She mimicked Etain's tone so exactly that it made several of the nearby women laugh.

"I'm a fool," Etain moaned. "Only a fool would send her husband away when she is so pregnant she could give birth at any moment."

"My friend." Fiona sat next to Etain and squeezed her hand. "Midhir will be here in time for the birth of his daughter. You know Moira will find him."

And she did. At least the Goddess Incarnate's mind told her that of course Moira, the Lead Huntress of Partholon, would be able to track and find her husband, whom she had shooed away yesterday in the company of several of his comrades for an all-night (and, she cringed as she remembered the crisp annoyance in her voice when she had told him to make it all day, too) hunting trip. But her heart and her laboring body said that this baby was coming soon. With or without her father's presence.

"I need him here, Fiona." Tears made her vision shimmer.

Before Fiona could reply another contraction began to build, and she tightened her grip on the other woman's hand.

"Oh! This one is bad." Etain gasped, feeling a little nauseous and panicky.

And then the Chosen One was blanketed with the cool, soothing voices of women as they hummed the melody of the birthing song. In harmony with the rhythm, several of them spoke joyously, one at a time.

"We are with you, my Lady."

"You are doing well!"

"Breathe with Fiona, Chosen One."

"Relax, Goddess. Remember each pain brings your daughter closer to this world."

"We cannot wait to greet her, my Lady!"

Their voices became Etain's rocks and she used them to anchor her concentration as she again matched her breathing with Fiona's calm breaths. She slid down the bottom side of the contraction and managed to smile her appreciation to the surrounding women.

The women laughed with a sweet sound that was infectious. Etain rested one hand on her taut stomach as a giggle slipped from her lips and she closed her eyes, willing her body to relax and rest.

Oh, please, please let him arrive in time.

Patience, Beloved. The voice tickled within Etain's mind. Her lips curved upward at the gentle admonishment. *The shaman will not miss the birth of his daughter.*

"Thank you, Epona," she whispered. Reassured by her Goddess's promise she felt a new surge of energy. "Fiona! Let us walk again."

"Are you quite sure, Etain?" Fiona's brow wrinkled in worry.

"You said walking would make the child come more quickly." Etain held out her hands and Fiona helped pull her awkwardly up from the chaise. "And quickly sounds wonderful to me at this moment." She winked and the concern in Fiona's face lightened. The Chosen One tossed her head and smiled at the attending group of women. "Ladies, please sing for me while I hurry my daughter's arrival."

The women clapped their hands happily. Some of them broke into a little celebratory dance that caused magic to sparkle in their wake. Linking her arm through Fiona's, the two women walked slowly through the diaphanous curtains.

Etain inhaled deeply. "This is something I *will* miss about being pregnant." Fiona looked at her quizzically. "My incredible sense of smell. All through this pregnancy my sense of smell has been amazingly acute." She lumbered to the nearest rosebush and gently passed a finger over the velvety petals before continuing down the path.

"Yes, this is amaz—" The word ended in a grunt as the next contraction took her by surprise.

"Slowly, remember not to fight it, Etain." Fiona spoke softly in her ear as her friend leaned heavily against her. "Should we go back to the other women?" she asked.

Etain shook her head and panted. "No. I feel like I can breathe better out here." The contraction subsided and she straightened slowly, wiping the sweat from her face with her sleeve. "And I like how their song sounds on the breeze—like the whole world is filled with the magic of this baby's birth."

Fiona's eyes sparkled suddenly with tears and she hugged Etain. "It is, my Lady, it is!"

The Chosen of the Goddess cleared her mind of pain by focusing on her blessings as they continued their halting trek through the garden. The nation of Partholon honored many gods and goddesses, but Epona would always hold a special place in her peoples' hearts.

Epona breathes life to the morning sky, and Epona's face is reflected in the fullness of the moon. She is Warrior Goddess of the Horse, as well as Benefactress of the Fruits of the Harvest. And Partholon would always revere her as their protectress. It was Epona's Chosen, along with her shaman lifemate, who repelled the invasion of demonic Fomorians and saved Partholon from enslavement. That it had been almost one hundred years since the Fomorian war mattered little in the minds and hearts of the Partholonians. Epona's largess would never be forgotten, and her Beloved would always be honored.

She was Beloved of the Goddess, Epona's Chosen One, Etain reminded herself as she panted through another contraction. And that meant that her firstborn would be a daughter, and that she, too, would be touched by the Goddess. She would be the granddaughter of the legendary Fomorian-slaying Rhiannon. The thought that her child would probably be destined to follow her as Epona's Chosen was exciting, and it made the tedium of labor somewhat easier to bear.

The wave of the next contraction scattered Etain's thoughts, and she quickly understood that it was different than the others. It was accompanied by a deep burning sensation and a need to push that was so overwhelming it made her gasp. Her knees buckled and Fiona struggled to help her gently to the ground.

"I have to push," she panted.

"Wait!" Fiona said sharply, then yelled over her shoulder in the direction of her bedchamber. "Women! Come to me! The Goddess needs you!"

Etain couldn't tell if anyone had heard her because her entire being was focused within. The urge to push was raw and primal, and it took all the strength of the fear for her daughter's life to struggle against it.

Then a sound pierced through The Chosen's concentration, and her soul leaped with joy as she recognized it. It was the sound of hooves beating against the firm ground of the path. Etain blinked the sweat out of her eyes as the centaur burst around a curve in the path and slid to his knees before her.

"Here, love. All will be well now. Put your arms around my shoulders." Her husband's deep voice seemed to chase away the pain as the contraction eased and then dissipated completely.

Wordlessly she wrapped her arms around his granite-like shoulders and let her head fall against him as he effortlessly lifted her. In a few long strides the bedchamber was in view. Seconds later he was laying his wife gently on the chaise longue. She clutched him, but needn't have worried. He had no intention of releasing her.

"I am so glad you are here," she said slowly, still trying to catch her breath.

"I belong nowhere but here." He smiled and brushed a limp curl away from his wife's sweaty face.

"I was afraid you wouldn't make it. I didn't think Moira would find you in time."

"She didn't," he said with a cryptic shrug of his shoulders. "Your Goddess did." And he kissed her softly.

Oh, Epona, thank you for bringing him to me in time—and thank you for fashioning him to be my lifemate. Through eyes filled with tears she watched her handsome centaur husband fuss with the pillows on which she was propped. Even after five years of marriage, the strength and virility of his centaur form still thrilled her. Of course, as High Shaman he had the ability to shape-shift so that they could truly mate, but she loved him completely, and reveled in the fact that her Goddess had crafted such a wondrous being to be her lifemate.

Before she could tell him once again how much she loved him, Etain felt the stirrings of the next contraction. Her moan summoned the Healer.

"My Lord, help us get her into the birthing position." She gave deft orders and Midhir's strong arms once again lifted his wife. This time he stood behind her with his hands linked under her arms and her back pressed firmly against him as he easily supported her weight. Fiona stood on Etain's right, holding her hand, and another woman took her left hand. The Goddess Incarnate looked down at the Healer who was crouched between her legs and was vaguely surprised to realize that somehow she had become naked. The Healer's fingers gently probed.

"You are fully ready. You must push with the next contraction."

And it enveloped her. Etain became nothing but a push. Brilliant colors exploded against her tightly closed lids. She saw splashes of gold and red and heard a guttural, inhuman sound, and with a strangely detached thought she realized it must be her own voice making that animal-like noise. For a moment she couldn't breathe.

Then a wordless humming registered through the fog of bearing down. Etain could not see the women, but she felt them. Their birthing song filled her and she was able to breathe again.

"Once more, Goddess. I see your daughter's head!" the Healer encouraged.

She heard Midhir's whispered litany of prayer. The words

from his old language, which always sounded so magical to his wife, seemed to mirror the rhythm of the birthing song just as the contraction took control of her.

Again Etain became nothing but a push. She was being torn in half. Struggling against panic and fear, her mind reached out to tap into the power that surrounded her. She let the enchantment of the birthing circle fill her, and focused on pushing with the combined power of will and magic. With a liquid feeling of release the warm wetness that was her daughter slid from her body.

Then time seemed to speed up and things happened very quickly. Etain struggled to catch a glimpse of her daughter, but was only able to see disjointed images of the Healer bundling the wet form against the folds of her robe. The old woman's hands shook as she cut the cord.

Silence.

Etain's knees buckled, and Midhir and Fiona supported her back to the chaise.

"Why isn't she crying?" Etain gasped.

Midhir's eyes narrowed in concern and he turned quickly back to the Healer who was still huddled on the floor over the small bundle.

Then the sweet, strong cry of a newborn pierced the air and Etain felt her fear thaw. But it was only a momentary reprieve because almost instantly she registered the look of shock that had immobilized the Healer's pale face.

The women who surrounded them had noticed, too, because their joyous song of welcome had fallen suddenly still.

"Midhir?" She sobbed his name as a question.

The centaur moved with inhuman speed to stand over the bundle that was his lustily crying daughter. The Healer looked up at him, confusion and dismay glazing her eyes. Swiftly Midhir dropped to his knees and reached out to unwrap the covering that concealed his child. And he froze.

His body was shielding the view of the baby from Etain and she fought against exhaustion to sit up so that she could see what was happening.

"What is it?" she cried, her stomach clenching with much more than the pains of afterbirth.

At her words a quiver ran through Midhir's muscular body, then he reached forward and scooped the baby from the floor. In one motion he turned to his wife, his eyes alight with joy.

"It is our daughter, my love." His voice was thick with emotion. "And she is a wee goddess!"

With those words he strode to Etain and gently handed her the now silent, but still kicking bundle. The Chosen of Epona gazed for the first time at her daughter.

Etain's immediate thought wasn't shock or surprise, but simply that she had never seen anything as exquisitely beautiful. She was perfect. Even though birth fluids still covered her, the infant's head was feathered with dark wisps of amber-colored hair. Her skin was a lovely creamy brown, a shade somewhere between bronze and gold. She looked exactly as if someone had poured her skin and Midhir's skin together, was the abstract thought that drifted through Etain's mind, which was hazy with wonder. Her gilded skin shaded down to her waist, where her body suddenly became covered with a fine coat of hair, the same color as the hair on her head, but in which speckles were already appearing in drying patches, as if it was the coat of a newborn fawn. She squirmed and kicked her two legs that tapered gracefully down to form two tiny hooves, which still glistened damply. Then she opened her perfect little mouth and let out an indignant cry.

"Sssh, my precious one," Etain cooed, kissing her face and marveling at the amazing softness of her skin. Love for her daughter poured into her, filling Etain more completely than she had ever believed possible. "I am here and all is well." At the sound of her mother's voice, the infant's incredibly dark eyes seemed to widen and her cries instantly quieted.

"Elphame." Midhir's deep voice was choked with emotion. He knelt beside them. One of his arms went around his wife so that she could rest securely against him, and his other hand reached down to touch his daughter's body. "Elphame," he repeated. His deep, wonderful voice added magic to the word, like he had just ushered the Queen of the Fairies into their midst. The name seemed to hang suspended in the air around them.

Etain gazed at him through her tears. The name was vaguely familiar, like she had heard it spoken in a dream. "Elphame… What does it mean?"

His warm lips first brushed his wife's forehead and then his daughter's forehead before he answered. "It is the shamans' ancient name for the Goddess as a maiden. It is She who is most exquisite, filled with the magic of youth and the wonder of life beginning anew."

"Elphame," she murmured as she guided her daughter's hungry mouth to her aching breast. "My precious one."

Yes, Beloved. The Goddess's voice drifted through her Chosen's mind. *The Shaman has named her truly. She shall be called Elphame—announce to Partholon the name of your newborn, who is also Beloved of Epona.*

Etain smiled brilliantly and raised her head. In a voice magnified by the power of Epona her words joyously split the air.

"Rejoice, Partholon! We have been given a gift worthy of a goddess in the birth of my child." Her gaze shifted from the staring women who still silently surrounded them to her husband, whose face was wet with tears. "Her name is Elphame. She is truly a wee goddess, most beautiful and exquisite!"

At the Goddess Incarnate's announcement there was a

stirring in the air, like a crackle of lightning. Then the breeze that had been pulling the billowing drapes out of the open doorway shifted direction, and the golden gauze blew into the chamber in a rush of fragrant, warm air—and suddenly they were enveloped in a gossamer cloud of delicate wings. Hundreds of shimmering butterflies fluttered around and above the gathering, fanning them with their magic.

"Thank you, Epona!" Etain laughed, delighted with the demonstration of her Goddess's pleasure.

Then the women began to hum and twirl. Slowly at first, then more quickly and joyously they took up the ancient ceremony that was the traditional greeting for the birth of a child of Partholon.

Etain rested within her husband's arms as he cradled his family against his strong chest.

"The magic of youth and the wonder of life beginning anew," she whispered to her daughter. Etain touched the infant reverently, unable to look away from her, not wanting to miss one breath or one movement. Her fingers ran down Elphame's body wonderingly, as she caressed her unique legs and learned the contours of each delicate hoof. Satyr. The name fluttered through her mind. But, no. She wasn't at all goatlike; she was too delicate and finely formed to resemble Pan. She was simply a perfect blending of human, centaur and goddess.

A sense of awe rushed through Etain, and laughter bubbled from her chest.

Midhir squeezed his wife's shoulders in response. "I, too, am filled to overflowing with the wonder of her."

She nodded her head, agreeing with him. Then, through more laughter she added, "Yes, but that's not why I'm laughing."

He arched an eyebrow questioningly.

She grinned and stroked one of Elphame's little hooves. "I

used to think that she must be clothed and wearing boots, as hard as her kicks sometimes felt. Now I see exactly what it was I was feeling."

Midhir's laughter joined his wife's as they reveled in the magic of their newborn daughter.

POWER. NOTHING WAS that good. Not Partholon's finest chocolate. Not the beauty of a perfect sunrise. Not even…no, she wouldn't know about *that*. She shook her head, purposefully changing the pattern of her thoughts. The wind whistled sharply through her hair, and some of the long strands blew into her face making her wish she had tied it back out of the way. She usually did, but today she had wanted to feel its heavy weight, and she admitted to herself that she liked the way it flowed behind her when she ran, like the flame-colored tail of a shooting star.

Her stride faltered as her concentration wavered and Elphame quickly regained control of her stray thoughts. Maintaining speed took focus. The field she ran in was relatively flat and free of most rocks and obstructions, but it wouldn't be wise to let her thoughts wander. One misstep could snap a leg all too easily; it would be foolish to believe otherwise. For all her life, Elphame had made it a point to shun foolish beliefs and behavior. Foolishness and folly were for people who could afford everyday, normal mistakes. Not for her, for someone whose very design said that she had been touched by the Goddess, and was, therefore, held apart from what was accepted as normal and everyday.

Elphame deepened her breathing and forced herself to relax her upper body. *Keep the tension in your lower body,* she reminded herself. *Keep everything else loose and relaxed. Let the most powerful part of your body do the work.* Her teeth glinted in an almost feral grin as she felt her body regather and shoot forward. Elphame loved the way the corded muscles in her legs responded. Her arms pumped effortlessly as her hooves bit into the soft green carpet of the young field.

She was faster than any human. Much faster.

Elphame demanded more of herself, and her body responded with inhuman strength. She may not have been as fast as a centaur over long distances, but few could outdistance her in a sprint, as her brothers liked to frequently boast. With a little more hard work, perhaps none would be able to best her. The thought was almost as satisfying as the wind on her face.

When the burning started she ignored it, knowing that she had to push herself beyond the point of simple muscle fatigue, but she did begin to angle her strides so that her run would take her in a huge spherical path. She would end up back where she had begun.

But not forever, she promised herself. Not forever. And she pushed herself harder.

"Oh, Goddess." Watching her daughter, Etain whispered reverently, "Will I ever get used to her beauty?"

She is special, Beloved. Epona's voice shimmered familiarly through her Chosen One's mind.

She pulled the horse to a halt well within the stand of trees

that flanked one end of the field. The silver mare stopped and
twisted her head around, cocking her ears at her rider in the
horse's version of a question. And Etain knew that her mare,
the equine incarnation of the Goddess Epona, really *was* asking
a question.

"I just want to sit here and watch her."

The Goddess blew imperiously through her nose.

"I am not spying!" Etain said indignantly. "I am her mother.
It is well within my right to watch her run."

The Goddess tossed her head in a reply that proclaimed she
wasn't so sure.

"Behave with the proper respect." She jangled the mare's
reigns. "Or I shall leave you at the temple next trip."

The Goddess didn't dignify the comment with so much as
a snort. Etain ignored the mare who was now ignoring her,
and muttered something about grumpy old creatures, but not
loud enough for the mare to hear. Then she squinted her eyes
and held her hand up to block the setting sun from interfer-
ing with her view.

Her daughter was running with a speed that caused her
lower body to blur, so that it appeared that she flew above the
brilliant green shoots of new wheat. She ran bent forward
slightly at the waist, with a grace that always amazed her
mother.

"She is the prefect blending of centaur and human," Etain
whispered to the mare, who swiveled her ears to catch the
words. "Goddess, you are so wise."

Elphame had completed the long loop in her imaginary
track, and she was beginning to turn toward the grove in
which her mother waited. The setting sun framed her running
body, catching the girl's dark auburn hair on fire. It glowed
and snapped around her in long, heavy strands.

"She certainly didn't get that lovely straight hair from me,"

Etain told the mare as she tried to tuck one of her ever-escaping curls behind her ear. The mare cocked an ear back attentively. "The red lights that streak her hair, yes, but the rest of it she can thank her father for." She could also thank him for the color of those amazingly dark eyes. The shape was hers—large and round, resting above high delicate cheekbones that were also copies of her mother's, but where Etain's eyes were mossy green, her daughter's eyes were the entrancing sable of her centaur father's. Even if Elphame's physical form hadn't been completely unique, her beauty would have been unusual—coupled with a body that only the Goddess could have created, the effect was breathtaking.

Elphame's pace began to slow, and she changed direction so that she was heading directly for the stand of trees in which her mother and the mare waited.

"We should make ourselves known so that she doesn't think we were lurking around in the shadows watching her."

They emerged from the tree line, and Etain saw her daughter's head snap in their direction in an instinctively defensive gesture, but almost immediately Elphame recognized them and raised her arm to wave hello at the same time the mare trumpeted a shrill greeting.

"Mama!" Elphame called happily. "Why don't you two join me for my cooldown?"

"Of course, my darling," Etain shouted back. "But slowly, you know the mare is getting old and—"

Before she could finish the sentence the "old mare" in question sprang forward and caught up with the young woman, where she pranced spryly sideways before easily matching her gentle canter with Elphame's gait.

"The two of you will never be old, Mama." Elphame laughed.

"She's just a putting on a show for you," Etain told her

daughter, but she reached down and affectionately ruffled the mare's silky mane.

"Oh, Mama, please. *She's* putting on a show..." Elphame let the sentence trail suggestively off as she quirked her eyebrow and gave her mother a knowing look that took in her glittering jewelry and the seductive wrap of her buttery leather riding outfit that fitted snuggly over her still shapely body.

"El, you know wearing jewelry is a spiritual experience for me," she said in her Beloved of the Goddess voice.

"I know, Mama." Elphame grinned.

The mare's snort was decidedly sarcastic, and Etain's laughter mingled with her daughter's as they continued compatibly around the field.

"Where did I leave my wrap?" Elphame muttered half to her mother, half to herself as she searched the edge of the tree line. "I thought I put it on this log."

Etain watched her daughter scramble over a fallen limb as she searched for the rest of her clothing. She wore only a sleeveless leather top, which was wrapped tightly around her full breasts, and a small strip of linen that hugged her muscular buttocks, and was cut high up on her hips, before it dipped down to a triangle to cover her in the front. Etain had designed it herself.

The problem was that although the girl's muscular body was covered with a sleek coat of horsehair from the waist down, and she had hooves instead of feet, except for the extraordinary muscles in her lower body she was otherwise built very much like a human female. So she needed a garment that would allow her the freedom to exercise the inhuman speed with which she had been gifted, as well as keep her decently covered. Etain and her daughter had experimented with many different styles before happening upon one that successfully accomplished both needs.

The result had worked well, except that it left so much of Elphame's body visible. It mattered little that the women of Partholon had always been free to proudly display their bodies. Etain regularly bared her breasts during blessing rituals to signify Epona's love of the female form. When Elphame uncovered her hoofed legs, people stared in outright shock and awe at the sight of the Chosen's so obviously Goddess-touched body.

Elphame loathed being the recipient of the stares.

So it had become habit for Elphame to dress conservatively in public, only shedding her flowing robes when she ran, which was almost always alone and well away from the temple.

"Oh, I found it!" El cried, and trotted over to a log not far from where they stood.

She picked up the length of fine linen that had been dyed the color of emeralds and began winding it around her slim waist. Her breathing had already returned to normal; the fine sheen of sweat that had caused the downy hair on her bare arms to glisten had already dried.

She was in spectacular shape. Her body was sleek, athletic and perfectly honed, but there was nothing harsh or masculine about its casing. Her lovely brown skin looked silky and seductively touchable; it was only after actually touching her that the finely wrapped strength of the muscles beneath the skin could be fully realized.

But few people dared to touch the young goddess.

She was tall, towering several inches over her mother's five-foot-seven-inch frame. During early puberty she had been thin and a little awkward, but soon the curves and fullness of womanhood had replaced that coltishness. Her lower body was a perfect mixture of human and centaur. She had the beauty and allure of a woman, and the strength and grace of a centaur.

Etain smiled at her daughter. As from the moment of her

birth, she had embraced Elphame's uniqueness with a fierce, protective love. "You don't have to wear that wrap, El." She hadn't realized she had spoken her thought aloud until her daughter looked quickly up at her.

"I know you do not think I need to." Her voice, usually so like her mother's, suddenly hardened with suppressed emotion. "But I have to. It is not the same for me. They do not look upon me as they do you."

"Has someone said something to hurt you? Tell me who it is and he will know the wrath of a goddess!" Green fire flashed in Etain's eyes.

Elphame's voice lost all expression as she answered her mother. "They do not need to say anything, Mama."

"Precious one—" the anger melted from Etain's eyes "—you know the people love you."

"No, Mama." She held up her hand to stop her mother from interrupting. "They love *you*. They idolize and worship me. It is not the same thing."

"Of course they worship you, El. You are the eldest daughter of the Beloved of Epona, and you have been blessed by the Goddess in a very special way. They should worship you."

The mare moved forward until her muzzle lipped the young woman's shoulder. Before she answered, El reached around the mare's head to stroke her gleaming neck.

She looked up at her mother and said with a conviction that made her sound older than her years, "I am different. And no matter how badly you want to believe that I fit in, it's just not the same for me. That is why I must leave."

Etain's stomach clenched at her daughter's words, but she forced herself to remain silent and allow her to continue.

"I'm treated like I am a thing apart. Not that I'm treated badly," she added quickly, "just apart. Like I'm something they are afraid to get too close to because I might…" Here she faltered and laid her cheek against the broad forehead of the silver mare. "…I don't know…might shatter. Or perhaps cause them to shatter. So they treat me like I am a statue that has come miraculously to life right in front of them."

My beautiful, lonely daughter, Etain thought, feeling the familiar ache of not having the solution to end her firstborn's pain.

"But statues aren't loved, not really. They're cared for and kept in a place of honor, but they aren't loved."

"I love you." Etain's voice sounded choked.

"Oh, I know, Mama!" Her head flew up and her eyes met her mother's. "You and Da, and Cuchulainn and Finegas and Arianrhod all love me. You have to, you're my family," she added with a quick smile. "But even your private guards, who adore you unquestioningly and would give their lives for either of us, believe I am something essentially untouchable."

The mare moved a step forward and El leaned against the side of the horse. Etain ached to take her daughter in her arms, but she knew that the young woman would stiffen and tell her she was no longer a child, so she contented herself with stroking her satin hair, willing Epona's comfort from her hands into her daughter's body.

"That's why you came out here today, wasn't it?" El asked quietly.

"Yes," her mother responded simply. "I wanted to try one more time to talk you out of going." Etain paused thoughtfully before she spoke again. "Why not stay here and take my place, El?"

Her daughter jolted upright and started to shake her head violently from side to side, but Etain doggedly continued.

"I have had a long, rich reign. I am ready to retire."

"No!" Elphame's voice was adamant. Just the thought of taking her mother's place sent a thread of panic through her.

"You are *not* ready to retire! Look at you. You look decades younger than your age. You love performing the rituals of Epona, and the people need you to continue. And you must remember the most important thing, Mama. The spirit realm is closed to me. I have never heard Epona's voice or felt the touch of her magic..." The sadness of the truth of her words settled resolutely on Elphame's face. "I have never felt any magic at all."

"But Epona speaks to me of you often," Etain said softly, touching her daughter's cheek. "Her hand has been upon you since before your birth."

"I know. I know the Goddess loves me, but I am not her Chosen One."

"Not yet," her mother added.

Elphame's only response was to lean against the warm familiarity of the horse's neck while the mare nuzzled her affectionately.

"I still do not understand why you must leave."

"Mama," Elphame said, turning her head so she could look up at her mother. "You sound like I am traveling to the other side of the world." She raised one dark eyebrow in exasperation, which her mother always thought made her look so much like her father.

Etain's answering smile was sardonic. From the moment of each of their births, she had been devoted to her children. Even now that they were adults, she preferred that they stay near her. She honestly enjoyed their company and appreciated them for the individuals they were growing into.

El spoke slowly, willing her mother to really hear her words. "I don't know why it upsets you so much that I'm going. It's not like I've never been away from home. I studied at the Temple of the Muse and that didn't seem to bother you."

"That was different. Of course you had to study with the

Muse. It's where all the most spectacular females of Partholon are educated. Arianrhod is there now." Etain's smile was self-satisfied. "Both of my daughters are spectacular, which is one reason I enjoy having you near me," Etain said logically.

"If I had married, I might have moved to his home." El's voice had lost its frustrated edge and she just sounded exhausted.

"Don't talk like you'll never get married. You're still young. You have years and years left."

"Mama, please. Let's not start this old argument again. You know no one will marry me. There's no one like me, and no one who wants to get that close to a goddess."

"Your father married me."

El smiled sadly at her mother. "But you're all human, Mama, and besides, the High Shaman of the centaurs is always mated to Epona's Beloved. He was created to love you—it's what is normal for him. It is obvious that the Goddess has touched me, but I am not Her Chosen. Epona has not prompted any centaur shaman to come forward as my mate. I don't think anyone, man or centaur shaman, was created to love me. Not like you and Da."

"Oh, Fawn!" Etain's voice broke on the childhood nickname. "I don't believe that. Epona is not cruel. There is someone for you. He just hasn't found you yet."

"Maybe. And maybe I have to go away to find him."

"But why there? I don't like to think about you being there."

"It's just a place, Mama. Actually it's just an old ruin. I think it is past time that it was rebuilt. Remember the stories you used to tell me at bedtime? You said that once upon a time it was beautiful," El coaxed.

"Yes, until it became home to slaughter and evil."

"That was more than one hundred years ago. The evil is gone, and the dead can't hurt me."

"You can't be sure about that," her mother retorted.

"Mama," El reached up and took her hand. "The MacCallan was my ancestor. Why would his ghost harm me?"

"There were more who died at the slaughter of MacCallan Castle than the Clan Chieftain and the noble warriors who gave their lives trying to protect him. And you know the castle is said to be cursed. No one has dared to enter its grounds, let alone live there, for over a century," Etain said firmly.

"But all of my life you have watched over the MacCallan shrine and its ever-burning flame," she countered. "We have kept alive the memory of The MacCallan, even though the clan was destroyed. Why should my wish to restore his castle surprise you? After all, his blood runs in my veins, too."

Etain didn't answer her immediately. For an instant she actually toyed with the thought of lying to her daughter, of saying that she had Goddess-given knowledge of the veracity of the castle's curse. But only for an instant. Mother and daughter had a deep reservoir of trust as well as love between them, and Etain wasn't willing to damage or take advantage of that—and she would never lie about knowledge given to her by Epona.

"I do not truly believe The MacCallan would harm you, though it is quite possible that restless spirits inhabit the old castle. And I admit that the curse is just a tale to frighten errant children. It's not so much that I fear for your safety—it's just that I don't understand why you must go with the workers who will clear out the ruins. Why not wait until the mess has been cleaned away and they have rebuilt it so that it is actually habitable? Then you can oversee the final stages of construction."

Elphame sighed fondly at her mother. The Chosen of Epona was used to living in luxury, surrounded by servants and handmaidens. It wasn't possible for her to understand her daughter's desire to get her hands dirty and live rough until the job was done.

"I need to be involved in every aspect of this. I'm going to rebuild MacCallan Castle, and I'm going to be mistress of it. As Lady of the Castle and of the surrounding lands I will have something of my own, something I've had a hand in creating. If I can't have my own mate and my own children, then I can at least have my own kingdom. Please understand and give me your blessing, Mama." Her eyes pleaded with her mother.

"I just want you to be happy, my precious Fawn."

"This will make me happy. You have to trust me to know my own mind, Mama."

You must let her go, my Beloved. The Goddess spoke the words gently within Etain's mind, but still it felt as if the blade of a knife had passed through her soul. *Trust her to find her own destiny, and trust me to care for her.*

Etain closed her eyes, struggling against second thoughts and loss. With a deep breath she opened her eyes, and wiped the wetness from her cheeks.

"I do trust you. And you will always have my blessing."

Elphame's face was transformed, and the lines of worry that so often clouded it dissipated, leaving her looking heart-wrenchingly young.

"Thank you, Mama. I believe that I am fated to do this. Just wait until you see MacCallan Castle alive again." She happily gave the silver mare's neck an enthusiastic squeeze. "Let's hurry back so I can finish packing. You know I'm supposed to leave at dawn tomorrow."

Elphame chattered brightly as she kept pace easily with the mare and her mother. Etain made meaningful, attentive-sounding noises, but she couldn't stay focused on her daughter's words. Instead it seemed that she already felt the weight of Elphame's absence as if it were a black hole in her soul. And, even though the late spring evening was warm, a chill marked its finger down the back of Goddess Incarnate's neck.

2

"CU, REMIND ME why I agreed to let you come with me."
Elphame looked slantways at her brother and tried to increase
her gait without being too obvious. He was singing what
seemed like verse five hundred of a semi-raunchy military
marching song and the never-ending chorus pounded through
her right temple in time with her headache, almost making her
wish she had not insisted that the two of them travel separate
from the rest of their party.

The big buckskin gelding on which Cuchulainn rode automatically picked up his pace to match El's long strides. Her
brother's infectious laugh rang around them. "I came, sister-
mine, to protect you."

Elphame gave an unlady-like snort. "Oh, please, spare me.
Protect me? It's more likely you needed a break from chasing
the temple maidens hither and yon."

"Hither and yon?" His handsome face broke into a boyish

grin. "Did you really say hither and yon?" He shook his head in mock seriousness. "I knew you were spending too much time reading those tomes in mother's library. And it's not the *maidens* I'd be after." He waggled his eyebrows suggestively at his sister.

Elphame tried unsuccessfully to hide a smile as she gave him a fond look. "Next you'll be reminding me that you don't have to *chase* any woman anywhere."

"Now that, sister-mine, is the simple truth…." He let the words trail off and grinned at her.

"Hmm, I thought you might be staying at home to welcome the…" Elphame cleared her throat and tossed back her hair, doing a perfect imitation of their mother's tone of voice as well as her body language. "…lovely and unmarried daughter of the Chieftain of Woulff Castle who will be sojourning at Epona's Temple on the way to begin her training at the Temple of the Muse."

Cuchulainn's mouth tightened, and for an instant Elphame regretted her teasing. Then, with his usual good humor he shrugged his shoulders and gave her a long-suffering grin.

"Her name is Beatrice, sister-mine. Can you image anyone named Beatrice not having a *high forehead and regal carriage?*" He spoke the words putting a simper in his deep voice, which made Elphame laugh out loud.

"She's probably a very handsome woman," El said through giggles.

"No doubt fertile, with ample hips and the ability to bear many children."

Brother and sister exchanged looks of complete understanding.

"I'll be glad when Arianrhod and Finegas are old enough for Mama to start matchmaking for them." El said in a tone that sounded more serious than she had intended.

Cuchulainn sighed heavily. "The twins will be eighteen

this summer. In three more years Mother will be in her match-making glory."

El slanted a look at Cu. "Poor kids. It almost makes me wish we hadn't picked on them so much when we were children."

"Almost!" Cuchulainn laughed. "At least we're all in this together—it's not like Mother singles out one of us."

Elphame just smiled at him and quickened the pace again, forcing herself temporarily ahead of her brother on the narrowing trail. *But it's not the same for me.* Thoughts whirred incessantly through her restless mind. Her siblings were humans—attractive, talented, sought-after humans. She didn't need to glance over her shoulder to picture Cuchulainn. His face was as familiar to her as her own—and very like her own. She smiled wryly. Cu was just a year and a half younger, and from the waist up they, too, could be twins. He had her high, well-defined cheekbones, but where hers were delicate and feminine, his were ruggedly masculine. Her chin was (according to their mother) rather defiant, and his was stubborn and proud (according to his eldest sister), complete with an adorable cleft. Instead of his sister's sable eyes and dark auburn tresses, he had eyes that were a unique color shaded somewhere between blue and green, and thick, sandy-colored hair that refused to give up its childish cowlicks. So he kept it slicked back and cropped short, which made their mother cluck and complain over the waste of not letting it grow like a proper warrior's.

But Cuchulainn, son of Midhir, High Shaman and Centaur Warrior Lord, did not have to be a "proper warrior." Named after one of Partholon's ancient heroes, he already looked and acted the part, whether he always behaved properly or not. Tall and well-formed, he excelled at tournaments, was the finest human swordsman in Partholon and had never been bested in archery. Elphame had heard more than one young maiden sigh longingly and say that he must indeed be Cuchulainn reincarnated.

No, Cu had never lacked for female companionship. He had just not yet found his lifemate. Elphame's shapely lips tilted up. "But not for lack of trying," she muttered to herself.

That was one way she was very unlike her brother. He was suave and experienced with the opposite sex. She had never been kissed.

Even her youngest siblings, whom she and Cu had nicknamed the Little Scholars, had no trouble finding partners for moon rituals. While Arianrhod and Finegas weren't as athletic as their older brother and sister, they were certainly growing into intelligent, poised young adults. Looking almost like mirror images of each other, their tall, graceful bodies were completely human—totally normal. And, Elphame admitted to herself, Arianrhod was as pretty as Fin was handsome.

The path that cut through the ancient forest curved to the right and widened. Cuchulainn urged his gelding to his sister's side.

"She reminds me of Mama," El said suddenly.

Cu looked around in surprise. "Who?"

El rolled her eyes. She always expected her brother to read her mind, and was annoyed the few times he didn't. "Arianrhod, who else? That's why the boys already moon over her. Of course it's not like she cares or even notices—not unless she's completely changed during her first term at the Temple of the Muse."

Her brother's turquoise eyes crinkled with his smile. "Arianrhod's head will always be in the clouds."

"Astronomy and astrology are inexorably linked to the Fates, and as such it is wise to study them carefully." El mimicked their younger sister.

Cu laughed. "That's one of our Little Scholars, all right. The irony is that young, besotted men will chase her all the harder because of her indifference. You see the maidens are already starting to follow Fin around, and his beard is still like duck's down."

"Well, for whatever reason they certainly like her a lot."

Cuchulainn looked closely at his sister. "Are you all right?"

"Of course," she answered automatically without meeting his eyes.

"It will be different here, Fawn," he said quietly.

"I know." She glanced quickly over at him, and then just as quickly looked away, afraid that he would see the tears that were beginning to make her eyes too bright.

"No, I mean it." His serious tone caused her to slow her stride so she could listen more carefully. "You will find what you have always desired at MacCallan Castle. I have had a Feeling."

Her brother's words hung in the fragrant spring air. She knew exactly what he meant. It was a part of the code between them. Just as she was her Goddess Incarnate mother's firstborn daughter, and therefore had been marked by Epona, Cuchulainn was truly the firstborn son of their shaman father. From an early age he had simply *known* things. When he was a child he had explained it to his sister by saying it was like he could hear words that were hidden in the wind. Sometimes this "wind" told him where lost items could be found. Sometimes it told him when someone was coming to visit the temple. And sometimes it foretold portentous news, like the untimely death of a beloved child or the breaking of a blood-given oath.

The preternatural knowledge had frightened the young Cuchulainn. It wasn't an enemy he could best with the prowess of his muscles or outwit through his cunning. It was something that made him feel like an aberration; it gave him power he hadn't asked for and didn't have any desire to wield.

It was a thing his older sister understood all too well.

So he had come to Elphame whenever he'd had a Feeling

about something or someone. And his sister had empathized with his fear. She had not turned from him—instead she had become his closest confidante, even though Elphame's attitude toward things of the spirit realm was decidedly different than his. She was, after all, a physical manifestation of the magic of the Goddess. She didn't understand why her brother would reject gifts from the spirit realm, especially when she longed to feel even a whisper of the power her mother wielded so easily, but she supported his desire to do so with a calm, no-nonsense attitude. As he grew older, Cuchulainn had learned to repress his burgeoning psychic abilities and not allow them to overwhelm him.

Now Elphame looked searchingly at her brother. He'd never lied to her before. And his Feeling had never been wrong.

"Do you promise?" she asked a little breathlessly, the sudden flush that suffused her cheeks the only outward sign that betrayed her inner excitement.

"Yes." He nodded tightly.

Joy surged through Elphame. "I knew restoring MacCallan Castle was the right thing to do!" Then she gave him a sisterly glare, thinking of all the cajoling it had taken to get their mother to agree to let her go. "You couldn't have shared this knowledge with Mama?"

"If I had told Mother that I knew you would meet your destiny at MacCallan Castle do you think there would have been any force on Partholon that could have kept her from accompanying us there?"

"Excellent point," Elphame agreed quickly. Then her thoughts navigated through her rush of emotions and she asked, "But why did you wait to tell *me?*"

Cuchulainn's forehead furrowed in thought and he answered her slowly. "The Feeling is indistinct." Then, seeing his sister's face fall in disappointment he hurried on to try and explain. "No, it doesn't make it any less certain. I know you'll meet your destiny at MacCallan Castle. I know that destiny is tied up in your lifemate, but when I try to focus on details about the man I get only fog and confusion." He shook his head and smiled sheepishly at Elphame. "Maybe that's because you're my sister and knowing details about your love life is actually pretty disturbing."

"I know exactly what you mean. When the maidens wax poetic about your various body parts—" she shuddered and made a face "—I cover my ears and run screaming in the opposite direction."

"Hrumph." He huffed at her succinctly, chuckling in spite of himself, glad his sister had stopped asking specific questions about the Feeling.

He had struggled with what to say to El about his vision. He knew it caused his beloved sister pain to believe that she would never find a mate, and he knew that he had to tell her about his Feeling. It was clear to him that she would meet her lifemate and her destiny at MacCallan Castle, but he also knew there was more to it than simply falling in love. A part of his premonition had been vague and ominous. It had been nothing like the typical "love" visions he had received in the past, which were usually glimpses of a friend in a young woman's arms, followed by a Feeling that the two people belonged together.

He had experienced a vision of his sister in a man's arms, but he had been unable to see the man. Maybe that was because the first thing he had been able to see clearly was the look of tender happiness that radiated from his sister's usually serious face, and that particular vision had been so surprising that his concentration had been irreparably fractured. Maybe not. And, yes, there had been a definite Feeling that the two were meant to be together. When he tried to refocus the scene and study the man, the vision had been bathed in a blinding scarlet light, as if the scene had been dipped in blood. Then, just as quickly, it had been covered in darkness, like the lovers had been wrapped in a velvet curtain, and the man had faded away, leaving his sister alone.

How very like the realm of spirits, to leave him with unanswered questions and a sense of unease. He had always loathed the elusive, slippery nature of the power. It wasn't like the sure weight of a sword, or the clear aim of an arrow.

Cuchulainn swallowed past a suddenly dry throat, glad Elphame had, once again, pulled ahead of him. She read his expressions too easily. He didn't want her to see that his latest vision had reached into his soul and truly frightened him with its strange, red-tinged whisperings. He flexed his right hand. He could feel the phantom weight of his claymore as in his mind he gripped it and held it at the ready.

Yes. Lifemate or not, Cuchulainn was prepared to protect his sister from all who might cause her harm.

$\mathcal{B}$

"I DO NOT understand why we couldn't have stayed in Loth Tor with the rest of the workers," Cuchulainn complained as he fed another dry log into their campfire.

"I thought warriors were supposed to be so thick-skinned that they could sleep on beds of thistles without wincing," Elphame quipped and tossed him the wineskin. "Have a drink. Remember, Mama packed the wine," she added meaningfully.

"Warriors like soft beds just as much as anyone else," he grumbled, but took the wineskin and drank deeply. "Mother's love of wine has been a blessing this trip. But it doesn't make up for the absence of a down-filled bed." Or a lusty young widow in that bed, he thought.

"Cu, you're just mad because that plump blonde was obviously offering you more than another helping of her excellent stew."

"Being a young widow is a lonely burden to bear."

"Not while you're around." She laughed. "Oh, come on.

Don't pout. I want to watch the sun as it rises over my castle, and I don't want to do it with a group of centaurs and men staring at me while they invent demons lurking in every shadow."

Cuchulainn grunted in response, took another long drink of wine and tossed the skin back to his sister. He poked the fire and quit complaining. He was used to Elphame's solitary ways, and he understood the reasons behind them. She had spent her life being revered because she had been touched by the Goddess; she was a being that had never before been created. It wasn't that she was ever treated cruelly—actually it was just the opposite. She awed people, especially people who were not accustomed to the sight of her. Most of the workers who had accompanied them were from the area around Epona's Temple, so they merely treated her with careful respect and kept their distance. But during the five days of travel from Epona's Temple to MacCallan Castle, Cuchulainn had noticed how the people would stop whatever they were doing and rush to the road, bowing so low as "the young goddess, Elphame" passed that they practically buried their heads in the grassy meadows surrounding the main road. And as they drew nearer their destination, new people and centaurs had begun joining their party, eager for the opportunities that would surround the reestablishment of MacCallan Castle. Their reaction to his sister was always the same—more awe and staring. Cuchulainn knew that was why Elphame had insisted that the two of them leave the road and follow the smaller, rougher path that ran through the forest. To El, fewer people equated to less chance of being worshipped, and that was a good thing.

Brother and sister had camped under the stars and hadn't stopped in any of the sleepy little villages that dotted the land between vineyards and pastures, until they had come to Loth

Tor, the village that nestled at the base of the plateau on which MacCallan Castle stood. That night they had rejoined their party and all of them had dined at the Mare's Inn, the town's only tavern, where it seemed the entire populace had paraded through, each reverently bowing to Elphame. Some asked if they could please touch the young goddess, some just stared openmouthed. Cuchulainn had watched his sister nod politely to each one of them, acquiescing graciously to their desire to worship her. Only he seemed to notice the unnatural tension in her shoulders and the rigid way she held herself. To Cu it looked as though if she moved too quickly she might shatter.

When the meal was over she had said she felt the need to sleep under the stars and to be alone with her brother and Epona. He knew she added the Goddess's name so that the town wouldn't follow her and continue to stare. Wordlessly he had saddled his tired gelding and kicked it into a gallop, scrambling to keep up with Elphame as she retreated from the village.

"It will get better after you've been here for a while, you know," he said quietly.

She sighed heavily. "You'd think I would get used to it." She took another sip of the excellent wine before tossing it back to her brother. "I don't, though." She raised her brows at him and added, "Hard to believe my destiny is around here."

"Stranger things have happened," he said lightly, not wanting to talk about his vision or her potential mate.

"Such as?" she asked.

"Such as the fact that we have the same parents, but I'm human and you're part-horse," he replied promptly.

She rolled her eyes at him. "I'm part-centaur, not part-horse." But she didn't argue further.

"Get some sleep," he told her. "You'll need all your energy tomorrow. I'll stay awake and watch over the fire." And over you, he added silently to himself. His sister's tension may have lessened with their departure from the town, but his own warrior instincts had him feeling wary and restless.

Why couldn't he get a clear picture of his sister's future? Why had his vision been so dark and indistinct? And why had it seemed to be drenched in blood?

Elphame curled up on her side, looking snug and comfortable in her bedroll. "You can't fool me, Cuchulainn." Her eyes were closed and her voice was a whisper, but the gentle night breeze brought her words clearly to him. "This is more of that I-must-protect-my-sister warrior stuff."

"Now that definitely sounds like something Mother would say," he told her, and then added under his breath, "It's about time you noticed."

His sister's lips were lifted in a soft smile as she fell deeply asleep.

Elphame dreamed that her lover came to her within a dark mist, which wrapped itself around her as if the night had grown wings, and though she trembled at his touch she wasn't afraid. Willingly, she offered herself to the mist, and it bent to her and drank of her love as they flew into the velvet blackness of the midnight sky and made their bed together amidst the stars.

"I knew it would be amazing." Elphame sighed happily. "Oh, Cu, look at my castle!"

They were standing at the edge of the pine forest that ringed the land side of the plateau on which the MacCallan Castle had been built. The tart, clean smell of pine mixed with the salty scent of ocean and seemed to wash everything in brilliance, making the green of the forest lush and layered, the blue and white of the ocean crystalline and elegant as it crashed against the rocks far below. The castle loomed before them, looking imposing in its rocky perch on the edge of the magnificent coastal cliff.

Elphame stared at her new home, letting her eyes drink in the wonder of that first sight. Surrounded by row after row of redbud and dogwood trees in full bloom, as well as overgrown scrub and clumps of blackberry bushes gone wild, the castle looked like it should have been housing a fairy creature who had been sleeping for centuries and was just waiting for the kiss of her true love to awaken her.

A little like me. Elphame surprised herself with the blatantly romantic thought. But the sight before her, coupled with her brother's premonition, had her feeling uncharacteristically romantic. And, she realized with a start, it was a feeling she thought she might enjoy.

Was this what she had been missing all those years? she mused silently. *This breathless, waiting excitement? Like someone was just about to turn a key within her and unlock something magical?*

The sun was beginning to climb above the trees. As Elphame watched, the dreamy pink and cream of the early morning sky morphed into the more mature gold and blue of a clear spring day. All at once she was filled with an incredible sense of hope, as if the dawn of that day was a promise of a new beginning for her, as well. A blessing that she had heard her mother offer to Epona many times drifted through her mind and suddenly she heard herself repeating it aloud—though her words were little more than a tentative whisper.

"Great Goddess Epona, my Goddess,
I stand here at a newborn day,
a day filled with Your magic.
I stand at a threshold, before Your veil of mysteries,
and I ask for Your blessing.
May I work for Your glory
and the glory of my spirit, also."

Cuchulainn was silent during his sister's prayer—partially out of respect for Epona, and partially out of surprise. Until then he had never heard his sister evoke Epona's blessing. Truthfully, Elphame had seemed to prefer to avoid all mention of the Goddess who had so obviously touched her. Until that morning. Then, although Cuchulainn could barely hear the words of her prayer, he could feel the distinct tingle of magic in the air—as he had many times when his mother performed Epona's rituals.

If she had looked at her brother, El would have seen the shock that widened his eyes, but she did not even glance at him. She was mesmerized by the beauty of the morning and the burgeoning feeling within her that she was just beginning to recognize as a sense of belonging. Suddenly the sun broke free of the tall pines and its rays washed the castle's walls in golden light, causing them to catch fire.

"Do you see it, Cu? It's like the walls are glowing."

"What's left of them, you mean." Still surprised by the new power radiating from his sister, his voice sounded gruffer than he had intended. He cleared his throat, squinting to get a better look at the crumbling edifice. To him the castle looked like a ragged old beast crouched precariously on the edge of the seaside cliff. "El, don't get your hopes up. Even from here I can see that the place is in ruins. We have a lot of work to do."

She punched his arm affectionately. "Stop being Mama. Come on, let's hurry." She leaped ahead, and Cuchulainn kneed his big gelding, scrambling to catch up with the lithe form of his sister.

They plowed determinedly through the sticky underbrush until they found the road that led to the castle's front entrance. It was easier going there, but Cuchulainn still muttered under his breath at the rough weeds and smattering of trees that choked the once wide, clear pathway.

"Oh, stop grumbling and look at these amazing trees!" Elphame chided her brother as she slowed down and spun in a circle, trying to look everywhere at once. "I had no idea it would be so beautiful." Even more than a century of neglect could not diminish the breathtaking sight of so many redbuds and wild cherries heavy with blooms. "It's like walking through a forest of pink clouds."

"Clouds don't usually have thickets of brambles in them." He pointed at the thorny plants that clustered amidst the scrub that proliferated between the trees.

"They're not brambles, Cu, they're blackberries. A little trimming and they'll be fine. Just think of the wonderful cobbler and pies we can have this summer."

"After you get a kitchen built, you mean," he muttered.

She flashed him a quick smile. "I'll get it built."

Cuchulainn thought that the determination in her voice was probably stronger than the walls of the castle to which she already seemed so firmly attached.

"And you know I've always liked the forest." She twirled again, head thrown back, dark auburn hair flying around her like a cloak. "The pines are wonderful, but I think these flowering trees are even more incredible."

He shook his head at her and spoke with a warrior's knowledge. "Surely you are not planning on letting this stand? For all your study of history, your memory doesn't seem very exact. One of the major mistakes of MacCallan Castle was that they allowed their defenses to weaken." The sweep of his arm took in the profusion of blooming trees. "MacCallan let this grow to his walls. The Fomorian army had no trouble staying undetected until they had breached the castle walls and begun slaughtering its inhabitants."

Elphame opened her mouth to retort that they weren't at war; there hadn't been a Fomorian in Partholon for a hundred and twenty-five years. No one would try to breach her walls. But Partholon hadn't been at war before, either. Not until MacCallan Castle had been taken by surprise. Yes, the Fomorians had been defeated, and what was left of their demonic race had been driven from Partholon through the Trier Mountains and into the Wasteland beyond. If she traveled northeast to the mountains she knew she would find that Guardian Castle still stood grim sentinel, eternally protecting the passageway to Partholon.

But one hundred and twenty-five years was a long time, and except for clan skirmishes and occasional raids from the barbaric, seagoing Milesians, Partholon had known a long era of peace and prosperity, and there was no logical reason why that wouldn't continue.

Elphame studied her brother, ready to remind him of the facts she had just ticked off in her head. He seemed tense; his usually clear brow was set in lines and she could see his jaw clench and unclench as he waited for her to speak.

"The Milesians, are they what is worrying you?" she asked slowly.

He shrugged. "I cannot tell. But your castle does overlook the sea. You would be proving yourself a wise and prudent leader if you made certain that MacCallan was defensible." As he spoke he didn't look at her, instead he scanned the forest around them as if he expected a barbaric horde to leap from the flowering trees and slit their throats.

Elphame felt a small shiver of unease. Something had obviously shaken her brother's normally calm center. He may not have experienced a true Feeling, complete with visions and a clear warning, but something was bothering him. Even though he consistently avoided the spirit realm and hated to tap into his psychic powers, he respected them—as did Elphame.

She nodded. "You're right, thank you for reminding me. Most of this must be cut and cleared." Her voice was sober and thoughtful. "I will, of course, need your advice on how the defenses of the castle should be rebuilt." She gave the trees one quick look of longing. "Do you think we could keep any of this, though?"

"A grove or two far enough away from the castle walls shouldn't hurt anything." He relaxed a little and smiled at her, surprised she had given in so easily. "And your blackberries can remain. They hold more thorns than protection for an enemy."

"Good, then we will have blackberry cobbler after all!" She smiled back at him, relieved that he sounded more like his playful self. Cu was probably just being ultracareful and overprotective of her, as usual.

The road curved gently to the left. When it straightened they found themselves standing less than fifty feet from the front entrance of the castle. The massive iron doors that legend still remembered as having never been barred to guests were gone. They had rusted and disintegrated. Elphame could see fragments of their remains lying amidst a tangle of weeds and vines. Only the jagged frame of the great entryway remained, giving the break in the thick walls the look of a mouth that was missing its front teeth.

The walls themselves were surprisingly intact, or at least what could be seen of them from their frontal view looked fairly sturdy and solid. Some balustrades were crumbling, and there were no archer's ramps. The parts of the roofing that had been made of wood were gone, but the skeleton of the castle remained standing, strong and proud.

"It looks better than I thought it would." Cuchulainn broke the stillness of the waiting air.

"It's perfect." Elphame's voice was filled with barely suppressed excitement.

"El, it is in better shape than I expected it to be, but it's still a ruin!" He was exasperated with her blind optimism. Not only was it a ridiculous attitude in the face of the rundown edifice in front of them, but it was totally unlike the sister he knew. Before he could say more she put out her hand, lightly touching his arm.

"Don't you Feel it?" Her voice was hushed.

Cuchulainn started in surprise. Although his sister had been physically touched by the Goddess, she had never exhibited any special link to Epona or the magical realm of spirits. Actually, except for her unique body, Elphame had no powers that attached her to the spirit realm at all. Her brother watched her closely.

"What do you mean, El?"

Her eyes never left the castle, but her hand still rested on his arm and he could feel the tremor that passed through her body. His horse stood suddenly very still. The gentle breeze had quieted; even the birds were preternaturally silent.

"It's calling me." His sister's voice sounded very young. "Not with words, but I can Feel it." She tore her eyes from the castle to look searchingly at her brother. "It's like the first time Mama had to perform a moon ritual at another Temple. Remember?" She rushed on before he could answer. "She had never really been away from us before, not for that long, and she was gone five nights. When she finally came home we called her name and rushed to meet her before she could even get to the Temple stairs. She hugged us and kissed us and laughed through her tears. Do you remember?" she asked again.

Cu nodded his head and smiled. "I remember."

Elphame's gaze was drawn back to the castle. "That's the Feeling it's giving me," she whispered. The magic that filled her words traveled up her brother's spine causing the hair at his nape to stand on end. "It's been waiting all this time for me to come home."

A

"I CAN'T WAIT to see the rest of it." Elphame shook herself from her happy trance and started determinedly forward.

"Not without me, you're not."

Cuchulainn dismounted quickly and looped the gelding's reins over the nearest tree. He jogged to her side and as they approached the burnt-out doors the sound of his claymore being unsheathed was deadly music in the morning's stillness.

Elphame stopped and frowned at the sword. "Do you really think that is necessary?"

"I would rather err on the side of safety than of foolishness."

She planted her hands on her hips and looked down her regal nose at him. "Are you saying I'm foolish?"

"No." He smiled, pleased that she was reacting more like the El he knew. "I'm saying that I'm *not* going to be."

She wrinkled her nose at him before striding toward the entrance.

"You are stubborn and hardheaded," Cuchulainn yelled, grinning at her when she glared over her shoulder at him. "But that's part of what I like about you."

"Hush and catch up with me. I'm sure there's some maniacal squirrel lurking within from which I need to be protected because I'm so very helpless…." She pretended a maidenly swoon, in the middle of which she leaned forward and bunched her powerful leg muscles, purposefully sprinting ahead of her brother so that he was breathing hard and muttering to himself about her being half-horse and definitely not helpless when he finally caught up with her.

She was waiting for him, standing silently just outside the castle's entrance. Weeds and vines had overgrown the space where the great doors had once rested, so that brother and sister had to hack a small path before they could force their way through. Elphame was the first to step within the confines of the walls. Her brother followed closely.

The tangle of weeds ended once they were within the castle's walls. They were in a spacious area between the outer walls and the beginning of the castle proper.

Cuchulainn glanced curiously around. To either side were the remains of what was once a sentry walk that must have stretched all along the castle's massive walls. Cu frowned. Too bad MacCallan hadn't posted lookouts there.

"Look, Cu, I'll bet there were beautiful wooden doors here once." Elphame's voice was hushed, like she'd entered a church.

Cuchulainn followed her through another gap in smaller, inner walls and they entered what had obviously been a grand courtyard. The floor was covered with debris and layered with filth and time, but here and there could still be glimpsed patches of the smooth stone that had held the muffled tread of the Clan MacCallan for decades. Huge pillars of carved stone ringed the area, rising up to meet what was once a

vaulted ceiling, but was now open to the brilliance of the
morning sky. The massive pillars still bore the black scars of
the fire that had been the death of the castle.

Elphame swallowed past the dryness in her throat. "Do you
think we'll find any—" she paused and met her brother's gaze
"—remains of the warriors?"

"I shouldn't think so. It's been a long time. What the fire
didn't consume, time and the elements surely would." Still, just
the thought made him peer suspiciously at some of the more
obscure mounds of leaves and dirt.

"But if we do find any trace of the MacCallan warriors, we
must give them a proper burial. They would approve of that."
Elphame spoke with quiet surety.

"Can you Feel them, El?" her brother asked.

"The warriors?"

He nodded.

She stood very still, cocking her head as if she were trying
to listen for a voice in the wind.

"Wait, I cannot be certain."

Slowly she moved to the centermost of the blackened pillars,
which was so broad that brother and sister couldn't have
touched fingertips if they had stood around its base, arms out-
stretched. That close, Elphame could see that the pillar had
been intricately carved in a circular pattern of interwoven
knots that linked together to form lovely designs filled with
birds and flowers and rearing mares. Even through the layers
of soot and filth the beauty of the workmanship was obvious.

"You must have been something to see," Elphame whispered
to the pillar.

Instantly a strange answering hum throbbed through her body.

"Oh!" she gasped.

"What is it, El?" In two strides Cuchulainn was beside her,
claymore gripped tightly in his strong hand.

She spared him a reassuring smile. "Don't worry, it's nothing bad." Then she refocused her attention on the pillar. "I can Feel something here—in this stone."

While she studied it Elphame suddenly became aware of a sentience. It was a listening presence. *It's where the humming comes from,* she thought. Ignoring her brother's restless watchfulness, Elphame placed her slender hands against the time-worn column. As her flesh met stone it seemed like the surface of the column quivered. In silent wonder, she caressed it. For a moment the massive column appeared to liquefy under her palms, almost as if her touch somehow made the stone claylike and malleable. Then her hands and the section of the column she touched began to shimmer, and the radiance moved up her arms in a rush of warmth to surround her body. She was filled with an astonishing sensation, like she had been immersed in a warm pool of emotion, or had been wrapped securely within her mother's embrace. Elphame's hands shook—not from fear, but from the sheer beauty of it.

"Oh." Her breath came out in a rush. "Oh, yes! I can Feel them." Her face beamed with emotion.

"It is not the warriors you Feel, Goddess." The deep voice came from behind them, splitting the silence like a hot knife through snow.

Cuchulainn moved with blurring speed to take a stand between his sister and the intruder, claymore before him held at the ready.

"Danann! That is an excellent way to be assured that you do not die quietly in your sleep from old age, Stonemaster." Cuchulainn's hand shook from unused adrenaline as he sheathed his sword, but the old centaur paid little attention to the warrior. His gaze was focused on Elphame, as was hers on him.

"If I am not Feeling the spirits of the warriors, then what is it that I Feel?" she asked.

At the sound of his voice, Elphame had broken contact with the pillar, but her hands still tingled with the residue of the stone's warmth. Now she waited expectantly for Danann's answer. All of Partholon knew that Epona had gifted the centaur with a special affinity for the earth. The spirits of nature spoke to him through stone, which was why Elphame had requested that the Stonemaster join the team to rebuild MacCallan Castle, even though at his advanced age he was more inclined to nap in the sun than to erect temple walls. But he remained the most revered stonemason in Partholon. He could hear spirits within stones, so he could literally choose the perfect stone for each building. With the renowned centaur Stonemaster to guide the renovations, she could be sure that what she rebuilt would stand harmoniously for centuries.

The centaur approached Elphame and the column that stood behind her with an energetic stride that belied his years. He studied the stone at first without touching it. When he spoke his voice had a dreamy, faraway sound.

"This is the great central column of MacCallan Castle. Once it was the strength of the castle." He smiled at her. "It is the spirit of the stone you Feel—the very heart of the castle itself—not the spirits of dead warriors."

Gently, he raised his hand and placed it against the column. "Touch it again, Goddess. You have nothing to fear."

"I'm not afraid of it," Elphame said quickly. Without hesitation she placed her smooth, unlined hand beside the centaur's age-creased one. Danann closed his eyes in concentration.

The glow began beneath her palm and it spread quickly to encompass both Elphame and Danann. Again, a surge of Feeling washed through her. She was ready for it and she concentrated, trying to sift through fragments of emotions that were almost spoken. *Joy*—she caught the word as happiness engulfed her…. *Peace*—Elphame wanted to laugh aloud… *An end to waiting*—the phrase flitted playfully through her mind. Then the glow faded, leaving Elphame breathless and giddy.

"I knew it! I Felt it as I stepped within these walls," the old Stonemaster shouted. He turned his head so that when he opened his eyes their clear, blue depths reflected her face.

"You are attuned to the heart of this castle, Goddess. The stones themselves welcome you. They rejoice that their mistress has arrived." His smile was rich with warmth. "Like your ancestress, Rhiannon, you have the ability to hear the spirits of the earth."

"Not until now I haven't! Not until I came here!" she cried joyously. Magic! She had finally been gifted with more than a physical aberration.

Impulsively, Elphame placed her hand over the hand Danann still pressed against the column and squeezed gratefully. Almost instantly she was sorry she had followed her impulse. Except for members of her family, she made it a point never to touch others. One of her earliest memories was of an incident involving the daughter of a visiting clan chieftain. The adults had been busy discussing whatever it was adults discussed. Young Elphame had become bored and had taken the opportunity to tap the arm of the Chieftain's daughter—she'd been trying to get her attention quietly so that the two of them could sneak off and play. The child had shrieked at Elphame's touch, screaming that the Goddess had marked her and that she was surely going to die. No amount of cajoling could dissuade the little girl from her hysterics. The clan chieftain had left hastily, casting fearful glances at Elphame—even after Etain had assured him that Epona was not interested in the life of her daughter.

Earth spirits might speak to her and the stones welcome her, but mortals did not like being touched by a living goddess.

With a little gasp, Elphame tried to take her hand from

Danann's before he could shrink from her touch, but instead of allowing her to pull away from him, Danann turned his palm up and clasped her hand within his.

"The spirits of the stone tell me that this is where you belong." Elphame felt her face flush. "For as long as I can remember, I have wanted to bring MacCallan Castle back to life," she blurted. "Thank you for joining us here, Danann. Your presence means much to me."

"I am honored to be of service to you, Goddess," he said simply, squeezing her hand before releasing it.

He did not pull away from her in fear or bow down before her in stunned reverence.

It's like she was just an ordinary clan chieftain asking for his help. The thought was so unexpected that Elphame blinked in surprise, and turned quickly to her brother to hide her awkwardness.

"Cu, can you believe that I can Feel the spirit in the stones?"

"Of course I believe it." He smiled at his sister, glad that she looked so happy and animated—almost glad enough to forget how disconcerting it had been to watch the magical glow of the stone engulf her. He had to remember that it was different for her. He was a warrior; he wanted no traffic with things he couldn't best with the stroke of a blade, but Elphame had never felt his unease for magic and the spirit realm. Though she spoke little of it, even to him, Cu knew that his sister had always yearned for a spiritual connection to the Goddess who had so obviously fashioned her body. Elphame was the first-born daughter of the Chosen of Epona. It was never a certainty, but often the Goddess called the eldest daughter of an aging Chosen to follow her mother as spiritual leader of Parthalon. Epona could be grooming Elphame for the day she would take her mother's place. It was the way of the world, Cu reminded himself. He shook off his trepidation and approached Danann, clasping the old centaur's hand in a warm greeting.

"I believe I am better at hearing spirits than I am at surprising a warrior guarding his sister," Danann said wryly.

"Oh, I would say you did a good job of surprising me," Cuchulainn said.

"Cu has been twitchy since last night. Just ignore him," Elphame said as she butted her shoulder against her brother's, grinning at him.

Cuchulainn ignored El's teasing. "Did you come alone, Danann?"

The Stonemaster shook his head and gestured toward the weed-strewn entrance. "No, I joined the rest of your party as they left Loth Tor. They chose to wait outside the walls of the castle. They were not overeager to enter." He shrugged his shoulders and smiled. "The young are often easily frightened by little more than bedtime stories and shadows."

Elphame felt a rush of gratitude for the centaur's common-sense attitude. "And isn't it just like *young* men." She gave her brother a look of sisterly annoyance, lumping him in the ne'er-do-well category. "Instead of getting busy they stand about waiting to be told what to do."

With practiced flair Danann bowed to her, bending one silver-tipped foreleg, while extending the other. Offering his arm in an old courtly gesture, he said, "Then, Goddess, shall I escort you so that you might give the young some direction before they waste their lives in idleness?"

Elphame hesitated. Was she really going to touch someone outside her family twice in one day? She looked from the old centaur's gallantly offered arm to her brother. Cuchulainn winked at her and nodded. She took a deep breath and rested her hand on the Stonemaster's forearm. Her fingers trembled only a little.

Just like a normal person, she thought, unable to contain her smile.

With Cu following close behind, they retraced the path from the ruins of the courtyard back through the gap in the ancient walls to where their party waited.

As Danann had noted, they were a youthful group—most of them younger sons who had been willing to embark upon the adventure of restoring MacCallan Castle because they had the desire to carve their own way in the world. There would be land and opportunity if MacCallan Castle lived again—and that had spelled excitement to their hot blood.

And then there was the young goddess, Elphame. All of Partholon knew that she had been given to them by Epona as a special blessing, but no one quite understood why. Epona's ways were often mysterious. She was a benevolent Goddess, but She did not often meddle with the day-to-day activities of Her people; instead She chose one woman—someone with whom She had a special bond, and it was through this Chosen One that Epona led Her people. That Elphame had been marked so obviously by Partholon's deity, especially while her mother still reigned as Goddess Incarnate, had been a source of awe and speculation since Elphame's birth. Epona had touched Elphame, and now Elphame was determined to restore MacCallan Castle. Surely the honor of accompanying her in her quest would bring them luck that even rumors of the MacCallan curse couldn't tarnish. Or at least that was what they had told themselves as they joined her. They had even believed it, until they had come face-to-face with the crumbling walls of the war-torn castle.

As Elphame stepped into view the men and centaurs who had been gathered nervously several feet from the entrance fell silent. Most of them were accustomed to the sight of the young goddess, but her appearance still affected them—and that particular morning she looked even more extraordinary than usual. Her face was alight and her skin seemed to glow. Several of the young men and centaurs found themselves thinking how spectacular she was, and when her full, sensuous lips tilted up in a brilliant smile, many of the gathered males felt an answering response in their blood—but only briefly— until they reminded themselves that they could not lust after a goddess come to earth. No matter how tempting she appeared.

When Elphame spoke her voice carried through the group like a firebrand. "From the blossoms on the branches, to the singing birds and the whispering breeze, to the pillars of this castle—we are being welcomed. The very stones of MacCallan Castle greet us with joy. It will no longer be a ruin." Elphame raised her hands over her head and shouted, "Rejoice! It will be our home!" Heat tingled through her arms as it had when she communed with the stone and her body felt deliciously on fire.

The group reacted as one, not so much to her words or to the idea of rebuilding MacCallan Castle, instead they responded to her—their spectacular goddess. With one voice they shouted a cheer that caused the ancient walls before them to echo again with the jubilant sounds of the living.

From his hiding place within the trees Lochlan watched the group. Men and centaurs—young and proud. He recognized the fire in their blood as they responded to her. And he recognized her, too. How could he not? He had known that he would find her here. Still, the sight of her jolted him. She looked so much more alive than she had in his dreams, and seeing her in person made him realize that he had never really comprehended the depth of her beauty.

Her body! It radiated passion and otherworldly power. He felt a surge of desire deep within his loins. His blood pumped hot and strong, and with his arousal he felt his massive wings quiver and begin to become erect. Quickly he forced himself to look away from her so that he could bring his lust under control.

Pain spiked in his temples and radiated throughout his body, carried by the blood that pulsed hard and hot within him. His body fought against his desire for control, but, as always, Lochlan pulled from his well of humanity to conquer his darker impulses. The pounding of his blood quieted. His wings shivered once more before refolding neatly against his back.

He ignored the familiar pain that continued to echo, phantomlike through his mind.

Once more in control, he allowed his eyes to return to her. At that instant she raised her arms over her head and the group shouted in response. He smiled, showing long, dangerous-looking canines. She made him want to shout, too. He had been right to come alone; the others could not possibly understand. But thinking of the others sent a tide of despair through him that threatened to engulf him. He could feel them. He could always feel them—their need, their pain, their belief in him. He shuddered and closed that part of his mind. Not now. He could not think of the others now. Not when everything within him that was honorable and true—everything that was human—wanted to rush to her and tell her that she had filled his dreams and his heart for as long as he could remember.

He took a ragged breath and raked his hand across his face. He couldn't go to her. Not in the open. Not yet. They would only see him as a Fomorian; they would kill him. He could not fight them all for her. No matter how desperately he ached to.

Remember your promise. His conscience whispered through his memory in his beloved mother's voice. *Remember the Prophecy.*

It is your destiny to find a way to heal your people and to bring them back to Partholon. It is you who must fulfill Epona's Prophecy.

Lochlan couldn't act selfishly. He had to consider the others. He had to end their pain, even if it meant...

Struggling against a crushing sense of loss he wrenched his gaze from her and soundlessly disappeared back into the depths of the forest.

5

"ARE YOU PURPOSEFULLY trying to spoil my fun and sentence me to a life of celibacy?" Cuchulainn grumbled at his sister.

Elphame grinned. "I hardly think that assigning you to oversee the outdoors, mostly male workers, while I interview women for staff positions at the castle will in any way affect your overactive love life."

"Come, boy. I'll join you and choose which of this sorry young lot might make passable stonemasons," Danann said, clapping him good-naturedly on his shoulder. "Then you can take the rest of them and begin clearing away the mounds of rubble within, as your sister directed." The old centaur winked at Elphame. "Keep this in mind—women will be more likely to grace your bed when the walls around it are sturdy and clean."

"You mean unlike this wreck," Cu said.

"That is precisely what I mean," Danann said.

"Hrumph." Cu snorted as he and the Stonemaster headed out of the main courtyard to return to the workers.

Elphame shook her head at her brother's retreating figure. His strong voice drifted back to her through the courtyard as he called to order the group of men and centaurs who were outside the castle walls. After she'd greeted the workers, Cu, Danann and Elphame had made a quick sweep of the castle grounds, and it hadn't taken long for them to realize that they could do little in the way of restoration before they cleared the debris that had accumulated over the course of the past century. So the first order of business was tedious, but necessary. Cleaning.

Hands on her hips, Elphame looked around her. Now that she was alone she relaxed her expression and narrowed her eyes. What a mess. It was true that the basic walls and structures of the castle were still standing, but everything else was a ruin. What The MacCallan's funeral pyre had missed, time had destroyed. Elphame felt her shoulders slump. It was so much bigger than she had imagined. The castle grounds, ringed by thick stone walls, took up an enormous area. How many people had once lived here? At least as many as currently populated the sleepy little village of Loth Tor. Could she really do it? Could she really restore all of it?

Feeling decidedly overwhelmed, Elphame's eyes were drawn back to the fire-scarred central column. She rubbed her hands together, remembering the warm sensation of communing with the stone. Magic...she had never Felt even a hint of it before, and today she had suddenly been bombarded with the knowledge that she had an affinity for the spirits of the stones. What did that really mean?

"Why not stay here and take my place...I have had a long, rich reign. I am ready to retire."

Her mother's words drifted out of her memory, causing her

stomach to tighten with anxiety. She couldn't take her mother's place! Whether she Felt the spirits in the stones or not, she wasn't ready to lead Partholon; she wasn't her mother.

"Stop it!" Elphame told herself severely. Her mother was Epona's Chosen; she was not. She was just feeling daunted by the enormity of the task before them, which was natural. She glanced at the fire-scarred, crumbling walls. "It's not like you thought it was going to be easy," she muttered, shaking herself mentally. She just needed to get started. Take things one step at a time. Stay in control.

It was her castle. Her home.

"Elphame!" Cuchulainn's voice boomed back along the empty courtyard. "The women are here!"

"This is where I begin," Elphame whispered. She could not lead Partholon—in truth, she had no desire to—but she could make MacCallan Castle live again. She gave the strong central column a parting smile before hurrying to the entrance of the castle.

The women were milling in a small group several feet from the gap in the castle walls. Unnoticed, Elphame watched them from the shadows. They looked young and scared. And they were so few! She quickly counted—just over a dozen. Nearly three times that many men and centaurs had volunteered. And all the women were humans. Not one centaur female had answered her call? Not even a young huntress in training? El allowed herself to feel the disappointment only briefly. She had a job to do and she would simply have to work with what was available to her. Maybe their smaller numbers would give her a chance to get to know them more personally. That would be a nice change.

She didn't allow herself the luxury of hoping that she might actually make a friend—she could hardly imagine such a thing. But maybe this little group of women could learn to interact with her as if she were a clan chieftain, or even a high priestess, instead of treating her like an object to be worshipped—goddess, untouchable and beyond mortal emotions.

When Elphame emerged from the ruin, the group curtsied nervously.

Elphame cleared her throat and put on her best welcoming smile. "Good morning. I am pleased to see that so many of you are interested in restoring MacCallan Castle and making it your home. The men—" she gestured over their heads at the groups that were already forming and beginning to clear rubble from around the castle walls "—will take care of most of the heavy work, but that doesn't mean that your jobs will be any less important. I will need cooks and women who are skilled with weaving and needlepoint." Without realizing it, Elphame's smile turned dreamy. "As MacCallan comes alive again I want to fill its walls with beautiful tapestries that will make even my mother jealous."

Responding to the goddess's sweet expression, several of the women smiled tentatively back at her. Bolstered by their positive reaction, Elphame continued in a strong, sure voice.

"And I will, of course, need women to help me with the daily care of the castle." Elphame laughed and looked pointedly at the weeds and refuse that choked the entry to the castle. "Some days it will definitely need more care than others."

One of the women giggled, and then covered her mouth with her hand and blushed furiously.

Elphame met her eyes. "Don't ever be afraid to laugh here. I know it doesn't look like it now, but the stones sing with happiness at our arrival. MacCallan will be a joyous home."

The girl took her hand from her mouth and smiled shyly at the goddess.

"What is your name?" Elphame asked her.

"Meara," she said, her voice breaking nervously.

"Meara," Elphame repeated. "What job is it that you are most skilled at?"

"I—I—" she stammered and then finally finished in a rush. "I am good at keeping things tidy."

"Then you have come to the right place. There is much tidying awaiting you." Her gaze traveled over the rest of the small group. "Those of you who are good at cleaning, please give your names to Meara." Elphame looked back at the girl she had singled out and saw her eyes widen with pride. "Meara, I will ask you to give me a list of your workers at the end of the day. Now," Elphame began again, "who are my cooks?"

With only a slight hesitation, four young women who had been standing in a little clump close together raised their hands. The one in the middle of the group took a half step forward. She had fiery red hair and lovely jade-colored eyes.

"We heard your call and came from McNamara Castle. The head cook there was…" She paused and looked at her friends for support. They nodded encouragement to her. "She was verra grumpy, and she dinna like young cooks. Aye, she especially dinna not like young cooks with new ideas." The redhead rolled her words with a soft, western brogue.

Elphame raised her eyebrows. "Well, I can assure you that I do not mind young cooks, and I especially *like* new ideas. I do not think I am grumpy, but Cuchulainn would probably disagree with me."

At the mention of her handsome brother's name, the girls tittered and smiled.

"So which among you is the best cook?" Elphame asked.

Three pairs of eyes shifted to the woman who had spoken for them.

"We are all fine cooks, but I admit to having a special talent in the kitchen. My name is Wynne. The lassies who join me

are Ada, Colleen and Ula." She pointed to each woman in turn
as she spoke.

"Wynne, I am pleased to announce that you are my new
head cook," Elphame said. "The first order of business for
you will be inspecting what is left of the castle's kitchens.
Take note of what must be repaired in order to get it into
working order as quickly as possible. You have many hungry
mouths to feed."

"Aye, Goddess," Wynne said, curtseying quickly.

Elphame could feel her jaw setting at the title. Goddess.
They would never see her as herself—Elphame, a young
woman who liked to run and laugh with her family and had a
tendency to be a little too fond of long soaks in her mother's
bathing pool—at least they wouldn't as long as everyone
insisted upon seeing her only as a goddess.

Perhaps this new beginning could change that. She made
the decision quickly.

"Ladies," she said, and the chattering that had begun silenced as all eyes turned to her. "I would like to ask a favor
of each of you. We are going to be working closely together,
and I would prefer it if you would call me by my name instead
of by the title of Goddess."

The women blinked at her, shocked expressions mirrored
on each face.

Elphame sighed.

"Or you could call me my Lady. Anything but Goddess,"
she said, feeling a little desperate when no one spoke. "Let's
see," she continued quickly. "What else? I know. Is there
anyone here who is skilled at weaving or needlepoint?"

Several hands went up. Elphame caught the eye of one
rather plump blonde whose rosy face seemed to have a per-
petual glow.

"What is your name?" El asked her.

"Caitlin."

"Caitlin, can you weave or needlepoint?"

"Both, Godde—my Lady."

"Excellent. I have several ideas for the new tapestries. Actually, I would like them to reflect a theme for each major room of the castle, beginning with the Great Hall." Elphame's voice lit with excitement. "And the theme for the Great Hall will be the castle itself. I want the tapestries to show MacCallan Castle living again in all of its grandeur and beauty."

Caitlin blinked several times before speaking. "But, Goddess…ur…I mean, my Lady, how will we know what to weave? It—" she pointed helplessly at the hulking structure before them "—it doesn't look so grand now."

Elphame frowned. She'd forgotten that everyone didn't have a picture of the restored castle imprinted upon their minds.

"I suppose I will have to find an artist…." She trailed off, staring at her beloved, tumbledown castle.

"I could sketch it for you, my Lady."

El's head snapped around and she searched the women, trying unsuccessfully to see who had spoken.

"Who spoke?" she asked.

The same soft voice answered from the rear of the group. "I am Brenna."

"Come here, I can't see you," Elphame said impatiently.

The group parted to let a petite brunette woman through. Her head was bowed and her face was obscured. Elphame noticed immediately that the rest of the women averted their eyes from her, as if the sight of her made them uncomfortable. Then the small woman lifted her head. Elphame felt an unexpected jolt run through her body as she looked the woman full in the face, and El had to force her expression to remain impassive.

Brenna was young, and had once been pretty, Elphame

could tell that from the left side of her face. The right side of her face was a ruin. A terrible burn scar ran from her neck all the way up to cover the entire right side of her face. It was thick and mottled with the shiny pink and white pigments that distinguished the deepest of burns. The right side of her mouth was missing its lip line, which was all the more horrible when compared to the smooth fullness of the unharmed lips on the other side of her face. Her right eye was clear and appeared unharmed. It was the same doe brown as her left eye, but the scars at the corner of it seemed to pull it down, giving it a droopy appearance.

She stood very still, letting Elphame study her. She met the goddess's gaze unflinchingly.

"I believe I can draw your castle for you," she said in a clear, confident voice.

"Are you an artist, Brenna?" Elphame asked.

"I have a small talent for sketching, especially for sketching things that I imagine in my mind." She smiled a crooked smile that Elphame was surprised to find endearing. "So I think I might be able to sketch things that you imagine, too, if you can describe them to me."

El nodded enthusiastically, but before she could speak Brenna continued, "But you should know that I do not consider myself an artist. I am a Healer."

Elphame's face split into a wide smile. "Then you are most welcome, Brenna. With all these workers lugging this and building that, we are bound to have several mishaps that will require a Healer's touch. I know my own brother, though an accomplished warrior, is uncommonly prone to cuts and scrapes."

For an instant Elphame saw Brenna's expression change, and it was as if a shadow passed over the young woman's ravaged face. But she responded with no hesitation.

"Of course, my Lady. I am always pleased to be where I am needed."

"Elphame!" Like a masculine tornado, Cuchulainn strode through the group of women. Eyes sparkling, he nodded to several of the prettiest before he reached his sister's side. "The supply wagons are bottled up in that mess that was once called the main road to the castle. I have dispatched the centaurs to meet them and to hack a path through to the front walls. When the wagons get here I think it best that we set up tents outside the castle walls, at least until we can make that monster inhabitable again."

Elphame raised on arched eyebrow at him and crossed her arms.

Cuchulainn laughed. "Okay! Forgive me for calling your palace a monster."

"It is not a palace. It is a castle," she corrected him.

"Well, your *castle* is not fit for man nor beast." He winked at the pleasingly plump Caitlin, who blushed a becoming shade of mauve. "Nor lovely lady." He gestured behind them. "The area of grasslands there, southwest of the castle that runs from the southern wall to the edge of the sea cliff, will be the easiest to clear. In a couple days we should have the tents erected and a camp set up. Until then the people of Loth Tor will be pleased to board us." Cu grinned at Elphame cheekily. "If that suits you, my Lady."

Elphame restrained herself from boxing his ears. "Yes, yes, that's fine. But I will need some men to accompany my head cook and her staff. It's important that the kitchens are restored quickly." She jabbed at his ribs. "Men need more than dried meat and hard biscuits in their stomachs if they are to work long days."

Cuchulainn chuckled and grabbed his side. He liked seeing his sister so relaxed in public—usually she kept their sibling banter to times when it was just the two of them. Restoring the hulking edifice might just be good for her if it taught her to loosen up.

"As much as I am loath to admit it, you are right, sister-mine. I will put several men at your—or rather your cook's—disposal." His eyes glinted mischievously. "Which means you will have to introduce me to your cook."

Elphame rolled her eyes at him before calling out her new head cook. "Wynne, this annoying young man is my brother. Cuchulainn, meet my head cook."

Cuchulainn gave her a rakish bow. "Well met, Wynne of the flaming hair."

"And the same to ye, my Lord," said the new cook, giving him a look of blatantly female appraisal.

"Now you know her name, Cu. Have some men come find her. She'll be inside the castle, as will the rest of us," she said, pushing him back the way he had come.

"Ah, you are forever all work, sister-mine." Cu backed away from the group, bowing gallantly. "Ladies, until later."

The women curtsied and called goodbyes to him.

"My brother is a rogue." She hadn't realized she'd said the thought aloud until Wynne, who was still gazing after Cuchulainn's retreating broad shoulders, spoke up.

"Aye, but a devilishly handsome one." Then, as if she was afraid she'd overstepped an imaginary boundary, her face paled and she muttered a hasty apology.

Elphame waved her hand dismissively and said with forced nonchalance, "Just keep the emphasis on devilish and you'll save yourself a wagonful of heartache."

Would they never be at ease in her presence? Would they always act like she was a holy conduit to be tiptoed around? She was trying her best to behave "normally" around the women. Hadn't she just teased with Cu in front of them?

It will take time to show them that I'm not that different, she told herself firmly. This was her new beginning, but she had to be patient. Years of living one way wouldn't be erased in one morning. Reining in her frustration she addressed the group.

"Let's get to work. I know each of you has special talents, and I do appreciate that." She smiled at the women, especially the individuals she'd already been introduced to, and noticed for the first time that Brenna was no longer standing near her. Instead she had disappeared once more into the rear fringes of the group. "But I'm afraid for now we must all emulate Meara—we must get things tidy before we can separate and focus on our individual talents. So, let us begin by clearing the entryway to our new home."

Without waiting for a response, Elphame walked purposefully to the overgrown gap in the castle walls. Grimly, she bent and grabbed a long section of rusted iron that once stood proud and straight as part of MacCallan's always-opened gate. She tugged, using her powerful leg muscles to give her added strength, and the piece of iron slid reluctantly free of the clinging vines.

She looked up to see the women's eyes flicking back and forth between watching her and peering into the shadows within the castle's walls. They looked anxious and afraid. No doubt they were thinking of the bedtime stories they'd been told about the curse of MacCallan Castle. Elphame could almost see the reflections of imagined ghosts in their eyes. She knew they needed words of encouragement, but she really wasn't good at that—the speech she had given to the men earlier that day had been a fluke; she had still been riding high on the magical tide of hearing the spirits in the castle's stones. Giving inspiring speeches was her mother's specialty, not hers.

But they needed her to reassure them; the nervous way their eyes kept returning to her said that they thought she had all the answers. And an idea came to her. She might not have all the answers, but she was completely sure of one thing. Mac-Callan Castle was her home. Now it would be their home as well. And suddenly she knew what to say to them.

"I think it's only right that we clear the opening to our new home. It's women who are the heart of a home, be it a castle, a temple or a modest cottage. Women breathe life into the family, as our Goddess, Epona, breathes life into our world with each dawn. As women of the castle, let's reopen MacCallan to the living, and, in turn, make it our home."

Elphame could hear the collective sigh as her words seemed to release the tension that had built within the group.

Meara hurried forward, grabbed a dead branch and tossed it on the pile Elphame had started.

"At least we know we're needed here," she said with a tone of satisfaction that made the others smile.

"Aye, that is a certainty," Wynne said as she began to pull at one section of the massive tangle of weeds that filled the opening. Without further hesitation, her three newly named assistant cooks joined her. Then the rest of the group fell to work, chattering and laughing and making slightly off-color jokes about women needing to open the way for men, or else they tended to lose their way.

Elphame stepped back and watched them. She could already tell that they were a hardworking group. No one complained about getting her hands dirty; no one whined about needing a break. El thought about what Meara had said: *"At least we know we're needed here."* Maybe that was it. This small group of women all had one thing in common—in their old homes, their old lives, they hadn't been needed, so they had come in search of the sense of belonging that being needed would provide.

They will always have that here with me, a home where they are needed and appreciated. As Elphame made the promise to herself, for just an instant she thought she heard the whisper of a voice on the wind that said, *Well done, Beloved.*

6

"IT LOOKS REALLY dark and scary." Caitlin's soft voice echoed against the empty inner walls of the castle.

The women were standing barely a step inside the newly cleared entrance to MacCallan Castle. They'd spent what was left of the morning removing a century's worth of rubble from the space, now it looked like a giant's mouth minus its cleanly pulled front teeth. Lunch had been a quick break that consisted of hard biscuits, cheese and dried meat, wolfed down hastily between weeding and chopping—Elphame could imagine her mother's shudder of disgust at the food and what she would label the barbaric way in which it had been eaten, but she had loved every hurried bite of it.

Now it was time for step two—actually entering the castle and beginning the decidedly more complex work of changing ancient destruction into a well-ordered home.

But first she'd have to rally her troops. Again.

"It's not really dark," she said, taking a few steps inside the protective outer walls. She pointed to the empty doorway that led to the interior of the castle through which could just barely be glimpsed the inner courtyard and the massive stone columns. "It looks dark because everything is still covered with soot from the fire. Not to mention dirt from years of standing open to the elements." She smiled encouragingly at Caitlin. "All it needs is a good scrubbing and some careful attention, and it won't be dark anymore."

Caitlin, as well as the rest of the women, still looked unconvinced. Well, she thought, she may as well face what all of them were thinking—get it out in the open so that they could deal with it.

"And about the curse." Elphame paused. It seemed to her that even the stones had stopped to listen to her next words. "There is no such thing," she said slowly and distinctly. "I have that assurance from the Incarnate of Epona herself, as well as my own intuition." As she spoke, Elphame backed a few more steps until she was standing directly within the inner doorway. She gestured behind her.

"There is still much beauty here. You just have to look for it. Please don't let silly stories told to frighten naughty children taint your trust in your new home." *Or in me.* She added the plea silently. She didn't want her people to skulk around Mac-Callan, jumping at shadows and being chased by imagined demons.

"I have never been afraid of bedtime stories, my Lady."

Elphame recognized the woman's voice even before she stepped from her habitual place in the shadows at the rear of the group. Brenna had stopped bowing her head and hiding behind a wall of hair—they'd all been too busy that day to care overly much about appearances. But El had noticed that Brenna kept to herself, and that she rarely was included in the easy banter that had already begun to link the rest of the women. Now her sharp gaze held Elphame's eyes.

"But I have found that sometimes fantasies and imaginings can be more powerful than reality. Because of that, it is wise to dispel the ghosts of *un*reality before they overwhelm that which is truth."

Elphame liked the quiet, confident way Brenna spoke.

"What is it you suggest, Brenna?"

"A simple cleansing ceremony, one that will clear any negative energy as well as protect and welcome us as the castle's new inhabitants," Brenna said.

The other women were watching Brenna with expressions of mixed curiosity and relief.

"Tell us what you need," Elphame said.

"The ceremony is simple. All we need to complete it is basil and containers with which to hold fresh water."

"It is possible that I might still find basil that has gone wild in the castle's herb garden," Wynne said.

"Herbs are resilient. Chances are good that you will find basil, if you can find the cook's garden," Brenna told her.

"I can find a cook's garden in any castle." Wynne put a flint edge to her melodic brogue.

"And there should be something left in there that can hold water," Meara added. "It is a place that was once filled with people, and where there are people, there must be housekeeping tools."

"Good ideas, Wynne and Meara. Half of you go with our cook to find the basil, the other half of you search with Meara for crocks or buckets or anything at all that can hold water," Elphame said briskly. "Then bring your finds back here and we will begin the ceremony."

Elphame really hadn't expected them to react so readily, but the women quickly divided into two groups and, like domestic warriors, they descended upon the ancient castle. Yes, they were talking and laughing in overly loud voices, as if to scare away anything that might be lurking in the shadows, but they had actually entered the castle itself, without cringing or crying or shrieking in fear. Elphame remembered how earlier that morning the men and centaurs had refused to follow Danann within the castle walls. Now those same walls rang with the sounds of busy women. It was certainly a step in the right direction.

"Fear can usually be overcome through common sense and tasks that are familiar and simple," Brenna said softly. She hadn't left with the women. She and Elphame were alone near the entrance to the castle.

El smiled at her. "It was wise of you to think of the cleansing ceremony. All I could think of was how silly it is to be afraid of a place that holds so much hope for the future. I wanted to yell at them and try to force them to see that the stories aren't true. Your way was better."

"Not better, my Lady, just easier for them to understand," Brenna said humbly, but she bowed her head slightly in acknowledgment of Elphame's compliment.

"Are you a shaman?" Elphame asked curiously.

Brenna smiled her crooked smile. "It flatters me that you would think so. No, I cannot heal the spirit, as a shaman can, but I do acknowledge that in order to treat the flesh I must have some knowledge of the spirit realm."

Elphame felt her smile widen. "You sound like my father—only he says the opposite. He cannot heal the body, but he must have a working knowledge of it to heal problems of the spirit."

"Midhir is a great shaman. I have only met him once, but that one time he showed me kindness that I will never forget."

"I didn't know…" Elphame clamped her mouth shut. She almost said that she didn't know her father had treated anyone who was so severely scarred. How insensitive of her! She coughed and cleared her throat to cover her awkwardness. "...Didn't know that you knew my father."

"I do not really know him, my Lady. As I said, I have only met him once."

Elphame nodded, still chagrined at herself, and said hurriedly, "Where are you from, Brenna?"

"Guardian Castle was my home," Brenna said.

"I'm glad you chose to join us, but I hope Guardian Castle won't feel the lack of their Healer too keenly."

Brenna looked away from Elphame, but not before she saw the pain that flashed through her mismatched eyes.

"It was time for me to leave. It was time for a new beginning," Brenna said quietly.

"I think I understand," Elphame said.

Brenna's eyes snapped back to her, and she opened her mouth to reply that Elphame, with her perfect, beautiful face, could not begin to understand. But the words would not come, and not because the Healer was afraid of this powerful woman. Slowly her gaze traveled down Elphame's body. She was dressed much like the rest of the women, in a plain, serviceable linen dress that wrapped across her chest and was held in place over each shoulder by simple brooches. The dress left her arms bare and free for working, and from the bodice it wrapped in soft, intricate folds—much like the kilts the men wore—to end, as was customary in Partholon, just above her knees. There Brenna's eyes stopped. Elphame was dressed like the rest of the women, but that was where the similarity ended. Instead of slim knees and shapely, feminine calves and ankles tapering down to leather-soled shoes, Elphame had powerful equine legs and hocks that were covered with a slick, lustrous coat of hair the same deep auburn shade as on her head. The incredible legs ended in hooves that glinted like polished ebony.

She was not a human, but she was most definitely not a centaur, either. She was something set apart from the rest of Partholon. Brenna's eyes lifted to meet Elphame's again.

"Yes, I think you might very well understand," she said slowly.

The two unique women smiled tentatively at one another.

The women returned much more quickly than Elphame had anticipated. Meara's group had found two usable containers. One was a chipped crock that had been half buried in filth, and the other was a blackened bucket that had somehow escaped being consumed by the fire.

"It's obvious neither have bathed for years," Meara said with distaste. "They need a good scrubbing." Then she added under her breath, "As does this entire castle."

Elphame stifled her grin. Meara was definitely the right choice to lead a formidable force of house-tidiers, and it was better that she was grumbling about the job ahead of her than running in fear from an imagined curse.

"There is a stream not far from here that runs from the forest to the cliff and empties into the ocean." One of the women spoke up.

"It's Arlene, isn't it?" Elphame asked.

The young woman nodded shyly. "Aye, uh, my Lady. I was raised in Loth Tor and I know this area well." Her voice was rich with western Partholon's thick brogue.

"Wonderful. You can show Meara the stream. Meara, take as many women with you as you need to give those a good scrubbing."

With a satisfied grunt, Meara motioned for several women to join her, and they trudged away, Arlene leading the little group.

"And I found plenty of basil." Wynne opened her skirts and several wide-leafed basil plants tumbled to the ground, filling the air with their distinctive aroma that brought to mind delicious red sauces and long, enjoyable meals.

Elphame inhaled deeply and noticed several of the other women did the same. She smiled at them and thought it must be nearing dinnertime if all of them were thinking of food.

"I also found the kitchens. They are in quite a shambles." The cook frowned down at the basil as if the herbs were responsible for the disarray.

Elphame's heart sank. "Can they be repaired, or must they be completely rebuilt?" She had hoped that the kitchens could be put back into working order in a relatively short amount of time.

"It willna be easy, but I believe they can be repaired. The foundation is strong, and much of it survived the fire."

For no explainable reason, Wynne's words brought tears to Elphame's eyes. She blinked rapidly, not wanting the women to misunderstand her emotional response. When she was sure of her voice, she said, "I think we will find that over and over again in our new home—the foundation is strong, and much of it has survived."

The women made little sounds of agreement, and Elphame felt her eyes well up again.

"El! Are you ready for those men yet?" Cuchulainn's voice boomed from behind them, causing the women to jump.

For once Elphame was glad of her brother's distraction, and she wiped quickly at her eyes.

Cu was too busy showing off his white smile to notice his sister's sudden display of emotions.

He winked at Wynne, who was hastily trying to brush the crushed basil and dirt from her skirts. "When I told the men what lovely ladies they would be assisting, I had many willing volunteers."

"Yes, yes, yes Cuchulainn, we get the idea." Elphame

frowned at him. At least he was consistently incorrigible. "We're almost ready for them. But first we have to perform the cleansing ceremony."

"Cleansing ceremony?"

Elphame gave her brother a smug look. Now that she mentioned magic, she had his undivided attention.

"That's right. Our new Healer thought a ceremony of ritual cleansing and protection would be a wise idea before we begin working on the interior of the castle. I agree with her."

It was Cuchulainn's turn to frown.

"It's just a simple cleansing ceremony, Cu. No one's going to cast any spells or summon any spirit guides." El winked at him and he grunted an unintelligible response. "Let me introduce you to our Healer…" She trailed off. A moment before Brenna had been standing beside her, but now her place was empty. El's eyes quickly searched the group of women and she caught sight of Brenna's brunette hair. Once again, she had melted silently to the rear of the group.

Elphame wanted to groan in frustration. If she was going to be their Healer, she was going to have to stop hiding every time a man came near. What did Brenna think, that her brother was going to shrink from her, or scream in horror? Then El remembered the look in the young woman's eyes when she had said that she needed a new beginning. Perhaps that was the exact response she did expect, especially from a handsome young man. Well, Brenna didn't know Cuchulainn as his sister knew him. He might be an incorrigible flirt, but he was a good man with a kind heart. He would never purposely hurt a woman.

"Brenna," she called. "I'd like you to meet my brother."

Slowly, the Healer moved from the rear of the group. Her head was bowed again, and she did not lift it until she was standing beside Elphame. Then, with a sigh, she looked up.

Elphame was watching her brother, and she saw his expression go flat at his first glimpse of the young woman's horrendous scares, but he didn't cringe and he didn't look away.

"Cuchulainn, this is our new Healer, Brenna."

"Well met, Lady Brenna," Cu said, bowing his head courteously.

"I thought the two of you should be introduced. I already told Brenna how accident prone you are," Elphame said, smiling warmly at Brenna, who seemed to be totally engrossed in studying her feet.

"I would be pleased to give aid wherever it is needed," Brenna said. Her voice was barely above a whisper, and Elphame had to strain to hear her.

"As I said before, it was Brenna's idea to perform a cleansing ceremony." Elphame's eyes swept through the little group of women, including them in her words. "And we thought it an excellent idea."

The women spoke bright, chattering agreement with Elphame, but she noticed that her brother was still looking intently at Brenna.

"Are you a shaman, Brenna?" Cuchulainn asked abruptly.

Reluctantly, Brenna pulled her eyes up and looked directly at the handsome young warrior. "No, Cuchulainn, I am not," she said with the same whispering voice. "But I do have some knowledge of the Spirit World, and I am familiar with the rituals which evoke its blessing."

"Good. I think it wise that we call upon the spirit realm to aid my sister in restoring MacCallan Castle," he said intently.

Elphame blinked in surprise. What was he saying? Cu hated any mention of the spirit realm—it always made him uncomfortable. She narrowed her eyes at him.

"Cu, are you feeling well?"

Before he could answer, Meara and her group of women

burst through the entrance. Their arms and skirts were soaked, but they were carrying two freshly cleaned containers that sparkled with water. When they saw Cuchulainn, they stopped and dropped into hasty curtseys, giggling as water sloshed onto the ground.

Cu grinned at the women. "How could I not be well, surrounded by such lovely faces?"

Now he sounded like himself. Elphame shook her head at him and told him to hush, but she made a mental note to ask him later about his sudden desire for spiritual backup.

"You can leave now, Cu." She shooed him off before turning to the Healer. "Brenna, what do we need to do?"

"Take the basil and crush it into the water." As she explained the ceremony, her voice grew from the halting, whispering tone in which she had spoken to Cuchulainn to the clear, confident voice of the Healer Elphame was already beginning to respect. "Each woman should be a part of this. Each of you take some of the basil leaves and smooth them into the water, and as you do so, concentrate on all of the wonderful things you would like your new home to hold."

Brenna beckoned to Meara, who was standing closest to the containers. A little nervously, the housekeeper picked up a sprig of basil, then she bent and immersed it into the cool, fresh water crushing the lime-colored leaves and gently swirling the water.

"Good," Brenna encouraged.

"It's soft and cool, and it smells wonderful," Meara told the rest of the women. Without further hesitation, Wynne, Ada and Colleen grabbed pieces of the little plants, and soon the bucket and the crock were surrounded by smiling women up to their elbows in green-tinged water.

"Close your eyes," Brenna told them, "think about your dreams for your new home—your hopes and desires for your future—think of what you wish for…what you long for."

As one, they closed their eyes and Elphame watched the women's faces grow faraway. Satisfied smiles tilted their lips.

"We must join them, my Lady," Brenna said.

Elphame nodded and she and the Healer each chose a sprig of basil. Elphame approached the crock, which was already well crowded with concentrating women. She squeezed in between Meara and Caitlin. No one gasped or shrank away from being in such close proximity with her. The women were so engrossed in their own thoughts that no one even seemed to notice her. It was nice, she thought, really nice to feel just like everyone else—even if it was only for a short time. Elphame closed her eyes and thrust her hand into the water, crushing the basil against her palm.

And all at once she could hear the silent desires of the women surrounding her. It was like the water was a conduit for their thoughts and dreams, and all of them emptied into her. Elphame held her breath, savoring each desire as it flooded through her.

Please bring my home happiness…. Let me know the joy of a good husband…. More than anything I want children…. Please let me never be hungry…. I want to always be safe…. I want to be accepted for who I am….

Their pleas washed through Elphame in a rush of emotions and she held them close to her heart and cherished them. Then she added her own desire, and almost without even being aware of it, Elphame's thoughts shifted from her constant plea to fit in and be normal. For the first time the desire that was foremost in her heart was not one that focused solely on herself.

Please let all who enter MacCallan Castle find it a safe haven and help me to be a wise and understanding leader.

"Now the rest of the ceremony must be completed by you, Goddess," Brenna said. Her confident voice rippled through the group of women, breaking the spell of thoughts that Elphame had been absorbing. They opened their eyes, blinking as if to reorient themselves after awaking from pleasant dreams, then they stood, wiping green-speckled hands on their skirts and looking expectantly at Elphame.

She felt a horrible shiver of trepidation. She had assumed Brenna would lead them in the ceremony, as she had in the preparations. El had never performed any type of ritualistic magic. Even during her education at the Temple of the Muse she had avoided the training that involved spellwork and the invocation of any deities. She knew that the other students had gossiped amongst themselves about her strange avoidance and that they all had assumed it was because she was so powerful that she need not have mortal guidance when she communed with the spirit realm. The people expected that she would follow her mother as Epona's Chosen—that she, as her mother and great-grandmother before her, would reign as the spiritual leader of Partholon. Just the thought made Elphame feel ill because, unfortunately, the truth was far from what they believed. Though she had longed for it, she had never felt any stirrings of magic—not from spirits, nor from the gods, and especially not from Epona. It would avail her nothing to study magic. She had no magic beyond that of her physical abnormalities.

Until she entered MacCallan Castle and the spirits of the stones had welcomed her, she corrected herself. Things were different here. MacCallan Castle was a new beginning for all of them. That did not mean that she would be forced to take up her mother's mantle; it meant that she had finally found where she belonged. Pushing aside insecurities that had haunted her for years, she met Brenna's eyes.

"What must I do?" Elphame asked.

"We will need to carry the containers to the entrance of the castle," Brenna said, and the task was quickly done. She positioned the containers within the newly cleared gap in the wide walls, and told Elphame to stand between them, facing outward. The other women were to stand just outside the entrance. "Now, you must call on each of the four elements in their turn—air, fire, water and earth. Ask them to cleanse this castle and fill it with protection as you scatter the herb-scented water to each of the four corresponding directions. There are no set words for you to recite, instead speak from your heart. We will follow your lead, Goddess." Thus saying, Brenna turned her back to Elphame and motioned for the rest of the women to do so, too. All of them were facing the east.

East...Elphame thought frantically. East was the beginning direction for all spellwork and for all circle casting. Its element was air—she knew that much, as did any half-grown Partholonian child. And east was the direction the castle faced. She drew in her breath with the realization. It must be a good omen.

She closed her eyes, settled her thoughts, and sent up a heartfelt prayer to a real Goddess. *Epona, if you can hear me, I don't ask that you speak to me as you do to my mother—I don't expect that. I just ask that you help me not to disappoint these women, and help me to honor the spirits I have just today begun to feel. Please give me the right words for the blessing and protection of our new home.*

She could do this, she promised herself as she opened her eyes and bent to cup the first handful of herb-filled water.

Looking out to the east she raised her hands in front of her and let the fragrant, grass-colored water slide from her fingers.

"I call upon you, Power of Air, to witness this rite. You are the element we encounter upon birth as we draw our first breaths. I ask that you fill MacCallan Castle as it is reborn and scatter any negative forces from it. Breathe within its walls protection and peace."

Suddenly a breeze ruffled Elphame's long hair. It twisted

playfully around her, catching the falling drops of water and making them appear to dance on the wind, clearly showing Elphame that her words had been heard and accepted. Elphame's answering smile was filled with stunned joy.

After the wind died she took a deep breath and turned to her right so that she was facing south—the direction of the element fire. The group of women followed her, turning to face south, too. She cupped another handful of water and held it out before her.

"I call upon you, Power of Fire, to witness this rite. It is from you that we draw warmth, light and energy. Your strength has already purified MacCallan Castle. I ask that you continue to guard it and us as we make it our new home."

As she spoke, she felt the sun's rays flash on her and it seemed that the magically enhanced warmth of it reached into her very soul.

Elphame and the women turned to the right again. She filled her hands with water.

"I call upon you, Power of Water, to witness this rite. You are present in our bodies as tears, milk and blood. You fill us and sustain us. Wash MacCallan Castle of the ancient pain of the past. Cleanse it and guard it with the joy of the present as it stands, ever watchful, above your shore."

The sound of the distant waves breaking against the cliff suddenly swelled and echoed with deafening intensity through-out the castle walls.

When the sound receded Elphame turned again, facing to the north and the element earth, completing the circle.

"I call upon you, Power of Earth, to witness this rite. You stabilize and shelter us. We feel your spirit in the very stones of this castle. I ask that you use your vast power to reject any lin-gering negative energy, and that you protect MacCallan Castle with the strength of new growth coupled with ancient wisdom."

The grass on which they stood rustled like a giant hand had just passed over it and the air surrounding them was filled with the rich fragrance of a bountiful harvest.

Then, acting on impulse, Elphame bent one more time. She cupped her hands and as she tossed the water high into the air directly above her, she said in a clear, joyful voice, "And I call upon you, Epona, to witness this rite and to gift MacCallan Castle, our new home, with your blessing and your protection."

The droplets of water exploded around Elphame like liquid stars and the women erupted into cheers.

"Come!" Brenna cried, hurrying to one of the containers of basil water. She dipped her hands and smiled her lopsided smile at the women. "Let us baptize our new home." So saying, she splashed the handful of water so that it rained against the ancient stones. Soon all the women were laughing and shrieking with joy as handfuls of softly scented water playfully washed away the last of their fears.

Hidden within the little grove of trees closest to the castle's entrance, Cuchulainn watched the women. The cleansing ritual had been powerful—that was easy to see. He could hardly believe that it was his sister who had spoken the words and invoked such an obvious, elemental response. But he had to believe it; he had borne witness to it. And the power within him—the power that he constantly had to repress in order to control—had leaped in response to her magical rite which had clearly been infused with the blessing of Epona. He had felt the cleansing, as well as the invisible walls of protection that Elphame had suddenly erected in a magical circle which encompassed MacCallan Castle.

He had thought briefly that perhaps he was feeling the psychic residue of Epona's anger at the Fomorian invaders.

Over a century ago the war had begun with the slaughter of the MacCallan Clan, an act that had so inflamed Epona that the Goddess's Chosen had rallied the people of Partholon. Centaurs and humans had joined together to defeat the demonic horde. Was that why Epona had touched his sister's ritual? To show the Goddess's approval of rebuilding Mac-Callan Castle? Was it as simple as that?

No. He knew that there had been more—something else had been present during his sister's ritual. And try as he would, he could not understand what it was. It was elusive, but he knew what it reminded him of. It was much like the Feeling he had experienced during his vision of Elphame's lifemate. It was dark. It was waiting. And it was here.

Cuchulainn was here, too, and he would protect his sister from harm. Even if that harm should come from one whose destiny it was to love her.

His hand rested on his claymore and his face was grim as he turned from the women and the castle. Ever vigilant, his warrior's eyes searched the forest that surrounded them, seeking the source of that which he feared would break his sister's heart.

7

ELPHAME THOUGHT THAT they smelled like a basil-filled garden after a spring rain. She brushed a damp strand of hair behind her ear, but not before picking a crushed leaf from it, and smiled to herself. The women—as well as the castle—had been cleansed. It had been a nice break, and a wonderful ritual. Elphame glanced up at the sky. The sun seemed to be sinking awfully fast. She stifled a frustrated sigh. She would be glad when the hearths were filled with brightly burning fires, and dusk would signal the lighting of the castle's brands—then the coming of evening would not call a halt to their work. But it certainly did now. Quickly she prioritized in her mind. The kitchens needed to be attended to, that should come first.

Then a niggling thought brushed at her. *Clear the Main Court-yard. Allow the heart of the castle to beat again.* Elphame felt a little jolt of surprise. Had that been her own thought? No, *thought* wasn't the right word. Her sudden desire to clear the courtyard felt more like a compulsion that beat in time with her blood.

"My Lady? What is our next task?"

Elphame broke from her inner musings and smiled at Brenna, pleased that the Healer had stopped calling her Goddess. She motioned for the women to gather around her. She searched for and found Wynne.

"Let's get the kitchen in working order. Rebuilding a home is hungry work."

Wynne's smile was bright agreement. "I know exactly where 'tis."

Elphame, of course, knew where the kitchen was located, too. She had glimpsed it on the quick walk-through she'd done with her brother and the Stonemaster, but she was content to allow her new cook the pleasure of leading them to what would become Wynne's personal territory.

"Show us," Elphame said.

And just like that the women surged as one into the castle. No hesitation. No trepidation. No nervous laughter. It was as if the air had been cleared of the emotional cobwebs of the past—now all that waited to be done was to clear its physical refuse so that the future could begin.

Elphame knew that Cuchulainn would tell her she was being an idealistic fool, but she was so happy that it felt like her heart might burst.

The women entered the Main Courtyard as a group, and suddenly their amiable talk was silenced. The great center column of Clan MacCallan stood silent and awe-inspiring, stretching to a majestic height well above their heads. Elphame left the group and approached it. She could still feel the phantom warmth of her commune with the spirits of the stone against her palms. But this time she didn't rest her hands against the granite surface, instead she faced the group of women.

"This is the center column of MacCallan Castle," she explained to them. "Always remember that this was once the home of the much-honored Clan MacCallan. They were warriors, but they also were poets and artists. Many of Epona's Chosen have had MacCallan blood pulsing in their veins. They revered beauty and truth, which is why Epona showed such rage at their slaughter." She pointed up the column's length. "If you look closely you can see that beneath the layers of grime and soot, it is decorated with symbols that were important to the MacCallans. Creatures and plants of the surrounding forest, as well as the Clan's symbol of a rearing mare, have all been intricately carved within the interlinking circular pattern."

Several of the women nodded and stepped closer, peering with open curiosity at the mighty pillar.

"This should be cleaned so that its original beauty can be seen," Meara said, with the same no-nonsense tone she had used when she ordered the dirty water containers to be scrubbed.

"It will be," Elphame assured her. "As will this entire courtyard. Look at the floor." The women's eyes drifted to their feet. Without stopping to consider that she might be drawing unwanted attention to her unique body, she pawed forward with one sharp hoof, loosening a small trench in the dirt that covered the floor. "See," she said with a satisfied smile. "Beneath all of this filth there is a thick layer of fine marble. When it is clean it will shine just as brightly as the pearl-colored halls of Epona's Temple."

The women talked together in excited little bursts of conversation as they studied the hidden treasure that lay beneath them.

The heart of the castle... Elphame's thoughts kept returning to the words that had seemed to resonate throughout her body. The women's reactions showed that they, too, were moved by it. It must live again. *Soon,* she promised herself and the time-scarred column.

"Lead us to your new kitchens, Wynne," Elphame said.

The cook flushed with pleasure before she strode purposefully from the courtyard through another empty arched doorway which led to an enormous room. There the women paused.

In the Great Hall the ceiling had been built of the same dull gray stone as the walls of the castle, so the fire could not consume it, but the walls were blackened and the huge room looked dark and sad. Mounds of burnt wood testified to the fact that long ago tiers of heavy wooden tables had stood in busy rows overlooking the ruined floor-to-ceiling frame that once was a wall of windows which let the castle occupants dine and hold court with a view of the austere Main Courtyard of the castle.

Now all that was left of it was rubble, but Elphame could still see the solid bones of the castle through what time had covered—and she could tell by the gleam in many of the women's eyes that they understood the potential there, too.

"There are two entrances to the kitchen from the Great Hall." Wynne's voice said she was more than ready to get down to business. "One there, and one there." She pointed to small arched doorways on opposite sides of the far wall. She talked as she walked toward one of the doorways. "They are connected by a long hall, which opens to the kitchen." She glanced at her three assistants. "We should designate one door to always be used as an entrance, and one as an exit. There will be fewer accidents that way."

The assistant cooks nodded in thoughtful response. Elphame had to stop herself from shouting with relief. They were beginning to see it as a living, working castle, too!

Because the kitchen was a part of the Great Hall, its stone roof was still intact, too. But, as in the rest of the castle, the room was a shambles. Elphame heard the distinctive rustle of birds and the scurrying of other small creatures, and she supposed that a whole tribe of animals had taken up residence in what used to be the castle's two enormous cooking hearths. Brick ovens lined one wall, and as Wynne peered within one of them a squirrel leaped out and rushed away in a chattering panic, causing the cook to stifle a shriek, which turned into a laugh.

"He probably thought I was a verra big, wet piece of basil," she said, and the rest of the women laughed with her.

The remaining wall held a large basin and a rusted pump through which fresh water had been available. To either side of the pump, stone cabinets gaped their open, debris-cluttered mouths. In the center of the room was a great marble island on which were piles of leaves and suspicious-looking droppings.

"Well, sister-mine, what's for dinner?" Cuchulainn's voice said in her ear.

She jumped and swatted at him. "Your hide if you scare me like that again!"

"His hide would be too tough to chew, Goddess," came a response from within the crowd of men who waited expectantly behind him.

"Ah, it has been such a short time, but they already appear to know you quite well," Elphame quipped.

Cu put his hands up in mock surrender. "I come in peace!"

"I hope you come to work," Elphame said with some asperity.

"That too," he said. "Command us, my Lady, and your will shall be obeyed." He bowed dramatically to her, as did the men standing behind him, which made his sister smile.

"Actually, it's not me who is in command in this particular chamber. It is our cook."

Cuchulainn's eyes sparkled as he changed the direction of his bow so that he was facing the buxom, redheaded Wynne.

Elphame noticed that several of the other men shot the young cook appreciative glances, too.

Wynne's attractively flushed cheeks were the only outward sign she showed that the attention pleased her. Straightening her shoulders and planting her hands firmly on her shapely hips she launched into a tirade of orders in her rolling brogue. "You men can start by clearin' the cooking hearths, as well as the ovens. Several of ye will have to go up on the roof and be sure that the flues are uncluttered and repair any stones that have come free. Also, I'll need this pump to be in working order, then we'll be needin' buckets and soap and rags and such for the general cleanin'." The room erupted into action.

Elphame stepped hastily out of the way.

"It's a good thing that the centaurs cleared the road to the castle and the supply wagons got through. I wouldn't have wanted to be the one to tell your pretty cook that the cleaning supplies were stranded in the forest." Cuchulainn had joined his sister in watching from the edge of the room.

"She may be pretty, but I think she might be more than a little feisty," El said.

"Redheads—they are a temptation," Cuchulainn observed with the voice of experience.

"Come on, Cu," she said, grabbing his hand. "I want you to help me."

"Where are we going?"

"To the Main Courtyard. Something tells me it's important to restore it as soon as possible."

As they started to leave the room, Elphame noticed the sudden silence. She glanced back to see that the activity had stopped and everyone was looking at her. "Carry on," she said quickly. "My brother and I are going to begin clearing the courtyard." Before she could continue walking away, Brenna's voice stopped her.

"May I come with you, my Lady?"

The Healer had stepped from a shadowy area at the far end of the room, and Elphame saw several of the men cringe and avert their eyes from her face.

"Of course you may, Brenna," she said quickly.

"I, too, would welcome you," Cu said. "As my sister has already observed, I am often in need of the services of a skilled Healer."

Elphame felt a rush of warmth for her brother. His words had caused the men to reassess the scarred woman by showing them that he, as well as his sister, valued and respected her.

Brenna didn't respond except to bow her head so that her hair concealed most of her face and followed them hurriedly from the room.

"El, you'll need to have these frames measured and then commission new windows," Cu observed as they walked back through the Great Hall. "Unless you prefer to have this wall rebuilt without the glass."

"No, I like the idea of looking out on the courtyard. I imagine it used to be a spectacular view."

The three of them came to a halt at the edge of the Main Courtyard. They could look up through the burnt ceiling to see that evening was rapidly approaching and the sky was shifting from brilliant blue to oranges and violets. The beauty above them was quite a contrast to the ruin that stood below it. Tree limbs and filth covered the marble floor. Mounds of scorched, rotted roof timbers littered the area, especially the very center of it. As she stood there, Elphame's eyes felt drawn to that center area. A memory stirred. Something about the central courtyard of the castle…

"Cu, Brenna, let's see if we can clear some of those old timbers from that middle area."

Without waiting for them to respond, she rushed to the

largest pile of rubble and set to work. Soon, Elphame pulled free one particularly long piece of wood and the lip of a basin appeared beneath it, looking like the edge of a giant's dirty bowl that had been discarded a century ago.

"Yes! I knew there was something under all of this mess," Elphame said with satisfaction.

They redoubled their efforts until, rising from the midst of rot and ruin, a delicate statue took form. It was a life-sized adolescent girl. She was standing in the middle of the basin, holding a large urn that was tipped up at the end as if she was pouring libations from it.

"It's a fountain!" Brenna exclaimed.

"Look at her, El, there's something about her…." Cu said, stepping within the basin to get a closer look. With a fold of his kilt he scrubbed at the face of the statue, until he exposed a small area of milk-colored marble which appeared luminous and ghostly. Then he drew in his breath sharply in surprise. "She looks like you."

8

ELPHAME STARED AT the statue. It did look like her. She and the statue shared the same high cheekbones, full lips and fine, arched brows.

"Rhiannon," Brenna said suddenly. "This fountain must be a statue of Rhiannon when she was a girl. I remember now. Before she became Goddess Incarnate of Epona, she lived here, as the only child of The MacCallan, and she was…"

"My ancestress," Elphame finished for her.

"She was also a great warrior," Cu said, still studying the statue carefully. "It was through her leadership that the Fomorians were defeated and driven from Partholon."

"Let us not forget that Rhiannon did have a little help from her lifemate, the centaur High Shaman, ClanFintan."

Elphame looked around in surprise, trying to locate the owner of the strong female voice that carried across the courtyard. From the lengthening shadow of the central column emerged the lithe form of a female centaur. Elphame couldn't stifle her gasp of surprise. The centaur must be a Huntress to be able to creep up on them so silently; Cuchulainn hadn't even been aware of her approach. The thought sent a rush of pleasure through Elphame. A centaur Huntress had joined them!

"You are right to correct me, Huntress," Elphame said formally. "My father would have done the same."

"I did not mean to correct you, Goddess, only to remind you."

As she came closer and more fully into the pool of light that illuminated the area surrounding the fountain, Elphame was stunned by her beauty. The equine part of her body was a sleek palomino, shading from cream to a blonde so light that she almost appeared to be silver, and El was suddenly reminded of the bright coat of Epona's Chosen Mare. She had never seen a centaur with such spectacular coloring. Even her hooves were a unique, snow-white shade. The human part of her body was just as lovely. Her hair matched her coat, and it streamed down her back in a thick, white wave. Her skin was alabaster, and she wore the centaur's traditional half-open leather vest through which could be glimpsed her full, well-rounded breasts. Her face was a study in classic perfection. Elphame met her eyes, which were an arresting shade of lavender.

The centaur stopped before her and executed a deep, graceful bow.

"I come to offer my services as Huntress to you, Goddess Elphame, and to MacCallan Castle. I am Brighid Dhianna."

"You are of the Dhianna Herd," Cu said. His voice was unusually sharp and his expression grim.

"I am of that Herd. I am not of that mind-set."

And her words suddenly made sense to Elphame. There was a growing sect amidst centaurs that disdained contact with humans. They rarely left the Centaur Plains and they rejected centaurs that chose to live within human communities as being little better than domesticated animals. She remembered her parents discussing the ramifications of the growth of such an exclusionist belief, and the disgust with which her centaur father viewed the segregationist ideology. And she also remembered him mentioning a particularly militant herd by the name of Dhianna, whose powerful shaman leader was stirring up a disturbing amount of support for her ideology, which explained Cu's grim expression.

"Brighid Dhianna, if it is a new beginning you seek, then I welcome you to MacCallan Castle, a place of new beginnings," Elphame said solemnly.

The Huntress met her eyes with a square, strong gaze. "Yes, Goddess, I am in search of a new beginning."

"Good, then you can start by calling me Elphame," she said briskly. "This stern-looking warrior is my brother, Cuchulainn." Cu nodded icily at the Huntress. "And this is our new Healer, Brenna." Elphame was pleased to note that Brighid did not flinch when Brenna lifted her scarred face at her introduction. "Grab a log, Brighid. It's getting late and I would like to have this fountain uncovered before we lose all of our light."

Elphame turned back to the pile of rubble, ignoring the suspicious looks passing between her brother and the Huntress.

"Enough, El! You can begin here tomorrow. Everyone left the kitchen some time ago—even your tyrannical cook and her harpies are on their way back to Loth Tor for a hot meal and a soft bed," Cuchulainn said, exasperated at his sister's unlimited store of energy.

He and the Huntress had just dragged another litter loaded with debris from the courtyard to the ever-growing pile outside the castle's walls. And had he returned to find his sister and Brenna stacking buckets and preparing to leave? No—his obstinate sister was filling yet another litter with filth, this time from the rear side of the basin.

"Cu," she said, barely looking up at him. "Why don't you go ahead? I'll just load this last litter and be on my way." She glanced up through the open roof at the sky that now held only the palest mauve light reflected from the dying sun.

"No. Everyone else is gone. I don't want you traveling through the forest alone."

"Oh, please. People have been clomping back and forth from here to Loth Tor all day. I'd be surprised if there are even any squirrels willing to stay through such noise."

"And she will not be alone. I will return with her," the Huntress said.

"As will I," Brenna added.

Elphame cocked one eyebrow at her brother. "Satisfied that I won't be alone?"

"Hrumph," he grunted. Then added firmly, "If you are not at the Mare's Inn by the time the food is being served, I will come and fetch you. And keep this with you." He unbuckled a thin belt from around his waist. Strapped to it was a small sheath which Elphame knew held one of his lethal throwing daggers. He tossed it to his sister, who caught it deftly. "You know I've told you before that you should carry a weapon." He turned and, mumbling under his breath about hardheaded women, stalked from the courtyard.

"Hey! It's your safety you had better worry about if Wynne hears you calling her assistants harpies," she called after his retreating back. "Overpossessive, annoying little brother," Elphame said in disgust.

"He loves you very much," Brenna said.

"But he is annoying," Brighid added.

"You haven't seen true annoyance yet. If I'm not back by the time he expects me he'll come charging through the forest, claymore drawn and ready, scaring the life out of small rodents and helpless songbirds."

Brenna began laughing. It was a lovely, musical sound, and soon Brighid and Elphame joined her.

As they worked companionably together on clearing the fountain's basin, Elphame thought how good it felt to have the courtyard filled with the sounds of laughter and life. She didn't need to press her hand against the central column to Feel that the atmosphere of the castle was changing. From her first glimpse of MacCallan Castle she had felt welcomed, but she also had to acknowledge that it had been a forlorn place filled with lonely waiting. Its history was rich with tradition and honor, as she had explained to the women earlier, but it had also stood silent and abandoned for more than a century. The span of a single day had begun to change that. In the very air surrounding them she could feel life newborn. It was as if each breath she breathed was filled with hope.

"I think that's enough," Elphame said, wiping her grimy hands on her skirt. She looked down at herself. "Ugh—I'm looking forward to bathing almost as much as I am to eating a hot meal."

Brenna nodded quick agreement as she tried to pick something sticky off her arm. Even Brighid's sleek coat was dusted with smears of soot.

The Huntress grabbed the leather leads that attached to the litter and linked them over her shoulder so that her powerful centaur body had no trouble pulling the weighty load.

"At least you two will actually get to bathe. I can almost promise you that Loth Tor will not have a bathing chamber large enough for me," she said as she started dragging the litter from the courtyard.

Elphame and Brenna helped balance the pile of rubble so that they didn't lose any of it on the trip out.

"I never thought about that before," Brenna said, panting a little as she jogged to keep up with the two more athletic females. "It would be awful if all the bathing chambers were too small for me," the petite Healer mused.

"Awful if you're a female," Brighid said. Then she grinned at Brenna. "If you're a male centaur, well, you don't so much mind."

"Ugh, boys!" Elphame said, remembering how her mother used to have to threaten Cuchulainn and Finegas when they were children to get them into a bathing chamber. "Centaur or human, they can certainly be disgusting."

The three women wrinkled their noses at each other and laughed.

"Can you believe how much this pile has grown?" Elphame said as they emptied the litter onto the growing mound of rotted timbers and ancient filth that was located a little way from the castle's outer walls.

"I believe it," Brenna said, pausing to rub her shoulders and roll her neck. "I hope Loth Tor has a decent mead brewer. We'll all need something to help relax our muscles tonight—" she glanced back at the hulking form of the castle "—and tomorrow."

"That's that." El clapped her hands together with satisfaction. "Let's head to Loth Tor and the Mare's Inn."

"And dinner," Brighid added.

"Absolutely," Elphame said. But they had only taken a few steps down the road when she stopped and slapped her forehead. "I left Cu's dagger inside. I'll never hear the end of it if I show up without it. Wait here, this will just take a moment." She bunched her powerful muscles and sprinted back up the road and through the castle's entrance.

Where had she left that thing? The light was really failing now, and every pile of leaves and heap of dirt could be mistaken for a casually discarded sheath and belt.

"I should have showed more sense and strapped it to my waist when he gave it to me," she muttered angrily to herself.

"Is this what ye seek, lassie?"

A cold shiver doused her body. The deep voice came from behind her; it had an odd quality, like it had to drift through a pool of water to reach her. As if moving through a dream, she turned.

He was sitting casually on the lip of the basin that held the fountain. She had no trouble seeing him because his body glowed softly, like candlelight on pearls. She could also clearly see the ruins of the courtyard behind him, as well as directly through his semisubstantial form.

"Oh!" Elphame hadn't realized she'd been holding her breath until it released in a rush. She felt her body begin to tremble as she tried to tell her numbed legs to get her away from there.

The specter raised one thick, well-calloused hand. *"Rest easy, Elphame, I mean ye no harm."*

He spoke with a gruff edge to his thick brogue, but the look in his eyes was gentle, and when she didn't bolt away he smiled at her. *"There, lass."* He nodded his head toward the belt that hung haphazardly over the lip of the basin not far from where he was sitting. *"Is it not what ye seek?"*

Elphame nodded her head woodenly, took a halting step forward, and snatched up the belt. "Th—" she had to clear her throat and swallow before she could get the words out. "Thank you."

He tipped his head gallantly at her. *"'Tis my pleasure."* His good-humored gaze slid from Elphame to rest on the fountain that was a statue of a girl. The specter's smile turned poignant. *"It pleases me ye have finally come, Elphame. Even the dead canna wait forever."*

"You know me?" Her voice didn't seem to want to work, and the words came out barely above a whisper.

"Aye, lass, I know ye. And a fine, braw lassie ye are, too." His eyes danced. *"Look at ye! A perfect blending of two. Ye are the right choice."*

"For what? Who are you?" El's power of reasoning was starting to recover along with her vocal ability.

"Use yer heart and intuition, lass. They will tell ye who I am."

Elphame took a deep breath and studied the specter carefully. He was well past middle age, but he was still a powerful figure in full western regalia with his blouse-sleeved linen shirt and his well-draped kilt. Even transparent, the bold colors of sapphire-blue and lime-green made a striking contrast on the tartan. Her eyes widened. She knew that plaid—intimately. Her mother had worn it for years whenever she traveled to the west. Elphame owned one herself. And she had every right to; the blood of the Clan MacCallan ran thick in her veins.

"You are The MacCallan."

His smile widened and he winked at her. *"Aye, lassie, I was. Now that position is held by ye."* Then his look sobered, and he stood, executing a dashing bow that suddenly reminded her of Cuchulainn. *"Your companions come for ye, and I canna stay. Another time, lass…another time…."*

And he disappeared into nothing more than a thin mist that hung like fairy fog around the fountain.

"My Lady! Is all well?" Brenna's voice drifted from the direction of the entryway.

"Yes!" Elphame called. She passed a shaky hand over her face. She had told her mother that she didn't believe that any of MacCallan Castle's lingering spirits would wish her harm, and she had meant it. But that hadn't meant that she had ever really considered that there might actually be lingering spirits to deal with. "I certainly never thought I'd meet The Mac-Callan himself."

"Did you say something, Elphame?" Brighid asked. Her

hooves thudded with a muffled clop against the dirt-covered marble and her silver-blond coat seemed ethereal in the darkness as she entered the courtyard. "By the Goddess it's black in here! No wonder it was taking you so long."

"I'll be glad when the wall sconces are repaired and the torches are lit," Brenna said nervously. She was just a slight, dark silhouette as she stayed close to the Huntress's side.

Elphame smiled and forced her voice to sound normal. "You're right, I was having a terrible time finding it, but I have it now, so we can finally go get that hot meal we've been tasting in our minds." With one final glance over her shoulder at the fog-shrouded fountain, Elphame hurried from the darkening castle.

9

THE FADING LIGHT softened the edges of the newly cleared road through the forest and the cool evening breeze filled the air with the sweet scent of flowering trees so that to Elphame it seemed like they were walking through a watercolor painting. Almost against her will she felt herself begin to relax. Out in the open with Brenna and Brighid talking amiably about the events of the day it was hard to believe that just moments before she had been conversing with the spirit of the Clan Chieftain who had been dead for more than a century. It wasn't that Elphame doubted what she had witnessed, it was just that for years nothing even slightly magical had happened to her. Until that morning the spirit realm had been dead to her. Now the spirits of the stones as well as the dead were talking to her—all in the span of one day. She surmised that her mind was probably in shock, which was why she was still able to walk and smile and chat with her companions, instead of standing frozen in one spot and drooling. She stifled a semihysterical giggle. Maybe the drooling was a slight exaggeration. She heard her name and nodded absently at a comment Brenna had just made.

"Wonderful! See, Brighid, I told you it was a good idea."

"Are you quite certain, Elphame?"

The tone of the Huntress's question broke through El's inner dialogue and she surfaced into the present to see Brenna's lopsided smile beaming at her.

"Of course she is. You already said that there would be no bathing chamber large enough to hold you and, look, the stream must pool just over there. It certainly should be big enough."

Elphame's eyes followed Brenna's pointing finger. The land was dipping steadily downward, creating a rocky, tiered area amidst the pine trees in the surrounding forest. And, sure enough, the stream that ran alongside the road, and even criss-crossed through it every so often, fell from one level to the next in a tumble of three waterfalls. As they peered through the forest foliage they could just glimpse a pool had been formed at the bottom level before the water continued to meander over the other side and disappear into the forest. Elphame looked at the Healer, trying not to show her shock. Brenna wanted them to bathe out there? In the pool? The three of them? She had never bathed around strangers—she didn't even allow the temple servants to be in the bathing chamber with her. Could she really bare herself in front of the two of them?

It sounded like something companions would do. It sounded normal.

"I think it's a good idea," Elphame said resolutely.

Before she could change her mind she stepped off the path, climbing down and around boulders and angling for the pool of water. Behind her she could hear Brenna and Brighid noisily following. She could do this, she told herself. If she wanted to be treated normally, she was going to have to act normal. And "normal" females bathed in front of each other—she'd been aware of that from the time she could toddle into her mother's constantly busy bathing chamber. Visiting priestesses as well as friends and acquaintances had all, at one time or another, joined Epona's Beloved in the luxury of her mineral springs bathing pools. Elphame's modesty was the exception, not the rule in Partholon.

She stopped at the edge of the pool, waiting for Brenna and Brighid to join her. It was larger than it had appeared from the road. The three waterfalls made a merry sound as they cascaded like liquid crystals over the water-smoothed rocks.

"It looks deep enough," Brenna said.

"It looks cold," Brighid said.

"Good," the Healer said, already unclasping the simple brooch that held her high-necked dress together over her right shoulder. "Then it should be refreshing after a long, sweaty day of work." She opened her bodice and shrugged out of her top while she began untying the knots that held her kilt-like skirt wrapped securely around her slender waist.

Elphame couldn't look away from Brenna's exposed body. The left side of her was covered with smooth, flawless skin, but as on her face, the right side of her body told a different story. The scars that disfigured that side of her face did not end at her neck. They traveled down, covering her shoulder and the top of her breast, so that in the evening light she looked like a beautiful, delicate wax statue that had been partially melted.

Brenna raised her eyes and looked from the goddess to the Huntress, who were both gazing silently at her. And sudden realization crossed her face. She had actually forgotten for an instant about her horrible scars. She glanced hastily away again, pretending to have trouble untying one of the linen knots, hoping that in the dim light they could not see her tears.

"I'm sorry," Elphame said quietly. "I did not mean to stare."

Still not looking up, Brenna's voice sounded muffled. "There is no need for you to be sorry. Everyone stares."

Elphame took a deep breath and unclasped the brooches that held her bodice together. Then she quickly unwound the length of material from around her waist, letting it fall to the forest floor. She bent and pulled off the small triangle of material that covered her most private parts. Totally naked, she stood very still so that Brenna and Brighid could study every inch of her exposed body.

"I understand exactly what you mean. That is why I apologized."

Brenna looked up, and her eyes shot wide in surprise. And for the first time in her life, the Healer couldn't help staring at another human being. Only Elphame's body wasn't human. It was much more. The upper half of her body was shaped with a feminine beauty that any woman would envy. Her waist curved in to swell back out into powerful hips that tapered down to what appeared to be the muscular forelegs of a well-built horse. From her waist down she was covered with a sleek auburn coat that glistened with health and youth. Her most private parts were shaped, as far as Brenna could tell, exactly like her own and they were covered with a thatch of dark auburn hair that swirled and curled into a triangle.

A violent stomping sound erupting from behind them made both women jump. At the edge of the pool Brighid was bashing one of her front hooves over and over again against a cluster of rocks that were beginning to froth and bubble.

"Soapstone," she explained. "I thought I would make myself useful while the two of you finished inspecting one another." She bent and sifted some of the soapy granules through her fingers. "I think it's crushed up enough now." Brighid unlaced her vest and laid it carefully on a dry rock.

"Why aren't you staring at us?" Brenna asked the Huntress.

"I was raised to believe that all humans are odd, misshapen creatures, so the two of you seem perfectly normal to me," she said with a sarcastic grin and surged into the water.

"I realize she didn't mean it as a compliment, but her attitude is a nice change," Brenna mused, gazing after the Huntress.

"Yes, it certainly is," Elphame agreed. Then she smiled at her new friend. "Are we finished inspecting one another?"

"I think so, although I would really like to touch your fur— if you wouldn't mind," she added hastily.

Elphame lifted a leg and held it out to the Healer. "I don't mind, but I don't think of it as fur, I think of it more as a coat."

Brenna ran one finger from Elphame's knee down her hock, hesitated, and then touched the shining black surface of her hoof.

"Oh, my…" she breathed. "It's as soft as it looks." Then the Healer part of her mind took over. "Does your skin cut easily, or is it tougher than a human leg? And how do you react to plants that usually cause skin to inflame, like poison ivy or oak?"

"If your brother comes looking for us and finds the three of us naked, I know at least two of us who will be very uncomfortable with that," Brighid called from the center of the pool.

Brenna blanched and looked hastily over her shoulder in the direction of the road. "You're right. That would be awful."

"We're coming," Elphame said. "You can quiz me later."

"I will." Brenna smiled.

"Bring some of that soapstone with you," Brighid shouted.

Quickly Brenna knelt and scooped handfuls of the rough, soapy stone. Taking a deep breath, she plunged into the pool. Slipping on the smooth, slick rocks near the bank she fell flat on her behind, gasping at the shock of the cold water that suddenly covered her body.

Elphame grinned at her, hesitantly flicking the water with the tip of one hoof. "Still think it's a good idea?"

Teeth already chattering, Brenna nodded enthusiastically. "It's not so bad once you get used to it."

"Don't worry about it. That coat of fur will protect you," Brighid said. Then her lips quirked and she added, "At least part of you."

"That's not particularly reassuring," Elphame said. But she couldn't stop smiling. They were bantering with one another easily as if they had known each other for years. She had friends. "Don't worry, I'm coming…."

But just before she stepped into the pool she paused. She felt something uncomfortable along the back of her neck. It was a feeling with which Elphame was much too familiar—the crawling-up-her-spine, breathless sense of being watched. Using the pretense of moving her pile of clothing, her sharp eyes scanned the surrounding forest. She didn't notice anything unusual. The trees were just trees, and they didn't appear to harbor anything more malevolent than chirping birds.

Still she felt the tingle at the back of her neck.

Her imagination was probably working overtime, which was understandable considering all that she had experienced that day.

"You know the longer you stand there, the colder the water is going to feel," Brenna said.

Elphame turned back to the pool. The Healer's lips were already blue, but she was happily rubbing the soapstone into her hair.

Ignoring her hyped-up senses, Elphame grabbed a handful of soapstone and then, squealing, plunged into the frigid pool.

When she took off her clothing Lochlan knew he should have turned away, or at the very least averted his eyes. It would have been the honorable thing to do. But he could not. She mesmerized him. He drank in her nakedness. Sometimes in his dreams he had flashes of touching her skin, or kissing her lips, but those dreams were always insubstantial and brief, leaving him throbbing for more. Now here she was—so very close to him. His dark wings quivered, reflecting his mounting desire. He felt hot and cold at the same time. Watching her was sweet agony.

When she turned from the pool and studied the forest with searching eyes, his body became very still, blending with the shadows of the trees, but his heartbeat pounded in his temples. She felt him. Her mind didn't know him yet, but her soul already recognized that he was there.

Then she waded into the water and her laughter filled the forest. She never laughed in his dreams. He had only seen her smile occasionally, usually at her warrior brother or one of her parents. Now the unexpected sound of her laughter was a gift that cooled his lust, but did nothing to lessen his desire for her. He felt his own lips turn up. Elphame should laugh more often. He wanted to see her happy; he thought he could make her happy. If only there was some way…

The Prophecy. It haunted him. It tormented him. How could he fulfill the Prophecy and live with himself? Yet if he didn't his people would be doomed to an existence filled with pain and torment, or madness. *No!* He couldn't think of what would happen if his quest did not succeed. His mother had been so certain. Her faith in her beloved Epona had been deep. He could still see her face, alight with remembrance as she performed the Goddess's rituals and taught him Epona's ways. She had been so sure. Sure enough to have survived a brutal rape, and, sick and weak from giving birth, she had gathered others like her to make a home for their hybrid children. Children whose mothers were not supposed to survive the births. They should have only served as incubators for their demonic captors, the Fomorian invaders, whose females had been mysteriously rendered sterile. Human women were not sterile; human women could be impregnated and be used to bring forth a new generation of Fomorians. It was inconsequential that the human mothers could not survive the birth of their horrible offspring.

But his mother had survived his birth, as had a small group of other women. Her Goddess had not forsaken her. How many times had Lochlan heard her say those words? Almost as many times as he had heard her repeat the Prophecy.

Determination filled him. His dreams of Elphame had brought him here; he just had to make his way through the maze of complications to actually be with her. He closed his eyes and leaned heavily against the thick trunk of the tree behind which he stayed hidden. They were alike, Elphame and he, a melding of two races.

The feminine laughter and the cool, fragrant breeze joined to play with his memory. He could almost see his mother, bent over the stream they used to wash their small supply of crude clothing. She had always worked so hard for so little, but when he thought of her, it was her smile and her sweet laughter he remembered first.

"You are my happiness." She had told him time and again. *"And someday you will lead the others like you back to Partholon to find their happiness, too, and you will be free of the pain and the madness."*

His mother had been such an idealist. She had believed that her Goddess would answer her prayers and that he would fulfill Epona's Prophecy. And soon he had quit trying to convince her otherwise. She wanted to believe the humanity within all of them was stronger than the dark impulses imprinted into their Fomorian blood, that goodness would eventually reign over madness and insanity.

"It will in me. It must," he whispered, needing the reassurance of the sound of his own voice. "I am more human than demon. My father raped my mother and impregnated her, but his race was defeated by the forces of Partholon, just as my mother's love defeated the pain and horror of my birth." Lochlan knew it was unwise to dwell on the past, especially to think about those he had left behind in the Wastelands. He needed to control his thoughts—to focus on the task at hand. A warning finger of pain lanced through his head. He told himself he didn't care, to think of the pain as an old friend. Its absence was what he must fear, what he must guard against. Its absence meant his father's dark blood had finally won.

He opened his eyes and crouched down so that he could peer at Elphame again. The females were leaving the pool, shaking themselves and laughing as they shivered and rushed back to their clothing.

He felt his blood quicken at her closeness. *Please, Epona, help me to find a way to fulfill the Prophecy without causing her harm.* He sent a fervent prayer to the Goddess of his mother even though guilt gnawed at him. Elphame's laughter floated to him again and he steeled himself against his conflicted heart and finished his prayer. *Allow me the chance to win her.*

If he could just find a way to talk with Elphame. Alone. It wasn't such an impossible task. Through his dreams he had watched her run often, and she usually ran alone. He would be patient. He had waited over a century for her. He could wait a few more days.

CUCHULAINN WAS SADDLING his gelding and preparing to ride back to find out what had happened to his sister when the three of them trotted up to the front of the Mare's Inn. He was all set to lecture Elphame about the dangers of disregarding his warrior senses, but the sight of them made all thoughts of brotherly lectures leave his mind.

They were laughing and chattering together, all three of them—which included his habitually solitary sister. By the Goddess she looked happy! And then what else he was seeing registered in his mind and he snorted in surprise. The little scarred Healer was riding the centaur Huntress! Centaurs did, from time-to-time, offer to transport humans, but usually it was under emergency situations. The noble race of centaurs were definitely not beasts of burden. But there was the Huntress, trotting nonchalantly along with a human perched rather precariously on her sleek back. Cuchulainn felt certain that the militant Dhianna centaurs would have a herd-wide apoplectic fit if they ever witnessed such a sight.

It made him want to laugh aloud. It also made him begin to wonder if he had judged the Huntress too harshly.

"El!" he called and waved her his way. She waved back and motioned for her friends to follow her.

"Sorry, Cu," she said breathlessly. "We didn't mean to take so long, but we found a wonderful bathing pool on the way back, and, well…" She shrugged her shoulders and squeezed some water from her wet hair.

His sister had bathed in front of others? He looked from the centaur to the Healer, and back to Elphame. They were wet. All three of them. And they looked flushed and very pleased with themselves.

"It was actually my fault," the Huntress said, giving Cuchulainn a challenging look. "I did not think the humans of Loth Tor would have a bathing chamber that could accommodate me—"

"So I suggested we stop and bathe before joining the camp," Brenna interrupted in a shy, soft voice. "Elphame kept reminding us that we should hurry." She didn't look directly at the warrior as she spoke, and she kept the right side of her face turned away from him.

"I see…" Cuchulainn said, scratching his chin. And he did. They were being protective of his sister, may Epona bless them. The smile that lit his face was dazzling. "I see that I should spend more time lurking around the area pools."

"Oh, Cu," Elphame curled her nose at him. "Don't be disgusting."

"Well, I wouldna be looking at you, lassie," he said, imitating the local brogue.

Elphame felt like her face must have lost all its color. He sounded unerringly like The MacCallan, reminding her that she needed to tell him about her encounter with the spirit of their ancestor; her brother would want to know.

"Where are we eating, Cu?" she asked hastily.

He nodded his head toward the rear of the Mare's Inn. "They've set up tables outside and they're bringing food out there." He glanced significantly at the larger-than-human Huntress. "Seems there wasn't room inside the inn to feed all of us."

Brighid made a rude sound in her throat and Brenna had to cover her laugh with a cough.

"Why don't you two go on, I need to catch up on the day's work with Cuchulainn."

"We'll save a place for you," Brighid said. The centaur hesitated, making an obvious pause before adding, "And for your brother."

"I can get down now, Brighid," Brenna said.

Not sure about the correct protocol for dismounting from a centaur, she started to gently slide her right leg over the Huntress's firm back, but before she began to drop to the ground she felt a strong hand steady her. Brenna turned, expecting to see Elphame helping her. Instead she was looking directly into the piercing blue-green eyes of Cuchulainn.

"May I help you dismount, my Lady?"

"I—uh—I—" she stammered, fighting the urge to duck her head and hide the right side of her face. She swallowed hard. She'd worked around Cuchulainn most of the day. He knew what she looked like. There was no reason to shrink from him. "Yes. You may," she finally managed to say.

Cu lifted the Healer from the Huntress's back. She was so light she felt as if her bones must be filled with air. And her wet hair smelled of rain and fresh grass. He placed her gently on the ground, and then bowed to her gallantly, but she wasn't even looking at him. She and the Huntress were already walking toward the rear of the inn. Brenna's sweet voice floated back to him on the breeze.

"Thank you, Brighid. I'm sorry I have such a poor seat. I've never been a very good rider…."

"What are you staring at?" Elphame asked Cu, butting his shoulder.

Wondering himself, Cuchulainn shook his head and blurted the first rational thought that came to his mind.

"A Dhianna centaur gave a human woman a ride?"

His sister raised one arched brow at him. "Yes."

"And there were no Fomorians hot on your heels?"

"I didn't notice any, but perhaps you should go back for a look— I'll be sure to save you a place at dinner," she said innocently. Then she laughed at his expression. "It was just easier, Cu. Brenna couldn't keep up with us, and we were in a hurry because I have an overprotective, bothersome brother I have to constantly check in with—so Brighid offered to give her a ride. I couldn't very well hoist her up on my shoulders. It was really the only logical thing to do."

"Unless you're a Dhianna centaur. Then the logical thing to do would be to let the human woman run herself into the ground."

Elphame's anger flared. "If Brighid was a typical Dhianna centaur she wouldn't be here. I want you to give her a chance. She's my friend."

She's my friend. Cuchulainn had never heard his sister say those words before, and hearing them was a miracle that made his mistrust of the Huntress seem like a selfish, petty thing.

"I'm sorry, El," he said, linking his arm with hers. "You're right. The only thing I can find truly offensive about the Huntress is her name." Of course he wasn't overly fond of the sarcastic tone she used when she spoke to him, but the look in his sister's eyes said he shouldn't mention that.

"Then you will give her a chance?" she said hopefully.

"Of course, El," he said. "And I have to admit that perhaps I have been jumping at shadows. I've had a vague, uneasy Feeling that I haven't been able to define." He met his sister's eyes, silently asking her to understand. "Maybe it was just the foreshadowing of the changes that were about to take place with you that were making me uncomfortable."

"Changes with me? What do you mean?"

"It's obvious you have chosen the correct path for your life. You belong at MacCallan Castle, El, even the stones welcome you. And look at you, you're laughing in public and making friends."

Happiness made Elphame's sable eyes sparkle. "I am making friends." She repeated the words as if they were a prayer.

"I may have been overreacting earlier," he said begrudgingly. "I suppose I'd been listening to too many children's ghost stories about the old place being cursed with spirits of the fallen dead. I'll try and loosen up some."

Children's ghost stories? She studied her brother's face. He was smiling at her with a pleased, open expression that said, even more clearly than his words, that he finally trusted that MacCallan Castle was where she should be. So what would happen if she blurted out that she had, indeed, been visited by the spirit of one of the fallen MacCallan dead—actually *The* MacCallan? She knew exactly what would happen. Cu shunned and mistrusted the spirit realm; he always had, though he'd been gifted with powers. If she told him about her spectral visitor she had absolutely no doubt that he would go back to being obsessively overprotective of her every move.

And besides that, she didn't understand herself why The Mac-Callan had appeared to her. His visit had felt benevolent—he had certainly seemed as gallant in spirit as history reported him being in life. He had called her The MacCallan. But what did his visit really mean? Was he welcoming her, or watching her?

She couldn't tell Cu about MacCallan's ghost. At least she couldn't tell him that night. She'd wait until they were more settled in and she knew more about The MacCallan's motives. Maybe the spirit would never appear to her again. If it didn't, why should she worry her brother needlessly?

"El," he said, nudging her. "Did you hear me? I said I'd try and loosen up some."

"I heard you," she said quickly. "I'm just in shock that you finally admitted the error of your ways. Now if I could get you to give up chasing women and settle down to father several dozen children, my life would be complete."

"You're scary when you sound so much like Mother. Be careful or your voice will freeze like that."

"Now it's me who's scared." She grinned. "Let's go eat."

"With your friends," he said.

"Yes. With my friends."

"The stars look so much brighter here than they do at Epona's Temple," Elphame said.

"It's because there is less light reflected from Loth Tor and the forest than there is at the temple and the city that surrounds it," Cu said.

"You should see the stars from the Centaur Plains. Sometimes they shine brighter than firelight," Brighid said.

"I've never been to the Centaur Plains, but it sounds beautiful." Brenna's voice was sleepy.

"Someday you must visit. There are open places there where you can run for days without stopping."

Elphame caught her brother's eye and shook her head sharply at him so that Cuchulainn bit off the snide comment she could tell he wanted to make. She sighed. Why did he find the Huntress so irritating? He seemed to like Brenna—actually, he went out of his way to be kind to her. But whenever he and Brighid exchanged more than a word or two it was like fire meeting ice. He had acted pleased when Brighid and Brenna asked if they could join their little makeshift camp after dinner, but since they'd settled down for the night he and the Huntress had been ruffling each other's fur nonstop. (Of course, the visual image of Cu actually having fur made her want to laugh.)

El relaxed into the bedroll that she'd fitted snuggly between two gnarled roots at the base of an ancient oak tree. Listening to the soft hum of Brighid's voice as she described the Centaur Plains to Brenna, El gazed contentedly up at the brilliantly lit night sky. She and Cu had chosen a clearing a little way into the woods where the huge oaks still superseded the pines. She'd wanted to be away from the rest of the group, but she hadn't felt the need to withdraw as completely as she had the night before. Dinner had actually been a pleasant experience, partially because Brighid and Brenna had chosen to situate the four of them around one of the several campfires that had been lit in the field behind the Mare's Inn. The main group of centaurs, men and women ate at long wooden tables, where they talked and laughed and generally got to know one another. When Elphame and Cuchulainn had appeared, the men and centaurs stood formally, all bowing respectfully to her. Elphame had set her jaw, readying herself for more unwanted goddess worship. But then a miraculous thing had happened. Wynne had waved and called a greeting to her—and she hadn't called her Goddess or even my Lady. She'd simply said, "Good evening to ye, Elphame." And Wynne's casual greeting had been joined by several others.

The women's acceptance had worked magic. Not once had a villager knelt in front of her and asked for her blessing. Surprisingly, it was Brighid who had received the unwanted attention. Elphame grinned to herself as she remembered how many centaurs had made it a point to find an excuse to speak with Cuchulainn, who was sitting across from the Huntress, when it was obvious that all they really wanted to do was to wrangle an introduction to Brighid. Elphame had watched the whole thing with great curiosity. The Huntress had been a study in graceful female aloofness. She had been cordial to her many potential suitors—cordial and disinterested. The centaurs had responded with obvious infatuation. Even the human males had sent appreciative glances to the beautiful Huntress. After several centaurs had presented themselves, Cu had muttered his annoyance to El, calling Brighid the Ice Princess. Elphame mused that apparently Ice Princesses were highly desired creatures.

"Hey," Cu whispered to her. "You have a silly grin on your face."

"It's not a silly grin, it's a happy grin."

"Go to sleep, El. Even your friends have finally stopped talking."

She glanced at the other two dark shapes, who had fallen silent, and she realized how heavy her eyelids felt. Then she rolled on her side and looked at her brother. "When are you going to sleep, Cu?"

"Soon, sister-mine."

He fed another limb to the little fire and settled back against the tree, watching as Elphame's eyes closed and her breathing deepened. He shifted his gaze to the other two females. Both seemed to be sleeping soundly. The Healer was curled up on her side with her back to him. People had left her alone tonight; he had sat beside her to make sure of that. He told himself that the fierce protective feeling he was developing for Brenna was because she was important to his sister, and part of the vows he had taken when he'd become a warrior stated that he would protect those who needed protection. Then he remembered the scent of her, and the way she had felt in his arms when he had lifted her from the centaur's back.

He looked away from Brenna's body and straight into the open eyes of the Huntress. He felt his cheeks heat under her silent, knowing gaze.

"I will take first watch. I'll wake you when the moon is at midpoint." Without waiting for him to answer, she stood and disappeared into the forest like a sleek silver wood sprite.

Cuchulainn could hear the muffled sounds of her body making its way through the underbrush as she slowly walked their perimeter.

"Damned Ice Princess," he grumbled to himself. "Let her take part of the watch. She's mistaken if she thinks she will get an argument from me."

Cu shifted his weight, trying to find a more comfortable position, thinking how glad he'd be when he could sleep in a bed again, and how annoying the Huntress was, and how much work they had before them...thinking about everything he could to keep him from remembering the soft-voiced Healer with the scarred face who smelled of rainwater and fresh grass.

Sleep enfolded Elphame like a fond parent, and she dreamed. In her dream she was running through a forest of ancient oaks which all looked exactly like the one her sleeping body was resting beneath. It was night, but the sky was brightly lit and the full moon illuminated the forest like a torch made of snow and fire. The floor of her dream forest was clear of underbrush, and there were no hidden holes or roots to trap her hooves. She breathed deeply and evenly, stretching her leg muscles and lengthening her stride so that the wind whipped against her face and the trees blurred as she sped past.

She loved to run. Her dream reminded her of how long it had been since she had gone on a good, hard run—since the day before she'd left Epona's Temple. Too long, her subconscious mind chided her.

The floor of the forest began a rolling ascent, and she pumped her legs, relishing the burn in her powerful muscles as she shot up the incline. She burst out of the forest and into a small clearing to find herself suddenly shrouded in fog. Breathing hard, Elphame came to a halt. The mist curled around her, thick and gray. She blew on it and suddenly the misty color changed and it became tinged with a hint of red.

The color beckoned her.

It swirled in an unending circular pattern that reminded her of one of Epona's holly-hedged labyrinths that decorated the temple grounds. In her dream the familiar comparison made her smile, and she stretched out her arms, spreading her fingers wide. Slowly, she began to turn and as the mist caressed her body she realized that she was naked.

"Elphame…" The disembodied voice floated around her on the mist. It was a man's voice, but she didn't recognize it.

"Come to me, Elphame…"

Instead of alarming her, the sound of the unfamiliar voice touched something deep within her and her body responded with a fierce rush of heat. The dampness of the caressing scarlet mist filled her, licking her skin and calling alive feelings that until then she had only imagined. The mist thickened and with it so did her desire.

"Yes…" The man's voice coaxed seductively. *"Let me love you."*

Elphame was wrapped in a gossamer web and everywhere it touched her nakedness her body came alive. No, she thought with a growing sense of awe, she wasn't covered with a web. She was wrapped within wings.

"He has wings!" she said aloud, and the sound of her voice jolted her suddenly awake.

In the dark woods north of MacCallan Castle Lochlan lurched to a sitting position, instantly awake. His body was burning with need. He'd dreamed he was with Elphame, and for the first time ever, she had felt his presence in return. He leaped from the snug shelter he'd made for himself within the cave formed by rocky outcroppings, unfurled his throbbing wings, and began the long, arduous climb up the side of the ridge, desperate to burn off his pent-up desire.

His mind flamed. The pain in his head pierced so hotly that he thought his mind would implode, but he maintained a rigid control over himself and concentrated on pushing his powerful body until sweat slid from his skin and his breathing came in ragged gulps.

He'd lived so long…one hundred twenty-five years. It was a curse, this longevity which had passed to him and the others from their Fomorian fathers. And who knew how much longer his heart would beat and the dark blood of his father would slither with its tempting madness through his body? The struggle. The constant struggle weighed on him.

Give in…the pain within him hissed. *Stop fighting. Let the madness take you. Revel in the power that is yours to command.* Lochlan could end the pain by embracing his dark heritage. He ground his teeth together. And then he would become like his father's race. He would be no better than a rabid animal or a demon. Either description would be accurate.

He wanted more—for himself, and for his people.

Elphame…her name was like cool water to his parched soul.

They'd met in the realm of dreams—he was sure of it. She'd heard his voice, and opened herself to him. He had wrapped her in his wings and stroked her. She had known him. She had recognized at least part of what he was. He'd clearly heard her speak.

"He has wings!"

Elphame's voice still shivered through him, and the wonder reflected in it filled him with hope and unspeakable joy, making the pain in his body temporarily easier to bear.

VESTIGES OF THE dream stayed with her throughout the morning, and even in the middle of the afternoon Elphame would find herself staring off into the distance, remembering the caress of the scarlet-hued mist. It was during one of those daydreams that she missed what the worker was saying.

"So that's it, my Lady."

"I'm sorry. My mind was elsewhere. Can it be repaired?" Elphame asked, annoyed at herself for her lack of attention. It had just been a dream. It was silly of her to be so distracted by it.

"As I said, it will take some work, but I believe it can." The young man had wide shoulders, thick hands and a rugged, sun-browned face that spoke of many years already spent exposed to the weather, but his brown eyes were warm and his smile confident as he looked up from probing around the rear base of the fountain. "I've already begun work on unclogging the castle's main well. When that is finished the water should once again run freely from it to the kitchen as well as to this fountain, my Lady. Unless there is a break in the underground system of channels, which I have yet to discover."

"Good, thank you."

The man bowed politely to her and left the courtyard. Elphame gazed at the statue of the pretty young girl who looked so much like her. The debris that had been hiding the fountain had been cleared, and now the task of cleaning the statue was at hand. Danann had recommended using sand and soapy water as well as a stoutly bristled brush to restore the statue—the same restoration technique that was being employed by several women who were standing atop hastily erected scaffolds to clean the massive columns that encircled the courtyard. The sound of their conversation mixed well with the noise of the reconstruction that was already beginning on the roof. The castle was alive with activity.

"I probably should be overseeing something terribly important instead of obsessing over you," she whispered to the stone girl. Elphame had already scrubbed the filth from Rhiannon's face. The marble from which the statue was carved was a luminous cream color, and the girl's newly cleaned face stood out in brilliant contrast to the rest of her body. "But for some reason I believe you are terribly important."

"I approve of you talking to the stone, my Lady." Danann's rich voice came from beside her, making her jump. She didn't know which one of them moved more silently, the Stonemaster or the Huntress, but she had a feeling that both were going to be hard on her nerves.

Recovering from her surprise, Elphame touched the statue's cheek. "It's not hard to talk to her. She seems real." El turned to face the old centaur. "There's something about this fountain, and about this courtyard that feels very important to me. I know that there are other duties to which I should be attending, but I'm drawn here, to the heart of the castle. I can't rest until this—" she opened her arms to include the entire area "—is revived."

"Heart…revived…" Danann said slowly, scratching his chin. "An interesting choice of words. When one speaks of building a new home, or even of reconstructing an old home, one does not usually use words that describe a living, breathing person— like *heart* and *revive*. Can you tell me why you do so?"

Elphame's eyes moved from the centaur back to the statue of her ancestress.

"That's easy," she said quickly. "The castle is alive to me. I don't see it as dead stone and rotted timbers." She thought about speaking with the spirit of The MacCallan, and she wanted to tell Danann about the encounter, but somehow it felt like a betrayal of her brother to confide in someone else what she had been unwilling to tell him.

"Yes, Goddess. You have an affinity with this castle."

"It's a new thing to me, Danann. I've never felt anything like it until I came here."

Danann smiled at the beautiful young creature. "That is because until you came here you were too caught up in your own life to feel the magic that surrounded you."

"That makes me sound like I have been shallow and silly," Elphame said.

"No, Goddess, not at all. What it would make you is like most of the other souls who are living out their current lives on Partholon. The trouble is, you are unlike most of the other souls."

Elphame didn't know how to respond to him. She hated being called "Goddess," yet when it came from the Stonemaster's lips it seemed more of an endearment than a title. And she had desired two things for as long as she could remember—to be like the rest of Partholon, and to be gifted with some form of magic. Yet what Danann was saying was that one excluded the other.

Elphame sighed. "It's hard to understand."

"Yes, for those of us who have been touched by the spirit realm, it is often a difficult thing to understand," Danann said kindly. Then he was silent, studying the partially restored statue.

"But I'd like to know more," she said, afraid the centaur might be done speaking. "Would you teach me, Danann?"

He gave her an appraising look. "You did not learn how to open yourself to the spirits of the earth when you studied at the Temple of the Muse?"

"No," she admitted.

"Ah, I see." Before he continued he considered his words carefully. "You must realize that I am not a teacher, nor am I a shaman. I cannot instruct you, I simply have a talent for hearing the spirits of the earth, most especially those that dwell within stones."

Elphame's face fell in disappointment, but the centaur was not finished.

"I cannot instruct you," he repeated, "but I can guide you."

"Oh, Danann, thank you so much!" Elphame took the old centaur's gnarled hand within both of hers.

"How could I refuse such an enchanting student?" Danann said fondly. "Why don't you take a break and walk a little with me? I feel my bones setting if I stand in one place too long."

"Of course, where would you like to go?"

Danann smiled enigmatically at the young woman who was such a unique blending of centaur and human. "Let the spirits guide you, Goddess. We will follow."

Elphame frowned. Let the spirits guide her? How? The Stonemaster was gazing expectantly at her, as if he had no doubt that the spirits would call her name, or pull her in a certain direction, or something...anything. She furrowed her brow, concentrating on the surrounding stone. She felt peaceful and happy, just as she had from the moment she'd arrived at the castle. But that was it. Nothing told her to go anywhere.

"I can't..." she began.

"You try too hard," Danann spoke quietly, raising his hand to silence her. "Begin slowly. Simply open yourself to the influence of the spirits, and start walking. They will guide you when you are not attempting to force their will."

Feeling ridiculously dense, Elphame asked, "Open myself?"

The centaur nodded patiently. "Take three deep breaths and then cease thinking."

Eager to comply, Elphame took three long, cleansing breaths and cleared her mind. Then she told her legs to move, and with the aged centaur walking stiffly beside her, they left the courtyard. Slowly, in a meandering pattern, El headed in the direction of the kitchen, but as she reached the hallway outside the Great Hall, she felt compelled to turn to her right and walk away from the beehive of activity that emanated from the rooms on the other side of the glassless windows.

"Remember that the world around us is imbued with soul." Danann's voice took on a melodic tone that was almost hypnotic. "From the stones of your castle, to the water that surges in the sea so close below us, the very earth is ensouled. It is living and breathing, and often simply waiting for one who has the stillness of mind to listen to its many voices."

Following a silent tug that pulled something deep within her, Elphame left the long hall and walked through an arched doorway which led to an interior courtyard that was much smaller than the one that held the fountain. El stopped and studied the area. She didn't remember passing through here the day before on their quick inspection of the castle. The courtyard was open to the sky, but not because the roof had been burnt off. In this particular area it had purposefully been left roofless. The floor there wasn't stone, but grass, which had

gone wild and grown almost to her knees. There were several
entrances to the little area, one of which was a steep flight of
stone stairs that led up to a large, low room that had once been
connected to the roof of the castle and its balustraded walls—
before fire had consumed it and left it only wreckage. It must
have been the warriors' barracks, she thought, and wondered
briefly about the men who had lived and died there.

Elphame's eyes were drawn to the foot of the stone stairs.
Her legs carried her forward of their own volition. Her hoofs
made a soft shushing sound through the overgrown grass. She
thought that perhaps the stones in the stairs were calling her,
but she stopped several strides from them.

The sadness that filled her was sudden and unexpected.

"Oh!" She sighed heavily, blinking back the tears that
filled her eyes.

"Breathe, Elphame." Danann was at her side, speaking
calmness through her surging emotions. "The natural world
is alive with power, information, counsel and wisdom. It is not
trying to harm you, it is trying to speak to you. Still your mind
and listen."

Elphame drew in another deep, cleansing breath and when
she exhaled, she released her trepidation—and listened.

"Come to me, you bloody cowards!"

She recognized the voice instantly—he'd just spoken to her
the night before. A jumble of images converged upon her, and
she struggled to stay calm as the little courtyard wavered, shifted
and, like a torch being lit within a night-darkened cave, the
shades of the past suddenly flared to life around her.

The MacCallan stood in front of her at the base of the stone
stairs. Horrible, winged man-creatures surrounded him. Blood
poured off open wounds that had been torn in his arms and
chest, but his huge sword was still swinging in an arc around
him. At his feet were two headless things, victims of his

strength. Snarling, the man-creatures circled him, careful to stay out of reach of his deadly blade.

"Come to me, you bloody cowards!"

He repeated his challenge. Entranced, Elphame couldn't take her eyes from him. His words had caught the attention of more of the creatures. One by one the ring around the old warrior grew until twenty man-creatures surrounded him, their wings taut, and their bloody mouths leering in expectation.

Elphame could feel her breathing increase and her heart beating erratically as the creatures began to tighten the circle and converge upon him. But The MacCallan didn't panic. His movements were calm and sure. She saw his sword flash and heard it slice through the first and second and third creatures, until it could no longer keep up. Then their fangs and teeth reached him. He fought with his fists, which were slick with his own blood—so much blood that the vision seemed framed in crimson.

Even as the Clan Chieftain dropped to his knees, he didn't cry out. And he didn't yield.

But Elphame couldn't take any more. Even though her mind knew she was only watching the shadows of the past, the scene was too real to her. She had just spoken with him the night before—she still remembered his gruff, good-humored voice and the warm sparkle of his eyes. When he fell to his knees, she fell with him and, sobbing, closed her eyes and covered her face with her hands.

The instant her knees touched the grassy ground, the sounds of the battle ceased.

"You witnessed the past for a reason." Danann's voice anchored her back to the present. "Be still and continue to listen—do not cause the spirits to have spoken in vain."

Trying to calm the trembling of her body, Elphame took

her face from her hands and opened her eyes. The day was peaceful; the courtyard was cheerfully lit by the sunlight of a warm spring afternoon. No more doomed ghosts of the past fought to their deaths. Elphame wiped her eyes and tried to clear her thoughts again, but the image of the noble Clan Chieftain kept filling her mind.

Had his death been replayed for nothing because she was an inexperienced fool who did not know how to listen to the spirit realm? Ashamed, she bit her lip and looked down. Something that lay amidst the tangled weeds and grass caught the sunlight and sparkled. Holding her breath, Elphame reached through the overgrowth and grasped the metallic object, lifting it from the dirt and into the sunlight.

It was a round brooch, heavily tarnished and crusted with dirt, but even a funeral fire and years of being exposed to the elements could not extinguish the beauty of the rearing mare on the silver shield.

"It is the brooch of The MacCallan," Danann said, bending to inspect the treasure. "It is what you were led here to find. Cherish it, Goddess, The MacCallan himself gifted you with it."

As she fingered the gift she thought she heard an echo of the Chieftain's response when she had named him The MacCallan.

"Aye, lassie, I was. Now that position is held by ye."

It seemed the old spirit was truly a welcoming one. She felt his approval through the warmth of the Chieftain's brooch, which she turned over and over in her hand as she and Danann walked slowly back to the Main Courtyard. The centaur allowed her time to digest what she had just experienced, but before they reentered the busy courtyard, he paused.

"It was a difficult experience for you," he said simply.

Elphame looked at the brooch and nodded, feeling a little light-headed and off balance.

"It would be wise if you took some food and drink now.

You have visited the realm of the spirits, and you will not feel wholly of this world again until you ground yourself amongst the living with nourishment."

She nodded, feeling another wash of dizziness.

"Seeing him die was terrible." Her voice was still strained.

"It happened over one hundred years in the past. Try to forget the horror and remember instead the wonder of the gift you've been given."

Elphame thought that she wished she could have been given the brooch without having to see The MacCallan slaughtered by the demonic Fomorians.

As if reading her mind, the centaur smiled and patted her shoulder. "You witnessed his death for a reason. It will be made clear to you in time. Until then, think of the gift. I must bid you goodbye now. The men should have returned with a new load of stone. I must oversee its placement."

"Thank you for teaching me, Danann."

"I did not teach, I only guided," the old centaur said with a slight smile. "But I will give you one last piece of advice. Tonight do something that gives your heart joy. Too often those who listen to the spirits forget to live their own lives. Keep in mind that the earth is ensouled, not entombed. Be filled with life, Goddess, not images of death." The old centaur bowed to her and departed.

12

"WHERE DID YOU say you found this?" Cuchulainn asked his sister as he inspected the brooch that bore the rearing mare of Clan MacCallan's crest.

"At the base of the stone steps that lead to what I think used to be the warriors' barracks."

She hadn't told Cuchulainn about the vision that had led her to the brooch, and she wasn't entirely sure why she hadn't, except that watching The MacCallan's death had been a very private experience for her. It had anchored her to her castle's past. She loved her brother with the same fierce loyalty he felt for her, but they were different, the two of them. She revered the past and embraced the Spirit World. Cuchulainn was a warrior who lived in the here and now. He mistrusted what he did not understand, what couldn't be bested with fists and weapons. El didn't want to hear her brother overanalyze or perhaps even reject outright what had happened to her this afternoon. She wanted to hold the past close a little longer, and that meant staying silent about her vision, and her ghostly visitor.

"This room looks wonderful," she said, pulling his attention from the brooch. And she wasn't exaggerating just to change the subject; with an open look of amazement she gazed around her. As evening approached, she and Cu had met to check on the progress of the workers. El had been pleased to note that the area south of the castle was almost totally cleared. Cuchulainn had assured her that the next night they would be camping there, instead of outside Loth Tor.

The top halves of the mighty columns that ringed the Main Courtyard had been cleaned, and the creamy beauty of their intricate carvings formed an odd contrast to the rest of them, making it appear that the restored tops had materialized out of the air. Brenna had taken a special interest in the ancient columns, and had personally been overseeing the women who were working on cleaning them. When Elphame and Cuchulainn praised the work they were doing, the little Healer had almost glowed with pleasure.

Now brother and sister were standing just inside the entrance to the kitchen, and though the activity around them was beginning to slow, Elphame could hardly believe the change that had been wrought in two days.

"'Tis good to see you, my Lady." Wynne approached Elphame and curtsied quickly. Her eyes slid appreciatively to Cuchulainn. "And you, too, warrior."

El watched Cu shift easily from concerned brother to rakish young man.

"It is always a pleasure to greet such a lovely lady, Wynne," he said.

"It's incredible what you've accomplished in so short a time." Elphame interrupted what she was afraid would be a long exchange of flirtatious remarks. "It doesn't even look like the same kitchen."

The huge hearths had been completely cleared of debris and scrubbed clean. The ovens had been emptied of rodents and dirt and the broken, fallen stones had already been replaced. Women were scrubbing the wall of cabinets and the imposing center island, as well as the stone floor.

"Wynne! We have water!" one of the cook's young assistants yelled. Elphame watched as she pumped the handle of the spigot, and water gushed into the marble sink. At first it was dark and discolored with dirt, but soon it cleared and cascaded in a sparkling river. Several nearby women cheered.

"My Lady, tomorrow evening ye will be feastin' on food prepared in MacCallan's own kitchen," Wynne said.

"That makes me very happy, Wynne."

The pretty cook smiled and curtsied before hurrying back to work.

"It sounds like it's time that Huntress started earning her keep," Cu said as they left the kitchen and made their way toward the front of the castle.

"That's where she is right now, Cu." Elphame frowned at him, exasperated at her brother's continued dislike of Brighid. "She said that she didn't like the thought of us eating up all of Loth Tor's food, so she went hunting this afternoon."

Cuchulainn grunted.

"You know, I'm amazed that you don't like her. She's a beautiful female, and you usually get along very well with beautiful females."

"Well, she knows she's gorgeous. She's too damn arrogant. And I still don't completely trust her motives," he growled.

Elphame rolled her eyes at him. "You just don't like it that she doesn't fall all over you."

Cu shrugged his shoulders. "You could be right, sister-mine. It is very unusual." He waggled his eyebrows at her, making her laugh. "But I don't want to talk about the Huntress, I want to know more about this Chieftain's brooch that miraculously fell into your possession."

They were stepping into the main courtyard and Elphame was saved from answering him by Brenna's excited voice.

"Oh, look at your fountain, Elphame!"

"Cu, it's working!" El grabbed his hand and pulled him with her to the center of the courtyard, where several women and men stood watching the fountain. Murky water tinkled from Rhiannon's urn to the surrounding basin, which was already beginning to fill, and as they watched, it cleared and caught the late afternoon sun and sparkled merrily. The room's massive columns gathered the sound of the fountain and the courtyard echoed the soothing, familiar noises of rainy days and laughing water.

"It really is wonderful, El," Cuchulainn said, sliding his arm around her shoulders and giving her a brotherly squeeze.

"Yes, I agree," Brenna said. She stood next to Elphame, smiling happily up at her. The young Healer's eyes danced with the reflection of the water.

Elphame couldn't speak. After years of feeling frustrated about her pointless life, suddenly it was like all of her wishes were being granted. She was almost afraid to believe it—almost afraid that if she spoke the spell would be broken and it would all dissolve like mist in a dream.

Mist in a dream. The comparison brought her dream back with sharp intensity, and for a moment she felt confused and dizzy. It was a little like how she'd felt earlier that day after experiencing the vision of The MacCallan's death. She blinked hard, trying to clear her eyes and her mind. She could feel her brother's concerned gaze, but she was careful not to meet his eyes.

"I think that's enough for today," Cuchulainn said abruptly. He singled out one of the men. "Dermot, pass the word that it's time to return to Loth Tor for the night."

"Yes, my Lord." Smiling, Dermot jogged from the room.

Talking amongst themselves, the men and women in the courtyard began to disperse, stacking buckets and brushes in tidy piles and hanging wet rags from the scaffolding so that they would dry by morning, and leaving Elphame, her brother and the Healer alone at the fountain.

"Are you all right, El?" Cuchulainn asked.

"Fine," she said, recovering her voice.

"You look pale." Brenna's experienced eyes studied her carefully.

Without looking at her brother or the Healer, Elphame said, "It's just all a little overwhelming, to see what I've dreamed about coming true. Sometimes it makes me emotional."

Cuchulainn grunted. "Now you sound like a girl."

His teasing lightened her mood and she was able to grin at him. "I *am* a girl, Cu."

Brenna, however, wasn't dissuaded from her concern by sibling teasing. "I think you should take your brother's advice, Elphame. You've done enough for today. You need a hearty meal and a good night's rest so that you will be invigorated for tomorrow. I will brew a tea that will relax you and help to ease your sore muscles."

"I don't have—ouch!" El said when Brenna reached up and poked her shoulder blade.

"Yes, you do," the little Healer said smugly.

"You better mind her, El," Cuchulainn laughed. "She's re-minding me of Mother."

"I will brew enough for you, too," Brenna told him sharply.

"How bad will it taste?" he asked. It pleased him that she was speaking to him with the same voice she used with his sister, instead of ducking her face and whispering into her shoulder.

"I am a Healer, not a cook." She gave him a disgusted look. Then she suddenly realized she was bantering with the handsome warrior. Brenna felt her face grow warm; she knew that the unscarred side of it was flushing, which would only accentuate the disfigured pink of the other side. "I need to collect the correct herbs," she said, and ducking her head she retreated from the courtyard.

Cuchulainn gazed after her. "Why does she do that?"

"You can't seriously wonder, Cu. You know why. Look at her face, and that's not all of her that's scarred, either," El said.

"I've seen her face. It didn't make me cringe or run away from her."

Elphame raised an eyebrow at her brother. What was that in his voice? "She hasn't confided in me, but my guess is that she has been treated harshly, and not just by women. I would bet that men have been very cruel to her, especially handsome men."

"If anyone treats her cruelly here, he will answer to me. The men know that." Cuchulainn's voice was flint.

Elphame raised her other eyebrow. "Really?"

"She's your friend. I will not have her treated with disrespect," Cuchulainn said, still looking in the direction in which Brenna had disappeared.

Elphame watched her brother. She had never seen him react this way to any woman outside his family. Was he beginning to care for Brenna? Could he? Instantly, Elphame was ashamed of her thoughts. Of course Cuchulainn could care for Brenna. He was handsome and talented, but he was not shallow and careless of others. Brenna was a lovely, petite young woman who just happened to be scarred. She should not doubt that her brother was man enough to see beyond the scars.

She smiled softly at him. "Thank you for looking out for her, Cu."

"You don't have to thank me. It's the right thing to do." His sister's words made him feel uncomfortable and his voice sounded sharper than he intended. He smiled apologetically at her. "We should go. Brenna will probably be worried if we don't join her soon."

Lost in their own thoughts, brother and sister walked silently through the courtyard and the empty doorway of the castle's inner walls. As they approached the outer walls, they were joined by a stream of workers coming from different parts of the castle. They nodded respectfully to Elphame and her brother, and she was pleased that several of them greeted her by name.

"The iron for the new gate should arrive before the new moon," Cu said as they exited the castle.

Elphame stopped and looked back at her castle.

"It makes you happy just to look at it, doesn't it?" Cu asked with a smile in his voice.

His words roused her memory. "Yes, it does." She glanced at her brother. "You know what else would make me happy?"

"What?"

"Running." She breathed the word. "I haven't had a good run since before we left Mama's temple. Cu—" she put her hand on his shoulder to keep him from interrupting "—I need to go for a run."

"You don't know this land. Where do you think you'd go? The road between the castle and the village is the only cleared area long enough to give you a decent workout."

She shook her head. No, she wouldn't run where others could see her. They were just starting to accept her. If they saw her true speed, they would probably go back to treating her like a goddess. She thought about it, studying the surrounding forest with an athlete's eye. Then she smiled.

"I'll run along the cliff. The forest ends several feet before the drop-off. It follows a fairly straight line, so I can see well far enough ahead. And anyway, all I need to avoid are the rocks, and they're large enough I can hardly miss seeing them."

"I don't know, El. I don't like the idea of you going off by yourself. Why don't you let me get my horse and I'll come with you?"

"Cuchulainn, weren't you just saying last night that you'd been mistaken about your paranoid feelings?" She ignored her twinge of guilt at using his apology against him—especially in light of all that she'd failed to tell him. "I'll take your throwing dagger." She patted her waist where she had it securely buckled. "There's still plenty of light. I'll be back at Loth Tor drinking Brenna's tea before the sun has set."

"I don't like it."

"Do you think I'm going to blunder off the side of the cliff?"

"No. I just don't like it," he said.

"Cu, don't be Mama."

He frowned. "I am *not* our mother."

She grinned at him.

Cuchulainn sighed. "Be back before the sun sets. That means in town, sitting next to me, drinking your Healer's tea—not heading in that direction or thinking about heading in that direction."

"Yes! Yes!" she said impatiently. She gave him a quick hug and brushed his cheek with a kiss. Jogging away she threw him a teasing glance over her shoulder. "Take care of Brenna till I get back."

She laughed and sped up, letting the wind swallow his terse reply.

ELPHAME JOGGED AROUND the side of the castle. MacCallan Castle had been built on a massive area of high ground that jutted out over the imposing shoreline of the B'an Sea. She followed the edge of the cliff north. Like the land to the south, the shore curved back into the forest, leaving Mac-Callan standing alone, silent and austere in its prominent position.

Well, it was silent for the moment. Elphame smiled into the wind as she thought about the castle being filled with the happy sounds of people going about the daily business of living. Her people and her castle.

When she was no longer visible to the castle, she stopped to unwind the skirt from around her waist and hang it over the side of a boulder. Then she began a series of stretches to warm the hard muscles of her legs. Elphame breathed deeply of the tangy sea breeze. Far below, waves rhythmically pounded the bottom of the cliffs. The sun was working its way down into the sapphire of the sea and the western sky was beginning to be streaked with the brilliant flush of evening. It felt so right for her to be there that Elphame wondered how she had lived so long elsewhere.

Muscles stretched and warm, she kicked into a brisk jog, following the cliff's edge and learning the feel of the land. It wasn't an easy run, like in her meadow near Epona's Temple. Here she had to dodge around boulders and leap over rocks, but the added exercise was satisfying. With the forest on her right, and the sea on her left, she seemed to be running on a ribbon of land created just for her. She leaned forward and increased her stride. Danann had been wise. She could feel the tension of the last several days sliding from her body as her legs pumped and her hoofs bit the ground in their familiar rhythm. When the burn started, it felt good and she leaned into the speed, drawing deeply from her reservoir of strength.

In front of her she saw a wide stream that ran out of the forest to cascade in a brilliant gush of white water over the edge of the cliff. She slowed, made her decision and turned into the forest, following the line of the stream. She loved the sea and the sound of the water, but the forest called to her. Beside the stream the ground was thick with pine needles and early moss. Her hooves crunched with a strong, satisfying sound as she sprinted deeper into the forest. The trees that grew in increasing thickness around her stretched far up into the sky. The pines were so ancient that their branches did not begin until more than a man's body length above her head. The enormous trees dazzled her—they were so much more beautiful than the tame willows and maples that grew around her mother's temple. She gazed up, drinking in their wildness. This was her home, where she belonged. For the first time in her life she was actually fitting in. Elphame felt free and happy and even, perhaps, a little giddy....

She did not notice the ravine until it was too late to stop. The ground opened beneath her and Elphame's body hurled forward and then down. Her arms windmilled frantically, trying to help her to regain any semblance of balance as she fell, tumbling over and over. Pain sliced through her side. Instinctively, she curled to protect her injury and something struck her shoulder and then her head. Blackness engulfed her quickly and completely.

Lochlan knew when she fell. He had been hunting—hunger was the only force that could pull him from his constant vigil of the castle. A young stag had passed close by his hiding place, and he tracked it into the forest, felled it with a single arrow and had begun the bloody job of dressing and cleaning it. He worked quickly and efficiently, sure that he would be finished in time to return and watch Elphame depart the castle as the sun left the sky. Perhaps she would bathe again. His wings quivered at the thought and he automatically repressed their stirrings, causing his head to ache with a maddening insistence. The passion of last night's dream had stayed close beside him all during that long day.

That is not all she is, he reminded himself furiously. She is not simply an object to be lusted after and used. From years of dreams he had learned that she was kind and thoughtful, and too often sad. She was more than a sensuous, beautiful female body. She was more than skin and blood— Blood... Unbidden, his wings quivered again.

Then he felt a jabbing pain in his side, followed by a sick jolt to his shoulder and right temple. Struggling against a wave of dizziness, he dropped the short sword he was using to dress the deer and clutched his side. And he knew.

"Elphame!" He cried her name, heedless of who might overhear him. Something terrible had happened. She was injured. She needed him. Frantically he tried to quiet his panic and regain control of his thoughts. Where was she? How could he get to her?

Your heart will tell you. Be still and listen to it.

A voice, very like his mother's, echoed within his mind along with the phantom pain of Elphame's wound. Was he finally going mad? He didn't care, he thought fiercely, as long as the madness led him to her. With the oneness of thought that had carried him into Partholon to find her within the ruins of Mac-Callan Castle, Lochlan focused on the young girl he had watched grow and mature. The young girl he believed was his destiny.

He felt the answer as surely as he felt her pain. Opening his wings so that they would carry him in the swift, gliding run he had inherited from his father's people, he raced into the north.

Elphame regained consciousness to the sound of distant thunder. She was going to be ill—violently ill. She tried to turn her head so that she wouldn't soil herself, and the pain that stabbed through her right temple caused her to suck in her breath with a sob. She retched—dry heaves that made her side feel as if it was on fire.

She opened her eyes slowly, wincing at the pain in her head. Her thoughts were disjointed, confused. What had happened? A shiver wracked her body and the fire in her side tore at her. Her vision grayed around the edges and she struggled to stay conscious. Why was she so cold? Her legs were frozen, almost numb. Was she paralyzed? She looked down. Her back was propped awkwardly against a mossy bank. The bottom half of her body was submerged in a stream—the stream she had been running beside—and her memory flooded back. She'd been running and hadn't been paying attention. She'd fallen into a ravine.

Cuchulainn was going to kill her.

Grimacing at the sharp ache in her shoulder, she slowly and carefully stretched her arms forward so that she could feel down the length of both her legs. Her hands were shaking terribly, but she felt no broken bones protruding from the wet coat of fur that covered her legs. Elphame shivered. Her side flamed again. There was a tear in her blood-soaked shirt. She pulled it open. And looked away again—quickly. A long, ugly gash that was bleeding freely ran from her waist across her ribs. Looking at it made her feel as if she might be sick again. She'd never been particularly squeamish about blood before, but she'd never seen that much of her own blood before, either.

Gritting her teeth against the pain she shifted her weight and tried to gather her legs so that she could stand up and climb out of the stream. The world grayed and a tide of nausea engulfed her. Panting, she slumped back against the bank. The right side of her head throbbed horribly. Her hand reached up to gently prod the site of the pain, and it came away sticky and red. She fought against another round of retching.

It was as she was shakily wiping her mouth with the back of her hand that she heard it—a strange, guttural, grunting noise. On the opposite side of the stream the incline of the ravine wasn't nearly as steep, and the trees grew almost to the edge of the bank, which was lined with rocks, browned with age and covered with fungus-colored lichen. Her vision was watery and Elphame blinked rapidly, trying to see into the shadowy forest. She could only make out vague shapes that might or might not be moving.

Thunder rolled again, this time louder. She squinted up at the sky. It was getting dark, but she couldn't tell if that was because enough time had passed for the sun to have begun to set, or because a storm was coming.

The underbrush crackled as if a large body was moving quickly through it. Had she been gone long enough for Cu to miss her? Could that be him?

Without truly believing it, she called tentatively, "Cu-chulainn? Is that you?"

The noise fell instantly silent. When it began again it was moving purposefully toward her. In the fading light a pair of red eyes appeared at the edge of the tree line just before the creature broke from the shadows.

Elphame felt a lightning jolt of panic. The wild boar was truly terrifying. Its mud-encrusted body was easily the length of a man's, with several times the bulk. Yellowed tusks protruded in deadly arches from its powerful jaws. The boar scented the air and pulled back its lips in a hideous growl that spewed frothy white spittle in an arc around it. Its stench reached her in a fetid rush and Elphame's stomach pitched dangerously. The boar's small eyes flashed with a feral gleam and it lowered its head. Elphame's leaden legs scrambled to support her and she tottered to her feet. Leaning heavily against the bank, she tried to blink her vision clear while she clawed her brother's dagger from the sheath around her waist, but her right arm wouldn't work properly and she dropped the dagger. The boar charged.

Elphame clenched her teeth and tried to push away from the bank. She knew she was going to die. *Epona, help me to be brave,* she prayed fervently.

"No!" Snarling the word like a curse, a winged shape launched itself from the bank behind Elphame, and crashed into the charging boar. The boar was knocked off its feet, but it righted itself with a terrible quickness. Now it was no longer focused on Elphame. Instead it faced a new foe, an attacker that crouched before it, wings spread and a blood-covered short sword drawn and held ready.

Elphame collapsed against the side of the bank. It seemed that reality had fragmented. She must have fallen through the fabric of the world she knew and entered another, for the winged being in front of her defied reason.

The boar charged, and the winged being leaped aside, raking his sword down the side of the monster's thick hide. The boar screamed its pain and rage, whirling to charge again. But again the winged being was too quick, and he drew second blood. Frothing at the mouth, the boar attacked wildly, trying to trap its enemy against the side of the bank. Elphame saw the winged being glance at her, and she saw, too, that he realized that the boar was driving him close to where she had fallen. With a terrible hissing sound, the winged creature leaped one last time, directly onto the boar's back. With incredible speed, his hand shot forward and the sword sliced neatly through the beast's throat. The boar squealed and fell heavily into the stream, blood pouring from the waterfall at its throat.

The winged creature rose from the back of the dead boar. He took two staggering steps toward Elphame.

"Stay away!" Elphame screamed.

As if he had run into a glass wall, the winged creature stopped.

Elphame was staring at his hands. They were covered in blood, as was the sword he clutched. He followed her gaze, and immediately dropped the sword, opening his hands to her.

"I will not harm you," he gasped, trying to steady his breathing so that his voice wouldn't frighten her. Her eyes were wide and glassy, and he could see that she was trembling violently.

"So much blood," she whispered through numbed lips.

She needn't have said anything; Lochlan was already intensely aware that the boar's blood covered him as well as filled his heightened senses. He could feel the animal's spirit, still strong and angry, within the slick redness that dyed his hands. It called to Lochlan with a barbaric voice that fired his own blood. The demon within him stirred; victorious, it wanted to sink its teeth into the boar's neck wound and drink deeply, absorbing its bestial essence. Lochlan struggled against the sensations. He had to get the blood off of him before he became lost to it. Fighting against the pain that spiked in his mind as he repressed the vicious longing within him, Lochlan bent quickly and dipped his hands and arms in the stream, rubbing frantically to rid himself of the animal's blood. Then, arms dripping, but no longer red, he again held them open in front him.

"It is gone now." Cleansed, the shield of his control was firmly intact and he was able to speak to her in a soothing voice, as if she were a very small child.

She looked from his hands to his body, studying him with a strange, breathless curiosity that was a result of shock and blood loss and utter disbelief. He was a man. A winged man. He was tall, several inches taller than she, and his hair was an unusual yellow color, like someone had tamed rays of the morning sun, she thought. It must be long, because even though it was tied in a queue she could see that during the battle with the boar, some of the strands had pulled free and hung past his shoulders. His face had been masterfully sculpted, with strong ridges and fine, high cheekbones. His eyes, which were watching her intently, were slightly slanted. Their color was a distinctive pewter-gray. With an increasing sense of wonder she realized that he was beautiful. His body was long and lean; his skin was very pale, but he didn't look sickly or sallow-colored. Instead he looked ethereal, as if he didn't belong to the mortal world. He was wearing a cream-colored shirt made of a coarsely woven fabric. Elphame thought that it looked like it needed to be washed. His breeches were brown leather that had been roughly tanned. He wore no shoes. There was something strange about his feet, but he was standing in the stream, and Elphame could not get a clear look at them.

Then her eyes shifted to his wings. Even now, tucked neatly

against his back, their size was impressive. She remembered how they had looked when he had fought the boar. They had spread around him as if he were a lethal bird of prey with a wingspan that must have been more than ten feet. They weren't feathered, but were made of a membrane that looked like it would be soft to the touch. The underside of the wings was light-colored down, like his skin and his hair, but the upper side was darker, more like the slate of his eyes.

"What are you?" She thought she asked the question in a normal voice, and was dismayed to hear that the words were only a weak whisper.

"I am called Lochlan. And I do not wish to harm you. Ever," he said, letting some of the urgency he felt creep into his voice. She was wounded. He looked away from the terrible amount of blood on her head and her side. Her lips were blue and her face was deathly pale. "Will you let me help you, Elphame?"

Her eyes widened and Lochlan thought she looked like a terrified woodland creature.

"How do you know my name?"

"I have always known your name," he said, taking a slow step forward.

"Is this really happening? Am I dead?"

He took two more steps and closed the space between them. "I promise you this is happening, and you are not dead."

He smiled then, and she was dazzled by the warmth that radiated from him.

"I understand what you feel, though. It is almost as if I dream, too," he said. One hand moved restlessly forward, as if he wanted to touch her, but when she flinched he stopped the motion and the brightness of his smile faded. He hesitated only a moment before saying, "It is too wet and cold here. I do not want to move you, but you are in shock and it is not safe for you to stay here."

The concern in his voice was real, and it penetrated through the fog of pain that threatened to overwhelm her.

"I don't think I can walk," she said, feeling strangely detached from the sound of her own voice.

He smiled again, and this time Elphame was surprised by a glimpse of very white, very sharp teeth.

"I can carry you," he said.

She had to be living a dream. What was happening to her was just another incredibly realistic dream like the one she'd had the night before. Soon she'd wake up to find Cuchulainn feeding the fire another log. He'd chastise her for not getting enough sleep, and then he'd pretend that he wasn't staying up most of the night himself to watch over her.

So, why not? It was her dream and she thought she might like it if the beautiful winged man carried her.

"You may carry me." She wanted to smile at him, but her lips wouldn't obey her.

Trying his best to be gentle, he knelt beside her. This close he could not ignore the blood that covered her head and soaked her side. Its living scent assaulted him—rich and strong, her blood ran thick with female power. Unbidden, he heard his mother's voice repeat the words of the Prophecy.

You will save your people from their madness through the blood of a dying goddess.

No! Elphame couldn't die. Not here—not now.

He gritted his teeth, rejecting the call of her blood, and embracing the pain that spiked through him as he turned away from his base desires. He slid one arm behind her back and the other under her knees. He hesitated. He was inhumanly strong, and he would have no trouble carrying her, but he dreaded the pain he knew he would cause her.

"Forgive me," he said.

In one smooth motion he lifted her into his arms. She

groaned, and the sound tore at his heart. He extended his wings for balance, and as quickly as possible, he carried her up the side of the steep ravine.

Thunder sounded, followed by a flash of lightning. He studied the sky; a storm was moving in from the sea. Elphame would need shelter as well as her wounds tended to. Lochlan clenched his jaw in frustration. He should carry her to his own shelter, but first he knew he must check her wounds. He searched the area. The canopy of tall pines would provide some relief from the storm, as long as the rain didn't become too heavy. He strode several feet into the trees until he found a spot under an ancient pine that was mounded especially thick with dried needles. He kicked more needles into a makeshift nest, then he crouched and carefully laid her down.

Her eyes were closed and she was trembling. She was wearing only a sleeveless bodice wrap and a small triangle of material. The sleek equine coat that covered her legs was soaking wet, but the legs themselves did not appear to be injured; he saw no blood or swelling marring their smooth surface. His eyes traveled up to her bodice. The wrap was torn open on one side and drenched scarlet with fresh blood. His stomach knotted and pain sliced his head with the effort it took to keep himself from acting on the dark impulse that was close to drowning him.

He would not taste her; his demons would not win. He looked away and steadied himself. When he turned back to her his voice was tight and controlled.

"Elphame, I need to examine your wound."

Her eyes opened only to narrow slits. "This isn't a dream."

"No. This is not a dream. I do not want to cause you any more pain, but I must see how badly you have been injured."

"Go ahead," she said, and pressed her eyes tightly closed.

He had to be calm. Now was not the time for trembling

hands and panicked thoughts. He was more human than demon. He could do this.

Lochlan took a ragged breath and pulled open the ripped edge of her bodice. The gash was long and ugly. He could see that it had opened her skin and sliced into her well-muscled side, but as he examined it he was relieved to see that it wasn't as deep as he had expected. He probed the area, making his touch as gentle as possible, and he felt no fractured ribs. It was bleeding freely. Lochlan ground his teeth together with the effort it took to keep the demon within his blood at bay. For once he welcomed the pain that filled his temples as he made himself observe the wound with clinical detachment. He would need to pack the gash and stop the bleeding. He glanced at her head, the side of which was matted with dried blood. The head wound frightened him far worse than the cut in her side, but there was little he could do for it.

Lochlan thought about what he needed. Over a century of living had taught him some lessons well—his kind had proven to be long-lived, but they were not immortal and certainly not impervious to harm. He had packed many wounds and treated countless injuries. Abruptly he started back to the ravine.

"Don't leave me!"

Her words brought him quickly to her side. He brushed her cheek with his fingers. "Never, my heart." Alarm at the clammy feel of her skin caused the endearment to slip from his thoughts into his words. "But I must pack your wound and stop the bleeding. That is all. I am not going far." He gestured to the ravine. "There is moss near the stream."

Silently, she nodded and then winced at the pain the movement caused.

He could feel her eyes following him as he hurried to the edge of the ravine and leaped, gliding swiftly to the stream where he retrieved his sword and then cut a section of healthy green moss from the bank. With the enhanced vision he had inherited from his Formorian father he could clearly see her watching for him, wide-eyed, and her look of relief as he climbed back over the edge of the ravine. Lochlan knelt beside her again.

"I would do anything not to hurt you, but I cannot allow you to keep bleeding. I have to pack the wound on your side. Do you understand?" He looked intently into her eyes. How clear were her thoughts? How severe was the wound to her head?

"I understand that it's going to hurt badly enough that you're already sorry," she said with a weak smile.

Her smile and clever words relieved him beyond measure. She sounded like the Elphame he knew so well from his dreams.

"Then there is nothing wrong with your understanding."

"I'm ready," she said, closing her eyes tightly again. "Today I discovered that I do not like the sight of my own blood."

The sight of her blood…the scent of it…the feel of it… He did not like what it did to him, either. Working quickly, Lochlan measured and cut a strip of moss to the length of her wound. Best to get it over with, he told himself. Carefully, he packed the moss into the open slash, trying to close out the sound of the pain he was causing her.

"Finished," he said in a voice that shook only a little.

Tears had seeped from her closed eyes and when she opened them she had to blink several times before she could focus on him.

"It's so cold," she said.

He silently cursed himself for being a fool. When he'd felt her pain, all other thoughts had fled from his mind. He'd left his pack containing water, knives and precious, fire-starting flint beside the corpse of the deer. Thunder continued to boom menacingly and Lochlan gazed uneasily at the bruised-looking sky. She could not walk to his shelter, and he didn't like the idea of carrying her, cold and fainting, through a thunderstorm. She needed to be warmed before shock set in and threatened her recovery. He would have to shelter her here, the only way he knew how.

"I can warm you, Elphame, but you must trust me."

She looked at him. Her head hurt with a sick throbbing that fractured her thoughts and eroded her ability to reason. Who was he? Lochlan—the name came to her mind. His wings drew her gaze again. But what was he? Had he already told her? Had she forgotten?

"Elphame, I give you my oath that I want no harm to come to you."

His voice called her eyes back to his. There was something about that voice, something familiar. She tried to concentrate, but the pounding in her head wouldn't allow it. All she was certain of at that moment was that Lochlan, whatever or whoever he was, had just saved her life.

"I will trust you," she said.

His fanged smile was disconcerting, but Elphame had little time to feel anything except surprise because Lochlan was suddenly lying beside her. He propped himself on an elbow and looked into her eyes.

"Do not be frightened."

Then one massive wing unfurled from where it had been tucked against the back of his body. Like a living blanket, it moved forward across her, and then down, until its scalloped edge met the forest floor. She was completely enclosed by him.

His warmth encompassed her. Elphame lay very still—even her shivering stopped. The wing was less than a hand's length above her. That close she could see that the light-colored underside was covered with small, fine hairs which looked soft as down. His scent came to her then. He smelled of pine and sweat and something musty and wild that she could not name, but was surprised to find pleasing to her senses. She turned her head, moving slowly and carefully. His face was very close to hers. He was watching her with silent intensity.

"What are you?" she whispered.

His eyes never left hers and without thinking he answered her from his heart. "I am the man who has known you all your life."

What he was saying made no sense to her muddled thoughts.

"But you aren't a man, and you don't know me."

"I've known you since your birth, Elphame. Through my dreams I've watched you."

Dreams…her eyes widened. She had dreamed of wings surrounding and caressing her. His voice! It was his voice that she had heard last night calling to her from within the fog.

"And part of me is very much a man," Lochlan said.

"And the other part?" Elphame asked breathlessly.

Lochlan continued to meet her eyes, but when he spoke his voice was filled with great sadness.

"My mother was human. My father was Fomorian. I carry the blood of both races in my veins."

Elphame's thoughts were spiraling erratically and she felt suddenly cold again.

"But, that's not possible." Even as she spoke her gaze drifted to the wing that covered her body and she shivered. An image flashed through her mind of the noble MacCallan surrounded by a ring of blood-drenched winged demons. How could Lochlan be a Formorian? Even if she hadn't witnessed the slaughter of The MacCallan, she had read enough about Formorians in her mother's library to know that their race had been poisonous to Parthalon. They had come perilously close to enslaving the entire world. Her eyes shot to his. "Fomorians were driven from Partholon more than a century ago."

He wanted to explain to her, to try to ease the fear and confusion that he read in her eyes, but his ultrasensitive hearing had caught a sudden sound. He raised his head and turned an ear into the wind. Within the noise of the coming storm he could hear pounding hooves. It had to be Cuchulainn.

"Elphame, listen to me," he said urgently. "Your people are coming. I cannot stay. They would see only a Fomorian, and not a man."

Elphame blinked. Through the pain that pounded through her battered body she forced herself to focus on his face. She did see a man—a beautiful, heroic man.

"Listen to me and remember. I am not really leaving you now. I will always be near you, awaiting your call. Do you understand?"

"I—" she began, but the sound of her brother's voice shouting her name cut clearly through the night. "Go!" she urged Lochlan.

His wing lifted from her. The chill of the night air struck her, leaving her feeling exposed and vulnerable. Before he stood, he stroked her cheek with his fingertips.

"Call to me, my heart. I will answer."

Then he glided silently into the forest, disappearing quickly from sight.

14

"CUCHULAINN! HERE!" Brighid's voice carried over the whine of the wind. The centaur Huntress galloped to the spot where Elphame lay and slid to a halt, Cuchulainn close behind her. He leaped from his horse before it could stop and fell to his knees beside his sister. Then Elphame was ringed in blazing torchlight as the night exploded with horses, riders and centaurs.

"El! Oh, no! Please, no!" He took her hand in his. It was cool, like carved marble. Blood—she seemed to be covered with blood. Her face was ghostly white, and if she hadn't blinked and whispered his name, he would have believed that she was dead.

Elphame thought he sounded very young, and she wanted to reassure him, but she was so cold again. It felt like with Lochlan, all of her strength had fled, too, and talking took such a great effort.

"Cuchulainn, move aside." Brenna's voice was calm and

firm and held none of the shy hesitancy with which she usually spoke to him.

He looked blankly up at her.

"Cuchulainn, now! I must see to your sister." Brenna's tone of command was so sharp that the warrior in Cuchulainn obeyed without thinking.

Brenna knelt beside Elphame. "Bring that torch over here," she ordered. "And bring something to cover her."

The light made Elphame squint painfully, but it was a relief to feel the concealing weight of several cloaks that were hastily thrown over her near nakedness. Strange that she hadn't thought about how little she was wearing when Lochlan had been there.

"Elphame, who am I?" the Healer asked, bending close and using the light from a torch to carefully study her eyes.

"Brenna," she whispered.

"And where are you?"

"Forest…" she managed to say. "The ravine, I fell." She tried to point, but the pain in her shoulder caused her to bite off a moan instead.

Brighid followed Elphame's half gesture. Holding her own torch high, the Huntress disappeared over the side of the ravine.

Brenna's sure, gentle hands traveled quickly over Elphame's injured shoulder, up to her head, and finally down to the moss-covered wound on her side.

"You did well to pack this. You've lost far too much blood as it is."

"I didn't…" Elphame started to say, but the Healer stopped her.

"Don't speak. You need to save your strength for the return trip. Drink this." Gently, the Healer helped Elphame lift her head while she pressed a wineskin to Elphame's lips.

Elphame sputtered, and then drank thirstily. The herbed wine was sweet and cold, and as its energy filled her she felt revived enough so that she was able to smile faintly at her brother.

"I'm fine, Cu," she said, wishing her voice didn't sound so weak.

"No," Brenna said sharply. "You are not fine, not yet. Cuchulainn, I need a strip of material to bind her shoulder and another to wrap around the wound on her side."

Relieved to have been given something constructive to do, Cu pulled off his shirt and began ripping the fine linen into long strips.

"He just wants to show off his chest." Elphame's voice shook, but she managed to make it carry. The men and centaurs surrounding her laughed, as did Brenna. Cuchulainn tried to frown at her, but he succeeded only in looking ridiculously happy, and El was afraid for a moment that he might actually cry.

"You have just relieved my mind greatly about the severity of your head wound," the Healer said.

Her brother's smile widened.

"There is a dead boar at the bottom of the ravine." Brighid had rejoined the ring around Elphame. "I believe this is yours." She handed the throwing dagger to Cuchulainn, but her eyes were studying Elphame with a curiously guarded expression.

"By the Goddess, El! A wild boar?" Cuchulainn's face, which had regained some of it color, paled again.

Brenna began carefully tying the linen strips around her waist, saving Elphame from having to respond to her brother. She closed her eyes and set her teeth against the pain—and tried to concentrate. Lochlan. He hadn't been an apparition; she'd seen him kill the boar, the same boar Brighid had found. He'd carried her up the ravine, dressed her wound, and covered her with his warmth. Shouldn't she tell them that he had saved her?

He said his father had been a Fomorian.

"They would see only a Fomorian, and not a man."

Lochlan's words echoed through her troubled mind. It shouldn't have been possible. The Fomorians had been defeated and driven from Partholon more than a century ago. The different races of Partholon had joined together to insure that the demon horde had been extinguished—that it would never threaten the peoples of Partholon, in particular the Partholonian women, again. Her pain-fogged mind shied away from remembrances of the historic record of rape and destruction. The being who had just saved her life couldn't be a Fomorian. It didn't make sense.

Yet she had seen his wings. They had covered her with their warmth. Clearly, the impossible had happened.

"You meet your destiny at MacCallan Castle…that destiny is tied up in your lifemate… The words rustled through Elphame's throbbing head. She tried to wrap her mind around the thought, but it was simply too bizarre. Her concentration fragmented. She couldn't think clearly about it now, and she wouldn't talk about it until she'd had time to sort it through in her mind.

"There," Brenna said, knotting the makeshift sling that held Elphame's arm securely against her chest. As she finished, the first drops of rain sprinkled through the canopy of pines. "That is all I can do here. We must get her back to the castle."

"El."

She opened her eyes to see her brother crouched beside her. His hair was already damp. He'd wrapped a fold of his kilt over his bare chest. Elphame thought he looked very dashing, like the ancient warrior for whom he'd been named. She smiled at him, wanting to ease the worry in his eyes.

"El," he repeated, spreading his hands over her head in an

attempt to shield her from some of the rain. "I know it's going to be hard for you, but you're going to have to ride back to the castle."

Brighid moved to Cuchulainn's side. "I will carry her."

"She can't ride by herself," Cu said. "She'll have to ride with me."

"Then I will carry you, too. You'll be too busy holding her to guide that empty-headed gelding of yours anyway," Brighid said. "And you can be sure that I won't misstep and cause her unnecessary pain."

Cuchulainn looked up at the Huntress. "You'd carry both of us?"

"Easily."

The sky boomed and the patter of rain came more insistently through the trees.

"I want her out of here. Now," Brenna told Cuchulainn. "And she should not sleep. Talk to her, Cuchulainn."

He nodded tightly in response to the Healer, then began shouting orders, "Angus, Brendan, lift her up to me." He stood and vaulted onto the Huntress's back. "Carefully!" He snapped when his sister moaned in pain as the two men began lifting her.

Elphame tried to help the men, but her vision had grayed again and each time she moved the wound in her side burned almost unbearably. She felt Cuchulainn's strong arms around her as she straddled the Huntress's smooth back.

"Ready?" Brighid looked over her shoulder at Cuchulainn.

"Yes." Cuchulainn tightened his grip on his sister and the Huntress moved easily into a smooth, ground-eating canter.

In some part of her mind, Elphame acknowledged that she would have liked to have been able to enjoy the novelty of a centaur ride. Instead she was plummeted into an unrelenting nightmare. Every stride the centaur took jolted through her body. Her head pulsed and her stomach heaved. She could feel warm wetness washing down her side and she knew her wound was bleeding through the moss. Soon she could not hold herself upright, and as they emerged from the forest to retrace her path along the rocky side of the cliff, she slumped against her brother, depending completely upon him to keep her from falling.

"It won't be much longer…. I've got you…." Cuchulainn kept up a litany of encouragement in his sister's ear. "Talk to me, El. Tell me about how beautiful MacCallan Castle will be when it's finally restored."

His sister's responses to his constant questioning were jumbled—sometimes she described rooms that he recognized very well as rooms they had grown up in, and sometimes what she said made no sense at all, like when she rambled about a bed of pine needles canopied by wings—but he did keep her talking, even though he could feel her growing weaker as she leaned more heavily against him. Then the sky opened and rain came down on them in heavy ropes. The torches the riders held sputtered and went out. Cuchulainn was almost thankful for the brilliant flashes of lightning that helped to illuminate their way. Brighid's decision to carry them had been a wise one. If he had been riding his gelding he wouldn't have been able to steer the horse through the stormy darkness and support his sister, too.

The Huntress soon outdistanced the rest of the group—even the male centaurs who had volunteered to join them on the search. Her determination and stamina were impressive. He had misjudged Brighid, Cuchulainn admitted to himself. When he had announced that he was going to search for his sister, she and the little Healer had been the first to join him. Without her assistance he could never have tracked and found Elphame as quickly.

If only he had reacted as quickly when he had had his

first premonition that something was wrong with El! Instead
he had ignored the growing Feeling because it had come
from the spirit realm—that area of his life that he tried his
best to repress and ignore. Well, this time the spirit realm
had refused to be ignored. The knowledge left the acidic
taste in his mouth that he recognized as part self-loathing
and part fear.

Cuchulainn clutched his sister more tightly within his arms.
Now he knew what had been bothering him since they had
begun their journey to MacCallan Castle. The nameless threat
that he had felt hanging over his sister hadn't been a hurtful
lover or an ancient curse. It had been something totally
mundane—an accident, and he'd been too busy imagining
faceless phantoms to foresee it.

Faceless phantoms? If he hadn't been so wet and miserable
he would have laughed aloud in self-mockery. Apparently,
some of them had faces all well as voices and attitudes.

Brighid slowed and Cuchulainn was relieved to see the dark
walls of the castle materialize before them.

"Take her to the kitchen. It's where they've done the most
work," Cu yelled over the storm.

Brighid nodded and trotted through the gap in the outer
walls, then entered the inner courtyard. Rain poured through
the empty roof, and, as they passed the fountain, lightning
forked across the sky, suddenly outlining the stone girl like a
ghost in the night. Cuchulainn eyed the statue uneasily—
glancing suspiciously at the area around it.

Brighid's hooves clattered into the Great Hall, where she finally
halted. She twisted at the waist and said quickly, "The kitchen
will be dark as a tomb. You and Elphame wait here where there
is some light. I'll get flint and torches from the wagons."

Brighid helped him as he lifted Elphame's unresisting body
from the Huntress's back to the floor, where Cuchulainn sat

leaning against the wall cradling his sister's head carefully in his lap.

"I won't be long," Brighid said, giving Elphame one last worried look before she hurried from the room.

"It feels good to be still," Elphame said faintly into the darkness.

"Brenna will be here soon," Cu assured her.

He wanted to fuss over Elphame, to do something that would make her feel better. He felt helpless and useless. He unwrapped the fold of his kilt that he'd thrown over his shoulder and used the end of it to gently wipe some of the rain from her face and arms. Talking...he had to keep her talking, but before he could ask another inane question about castle decorations she surprised him with a question of her own.

"How did you know to come after me, Cu?"

He looked down at his sister. In the dimness only the vague outline of her face was visible. Occasional flashes of light stole into the Great Hall from the open courtyard, and Cu could see the bright reflection of her eyes as she stared up at him.

"I was uneasy about you."

Elphame smiled weakly. "You've been uneasy about me since we arrived here. What made you come after me?"

"I wasn't going to; I told myself that I was imagining things. Then the storm began moving in. I was restless, so I thought I'd come back here and keep a lookout for you." He paused and brushed a wet strand of hair off of her face. "I thought I'd challenge you to race my gelding to Loth Tor, and since you'd already been for a long run, he might have a chance at beating you."

He saw her teeth flash, and he grinned back at her.

"So, I was waiting by the main entrance when I heard a noise coming from inside the castle. Unlike my restless unease about you, the noise was impossible to ignore."

"Why?" Elphame asked.

"Because it was the sound of someone bellowing my name." Cu shook his head, remembering the massive voice booming his name from within the empty castle and the terrible feeling caused from hearing an all too real spirit demanding his attention. Cu's voice was tight with anxiety. "El, I have to tell you that the rumors about your castle were at least half-true. It might not be cursed, but I can promise you that it is haunted."

The next flash of lightning illuminated his sister's widened eyes.

"The MacCallan talked to you, too?" she asked in a rush, with decidedly more animation than she'd shown since they'd found her by the ravine.

Cuchulainn frowned.

"Are you telling me that he has appeared to you and you said nothing to me?" he said incredulously.

"Well, Cu…" She hesitated, suddenly almost glad she was injured. At least he couldn't get too mad at her. "I know how you dislike the spirit realm."

"Dislike!" he shouted. When his sister winced in reaction he closed his eyes and took a deep breath. "El," he said slowly, "it isn't simply a matter of my dislike for the spirit realm. Think about all that has happened since we have arrived. You have never felt even the slightest touch of magic from the Goddess, and suddenly it is as if you have become a living conduit to Epona. There are forces at work here that we do not understand, El."

Elphame made a weak gesture with her hand and tried to shake her head, but the motion ended in a grimace.

"Shhh." Her brother was instantly apologetic. "I didn't mean to upset you. I'm not angry at you."

"I know, Cu," she said, blinking hard to clear her vision and order her thoughts. "But you must remember that it is different for me. I do not fear the spirit realm. And you cannot believe that The MacCallan or Epona wish us any harm."

"Of course not," Cu said, wiping more bloody water from her face. "But I want you to remember that just as good exists, so does evil. And evil in the realm of spirits cannot be defeated with strength of arms."

"No," she said softly. "It must be defeated with honor and truth and strength of will."

Cu studied his sister in the dim light. He realized that she was changing. He didn't want to admit it, but that realization made him uneasy. Lightning flashed again and he could see that she was smiling up at him. His heart wrenched. She had been his best friend for as long as he could remember. Didn't he love her enough to allow her to become the woman of her destiny, even if part of that destiny seemed foreign and incomprehensible to him?

"Just promise me that you will tell me about any more of your spiritual visitations. Especially if they are with any of our ancestors."

"I promise," she said, sounding relieved. "By the way, did you notice the resemblance between you and The MacCallan?"

Cuchulainn snorted. "Please! I am nothing like that caustic old ghost."

"What did he say to you?"

"Let me see if I remember it correctly…yes, it was something like, *'Cuchulainn, are ye no more than a muscle-bound clotheid? Go after yer sister, the lass has need of ye!'*" He growled in an excellent imitation of the gruff old spirit.

Elphame was still alternating between giggles and grimaces from the pain they caused when Brighid and the rest of their party clattered noisily into the Great Hall. Brenna climbed awkwardly from her horse and moved to Elphame's side, frowning severely at Cuchulainn.

"I told you to keep her talking, not to make her hysterical."

★ ★ ★

Lochlan shadowed the three of them, watching through the
pelting rain to be certain that Elphame arrived safely at her
castle. They disappeared within, and were soon joined by the rest
of the group that the female centaur had so easily outdistanced.
He continued watching all through that grim night, and only
allowed himself to return to his shelter to sleep when Elphame
emerged from the castle the next morning leaning heavily upon
her brother to walk stiffly to the tent the workers had hastily
erected as soon as the sun had begun to lighten the sky.

Lochlan smiled. He had known that Elphame would not be
content to retreat to the village and be cosseted and cared for
there like a delicate flower. He was a little surprised to see her
leave the castle walls, but that was probably a compromise she
had agreed to make with her brother. His sharp eyes focused
on Cuchulainn's stern expression. Yes, the warrior would prefer
that she recover in the village. Did he not understand that she
drew her strength from the very stones of her castle?

He should not judge the brother harshly, Lochlan chided
himself. Cuchulainn loved her dearly, and only wished to save
his sister from harm, just as he did. If only the two of them
could be allies....

Far to the north Keir raised his pale head as if he was
scenting the air, but in truth the gesture was unnecessary. It
was not a physical trail he detected, but a spiritual string, a
strand of which lay unwound at his feet.

"Yes." His voice was a hiss of triumph. "Lochlan took his
departure through here."

Beside him, Fallon's wings stirred with excitement as she
gazed at the small, partially hidden trail that led deep into the
mountains. "Are you quite certain?" she asked, hardly daring

to believe. "We have searched this area before and found nothing of him."

"He has been away too long and he grows careless. I have said many times that his obsession makes him weak, and this only proves it. He has relaxed his thoughts and I sense him again. If you would concentrate, you would know that it is so," he said, his voice a steely admonishment.

With an effort, Fallon did not cringe. It would only make him angrier, and Keir's anger hovered too close to the surface without enticement. Fallon could sense the madness too clearly in Keir. She could feel how it waited for her mate to give in—to be finished fighting for his humanity and to embrace the dark heritage of their father's demonic blood. She could see it lurking like an oily stain within his eyes. The longer Lochlan was gone, the wilder Keir had become. It seemed that Lochlan had taken with him a piece of her mate's humanity. Yet another reason that they must find Lochlan and the hoofed goddess of his dreams....

Fallon closed her eyes, ignoring the insistent pain that tapped at her mind as she beat back her instinctive flare of anger. Lochlan should have allowed them to accompany him. His quest was too important. One slip—one mistake—and they would all be doomed to the madness that lived within their blood. Keir might be right; Lochlan could have become too obsessed with his dreams to be trusted completely. With an enormous effort she cast aside her whirring thoughts and concentrated on gray eyes that sparkled with humor and patient understanding—and she felt it. A small tug that beckoned her forward. She opened her eyes and smiled at her mate.

"I do feel him!"

Keir's scowl relaxed, and the blackness within his gaze lightened. He nodded, satisfied with her response. "Let us tell the others."

15

THE SUN HAD just broken over the tall pines of the forest when Brenna announced that Elphame could sleep.

"Drink this." The Healer held a mug to Elphame's lips.

The tea was warm and thick and tasted vaguely of honey and mint. Almost instantly Elphame felt her eyelids become unnaturally weighty.

"You didn't need to drug me. I'm already tired," she slurred.

Cuchulainn smoothed a thick strand of hair back from his sister's pale face. "Just sleep. Brenna knows best."

El tried unsuccessfully to focus on her brother. He still looked so worried. Dark shadows bruised the area beneath his eyes.

"You need to sleep, too," she said faintly.

"Soon, El."

Elphame sighed and closed her eyes, allowing sleep to finally claim her.

Cuchulainn dropped into the chair next to his sister's bed.

He rubbed his temple and rolled his neck, trying to work out the stiffness.

"She was right, you do need to sleep, too," the Healer said without looking at him while she straightened the linens around Elphame's sleeping form.

Cuchulainn noticed that Brenna's voice had softened again and she turned away from him as she spoke. Actually, she hardly sounded like the same woman who had not long ago been firing orders like a warrior. He watched Brenna as she tidied the little piles of herbs she had steeped into his sister's tea. The Healer's growing friendship with Elphame had already made Cu predisposed to think kindly of her, but the expertise she had shown in dealing with his sister's accident had solidified his respect for her. And, he admitted to himself, she fascinated him. One moment she made him feel as if he should protect her, as he would his sister, and the next she was shouting orders and showing a confidence that was reminiscent of his mother's no-nonsense attitude. She was a mixture of women, and like no one else he had ever known.

The light in the tent was muted—only a single candle flickered on the small bedside table. As usual, the bodice of her shift was modest and completely covered her breasts, ending just under the line of her throat. He was used to seeing women's breasts; traditionally, the women of Partholon felt free to display as much enticing cleavage as they desired. Even his sister, who habitually covered the bottom half of her body from prying eyes, wore filmy bits of silk that often left little of her upper body to the imagination. Just as her personality stood out as different, Brenna's conservative dress stood out as unusual, especially in such a young woman. Cu understood that she must be covering more scarring, but the thought came and went quickly through his mind. What lingered was his desire to see beneath the concealing cloth—and not because he was curious about her injury. He wanted to really see her, to know the woman beneath the scars. His eyes lingered on the ivory skin of her delicately rounded upper arms.

Brenna felt his gaze. She knew when a man was staring at her; she'd had a decade of experience with men and their poisonous looks. She felt her stomach tighten. During an emergency they tended to forget how she looked, but when the illness or accident or birth was over, the Healer once again became the Scarred Woman. It wasn't that their stares were that awful. It was that, for all of their looking, they never really saw her, especially not the handsome ones like Cuchulainn; they saw only the ruin that the fire had left. Yes, he was kind to her, but Brenna knew that it was his devotion to his sister that prompted his compassion. The naked truth would be easy to read when she glanced up from the pile of herbs and met his eyes. She had pulled her hair back out of the way before she changed the dressings on Elphame's wounds, and even though long habit caused her to automatically keep the scarred half of her face as hidden as possible, he was sitting very close to her. Her scars would be clearly visible to him. He would be staring at her with the look of mingled fascination and disgust that she knew all too well. Brenna sighed and lifted her chin to face him.

Cuchulainn felt his cheeks heat. She was looking directly at him, and he had been staring at her body like a gawking youth. He rubbed his hands over his face before lurching to his feet.

"Sleep, uh, yes. I should sleep," he said, feeling like an utter fool.

Brenna's candid gaze never wavered, and he found he was unable to look away from her gentle brown eyes.

"I will stay with her. If she awakens I will give her more of the tea. Sleep is what she needs most right now," Brenna said.

"But aren't…what… aren't you tired, too?" He tripped over

the words and finally blurted the question. What had happened to his renowned charm and witty, impressive banter? Even to his own ears Cuchulainn sounded nervous and inexperienced. If he kept going like this he would revert to voice-cracking and sweating palms.

"It is my gift. I care for those who are injured."

"Oh, right. Yes."

Brenna cocked her head sideways and gave him a peculiar look. What was wrong with the warrior?

"You can trust me to care for your sister, Cuchulainn," she said.

Cu's look of surprise was obviously not feigned. "I have no doubt of that." He cleared his throat. "I'll go now. I won't be gone for long, though." He turned and fumbled with the tent flat, but before departing he looked over his shoulder and caught the Healer's quizzical gaze. "I do not believe I have thanked you for the care you have taken with my sister. Thank you, Brenna." He smiled nervously and ducked out of the tent.

Brenna shook her head. Elphame's accident had obviously affected the warrior greatly; he didn't seem himself. And what had been that odd expression on his face when he had been staring at her? And then he'd blushed. She felt her own cheeks warm in remembrance. No, she had to be mistaken. Why would Cuchulainn want to look at *her* body? Perhaps he'd caught a chill during the wet ride. That would explain the brightness of his eyes and his flushed face. Brenna made a mental note to check on the warrior's health as she curled comfortably within the chair that was still warm from his body.

She leaned forward and snagged the strap of her Healer's bag from the edge of the table. Rummaging through it she found the pad of raw paper and fished out a charcoal pencil. It would be a long day. Sketching would keep her awake and help the hours to pass. It would also calm her nerves, for she felt suddenly, inexplicably restless and out-of-sorts. Her pencil moved over the surface of the paper in smooth, sure strokes as her mind wandered. Without conscious thought her hands sketched the image that had settled into her subconscious and as the day lengthened the strong lines of Cuchulainn's handsome face took form beneath her restless fingers.

In Elphame's dream she was being cradled by a soft warmth that she had no trouble recognizing. Wings, her sleeping mind thought, Lochlan's wings. A delicious thrill hummed deep within her body and in her dream she could feel his gentle touch again, only this time he was not ministering to her wounds, he was caressing her body. Her desire built as she gave herself over to him…

…And her mother's voice shattered the erotic dream, dashing guilty cold water over her growing need.

But she has been injured! I must go to her.

You cannot. She must learn to grow without you.

Confused, Elphame tried to open her eyes, but her drugged body resisted. She was in the nebulous realm of dreams, surrounded by clouds that swirled around her like half-formed thoughts, and echoing from within the clouds she could definitely hear her mother's voice, as well as another woman's.

She is my daughter; of course I need to go to her.

But she is no longer a child, Beloved.

That doesn't make her any less my daughter.

Elphame thought her mother sounded uncharacteristically petulant. It almost seemed as if she was a child arguing with an adult.

She will always be your daughter, but she must grow into her own woman so that she can embrace her future, which is a thing she cannot do if you shield her from life's difficulties.

*But she—*her mother began but the other woman interrupted.

Do you trust her, Beloved?

Elphame felt as if she was holding her breath as she waited to hear her mother's answer.

Yes, I trust her.

Then you must free her to claim her own destiny, just as it is part of your destiny to trust her, Beloved, and to trust Me to watch over her for you.

Elphame felt a jolt of surprise as she realized who the other woman must be. Epona! Was she actually listening to a conversation between her mother and the Goddess, or was she simply dreaming? Fascinated, Elphame heard her mother draw a long, shaky breath.

Parenting was easier when she was a baby.

The Goddess's laughter caused silver glitter to sparkle throughout the snow-colored clouds.

May I at least send her a special shipment of wines and linens? The way she's living is simply barbaric.

Of course, Beloved...

As the voices faded and swirling clouds darkened, Elphame's sleeping lips tilted up in the hint of a smile. It was so like Mama to believe good wine and expensive linens would heal every wound.

In his sleep Lochlan felt her touch his dreams. Without waking, he responded, reaching for her. He could not see her, but he could feel her soft skin under his hands and in his dream he wrapped her within his wings.

Then she began to fade away from him.

He shifted restlessly, trying unsuccessfully to regain the dream, but the exhaustion of the past day took its toll on his concentration and her image slid from his grasp like sands through a loosely woven basket. Lochlan woke. He stared into the darkness of the cave. His desire for her was a tangible thing—a force that had been building for a quarter of a century. He breathed deeply. The scent of her blood lingered on his body. When his wings began to quiver with his arousal, he did not try to stop them—he did not fight the darkness and cause the answering pain to slide through his mind. Instead he loosened the rigid control under which he usually held the strongest of his emotions. His body hardened. He closed his eyes and stroked himself, picturing Elphame, not as she had been the night before, injured and frightened; instead he remembered how she had looked the morning she had claimed MacCallan Castle as her own. She had blazed with power.

The force of his climax shot through him, pulling Lochlan into a vortex of hot, pulsing passion. When he regained his senses and opened his eyes his first thought was that he smelled fresh blood, which he instantly recognized as his own. The fingers of one of his hands stung. He turned his head to see that he had raked his fingernails down the side of the cave with such force that they had left a long, bloody trail as well as evil-looking scratches within the rock. His spent body slumped in despair as he cradled his hand. How would he ever be able to love her? He hadn't even realized he had gouged the wall. What if she had been there? Would he have torn the soft skin of her body without being able to stop himself?

The words of the Prophecy mocked him. Elphame was the incarnation of a goddess; he could not deny that. And the Prophecy of his people, passed to them from his mother's lips, was that only the blood of a dying goddess could save them from the madness that was the legacy of their dark heritage.

It was preordained that he would kill her.

Lochlan clenched his jaw. No! There had to be another way. *Please, Epona, do not let me harm her. I would rather die first.*

Lochlan curled on his side, trying to bury his fear and loneliness in the remembrance of the kindness he had glimpsed within Elphame's eyes. She had not looked at him as if he was a creature of evil—she had seen the man, not the Fomorian.

He had been alone too long. He closed his eyes. Loneliness gnawed at him. How were his people? It was early spring. They should be planting the food that would help sustain them through the long winter. The hunters would begin the first of many treks to the sea so that fish could be caught and smoked. The snow would soon be melted enough so that wild mountain goats could be trapped to replenish their own domesticated herd. So much to do to survive in the harsh Wastelands... Were the children well? How quickly was the madness encroaching? He knew that Keir would have taken over his position as leader. Keir had coveted Lochlan's position and the power that went with it. He could only hope that Fallon's influence was helping him to lead wisely, and keeping a check on Keir's dark side, which always seemed too close to the surface.

Lochlan's eyes snapped open. What was he doing? Like water on flame he extinguished all thoughts of home. He knew how dangerous it was for his mind to dwell on his people. The psychic ribbon that tied his blood to theirs was naturally strong. Thinking of them would only reinforce it— and the last thing he needed was for them to discover the hidden pathway through the treacherous Trier Mountains into Partholon and track him here. To the people of MacCallan Castle a group of hybrid Fomorians would be viewed in only one way—as an invading army. And they would be an army, he admitted to himself, an army that had a single mind and purpose—to capture Elphame and to fulfill the Prophecy.

Think of her instead, he ordered himself. Think of her beauty and her strength. There must be a way to do both, to save his people and to have Elphame.

16

"IT'S BEEN FIVE days. I'm going to go mad if you don't let me out of here." Elphame snapped the words at her brother. Then she narrowed her eyes and cut him off before he could reply. "No! I don't want to hear about how badly I've been hurt. I know exactly how badly I hurt. My side is itching like I've been bitten by fire ants. My shoulder aches. And I am well into day five of a five-day headache. But I'm telling you that I have to get out of this tent, and I mean farther out of it than just sitting in front of the awning."

The tent flap opened and Brenna bustled in carrying a tray that held fresh bandages and a mug of steaming tea.

"Oh, no! I'm not taking any more of your sleeping poison. I'm tired of sleeping. I'm tired of lying in bed. I'm tired of this tent. And I'm especially tired of how I smell."

Brenna glanced at Cuchulainn who was looking harried. He

threw up his hands and turned away from his disheveled, frustrated sister.

"You're the Healer. You handle her," he said a little too quickly, starting to sidle toward the exit.

Both women frowned at him.

"And to think maidens swoon over your bravery," Elphame said in disgust.

"Said swooning maidens aren't my sister. You are a different thing altogether. Brenna, I admit she is a terrible patient, and I leave her in your capable hands with my most humble apologies." He managed a quick grin at his glaring sister, bowed to Brenna and, with a flourish, retreated from the tent.

Brenna had to make herself quit smiling at the empty doorway.

"Overprotective oaf!" Elphame said, grimacing as she brushed one long, greasy strand of hair from her face. "I'm disgusting. I smell bad." She rubbed absently at the bandage that covered the wound in her side. "But he's right. I am a terrible patient."

Brenna smiled. "You aren't a terrible patient. You're just bored and healing. If you weren't going a little mad I'd be worried about you."

"Somehow that is not much comfort." Elphame scratched her scalp.

"Would a bath help?"

"Oh, sweet Goddess, yes!" Elphame swung her legs over the edge of the bed and stood a little too quickly. She gritted her teeth as the world pitched around her.

"Easy. You must go slowly." Brenna's firm hand caught El under her elbow, steadying her with the knowing touch of an experienced Healer.

Elphame breathed deeply and slowly until the dizziness passed.

"Better?" Brenna asked.

"That was foolish of me." El gave her friend a sideways look. "Am I still allowed to bathe?"

"Later this evening."

"But—"

Brenna put a hand up to stop her. "It's a surprise. Do not argue with your Healer."

"That's good enough for me." El glanced at the tray Brenna had set on the table. "I'll even drink your awful potion if it'll hasten my way to cleanliness."

Brenna laughed. "Now you sound almost as dramatic as your brother. And, yes, I do want you to drink the tea, but you need not fret. There is nothing in it stronger than willow bark to help ease your headache."

Relieved, Elphame sat on the edge of the bed and sipped the surprisingly harmless-tasting tea.

"And when you've finished your tea, how would you feel about going on a short walk?" Brenna asked, although she knew very well what Elphame's answer would be.

"You mean outside?"

"Definitely outside."

Elphame gulped the tea. "You are wonderful."

"You mean I'm not a horrid, potion-brewing jailor?" Brenna said with feigned innocence.

Elphame cringed. "You heard that?"

"I know you meant it only in the kindest of ways, my Lady." Brenna's eyes sparkled as she curtsied to Elphame.

"I have been a terrible patient."

"Yes." Brenna laughed. "You have."

Elphame swallowed the remainder of the tea and stood, slowly and carefully. Brenna hung her Healer's bag over one shoulder, and linked her other arm firmly through her patient's.

"Going to keep me in check?"

With a mischievous glint in her eyes, Brenna nodded at her charge and then tugged gently at El's arm. Both women were smiling as they emerged from the tent. Brenna took only a couple of steps before she halted, letting Elphame's eyes adjust to the bright afternoon light. Then she began guiding her slowly to their left, the direction that led away from the castle and toward the edge of the forest that flanked the southern-most grounds of the castle.

Elphame cleared her throat. "You know how I hate to complain…"

Brenna's eyebrows shot up in silent sarcasm.

"…but I was rather hoping we would take our little walk into the castle. I haven't seen the inside of it for five days, and I am just mildly curious about the progress of the renovations."

"You'll see the inside of the castle. This evening."

"Not now?"

"Not now," Brenna replied cryptically.

"Hrumph," Elphame said, borrowing one of Cu's favorite expressions.

"I thought you were fond of the forest."

"I am!" Elphame assured her. The forest…her heartbeat quickened. *He* was in the forest.

"Good. I found a smooth set of boulders a little south of here, just edging the forest. From there you will have a lovely view of the sea and the castle. It seemed a good place for us to walk to. Once there, I can work on those sketches for the castle's tap-estries while you relax and work on your frustration level."

"It sounds nice," Elphame said and smiled absently at Brenna, but her thoughts were humming.

They would be near the forest. Lochlan waited somewhere within the forest. Or did he? For what seemed like the thou-sandth time she silently cursed her incomplete memory. He had been real; the physical proof was undeniable. Lochlan had killed the boar, carried her up the ravine, packed her wound and covered her with his warmth, but the entire experience

was shrouded in a fog of pain and confusion. When she tried
to remember specific things he had said to her, she could reconstruct only halting bits of their conversations.

He'd told her he knew her from his dreams.

He'd said he would be waiting for her.

He'd admitted his father had been a Fomorian.

A visual memory flashed suddenly through her mind and
she clearly saw Lochlan, wings spread, his handsome face
twisted in a feral snarl as he plunged his knife into the attacking boar. Despite the warmth of the afternoon, Elphame
shivered.

Brenna's probing eyes fastened on her.

"I feel fine," El assured her. "I—I was just thinking about
the accident."

The Healer's gaze softened in sympathy. "Brighid said she
had never seen such an enormous boar. The battle must have
been horrible. I hate to think of the pain you were in."

"I can honestly say I have never been so afraid." Was an
omission a lie?

"Thank Epona you survived."

Elphame made a vague noise of agreement, wishing Brenna
would change the subject.

"I haven't wanted to mention this in front of your brother,"
Brenna began slowly, "but I have noticed that your sleep has
been rather restless. I think you should know that it is normal
for your dreams to be troubled after a traumatic experience."

Elphame met Brenna's compassionate gaze, then she looked
hastily away. It wasn't nightmares that were causing her dreams
to be restless. She felt the flush of heat color her face.

"There is no reason to feel shame, Elphame," Brenna said,
squeezing her arm gently. "But if the dreams trouble you I
could give you a stronger sleeping potion, although that would
not be my preference."

"No!" Elphame said, feeling more and more guilty at the honest concern in her friend's voice. "The dreams aren't bad." Well, at least that much wasn't a lie. The dreams she had experienced for the past five nights had been delicious, not disturbing. "I think I'm restless because I'm not used to so much inactivity. I'll be fine when I can get back to a more normal schedule."

"That will be soon. Your wounds are healing with almost miraculous speed."

Elphame rolled her eyes. "Oh, please don't tell anyone."

"I never divulge a Healer's secrets."

"That's a relief. I don't want the people to go back to treating me like I'm a goddess on a pedestal."

"It is difficult to be set apart from others." Brenna soft voice was introspective.

This time Elphame had no trouble meeting her eyes. "Yes. It is difficult."

They walked on silently, both lost in their own thoughts. It was a spectacular afternoon. It had rained early that morning and the forest was even more brilliant than usual, as if it had been newly washed by the Goddess. They were traveling through the grassy grounds that adjoined the southern side of the castle, and Elphame was impressed by how much work the men had accomplished. The concealing shrubbery and trees had been cleared, leaving no greenery other than meticulously cropped grass within several hundred paces of the castle's outer walls. After what Cuchulainn must have decreed as a proper distance, a few well-trimmed groves of still-blooming dogwood trees had been spared. They lined the road that led into the forest with a halo of blushing pink blossoms. Elphame smiled when she noticed that Cu had also left a dozen or so tufts of thorny blackberry bushes, which looked maniacal in their haphazardly entwined vines when compared to the newly established order around them. The grounds appeared to have been lovingly cared for, which pleased Elphame. She'd have to remember to praise Cuchulainn and the men for a job well done.

Brenna angled their walk in a direction that led toward the cliff where the forest softly kissed the sheer, rocky edge.

"Here's our spot." She pointed to a cluster of smooth boulders that perched near the cliffside just within the shade of the tall pines. The rocks varied in size from imposing heaps of rock that towered over Elphame's head, to small lumps that were no more than waist high. "If you sit here—" Brenna gestured to a medium-sized rock that butted up against one of the massive boulders "—you can rest comfortably and have an excellent view of your castle."

El gingerly sat. Being careful of the still sensitive wound in her side she slid slowly back until she could lean again the boulder, which formed a surprisingly comfortable backrest. Brenna hiked up her skirts and with a nimbleness that reminded Elphame of a scampering mouse, she climbed up the side of one of the larger rocks. El saw that her friend's boulder had a convenient edge that lipped up in serrated ridges so that she could rest her sketchbook within its grooves almost as if it were an easel. After she positioned herself, Brenna searched through her bottomless bag until she found her charcoal pencils. Then she considered for a moment before returning her hand to dig farther. With a slight smile she produced a floppy wineskin, which she tossed down next to Elphame.

"I think you're well enough to enjoy a little fruit of the vine."

"It's a nice change from your never-ending teas," El mumbled after taking a deep drink of the rich red wine.

"The tea is good for you. Stop complaining and enjoy the view. I'll show you the sketch I've been working on as soon as I correct the tower detail."

"I will do exactly as you say." Elphame smiled happily. She

sincerely enjoyed Brenna bossing her around. It meant Brenna felt comfortable with her; it meant she treated her like a normal patient. She was also coming to understand that it meant that Brenna cared deeply about her. Elphame took another long drink of wine and breathed in the crisp spring air, pleased that just that morning her side had stopped aching each time she took a deep breath.

Saltwater and pine filled her senses, and she drank in the pungent scents as she gazed at her castle. It looked like a hive covered with busy worker bees. The pointed roof of one of the four lookout towers was complete, and two others were actually taking form, as was the massive roof that would eventually cover the center-most area of the castle. For the past several days she had, of course, been restlessly watching the construction from the chaise longue that Brenna had allowed her to recline upon just outside the front flap of her tent, but Elphame had had no way of comprehending the extent of the ongoing construction while she had been so near the castle walls. From her new vantage point she could see her home literally coming alive before her eyes. She felt suddenly overwhelmed with emotion at what her people had accomplished while she had been recovering.

"It really is beautiful, isn't it?" she said reverently.

"Yes," Brenna slurred, tongue tucked against the side of her mouth in concentration as her charcoal pencil flew across the page. When she stopped, she blew across the surface of the sketch and narrowed her eyes critically at it even as she reluctantly set her pencil aside. "That finishes it. I think I have that fourth tower in the right position now." She bent and gently tossed the open pad of thick, crude paper to Elphame.

MacCallan Castle seemed to leap from the linen-colored page. Brenna had drawn in the mighty outer walls, complete with the restored wrought-iron gate, although in reality it had yet to be installed. Flags that were currently being stitched flew proudly from each of the four watchtowers—Brenna had even thought to sketch in a plunging mare on each waving banner. There were no bare, fire-scorched timbers or crumbling stone breaches in the battlements. The castle looked young and vibrant and very much alive.

"Oh, Brenna! It's perfect. It's like you got inside my mind and saw what I saw."

Brenna blushed. "You're just good at describing what's in your mind."

"No, you're really a wonderful artist." Before Brenna could stop her, Elphame began to leaf through the sketch pad. There were preliminary drawings of parts of the castle and some close-up studies of hands and feet. And then there was Cuchulainn—page after page of Cuchulainn. Elphame felt a little start of surprise. Well, she thought, *that* was how it was. The drawings of her brother were tenderly rendered, and they captured several of his different moods. She lingered over one of him looking sad and tired in which he appeared to be a decade older than his true age.

"This was how he looked the day of my accident," Elphame said.

"He's—he is—I just wanted to—" Brenna paused, swallowed nervously and started again. "Your brother is an interesting study. He has all those proud, perfect lines in his face and so many differing emotions."

Elphame couldn't look away from the lifelike rendering of her brother that so clearly showed his love and concern for her.

"You capture him perfectly." Finally she glanced up at Brenna, who looked quickly away from her. "May I have this one?"

Brenna's eyes shot back to meet her friend's. She gazed intently at Elphame. She saw no pity in her open expression, nor did she see any reproach.

"Of course. You may have any of them you desire."

"Just this one. The rest are yours." She met Brenna's timid gaze and smiled warmly, thinking how very much their mother would approve of Brenna.

The sound of pounding hooves surprised both of them, and, as if thinking of him had conjured him into their presence, Cuchulainn thundered up. Brenna instantly read his expression.

"An accident?" she asked, already climbing down from her perch.

"Angus was cutting a new section of raw timbers and the saw slipped. I'm afraid it's a rather nasty wound." Cu leaned down to offer his hand to Brenna. Without any hesitation she placed her small hand in his and he lifted her behind him. He gave his sister a stern look. "Don't go anywhere. I'll be back to get you soon."

"No need for you to hurry. It feels good to be out of captivity." Elphame shooed him away with an impatient gesture.

Cuchulainn frowned at her before kicking his gelding so that they raced back to the castle. El watched Brenna's arms tighten around her brother's waist and Cu reach a possessive arm back to steady her and hold her more firmly against him.

Yes, that's how it was—Cuchulainn and Brenna—her instincts had been right. She wondered if either of them realized it yet. Probably not. For all his experience with women, Cuchulainn would be as unprepared as his sister for love.

"Unprepared," Elphame whispered. That certainly described her. But how could she have been prepared for Lochlan? Had he been a hallucination? No, he couldn't have been. There was tangible evidence that he had been there— the boar was dead—her wound was packed with moss. But did he really have the wings of a Fomorian? She shivered and her gaze turned from the castle to the forest. She hadn't been afraid of him, she did remember that much. Why hadn't she been?

Because his presence had Felt right. She already knew that answer—she'd thought about it over and over again during the past five days. But was she being a fool, depending on an ability that had recently fledged within her?

"Lochlan," she said, unable to keep from speaking his name aloud. An unexpected breeze caught his name, and Elphame felt the skin on her forearms prickle. For a moment Lochlan's name seemed to hover, frostlike and almost visible, before the playful wind whisked it up and sprinkled it into the waiting forest.

She shook her head, ashamed of her overactive imagination. A lover's name didn't become visible when spoken aloud. And Lochlan was not even her lover.

"That bump on my head is making me imagine things," she said, lifting the wineskin to her frowning lips.

"What is it you are imagining, my heart?"

Elphame sputtered in surprise, gagging on the half-swallowed wine. Eyes wide, she peered into the forest.

Like an enormous bird, the winged man dropped from the concealing boughs of a pine, mere feet from where Elphame sat. He remained within the shadows of the forest while his wings tucked themselves neatly along his back. His smile was tentative.

"I did not mean to startle you."

"By the Goddess, you *are* real!" Elphame blurted, and then instantly felt like a fool.

"Did you truly doubt it?"

Elphame nodded vigorously. "Constantly."

Lochlan laughed, a sound so honestly joyous that Elphame smiled and felt some of her nervousness slip away.

"I understand your confusion. My mind was clear and un-injured, yet in the five days since, the memory of our meeting seems to have become a thing that belongs to a different realm."

"Like a dream," Elphame said.

Lochlan shook his head. "No, my heart, our dreams are something unique, something unlike anything else."

Elphame felt herself blush but she had no desire to look away from his penetrating gaze. Lochlan stepped from the tree line. Even with his wings held tightly against his body he moved with a feral grace that mesmerized her; for a moment all she could see, feel or hear was Lochlan. And then her mind began working again and realization flooded her. What if someone saw him? She thrust up one hand, instantly causing him to halt his approach.

"I want you to explain all of this to me. I want to know who you are and what is happening between us." Elphame looked around nervously. "But you can't be seen. I haven't even told Cuchulainn about you."

Disappointment darkened Lochlan's expression, but he nodded tightly and retraced his steps so that he stood back within the opaque semidarkness at the edge of the forest.

Elphame felt a rush of shame, followed by a flood of irritation. Days of boredom and frustration had her nerves on edge and suddenly she wanted to lash out at him and shout that she had just met him, and that he was nothing to her except an intriguing stranger. But the false words wouldn't come. Elphame stared into his storm-colored eyes and knew with an almost terrifying certainty that she was seeing her future.

With a clear mind, she remembered that Cuchulainn's own words had foretold him. *I know you meet your destiny at Mac-Callan Castle. I know that destiny is tied up in your lifemate....*

Lochlan was that lifemate.

Then, unbidden, the rest of what Cuchulainn had said played through her mind...*but when I try to focus on details about the man I get only fog and confusion.*

At least now she knew why her brother's vision had been

incomplete, and she couldn't help but think that the Goddess had been wise in hiding Lochlan's visage from Cu. If he knew that her lifemate was the son of a Fomorian demon… Elphame didn't even want to finish the thought.

"This is going to be very difficult," she said uneasily.

Her words made Lochlan smile. "My mother would have said that then it must be something that is worth doing."

The warmth in his voice when he mentioned his mother touched her, evaporating her irritation.

"You loved her very much," she said.

"She gifted me with humanity, and then she taught me what that gift meant. She never saw the monster, she saw only her son."

"You aren't a monster," Elphame said emphatically.

Lochlan's smile was bittersweet. "No, I am not a monster, but I do have the blood of a race of demons within my body, and that is something that neither of us can ever forget."

"Should I be afraid of you?"

"I cannot answer that question for you." One of his hands lifted as if to touch her. "All I can tell you is that I would rather die than harm you."

The thickness of foreboding clogged her throat. Her mind and her heart felt like a kingdom in civil war. She should demand that he leave. She'd give him an honorable head start before she informed Cuchulainn that a creature of Fomorian descent had entered Partholon. She needed to stop thinking like a romantic fool. He was nothing more than a dangerous dream.

"I will leave if that is truly your wish," Lochlan said solemnly.

"Must you read my mind?" she snapped.

"I cannot, I can only read your face and your eyes. I have dreamed of you since you were born. It was enough time to learn the expressions of your face and to understand your moods."

Elphame's eyes found his, trying to ignore the sadness she saw there. She could do it—she could send him away. It was her destiny to be Clan Chieftain, The MacCallan, and she had been touched by the power of the Goddess. She was a being set apart.

As is Lochlan, her mind whispered.

She looked at him, making herself see the truth of the creature that stood before her. His body was very human. He was tall and muscular and well-formed. But men didn't have down-lined wings that tucked against their bodies, and they didn't have skin that seemed to glow faintly as if it had been lit from a pale light within. She couldn't remember ever seeing any man who had eyes that slanted such a stormy shade of gray. Her reflective gaze slid slowly down his body. His feet—they were bare and looked odd. With a little jolt she remembered that she had thought the same thing when he had been standing in the stream after his battle with the boar.

"Talons," Lochlan said, following the path of her eyes. He lifted one foot from the green of the forest floor and shrugged. "I have talons. You have hooves. If I had my choice I think I would rather have either than the feet of a normal man. I cannot imagine liking to wear shoes."

Unexpectedly, Elphame laughed. "This is the first time I've ever admitted it aloud, but I have often thought the same thing. You would not believe the small, tortured contraptions my mother lashes her feet into. When I was a young girl it made her sad that I couldn't wear frilly little stockings and silly, awkward shoes, so she used to buff and polish my hooves until they glistened. I tried to explain to her that it didn't matter, that I liked my hooves, but she never seemed to understand."

He smiled back at her. "My mother simply told me to keep my talons trimmed because she was tired of mending my bed linens."

He was easy to talk to. When she stopped dissecting his

humanity, and simply reacted to him as a woman to a man, she found that it was already easy to forget that he was so different. By the Goddess! *She was different.* Her heart said that he could not be a monster, but could she trust her heart?

Do you trust her, Beloved? Epona had asked.

Yes, I trust her. Her mother had answered with calm certainty.

Elphame had trusted herself when it came to restoring MacCallan Castle—and that had been the right choice. How was this any different? Lochlan was just another life-altering choice she had to face. Perhaps it was time that she grew up and began to truly trust herself.

Waiting within the shadows of the pines, Lochlan showed no outer sign of his own inner turmoil as he watched her struggle silently with her conflicting emotions. What could he say to her? He couldn't ask her to accept him. How could he? What if he could find no other way but through her blood to fulfill the Prophecy? He should leave her—now. He should turn and flee, and never see her again, even if in doing so he was damning his people to eternal madness.

He could feel the ever-present pull of the demon that surged deep within his veins. Steal her, the currents of his dark blood murmured erotically, take her and do with her as you will.

No! Lochlan welcomed the pain that was always the response when he suppressed the demon in his blood, the pain that was causing his people to lose their humanity and slowly embrace the madness and the never-ending blood lust that was at the core of the Fomorian race. Pain was the price they paid for striving to be more than their demonic fathers. They had been born different, unique. In their mother's womb each of them had somehow been altered. Instead of being fashioned after the race of Fomorians, they had evolved into something that was almost human. But the call of their dark heritage was an ever-present lure they struggled against. A lure filled with dreams of death soaked in the maddening scent of blood.

How could killing Elphame save his people from the violence that was destroying them? How could the Goddess ask that of him? It made no sense. There had to be another way for the Prophecy to be fulfilled.

She was so near. No longer an insubstantial woman from his dreams; she lived and breathed and was standing mere feet from him. He couldn't leave her, not yet. He'd spent a century fighting darkness; he would not retreat now.

Slowly, Elphame raised her eyes to meet his, and Lochlan read the confusion and the questions there, which mirrored the turmoil within his own soul.

"I do not have all the answers you need. There is much happening here that I, too, do not understand, but I swear to you that my heart, perhaps even my very soul, is linked with yours. If you are not by my side, I will ache for you until I cease to breathe," Lochlan said.

He ached for her. Elphame was just coming to know that wonderful, terrible feeling. Suddenly she wanted to touch him; she wanted the reassurance of feeling his heartbeat and his warm, living flesh under her hands. He had been dreaming of her for all of her life. She had only dreamed of him for a fraction of that time, but already she knew that she wanted more than ethereal dreams and half-realized hopes.

Without allowing herself second thoughts, she slid from her rocky seat. She studied the castle. The distant workers were busy, no one was even glancing in her direction—and there was definitely no sign of Cuchulainn charging up on his gelding. And anyway, she told herself, if anyone was watching her, the fact that she stepped into the forest for a moment of privacy would not seem unusual at all.

She turned to Lochlan. He was watching her with an expression that made her suddenly want to weep. He radiated a feral, masculine power, yet at that moment he looked heart-wrenchingly vulnerable.

"Elphame—" his voice sounded choked "—I should not stay."

Elphame felt his words quiver low in her stomach. Her pulse pounded in her ears and her body moved toward him as if he were drawing her on an invisible string. She stopped a little less than an arm's length in front of him.

Elphame shifted her legs nervously and her hooves made a liquid sound against the long grass.

"I know you shouldn't stay, but I don't want you to leave," she said in a rush. Then she tried to smile, motioning to her head. "But maybe the bump on my head is tainting my judgment."

Lochlan's lips twitched. "Then it seems your wound has spread to me." He raised his chin and peered at the side of her head. "And it appears that you are much improved. You heal quickly." He glanced at her shoulder, glad that they had something less emotionally charged to talk about. "And I see the Healer has given you leave to stop using your sling."

"Brenna," she said. His nearness was intoxicating and she tried to dilute the effect he was having on her with simple, normal conversation. "The Healer's name is Brenna. She is very gifted, and she is also my friend."

He nodded his head thoughtfully then pointed at her side. "I would like to see how she has dressed that wound."

Elphame held her hand protectively over the bandage that rested snuggled beneath her linen shift.

"I think you'll just have to take my word that it's healing well, too."

Lochlan's lips twisted in a lopsided smile that made him look like a mischievous boy. "I have already seen your naked side."

Oh, Goddess… Her stomach rolled and she wished desperately that she had her brother's gift for light, flirtatious repartee.

And Lochlan was no simple-minded maiden.

"Well, that was under duress. There's no boar getting ready to attack me now," she said, feeling ridiculous. She wanted him to touch her, but thought that if he actually did she might bolt back to the castle. "And anyway," she continued. Her thoughts were like fireflies, flitting around in her head and she was unable to stop herself from babbling. "I'm not a very pretty sight right now, naked or otherwise. I haven't really bathed since the accident." She told her mouth to be quiet and nervously ran a hand through her long hair. It felt hopelessly dirty and lifeless. She even took a small, half step back, afraid she might actually smell as bad as she thought she did.

But Lochlan would not let her retreat. Without coming toward her, he reached out and snagged her wrist as her hand lifted to pat at her hair again. His hand felt warm and strong. He pulled gently, and she moved one step closer to him.

"How can I make you understand what I see when I look at you?" Lochlan asked. "My mother raised me with her beliefs. She taught me the ways of her people, the people of Partholon. And she passed on to me the love of her Goddess, Epona. I cannot count the times I heard her beseech Epona's protection and aid—and ask special blessings for me and the others like me. She had a bond with her Goddess which stayed strong throughout her life." He paused, his throat suddenly tight with the remembrance. "My mother was a woman of great faith. She died believing that her prayers would be answered." Lochlan pulled insistently on Elphame's hand, drawing her nearer. This time she followed the beating of her heart and came to him. "So you see, to me you have stepped from my mother's prayers into my heart. When I look at you I see the love of my past coupled with the fulfillment of my deepest desires."

Gently, as if he feared that she would shy away from him, he touched the side of her face with just the tips of his fingers. Slowly, he traced the smooth line of her jaw and let his hand slide down, caressing her neck and finally letting his palm come to rest lightly on her injured shoulder.

"Does it still cause you pain?"

"It?" She was so close to him that she could feel his body heat.

"Your shoulder." His touch had shaken her, Lochlan could see that—her lips had parted and her eyes looked dewy and dazed. The thought that his touch could so obviously affect her made him smile, exposing very white, very pointed incisors.

Elphame looked away quickly, but Lochlan put one finger under her chin and turned her head back so that she had to meet his eyes.

"They are just teeth."

"Stop reading my mind!" She covered her unease with irritation.

"I already told you that I cannot."

"Then stop reading my face."

"I cannot help it. It is a lovely, expressive face."

When he smiled again she did not look away.

His teeth were definitely different—sharp and dangerous. Fragments of information from the history books in her mother's library rattled through her brain. Fomorians were demons...were filled with uncontrollable bloodlust...especially during mating...fed on a living creature's blood to live...preyed on humans....

"Can you—" she began abruptly and then paused, regrouped her thoughts and rephrased the question. "Do you feed on the blood of others?"

Lochlan blinked once, clearly surprised.

"No, I do not feed on the blood of others. I prefer my meals cooked." The corners of Lochlan's eyes crinkled, but he didn't smile. "And dead."

"Then why?" She looked purposefully from his eyes to his mouth, and then back to his eyes.

"Why do my teeth look like this?" he finished for her.

She nodded, watching him carefully.

"It is part of my heritage, Elphame. I am human enough that I do not need to feed from the blood of the living to survive, but I am Fomorian enough that I still carry within me the vestiges of that bloodlust."

She drew a deep, shaky breath. "I have read that Fomorians drink each other's blood."

He sighed. "Your books are correct. A Fomorian lusts to taste his mate's blood, as she, in turn, desires his. The blood exchange is a part of the bond they form together." His smile was sad. "Does that seem a terrible thing to you?"

She looked at his mouth—his lips—the strong line of his jaw. "I don't know," she whispered. Then her gaze traveled up to look into his smoky eyes. What would it be like to kiss him?

Ask him. The thought swept through her mind like dancing autumn leaves. *Ask him,* it echoed through her blood.

And to her surprise she heard her own voice ask, "If you kissed me, would your teeth cut my lips?"

"No. I would not cut you," he said softly.

He mesmerized her. She heard the pounding of her blood in her ears.

"You said that you still carry the bloodlust within you. Do you want to taste my blood?"

Through their joined hands she could feel the tremor that passed through his body as an instant response to her question, but his eyes remained steady, holding hers.

"There are many things I want from you, Elphame, and

much that I desire. But I will not take anything from you that you do not wish to give."

"I—I don't know what I wish. I've never even been kissed before," she blurted.

"I know you have not." Lochlan's eyes darkened from slate to thunder.

"I think I have been waiting for you."

She spoke so softly that he felt the words more than he heard them.

"As I have been waiting for you," he whispered back.

Go gently…don't rush her…the rational part of his mind ordered. She is young…inexperienced…easily frightened.

But he had to taste her.

Slowly, giving her time to pull away from him, he bent and brought his lips to meet hers.

It was so different from what she had imagined. She had thought that kissing would be awkward, especially at first. She had been so naive. Lochlan's lips were warm and firm against her softness, but they were also inviting. Her mouth fit against his perfectly, and when their tongues met her mind stopped thinking and she let her body take over. Elphame closed her eyes and drank him in. He was the forest—wild and beautiful and untamed. And he beckoned to her. He deepened the kiss. He buried one hand in her hair, and with the other he pulled her against his body. Elphame came willingly, pressing herself along the length of him. Automatically, her arms reached up to wrap around his neck.

Even lost in the kiss she was aware of something brushing against the outside of her forearms, and the foreignness of the sensation brought her eyes open as she broke her mouth from his.

His wings. They were what she had felt against her arms as they had begun to unfurl and spread over him. Her eyes darted from the erect wings to his face. His breathing had deepened with hers and his gray eyes were dark with desire.

"They mirror my passion." His voice was thick. "I cannot stop them. Not when you are so close, and I desire you so much."

"You make it sound like they are not a part of you."

"They are from a darker part of me, a part I struggle against."

Her eyes slid back to his wings. They were spread over her, as if he was poised to carry her away. She thought that the downy underside was the exact color of a harvest moon.

"They're beautiful," she whispered.

Lochlan jerked his head back as if she had slapped him. "Do not say such a thing in jest."

"Why would I be jesting?" Hating the hurt she saw in his eyes, she unlaced a hand from around his neck. "May I touch them?"

He could not speak; he could only nod his head slowly, as if he were moving through deep water.

Without hesitation, Elphame's hand lifted to touch the part of one wing that was spread over his left shoulder.

"Oh," she breathed the word. "They *are* soft. I thought they would be." She opened her hand so that she could brush her palm gently across the creamy fluff. The wings shivered under her touch, and then they seemed to fill and expand as Lochlan's breath exploded from his lungs in a wrenching moan.

Instantly, Elphame pulled her hand away.

"Did I hurt you?"

His eyes were pressed tightly closed and a thin sheen of sweat had broken out across his face.

"No!" He half laughed, half sobbed the word. "Don't stop. Don't stop touching me."

The raw desire in his voice intrigued her almost as much as his exotic body. She didn't want to stop touching him—ever.

Elphame lifted her hand back to the seductive softness of his wing, but before she could stroke him again he stopped her by capturing her hand in his.

Surprised, she looked up to see him staring over her shoulder, eyes narrowed.

"Someone approaches," he said. He cocked his head to the side and added quickly, "It is the centaur Huntress."

"You have to go! She can't see you." Fear for him jolted through her.

"I must be with you again. Soon." His voice was a sharp blade of frustration.

"I'll find a way. Just go now, please. The Huntress would think you're attacking me." Her eyes beseeched him to understand.

"Call for me, my heart. I will never be far from you."

Lochlan bent and kissed her once more, pressing his lips to hers with a desperation that threatened to leak over into violence. But Elphame did not flinch or pull away from him. She answered his passion with her own inhuman strength.

He forced himself to break away from her and with a low cry of despair he turned and let the forest swallow him. He did not look back at her—he could not.

17

ELPHAME WIPED A trembling hand across her lips as she hurried from the edge of the forest back to the cluster of boulders. She just had time to heave herself up on the rock and take two long, deep breaths before Brighid trotted around the curving tree line, calling a greeting to her. Elphame waved a hand in response and forced herself to smile. No one would know just by looking at her that she had just been kissed, she reminded herself—not even a Huntress. A Huntress couldn't read faces, she could only read tracks…

…Elphame's mind jerked like a frightened colt. Oh, Goddess! Brighid could read Lochlan's tracks. The Huntress's bright look of welcome changed to a worried frown when she noticed how pale Elphame's face had become.

"Cuchulainn said I should fetch you back to the castle, that you had been gone long enough to tax your strength. By the look of you, he was right."

"I hate it when he's right," Elphame tried for nonchalance, all the while being careful to stop her eyes from obsessively scanning the forest for the smallest telltale sign of Lochlan.

"We all hate it when he's right. Come on, I'll give you a hand down." Brighid steadied her as El slid from the boulder. Then she cocked an eyebrow at the disheveled, breathless young woman. "Do you need to ride back to the castle?"

"No, I'm fine."

"Are you certain? You know I truly do not mind," Brighid said.

"Yes, I know." She smiled at the serious-looking Huntress. "Thank you, Brighid, I appreciate the offer, but I think I'm just stiff from sitting so long."

Elphame was touched by Brighid's offer of aid, just as she would not forget the night Brighid had carried her—and Cuchulainn—from the forest to the castle. During the past five days Brighid had visited her as often as possible, even though her hunting schedule was taxing. Brenna and Brighid had done everything they could to make her forced captivity bearable. And Elphame felt like a traitor as she prayed to Epona that Brighid wouldn't notice Lochlan's unusual tracks.

Relax and talk to her, Elphame ordered herself. Stop acting so guilty.

"I'm glad you came to get me. I've missed your company the past day or so," Elphame said.

"Yesterday five more men, all with young wives, joined us."

"I hadn't heard." Elphame's eyes narrowed. "Cuchulainn…" She drew out her brother's name like a curse. "That overprotective oaf! He didn't tell me more people had joined us. He's treating me like I am a damned invalid."

"Your brother is most definitely annoying," Brighid said, but she couldn't help grinning at his sister. At least he was never boring or, for all his irritating faults, awkward to be around.

Except for Elphame, Brenna and a handful of others, too often she found humans difficult to interact easily with. They were, of course, not as powerful as centaurs physically, but it seemed to her that their limited physical abilities too often defined their personalities, too. She'd spent little time with humans until lately, but even in that short time she'd noticed that humans tended to act unnatural around those of her race. The humans either went too far—to the point of embarrassment—in exuberant displays of acceptance and brotherhood. Or they seemed to need to puff up, to preen, and to try to act superior. Mentally, Brighid shook her head. She didn't agree with the Dhianna herd's views on the separation of species, but they were right about one thing—most humans were difficult to understand.

She glanced at Elphame, who was neither human nor centaur, and smiled at her sullen expression. Although she disliked being set apart, Elphame never tried to pretend to be anything except what she was—a natural leader who had been touched by Epona. Brighid respected that about her, even before she had begun liking her.

"If you're feeling well enough to fight with Cuchulainn you must be healing. That will certainly make Brenna happy," Brighid said.

"But not Cu," Elphame said with a satisfied smirk.

They were walking slowly back to the castle, with the Huntress being sure to shorten her long strides to accommodate Elphame's injuries. When Brighid started angling more toward the forest than the sea, Elphame felt alarm bells go off in her head and she hastily pointed to the imposing cliffside.

"Let's walk along the edge. I like looking at the sea."

Brighid changed direction, but she shook her head as they made their way slowly along the treacherous edge. "I do not know why you like it. It makes me nervous."

Elphame gave her a surprised look. "I didn't think anything made you nervous."

The Huntress snorted. "Falling does—very nervous." She gave Elphame a gentle nudge with her elbow. "That should be something you understand."

Elphame shivered in not so mock horror. "You're right about that. It's not an experience I ever want to repeat."

Brighid was silent for several more strides. She needed to talk with Elphame about the accident, or more specifically, about the disconcerting evidence she had discovered. Elphame seemed more relaxed than she had been earlier. She was walking comfortably beside her, letting her hands trail over the longest of the grassy tufts that grew in bunches near the cliff. Now seemed as good a time as any. Brighid cleared her throat and shot her a sideways glance.

"I've wanted to ask you something about that night, but I thought I should wait until you were recovered—or at the very least thinking clearer."

"By the Goddess! I couldn't be more tired of having my thinking questioned. I promise you I'm thinking clearly. Would you like me to recite an epic poem or two as proof?"

Brighid put her hands up as if fending off an attack. "I'll take you at your word, Goddess."

Elphame scowled at her. "You've hauled me around on your back. You should know better than to call me Goddess."

"You're right. A proper goddess wouldn't be so heavy," Brighid said without thinking.

At the horrified expression on the Huntress's face, Elphame burst into laughter, holding her side and wincing at the unexpected pain.

"Oh, stop! Don't make me laugh." She leaned against Brighid, trying to catch her breath, but every time she looked at the Huntress she started laughing again.

"You can quit laughing now. It wasn't that funny." Brighid frowned at her. "Or are you hysterical?"

Elphame shook her head, gulping air. "No, it's just that what you said is so true. I'm not exactly petite."

Brighid snorted. "Someone called you petite?"

"No." El got herself under control and limped slowly on, holding her aching side. "Until I came to MacCallan Castle no one except my family called me anything normal at all. I've always been The One Touched By Epona, The Special One. It's a lovely change to be nagged and told that my butt is too big."

"I do not nag and I said nothing about your hindquarters." Brighid huffed.

"Not directly you didn't, but it's nice that you feel free to tease me a little. And you're not the nag, that's Brenna."

"She certainly is," Brighid said. "Do you know she has been insisting that I drink one of her herbal concoctions? She said it will help boost my strength so that the hunting will not overfatigue me."

"It tastes terrible?" Elphame asked sympathetically.

"Yes." Brighid grimaced.

"Does it work?"

"Of course."

The two shared a long-suffering look.

"Perhaps we should tell her Cuchulainn's looking overtired lately," Elphame said mischievously.

"Excellent idea." Brighid laughed. "And you're right, there's nothing wrong with your thinking."

"Well, do me a favor and pass the word. I'm tired of people treating me as if the fall permanently disabled my powers of reasoning."

"It would be my great pleasure."

"And now that we have established that I can give you a coherent answer, what was it you wanted to ask me?"

Brighid paused and collected her thoughts before speaking. When she did her voice had lost its teasing edge.

"That night, when you killed the boar, were there any other creatures in the ravine with you?"

"Other creatures? What do you mean?" Elphame had to fight to keep her expression open and neutral.

"I'm not sure," Brighid said slowly, as if trying to put a puzzle together aloud. "I found the boar with its throat slit, dead, in the middle of the stream. And I could easily see where you had fallen. But I saw other things, too. Tracks that I did not recognize very near your own."

"Other tracks? I don't understand," Elphame said, feeling her chest constrict. She did not like to lie. Until the accident she'd had no practice at it, and it pained her to mislead her friends.

"I don't understand, either. Granted, it was dark and the rain had already begun washing away the tracks, but I'm sure what I saw was unusual. They were the tracks of an animal I have never before encountered." Brighid looked at Elphame, concern clearly showing in her eyes. "And I have seen similar tracks since in the forest surrounding MacCallan Castle."

Elphame fought down the panic that threatened to choke her throat. In the most nonchalant voice she could muster, she said, "Could it be some kind of large bear? You know these woods have been underhunted for most of the past century. There's no telling what wild animals have been allowed to thrive unculled and roam free."

Brighid sighed. "It could be, but the tracks are not a bear's. It is a two-legged creature. I know it sounds far-fetched, but I wonder if dragons have returned to Partholon."

Elphame did not have to pretend her surprise. Dragons had been the stuff of bedtime tales and ballads for centuries. If they had ever existed, they hadn't been seen in hundreds of years.

"You do think I'm imagining things," Brighid said.

"No! I don't doubt your word. Maybe there are dragons in this forest." Elphame looked up at Brighid and gave her an impish grin. "Just don't tell Cuchulainn. He'll insist on a lance and a dragon-slaying party."

Brighid laughed.

"Brighid, it would put my mind at ease if you would promise me something."

The Huntress raised her eyebrows at her friend.

"Whatever this creature is, don't go after it. Just let it be— at least until we're more settled here and you can call in extra Huntresses to join you." Elphame felt that her dissembling words branded her as the blackest of traitors, to both Lochlan and her friend, but she didn't know what else to say—or what else to do.

Brighid shrugged her shoulders. "As you wish, Elphame. I'm busy enough providing the daily meat for this growing horde."

They walked on in silence, both thinking of the talon-edged tracks in the forest.

8

"EL! THIS WAY." Cuchulainn raised his hand, beckoning for his sister and the Huntress to join him near the entrance to the castle.

Chagrined to realize just how tired the relatively short walk had made her, Elphame forced a smile firmly on her face and straightened her shoulders. She stifled a grimace as her right shoulder reminded her that it was still far from healed. As she and Brighid approached her brother, Brenna emerged from the interior of the castle, wiping her hands on her blood-spattered apron. She caught sight of Elphame and Brighid and called an enthusiastic greeting, but she instantly changed from friend to concerned Healer when they were close enough for her to get a good look at her patient.

"How is the worker's hand? I hope the injury wasn't too severe," Elphame asked Brenna.

"He will recover, but I believe he will rethink the impulse to wink at an attractive maid while he's cutting logs." She narrowed her eyes at Elphame, taking in her pale, drawn face. "I can see the surprise we planned for you comes none too soon," she huffed. Ignoring her protests, she raised Elphame's bodice and checked the dressing on her wound.

"Is she well? Should we call a chaise for her?" Cuchulainn asked, peering over Brenna's shoulder.

"No, *she* doesn't need a chaise!" Elphame snapped, pulling down her shirt and sending Brenna and her brother twin looks of annoyance. "*She* needs a bath, something besides broth to eat and some privacy."

Brenna's lips tilted in her endearing lopsided grin. "Then your surprise will be most welcome."

"What surprise are you talking about?" Elphame said, trying not to grit her teeth. Honestly! The three of them were going to drive her mad. She just wanted a bath and dinner—and some time by herself to sort through her turbulent emotions.

"Come with us, sister-mine," Cu said mysteriously. He looped an arm through hers and led her into the castle.

"Elphame! Good to see you up and about again, my Lady!" El looked up at the voice coming from the newly rebuilt soldier's walk just inside the main castle walls. She waved at the man, and searched through her memory for his name.

"Thank you, Brendan," she called.

Then his voice was joined by many others, which she answered in kind, as she walked slowly through the gap in the inner wall and into the center of her castle, where she stopped in wonderment at the change five days had wrought.

The great heart of the castle looked newborn. The fountain was gurgling merrily. Someone had brought in huge ferns from the forest floor which had been potted in large clay containers and arranged in a curving pattern around the marble girl. Sconces newly attached to the walls and columns held torches that burned brightly, bringing light and warmth and a fire-colored pulse to the castle. The floor was spotless, smooth and soft, and now that it had been cleaned, the stone looked as if the weathering of more than a century had simply served to hone its beauty.

"Oh, Cu! The columns!"

She squeezed his arm affectionately before hurrying to the giant central column. It stood like a newly commissioned sentinel, watchful and proud. It had been lovingly restored. The dancing torchlight stroked the intricate carvings of interwoven knots and the lovely designs they formed of birds and flowers and rearing mares.

And the stone hummed, with a musical, resonant voice that seemed to echo through her soul. Without even touching it she could feel the pull of its call.

Automatically, Elphame drew closer to the pillar, eager for a more intimate communication with the stone. Then she felt the dozens of watching eyes and remembered that she was not alone. Elphame fisted her hands at her sides. What had she been thinking? She hadn't meant to put on a performance for the entire castle.

The centaur's hooves clopped solidly against the stone floor as Danann stepped from the group of workers that had congregated near the fountain.

"The stone calls you. It is a unique gift, one you should not hesitate to answer." The old centaur didn't raise his voice, but it carried throughout the increasingly crowded room.

Elphame looked nervously from Danann around the room.

"No," he said, joining her beside the column and lowering his voice for her ears alone. "Do not fragment your attention. You have only one course of action. When the stone speaks, you answer." He softened the admonishment of his words with a kind smile. "You are destined to be The MacCallan. Your castle has called you from a great distance and across a gulf of time. Now you must answer with your soul, as well as your body."

Elphame licked her lips and swallowed past the dryness in her throat. His words made sense to her. She was connected to this castle—to its walls and floors and columns, and to the spirits of its past. She wanted that connection, her very soul craved it.

She spared one more look at Danann. He nodded encouragement.

Elphame cleared her mind and pressed her palms against the central column. The ancient stone became fluid under her hands as the warmth began. The heat grew rapidly, spreading up her arms and enclosing her body—and the rush of feeling filled her mind with a single shout of joy.

Faith and Fidelity!

Her heart leaped in recognition of the motto of Clan Mac-Callan which the stones of the castle—her castle—had cried with a single, victorious voice. Elphame gasped at the sweet intensity of happiness. From a detached part of her mind she noticed that Cuchulainn had moved toward her, and that Danann had stayed him by laying his gnarled hand against the warrior's arm.

"Your sister is safe. She draws her strength from these stones."

Elphame heard the Stonemaster's voice as if it came from a great distance, but his words registered deep within her consciousness.

She could draw strength from the stones? What an incredible thought, but how could it be possible?

The instant she wondered the heat filling her changed, shifted and reacted to her unspoken request. The heat under her hands increased and Elphame felt them actually slide a little way into the temporarily malleable stone.

Energy surged into her body. Like a diver surfacing after an unbearably long underwater search, Elphame drank in strength from the stone. The ache in her shoulder and side was soothed, and the headache that had dogged her for five days evaporated.

Elphame closed her eyes, and took several deep, cleansing breaths, centering herself as Danann had taught her all those days ago. Then she concentrated on her connection with the living stone. *Thank you. I don't know why you are allowing me this magical gift, but thank you.*

The spirit of the castle's central column answered her—this time in more than fragments of feelings and tides of emotions.

We have long awaited the return of The MacCallan and the pulse of life within our walls. We rejoice that you have come to claim your birthright. Behold what is yours, Goddess!

With a force that almost frightened her, Elphame felt her senses stretch as her spirit joined with the spirits of the stone. There was a moment of confusion and swirling vertigo while she became accustomed to her new awareness. Then more power filled her and with a burst of energy she was suddenly as one with the castle. Its walls became her skin, her limbs were towers and partially rebuilt chambers, and her spine was the central column itself. She could feel every nook and alcove of the castle. They were tissue and blood, just as she could feel what a sublime pleasure it was that her "body" was alive and being cared for. *This is my home.* The loving caress of her thoughts flowed throughout the foundation of MacCallan Castle. Her clan's ancestral home lived once more.

Cuchulainn watched as the spirit realm enfolded his sister. Danann's firm hand remained a constant pressure on his arm, as if the old centaur knew how difficult it was for him to release his sister to a realm that he had so completely rejected. But even he had to admit that she was awe-inspiring. Just moments before she looked weary and strained. Now, he watched her change before his eyes. She glowed with the power of the ancient heart of the castle. Her cheeks flushed and her hair snapped around her with the indwelling of her castle's spirit.

For the first time in his life, Cuchulainn saw the Goddess within his sister come fully alive, and for a moment it was as if he was watching an awesome stranger take her place. He knew it was what she had always desired, this connection with the spirit realm, and he knew he should feel happy for her—she was finally experiencing her destiny, but it saddened him almost as much as it awed him.

He broke his eyes from Elphame to study the people and centaurs surrounding them. Many of them had joined hands. Two women had fallen to their knees. On all of their faces Cuchulainn saw reflected the awe and love he felt for his amazing Goddess-touched sister. They would follow her anywhere. *We,* he amended, *we* would follow her anywhere.

At that moment Elphame threw back her head and in a voice magnified by the power of the spirits of the castle shouted the words that filled her to overflowing.

"Faith and Fidelity!"

"Faith and Fidelity!" Automatically, Cuchulainn's voice joined his sister's in their Clan's ancient battle cry, and soon all the voices of MacCallan Castle blended together in a shout that echoed from the walls of living stone and out into the listening forest.

"Faith and Fidelity!"

19

ELPHAME LOOKED AROUND her while she rubbed her tingling hands together. Still exuberant from the communion with the spirits in the stone, she found it almost impossible to stand still. She was filled with strength and hope and joy, but her restless eyes searched the people that crowded around her. She braced herself for her people's reaction to what they had just witnessed. Yes, they had responded to her cry, and had been caught up in the magic of the moment. But at what cost? Would they see her as a Clan Chieftain and accept her as such, or would they begin to shy away from her? Or worse, would they try to worship her?

The little housekeeper, Meara, was the first to speak. Her plump face dimpled adorably when she bobbed a quick curtsey and smiled at Elphame.

"I supervised the cleaning of these columns," she began in a soft, hesitant voice, but as she continued to speak her nervousness calmed. "I restored the central column myself." Meara's gaze touched the magnificent column with a loving look of pride and accomplishment. "I cannot communicate with the spirits in the stone as you do, but on my oath I swear that I could feel them—their strength and most of all their welcome." Impulsively, she reached out and squeezed Elphame's hand. "You were right. This is our home. The very stones do welcome us."

Through a surge of emotion Elphame struggled to find her voice.

A young man stepped up beside Meara. He bowed to Elphame and she thought she recognized him as one of the men who had lifted her to Brighid's back the night of her accident. But before Elphame could greet him, he dropped dramatically to his knees. Locking his eyes with hers he spoke in a voice rich with the passion of youth.

"I have never had a home to call my own. I am the youngest of ten sons and all my life I have felt displaced, transient. I think many of us have felt that way." He paused and looked around at the mixed group of humans and centaurs. Several heads nodded and Elphame heard general sounds of agreement. "But no longer. I was not born of the Clan MacCallan, but as I have labored to rebuild its walls, I, too, have felt the pull of the stone. I fit here, as I never have before. This castle has set its foundation within me, and if The MacCallan will accept me, I will swear allegiance to you and will proudly bear the clan name until my death and beyond, if Epona so grants it."

"As will I!" cried a voice from Elphame's right and another man sank to his knees.

"And I!"

"I, too!"

Overwhelmed, Elphame watched as each person in the great central chamber of the castle, men, women and centaurs alike, including the proud Dhianna Huntress, dropped to their knees, until only Cuchulainn and Danann were left standing. Then Cu stepped to his sister's side.

"I am, of course, already of the Clan MacCallan, but on this day I join those here in swearing allegiance to you, my sister and my Chieftain." Cuchulainn knelt before her.

"Decades ago I swore allegiance to the Temple of Epona, and it is a bond I cannot break," Danann said slowly. "But I do hereby acknowledge that you are the rightful heir of the Clan MacCallan, and I stand as witness to the oaths sworn to you on this day." He bowed gallantly to Elphame.

"Thank you, Danann. Then bear witness that as The Mac-Callan I accept the oath of each human and centaur present today." Her words were clear and filled with the strength of the castle, even as tears of happiness threatened to spill from her shining eyes. "And I bind their allegiance the ancient way." Elphame raised her hands and invoked the timeless words of clan binding.

"Through the deep peace of the flowing air
    I bind you to me.
Through the deep peace of the crackling homefire
    I bind you to me.
Through the deep peace of the flowing wave
    I bind you to me.
Through the deep peace of the quiet earth
    I bind you to me.
Through the four elements you are bound to me, The MacCallan, and through the spirit of our Clan the bond is sealed. Thus has it been spoken; thus will it be done. Rise, Clan MacCallan!"

With a shout, the room erupted into cheers as the newly made clan surged to its feet. Elphame wiped tears of happiness from her face as she watched her clan congratulating one another. Wineskins suddenly appeared and they were enthusiastically passed around while toasts to The MacCallan's health were proclaimed.

"Well done, sister-mine," Cu said into her ear as he hugged her tightly.

"It's like I'm living in a dream, Cu." A dream…the word echoed through her mind, evoking images that made her wish suddenly and unexpectedly that Lochlan was there beside her. Would he have sworn allegiance to her? And if he had, would that make a difference to Cuchulainn? Would that make Lochlan one of them? Could Cu ever see that Lochlan was something more than an ancient enemy? Or would he only be viewed as a threat, something that could drive a wedge between her and her clan?

"They're mine," she said fiercely.

"That they are—that we are." The warrior smiled at his Chieftain.

They belonged to her, and through them she finally belonged, too.

One of the men produced a flute and began playing a light, lively melody, which was soon joined by another flute and the distinctively liquid sound of a lyre. Elphame grinned. She wanted to dance and sing and rejoice all night, but before she could grab Cu's hand and make him dance with her, Elphame felt a restraining hand on her arm. She looked up into the wise eyes of Danann.

"It is only temporary," he said quietly. "The strength you borrowed from the stone will soon fade."

Instantly attentive, Cuchulainn linked his arm with his sister's and searched through the crowd until he spotted Brenna's small dark head where she stood quietly beside the Huntress, her head tilted down so that her thick hair concealed the scarred half of her face. As if she felt his gaze, she looked up and read the familiar look of worry on Cuchulainn's handsome face. She nodded, spoke to Brighid, and the two of them began making their way through to Elphame.

Satisfied, Cu turned to his sister. "I recognize that look in your eyes, sister-mine, but unless you want to turn pale and faint in front of everyone, I think you should rethink the dance you're going to try to drag me into."

Elphame curled her lip at him and would have shot out a quick retort reminding Cu that she didn't faint, if her headache hadn't chosen that instant to pound back with a stomach-sickening vengeance.

"Your face just lost color," Brenna said as she bustled up to Elphame. "Is it your head?"

"If I say yes do I have to drink more of your tea?"

Brenna tried to hide her smile. "Of course."

"Then my head feels fine." Elphame grinned, and then winced as a spike of pain pounded through her temple in time with her heartbeat.

"You lie poorly."

"I would say it is the perfect time for her surprise," Danann said.

Cuchulainn, Brenna and Brighid beamed in agreement.

"Clan MacCallan!" Cuchulainn's voice broke through the celebratory noises and the room quieted. "Your Chieftain will retire to her chambers to rest and refresh herself before the evening feast."

Elphame's brow furrowed in confusion. Her chambers? Didn't he mean her tent?

The bright looks from the crowd and the cheery cries of "Rest easily, MacCallan!" said they were in on it, too—perhaps Cu had fashioned a makeshift area within the castle grounds for her. She admitted to herself that the idea appealed to her, no matter how crude the temporary shelter. So Elphame simply smiled and waved as Cu, followed by Brenna and Brighid, led her from the central hall through a passage that curved off to their right, well lit by brightly burning wall sconces. She glanced around curiously. She hadn't spent much time in this side of the castle. She knew it housed what used to be the personal quarters of the MacCallans, but she had been more concerned with the renovation of the kitchen and public meeting rooms—and, of course, she had also been so enthralled by the fountain and the heart of the castle, that she had given little thought to the private quarters.

"Where are you taking me?"

Cuchulainn just smiled enigmatically. Elphame sighed. She knew that look; she'd get nothing out of him.

"Stubborn," El said. "You've always been so stubborn."

Behind them Brighid snorted and muttered, "Like brother like sister."

Brenna giggled.

Elphame glanced over her shoulder at her two friends. "I'm the eldest. So if it's anything it's like *sister* like *brother.*"

The Huntress raised one perfectly arched brow. "I stand corrected."

It was Cuchulainn's turn to snort.

To the left a smaller corridor branched from the hallway, and Cuchulainn turned into it. Elphame blinked in surprise as it dead-ended in front of a thick, wooden door onto which was carved the plunging mare from the MacCallan crest. Twin sconces burned on either side of the door so that the newness of the polished pinewood glistened in the firelight with a rich luster. Elphame traced her fingers over the outline of the mare.

"This is beautiful. It couldn't possibly have survived the fire," she said.

"It didn't. Several of the men cut it from one of the trees

in your forest, and Danann carved it. He said it is only fitting that the MacCallan Crest adorn the door to the Chieftain's chamber," Cu explained.

"The Chieftain's chamber?" Elphame repeated. The words held unending magic.

"It is a gift from your clan." He opened the door.

The first thing she noticed about the room was that it was alive with light. Burning sconces illuminated the walls—tall, metal candelabra held lighted tapers, and on one wall a huge fireplace crackled cheerfully. High, narrow windows were spaced all along two of the four walls letting in the muted light of late afternoon. The huge room was furnished with only a plain wooden table and chairs, a small vanity over which hung an ornate mirror, and a golden chaise which sat adjacent to a large bed covered with thick linens and comforters that glistened with a brilliant golden shine as the flickering candlelight caught the meticulously embroidered shapes of interwoven knots.

Elphame walked to the bed and ran a hand across the closest down-filled comforter.

"Mama." She smiled at her brother. "Mama sent these."

"Yes, they arrived this morning, along with several barrels of her excellent wine and those two things." He pointed to the gilded chaise and the gaudy mirror.

Elphame felt laughter bubble from her chest. "Mama sent the essentials." And with a rush she remembered her dream and her mother's voice asking Epona, *May I at least send her a special shipment of wines and linens? The way she's living is simply barbaric.* It had been true! By some whim of the Goddess she had listened in to her mother's conversation. Her mother did trust her, and Epona was watching over her.

How could you ever doubt it, Beloved?

The voice that filled her head was almost as familiar as her mother's, even though she had only heard it once. Epona! She belonged to the Goddess—not in the way her mother did, but in a way that was uniquely her, just as her body was uniquely her. And finally she felt a letting loose within her, an acceptance of herself that had been a long time coming. With a shaking hand, she stroked the soft comforter again and gave silent thanks to her Goddess.

"I told you she would be speechless," Cu said, grinning like a naughty boy.

"Of course she's speechless," Brenna said, smiling through tears. "Let's show her the rest."

"There's more?" Elphame asked.

Three heads nodded. Elphame thought they looked like gleeful children. Brenna took her hand and led her to a small stone doorway that arched as the two outside walls met. It opened to a rounded tower within which steep stone stairs wrapped up and up, winding against the thick stone wall. Elphame tilted back her head. She could see that the stairs fed into a landing of some sort.

"Remember the tower I had to finish sketching today? The only one that the workers had completed?" Brenna asked.

Elphame nodded.

"This is it. Your tower is restored."

"We all wanted the Chieftain's Tower restored first," Cuchulainn said.

"Everyone agreed that it felt right," Brighid added.

"It's pretty bare right now, but some day you'll fill it with all of your books and such. You'll make it yours," her brother said.

"I—" El had to stop and clear her throat. "I can't wait to see it."

Brenna caught her wrist, changing from friend to Healer again. "I don't think that would be a good idea. I realize I just swore allegiance to you, but in matters of your health I still overrule you. And right now your body needs rest and food, not the exercise of climbing up all those stairs."

Before she could argue Cu said, "The tower has been there for more than one hundred years. It can wait one more night."

"And I thought you wanted a bath," Brenna said.

Elphame's eyes lit. "If you can drag a tub in here so that I can bathe, I promise I'll forget about the tower—at least until morning."

"Drag in a tub?" Brighid laughed and the other two joined her. "I think we can do better than that for The MacCallan." The Huntress nodded toward the wall in which the fireplace had been built. "This is my favorite part. Follow me, my Lady." She grinned, swishing her blond tail as she led Elphame to an unnoticed gap in the wall situated near the far side of the fireplace. It looked as if a part of the wall had been sliced open by a giant's hand.

Intrigued, Elphame watched as the Huntress disappeared into the dark void. Her voice drifted back, eerily muffled by the thick stone walls.

"Be careful. There's plenty of room, but it's a little damp and tends to be slick on the hooves."

Elphame stood within the sectioned off wall and blinked in surprise. It wasn't another room at all. Wide stairs opened at her feet. They were lighted by wall torches, and she watched Brighid's withers disappear as the stairwell dipped down and turned gently to the left.

"Go on, you're going to love this," Cuchulainn coaxed when she hesitated.

Elphame stepped carefully down the stairs, followed the curve to the left, and went down several more steps before it bottomed out by emptying into a small, cavern-like room. The Huntress stood next to a deep pool of water from which waves of steam hung suspended in the thick, warm air. Elphame could see that the pool was fed by a waterfall that ran lazily from the wall above it, and drained off at the other end through a groove carved in the stone floor. Open braziers held smooth, round stones which Elphame knew would replace the hot stones that must have already been placed in the pool to heat the normally cool water.

"The oils and soaps are from the women," Brighid said, pointing at an impressive collection of small bottles and jars that sat beside the pool. "We each brought our favorite." She bent and tapped a large glass jar with her finger. "My offering is soapstone."

Brenna gestured at a fat round bottle. "I chose an oil infused with chamomile of which I'm particularly fond. I always find it soothing. Be certain that you rub some of it into your side." The Healer looked carefully at Elphame. "And I do not want you soaking too long."

"I promise," Elphame said, raising her hands in surrender.

"I didn't bring oil or perfume," her brother said. "But I did manage to talk the innkeeper into donating those towels."

"It's perfect," Elphame breathed.

"No," Brighid said, backing toward the stairwell. "It will be perfect when we have left you alone so that you can bathe without an audience checking your every pulse and breath."

Brenna frowned, but didn't argue when Brighid took her shoulders and pushed her toward the exit. Then she shifted her gaze to Cuchulainn.

"Your sister can bathe herself."

"Hrumph," he said, and ducked from the room.

"Thank you, Brighid," Elphame said. "You are a good friend."

"Anything for The MacCallan." The Huntress sent her a jaunty wink. She started up the stairs, and then stopped and swiveled at the waist so that she could meet Elphame's eyes. "I almost forgot—we are planning a special dinner tonight to honor your recovery. It's a little something I hunted especially with you in mind. But take your time, Wynne promised to keep a plate warmed for you."

"You hunted it just for me? What is it?"

"Wild boar."

Ignoring the dull ache in her temple, Elphame threw back her head and laughed.

ELPHAME CLAMPED A hand on her side and breathed deeply, trying to catch her breath. Brenna had, of course, been right; the steep, winding stairs were probably too much for her to have attempted that night, but she hadn't been able to resist the lure of the famous Chieftain's Tower—her tower. The truth was that except for the shortness of breath and the dull aches of her body, she felt wonderful. Tired, yes, and perhaps overfed, but wonderful. The long soak—during which she had washed and rinsed her hair three times—had been exactly what she needed, as had been the excellent meal of roasted boar. The thought of it still made Elphame smile. They'd sat on the newly made tables, fashioned in length and depth to accommodate both centaurs and humans, and feasted. There was no glass in the windows that lined the Great Hall, and the walls were still blackened from the fire and as yet unadorned by tapestries which were still being woven, but the sense of comradeship was palpable. With Brighid and Brenna on one side of her, Cuchulainn and Danann on the other, and her clan clamoring noisily all around them, the aches in her body had been easy to forget…unlike Lochlan.

If she had stared into the distance occasionally and lost the thread of the conversation tangling around her, no one thought anything of it. The MacCallan was strong and healing, but she had been through a terrible injury. They could never have imaged where her thoughts had drifted.

She would have stayed there all night, surrounded by her clan and immersed in winged thoughts had Brenna not insisted that she retire and get a full night's rest—threatening to brew a new batch of medicinal tea if Elphame insisted on staying.

She'd retreated amidst warm good-night wishes, and though her chamber was private and wonderfully comfortable, and her body was definitely tired, her mind would not be still long enough for her to rest.

She had her home, and she had her clan, now all she lacked was her lifemate….

Her lifemate. But was he really? As she climbed the winding stairs to the Chieftain's Tower her mind was filled with doubts. In the forest when she had looked into his eyes it had been so clear. She had felt that her future was reflected there, but now—in the light of reality—she had only questions. She wanted to see him again. She needed to be with him, to talk to him and spend time getting to know him. He seemed to know her so well; he could read her moods as if they had spent a lifetime together. But he was a stranger to her—a mysterious, winged stranger. And how *could* she be with him? Her clan wouldn't understand—she didn't even understand. Could they ever accept him, any of them?

Before the staircase ended the fitful night breeze swirled down around her, dousing her with the scent of newly cut wood from the roof. It smelled of the forest—the forest in which her lover watched and waited. She breathed deeply, automatically savoring the scent that already reminded her of Lochlan.

She climbed up through the floor. The Chieftain's Tower was larger than it looked from below. The room was perfectly round; its windows were floor-to-ceiling slits evenly spaced around the circumference. The walls held torches, and a wide fireplace, none of which were lit. A half-moon cast a shy, pale light into the dark tower, and Elphame turned slowly in a circle, allowing her eyes time to accustom themselves to the night. One window slit was obviously larger than the others and she made her way slowly to it, savoring the happiness of belonging.

When she reached the opening she realized that it was not a window at all, but an exit that led to a small balcony. Smiling, she stepped out into the night sky. Elphame inhaled the view. The tower's balcony faced the front of the castle and looked eastward out on the forest. From her vantage point she gazed across an endless sea of pine. Boughs moved restlessly in the wind. Shadows stirred and flitted across her vision. Elphame strained her eyes. Was that the outline of a wing rustling in time with the darkened limbs?

Impossible.

She sighed and let her gaze slide down to the castle that nestled beneath her. Music and light filtered up through the breaks in the unfinished roof. She could see that some of the clan had begun to disperse. Sporadically, clumps of people and centaurs, usually in couples, exited the castle and headed to the group of tents that littered the grounds. Cuchulainn had said that within two more passings of the full moon there should be enough renovated quarters that the majority of the clan would be housed within the castle walls. The thought pleased her; she wanted her people within her walls. She rested her arm on the balustrade and felt a faint tingle of warmth against her skin as the spirit of the castle acknowledged her presence. MacCallan Castle mirrored her feelings—it longed to live again.

A movement at the bottom edge of her vision caught her attention, and Elphame saw a slight figure emerge from the castle. Though she couldn't see the woman's face, the torches that hung from either side of the toothless entrance illuminated her figure well enough for Elphame to recognize Brenna. The little Healer stood very still, as if she needed to catch her breath, and then she slumped against the thick wall. Her back bowed and she put her face in her hands. Even from a distance, Elphame could see that her shoulders were shaking with her sobs.

Worry lines creased Elphame's brow. What was wrong with Brenna?

The thought had hardly formulated in her mind when the side of her arm resting against the balustrade warmed, and suddenly Elphame felt her mind connect with the stone, much as it had connected earlier with the central column. *What was wrong with Brenna*…slid through the skeleton of the castle in a powerful rush. Elphame gasped. She could see a ghostly sliver of golden thread that stretched from her body, through the conducting rock, and directly to the place where the little Healer slumped against the castle's outer wall.

Despair…loneliness…yearning… Snippets of heart-wrenching emotions burst back along the thread and bombarded Elphame. Instinctively, she started to break contact with the stone—to end the connection with such painful emotions, but almost instantly she was sorry for her cowardice. These were Brenna's emotions. Someone had wounded her, and instead of running from the pain Elphame discovered within her friend, she should want to help her—as Brenna would do for her.

Elphame gritted her teeth and breathed deeply, centering herself. She watched Brenna's shoulders shake with sobs, and felt her friend's heartache. It made her angry. When Elphame had left the Great Hall, Brighid had been chattering gaily to a smiling Brenna. What had happened? Who had hurt Brenna so deeply and in such a short amount of time? By the Goddess! And where had her brother been while someone was causing Brenna pain?

Righteous anger boiled through Elphame's blood, burning down her body and pouring like molten lead into the stone, turning the slender golden thread scarlet.

Brenna's head snapped up. Her shoulders stopped shaking and Elphame watched as she swiped at her face with the back of her hand. Then the Healer's spine slowly straightened, and she stepped resolutely away from the wall. For a moment she turned back toward the interior of the castle and it looked as if she might be considering returning. But instead she backed away, finally fading into the shadows that ringed the tents.

Just as she disappeared from sight, a man rushed from the castle. Elphame didn't need the torchlight to recognize him; his form was as familiar to her as her own. Cuchulainn paused, peering into the thick shadows that surrounded the castle. Even from a distance, Elphame could hear the echo of her brother's curse as the shadows revealed only the empty night. Cuchulainn cursed again, and stalked off in the direction of the tents.

"We canna choose where we will love. 'Twould be easier if we could, but we canna."

The spectral voice came from beside her, rich and gruff with its rolling brogue. Elphame took two skittering steps back, clutching her side against the sharp pain that the sudden movement caused.

"Have a care for your wound, lassie. It isna fully healed yet."

"My wound!" Elphame felt her heart galloping in her chest. "You almost scared me breathless. It's lucky I didn't fall from the tower."

He chuckled. *"I dinna mean to startle ye, but yonder boyo caused me to forget myself."* The spirit jabbed his chin in the direction Cuchulainn had taken. *"Wi' that thick head of his the lad is in for a verra hard fall."*

He shrugged his broad shoulders in a gesture that reminded Elphame so much of her brother that it made her breath catch in her throat.

"But there's naught to do. Love makes fools of us all. Though I do worry after the wee Healer. If she canna trust, she canna love." Suddenly his sharp gaze shifted from the tents to Elphame. *"What do ye think, lass?"*

Elphame blinked, disconcerted by the question.

"Ye canna answer? Dinna tell me ye are as thickheaded as yer brother."

"Cuchulainn is not thickheaded," she said, instantly annoyed. "He's stubborn and loyal. And if I remember my history correctly those are two traits he shares with you."

The MacCallan laughed heartily. *"Aye, lass, you remember yer history well."*

Elphame felt herself relax as his laughter rolled into good-natured chuckles. He leaned against the balustrade.

"But ye dinna answer my question."

"I'm aware of that. Remember, you're talking to a Clan Chieftain, and we do not appreciate being asked patronizing questions." She folded her arms and met his eyes.

The old spirit shook his head appreciatively. *"Ye are right to remind me, lass. Yer good, strong backbone is one of the things I like best about ye. Allow me to rephrase the question. As Chieftain of this Clan, do ye approve of the match between yer brother and the wee Healer?"*

"Yes, I think that they make a good match."

The MacCallan nodded. *"I think so, too. But that wasna all that I wished to ask of ye."*

"What else do you want to know?"

"I want to know if ye believe that love can truly live without trust. And before ye get yer fur in a ruff, know that it isna a trite question, lass. It is a question all Chieftains must think on."

Elphame returned his steady gaze. How much could the spirit see? Was his realm limited to the castle, or did he watch the surrounding grounds, too? Could he know about Lochlan? She felt a tremor of worry. But what could she do if he did know? She was already hiding from her brother and her clan; she couldn't hide from the spirit realm, too.

"I have little experience with love, but I do know myself. I don't think I could love someone unless I trusted him."

"Ye sound wise, lass. And ye remind me of yer great grandmother. Hold to that wisdom. Place yer love as carefully as yer trust and ye will make a strong Chieftain, as well as a loyal mate."

"But how do you know for sure?" The question slipped out before she could stop it. "How do you know if you're wise to trust when love—and lust—" she could feel her cheeks warm and she rushed on "—get mixed into it? I mean I'm a good judge of character, but my heart's never been involved in the judgment. Doesn't your heart skew everything?"

"Aye, that it does lassie." He laced his fingers together and cocked his head, contemplating her. *"How did ye know that ye must come here to restore MacCallan Castle?"*

"It felt like the right thing to do." She hesitated, looking below them at the sleepy castle. "No, it was more than that. The idea wouldn't leave me alone. For as long as I can remember, stories of MacCallan Castle have intrigued me. It was like it called to me until I couldn't find peace anywhere else."

The MacCallan nodded his head. *"Love is much like that. When you canna find peace anywhere but by his side, you will know."*

"So you're saying to trust my heart?"

"Not yer heart, lass!" He gravely voice ground the words out. *"Do not be foolish. Yer heart dinna lead you to be The MacCallan. That was in yer blood—yer soul. Listen there, not wi' somethin' as fickle as yer heart."*

Elphame sighed. One might think that talking with the ghost of an ancestor would be an illuminating experience. One would be wrong. She should listen to her blood and her soul? She had no idea what that meant.

"It pleases me that ye wear my gift." With one transparent finger he pointed to the brooch that held in place the fold of pale saffron-colored material that wrapped across her chest.

She touched the brooch lightly. "It is very important to me that you gave it to me." The memory of watching his death crossed her face. "But I would rather not have watched your death. It—it was…" She cleared her throat. She had only spoken to him once before, but already she felt connected to the old spirit. *Through their shared blood…* The thought came to her suddenly and she realized it was true. She felt linked to him through her blood, much like she felt linked to the foundation of the castle. "It was terrible. I know you're dead." She smiled sheepishly at his snort. "But having to watch you die was a very hard thing."

The MacCallan met her eyes. *"If it isna hard it isna worth doing."*

Elphame felt a jolt at his words. How could words spoken by the spirit of her ancestor so closely resemble those spoken by a creature who was part Fomorian? Creature…her heart rebelled even as her mind labeled him thus.

"Ye look tired, lass. I will leave ye to yer rest. And do not think I'll

be spying and peering in at ye. The castle and the clan belong to you now."

"But you won't go for good, will you?" she said as his form began to waver and fade.

"Nay, lassie. I'll be here when I'm needed…"

Slowly and carefully Elphame made her way back down the winding staircase. The MacCallan had been right; she was exhausted. Thankfully, the effort it had taken to climb to and from the Chieftain's Tower worked on her like one of Brenna's infamous brews. When she dropped into her newly made bed, sleep was easily granted to her and she slid gently into unconsciousness.

She dreamed that she was walking through MacCallan Castle. It was fully restored and glorious. Colorful tapestries covered the walls. Beveled glass reflected back the light of hundreds of chandeliers suspended from the perfectly intact roof. She entered the heart of the castle, the Main Courtyard where the massive columns stood as silent protectors. Smiling, she approached the tinkling fountain, but the unexpected sight before her made her come to a stumbling halt. The statue was no longer the child version of her ancestor, Rhiannon. It had been replaced by a life-sized replica of Elphame. Her image was standing in the middle of the basin. Scarlet-tinged water poured from the open mouths of wounds that covered her body. Iridescent winged figures crowded around the basin, silently dipping their hands in the bloody water and then drinking of it, but in her dream Elphame hardly noticed the winged creatures or the blood pouring from her marble body. Her attention was locked on the statue's face—her face. In the midst of chaos and blood the statue's face was radiant and serene. Elphame felt the pull of that face and she began walking forward again until a single word shattered the dream.

"No!" Lochlan's voice shrieked.

Her sleep interrupted, Elphame tossed fitfully until exhaustion reclaimed her and she slept dreamlessly on.

CUCHULAINN HAD NO idea how it had happened. Everything had been going so well. There were times when Brenna
seemed almost as relaxed around him as she was around his sister.
And he'd worked hard to make it so. He rubbed at the stiffness
in his neck and took another long drink from the half-empty
wineskin. Then he fiddled restlessly with the little pots of herbs
and tea leaves that sat on the desk. Brenna had left them there.
She must have forgotten them in the haste with which they'd
moved Elphame's things from this tent to her new chambers
within the castle walls. Cuchulainn had tried to get Brenna to
take the tent as her own, but she had insisted that he have it.

"She likes her own tent," he growled. "She likes it because it's on the fringe of the others—well away from
everyone else. Alone."

In his opinion she spent too much time on the fringes of
life. Unless someone was sick or injured, of course. Then she

strode into the middle of the fray, metamorphosing from shy, unsure maiden to someone who could command an army with a single look.

Or at least the heart of a warrior.

Cuchulainn breathed out his frustration in a noisy burst of air. It had never been this difficult before. If he'd wanted a woman, she'd come to him. He only had to smile, flirt, perhaps tease and cajole. They came willingly. But not Brenna. He'd known it would be different with her. First of all, she was so inexperienced. He didn't usually prefer virgins, unless it was during a festival of the Goddess when the spirit of Epona walked freely, inhabiting maidens, guiding their bodies and soothing their nerves. But again Brenna was different. Her innocence captivated him. He thought about her ceaselessly.

He took another long pull from the wineskin.

So he'd been careful with her, coaxing gently as if she were a timid bird he was trying to entice into his hand. Her response had been confusing and frustrating. The more attention he lavished on her, the farther from him she flew, but when he wasn't trying to charm her—like when they were working together to make ready Elphame's chamber, or when he had to fetch her because of an accident with a worker—she spoke easily with him. It was as if during those times she forgot who he was, which seemed the only way she could be relaxed around him.

The thought was not flattering.

He tried to understand her. He knew her reticence around others, especially men, was caused by her injury. As Elphame had said, her scars were extensive, and they had wounded her soul as well as her body. But he was finding it increasingly difficult to remember that.

"I've stopped seeing the damned scars." His words were slurring, but he didn't care. He was alone. Just like she was alone. "How can I tell her that if she won't let me close to her?" How could he tell her that her face was just a part of her to him? That the scars were like her eyes and hair and the rest of her body. They were *her*.

The irony of the situation was not lost on him. Words usually came so easily to him. He'd always thought that his ability to talk to women charmed them more than his body or his face. He knew that the easiest path to a woman's body was to seduce her mind first. Women wanted undivided attention; they wanted to be treated with respect, which translated into a man who could focus and really listen to their individual needs and desires. He had become a master at that game. Now he found himself obsessed with a woman who shied away from his words and was only easy in his presence when his focus was distracted from her and they were not talking.

"By the Goddess! I don't know what to do."

He wanted to get up and pace, but the floor of the tent had unexpectedly become a little unsteady, so he contented himself with drumming his fingers on the tabletop.

That night had been a perfect example of his ineptitude. He'd thought all was well. Brenna had surprised him by agreeing to sit at the head table with the rest of them, and he had thought that that was a definite move in the right direction. Hindsight told him that she had agreed to the public placement so that she could keep a close eye on her prominent patient, and that it had had nothing to do with him, but Elphame's swearing in of their new clan and the exuberance of the evening had filled him with a sense of blind optimism.

It had also, he admitted blearily to himself, filled him with too much wine.

After his sister had retired, as directed by her attentive Healer, the music had begun. One of the workers produced a drum, and when he joined the other musicians, the clan roared its approval. They pushed aside tables and began pairing off and moving in time to the beat of the music. Cuchulainn had felt flushed and ebullient—all he could think of was how much he would like to dance with Brenna. She'd been laughing easily at something the Huntress had just said when he'd approached her and with a gallant bow begged her indulgence in allowing him a dance.

He'd watched as all of the color drained from the unscarred side of her face, leaving the other side even more livid in contrast. In a gesture that Cuchulainn was learning to hate, she'd ducked her head forward and hid behind the wall of her dark hair.

"No, I cannot dance."

Her voice had drifted back to that tremulous whisper with which she used to address him. For some reason hearing it again had made him feel suddenly very angry.

"Cannot dance? The woman who can stitch up a wound, set a broken arm and birth a babe cannot dance?"

He hadn't intended his voice to sound sarcastic—truthfully he hadn't.

Brenna's dark eyes had lifted and through the veil of hair he thought he had caught a flash of anger within them. He remembered being glad, thinking that any emotion was better than her withdrawal.

"The skills you mention are ones I have had the opportunity to learn. I have not had the opportunity to learn to dance."

"Now you do."

He cringed, remembering the arrogant way he had held out his hand, certain that she would take it. So certain that he had not noticed that the people closest to them had gone silent to watch their exchange. Brenna's eyes had darted around like a small bird looking for an escape, and he ground his teeth at the memory. His arrogance had caused her to be the center of attention.

"No. I—no," she said.

"It's just a dance, Brenna. I'm not asking you to be my lifemate." He'd chuckled, hating himself even as he heard the flippant words escape from his own mouth.

"I did not...I would not ever think..."

"I know what the problem is," Brighid broke in, covering Brenna's soft, stumbling words. "Cuchulainn has never heard the word 'no' uttered from a woman's mouth. He obviously is unaware of its meaning."

Laughter traveled through the listening group. Cuchulainn just had time to catch a flash of color out of the side of his eye, and then Wynne stepped jauntily from the circle surrounding them. She walked with a rolling, teasing gate that was an open invitation, tossed her flaming hair, and placed her hand firmly within the one he still held out to Brenna.

"The Healer is right, Cuchulainn. Perhaps ye should choose a lass who has learned the skills ye require and willna tell ye no." She rolled her words seductively.

The crowd erupted into raucous shouts of encouragement as she pulled Cuchulainn onto the makeshift dance floor and she began to move around him in a slow, seductive circle. Cu easily caught the rhythm, mirroring her movements with the same sensuous, earthy grace he brought to the battlefield. Wynne teased and promised, all in time to the pulsing beat of the drum. She brushed her lush body against his and through the fog of wine he caught her scent. She smelled of fresh baked bread and spice and woman, but instead of enticing him as it should have, her scent only reminded him of what she was lacking. She did not smell of newly cut grass and spring rain. She was not Brenna.

Still dancing, he turned and looked back at the table. Brighid was still there, and for a moment their eyes met. Then hers slid away from his in disgust and she turned her back to him. The seat next to her was vacant.

That was when the sick feeling in his stomach had begun. He'd made hasty excuses to a disappointed Wynne, and left the dancers. He needed to find Brenna—that much he knew. He didn't know what he would say to her. She wasn't in the Great Hall, nor was she in the Main Courtyard. He interrupted a couple who were embracing in the shadow of the central column, and they told him rather gruffly that the Healer had hurried from the castle a little before him.

He'd tried to catch her before she made it to her lone tent, but he had been too late. He remembered standing outside her tent, watching her small shadow pass in front of the single candle she had lit. If she had been any other woman he would have entered the tent, begged her apology and called himself a fool, drunk on wine and desire. Then he would have made love to her.

But Brenna was not any other woman.

Instead he had retreated unsteadily to his own tent to drink himself quietly and thoroughly into oblivion.

"I was right about one thing. I am a drunken fool."

His last thought before blessed unconsciousness claimed him was that tomorrow he'd have to make it right with her, and that he had no idea how he was going to do that.

Before she slept Brenna always talked to Epona. She didn't call it praying; she didn't make requests of the Goddess, instead she just spoke to her as if she were an old friend. And, truthfully, Brenna had been speaking to her for so long that that was how she thought of the Goddess. Her conversations with Epona began after the accident. She had known that there was nothing that could be done about her wounds—actually the ten-year-old Brenna had believed with absolute, single-minded certainty that she was dying. Her pain had been so intense for so long that she had not thought to ask Epona to save her; she had not wanted salvation, she had simply wanted relief. Instead of sending up prayers begging Epona to heal her, Brenna had spent long hours talking to the Goddess who she believed she would soon meet in the spirit realm. Even after she surprised everyone, including herself, by failing to die, she could not give up her conversations with Epona. It became a lifetime habit that calmed her mind and soothed her body.

That night she needed to be calmed and soothed.

Her hand shook with the remnants of suppressed anger as she lit the small bundle of dried herb and breathed in the familiar smoky scent of lavender. She sat in front of her little makeshift altar and fingered each item, trying to clear her mind and ready herself to speak to Epona. But that evening she found no solace in the lovingly chosen items—the turquoise stone that was the color of sea foam, the small likeness of a mare's head that she'd meticulously carved from soft wood, the single, perfect drop-shaped pearl and the feather, which glistened the same unique blue-green as her stone…

…The same color as his eyes.

Brenna closed her own eyes in disgust. Stop thinking about it, she ordered herself. But her thoughts, which were usually well-disciplined and logical, failed to obey her.

Anger surged through her again and she relished the coldness of the emotion; it was so much easier to bear than despair and loneliness.

How could she have been so naive? She had thought that she had found peace within herself, that years before she had accepted her life. She was a Healer. She would never know the joy of having a husband and children of her own, but her life— the life that should have ended a decade before—had meaning. She had dedicated herself to fighting her two old acquaintances, pain and suffering.

What had happened to her recently? How had her placid core become a turbulent ocean?

Absently, Brenna touched her right cheek, feeling the slick, uneven surface of her scars. When was the last time she'd thought about love? It had been years ago, right after she'd begun her monthly flux. During that transition into womanhood she'd thought about what her life might have become if she'd been just one step farther from the hearth—or if her mother had known the bucket contained oil instead of water—or if her mother had waited to see if she would live—or if her father had been able to go on with his life....

It had been more than a decade, but tonight the memories felt suddenly fresh. It had been such a long time since she had allowed herself to dwell on "ors." She was usually more logical than that, and there was no logic in yearning for the impossible, or in wishing the done, undone.

Then why now? Why had desires, which had been cremated in another life, been reborn within turquoise eyes and a boyish smile?

Brenna reached to touch the stone, but her hands still shook, so she clasped them together in her lap. She looked away from the altar. That night she didn't see the Goddess reflected there, instead she saw shades and shadows of Cuchulainn.

She breathed in the lavender incense and forced her thoughts to focus on Epona. Thankfully, her mind cleared and the tension in her shoulders eased. She took another deep breath of incense. As was her wont, she didn't pray, she simply talked to the Goddess, although that evening her voice had an uncharacteristic hardness about it.

"It felt so right today to swear my oath to become a part of a clan which has always been close to you. The sense of belonging is…" She paused and squeezed her hands together so tightly that her knuckles whitened. "It is something I haven't known in so many years that I'd forgotten the joy of it. Thank you for that, for allowing me this new home."

Spoken aloud, her words became the lost pieces of a troubling puzzle. Her eyes widened in sudden understanding, and she felt some of the anger within her begin to thaw.

"Perhaps the lure of belonging caused my errant thoughts." Her smile was grim. "Like a child, I have allowed pretty fantasies to sway my common sense. Pretty fantasies that centered around a handsome face." Brenna sighed. She couldn't avoid the subject any longer, not when she was speaking to the Goddess who knew her so well. Deliberately, she unclasped her hands and stroked her finger down the side of the turquoise-colored feather.

"It wasn't just his face, Epona. It was the kindness I saw in his eyes. It made me forget that all he can feel for me is pity, and not true caring." She gave a slight shake of her head and her voice hardened again. "They think pity is caring. Not true. Pity is a foul sweetmeat—something meant to cover what is better kept hidden. But life eventually washes away layers, exposing even buried truth." She steeled herself before she continued speaking her most secret thoughts. "Truth was exposed tonight. He thought he would take pity on the scarred Healer and dance with her. As usual, handsome men—" Brenna blew out a breath through terse lips "—think of very little except their own desires. I knew better. I should never have believed…"

Her voice faded. How could she have believed that he was beginning to care for her? But she already knew the answer to her silent question. It had been in his eyes—in those amazing eyes, which were the same color as turquoise and exotic birds. He had looked at her with—

"No!" The word burst from her mouth. "I'm finished with vain longings that only open old wounds."

Brenna welcomed the return of the anger that had suddenly

broken though her grief that night. With a hard-edged sense of finality she rose to her knees so that her body was positioned over the burning lavender. Resolutely, she watted her hands through the sweet smoke, bathing her body in the scent of the herb. She repeated the ritualistic action three times. Then she picked up the carved mare's head, closed her hand around it, and pressed her fist against her breast.

"Great Goddess Epona, for the first time in all our many years together I wish to beseech you with my own orison. I ask that you help me to find my calm center again so that peace may return to my heart and soul. I seal this prayer by calling upon the four elements. Air, which holds the breath of life. Fire, which burns with the pureness of loyalty. Water, which washes and restores. And Earth, which comforts and nurtures."

Brenna's words caused no magical stirring in the air around her, but she thought she detected a new warmth in the smooth wooden figure she clenched, and with that warmth the remaining coldness of the anger that had blossomed within her melted and died. Brenna closed her eyes and sighed sadly. Anger was not the way—it was only a temporary balm that dealt only with the symptoms and not with the problem itself.

She would find peace within herself again. She would avoid Cuchulainn, which shouldn't be difficult. Brenna had stayed in the Great Hall long enough to see his body react to Wynne's seduction. The beautiful cook would be keeping him very busy.

As she fell asleep she ignored the pain thinking of Cuchulainn with another woman caused her.

22

IT WAS A TRUE pleasure to wake in her own chamber to the muffled sounds of workers already busy with the day's business of restoration. Elphame stretched slowly, testing the soreness in her side and shoulder. Pleased, she rubbed at the puckered scab that slashed across her waist. The sharp pain was gone, replaced by an itchy numbness. Would it be too decadent for her to begin her day with a long soak in her private bath? She grinned. Not if she made it a short soak. She nearly vaulted from her bed, and hurried to the entrance to the bathing chamber, slowing only when she began the sharp descent down the stairs. She didn't even want to imagine what Cuchulainn would say if she tripped and had another fall. For balance, she let her hand slide over the rough skin of the stone wall. The instantaneous connection with the spirit of the castle thrummed under her palm.

Home, it said to her. *The MacCallan is home.*

The castle filled her with a sense of belonging. Had she ever been happy before? She didn't think so—not really. Before she had come to MacCallan Castle her happiness had been an infant compared to the adult her joy had become. Now, if only she could complete her home.

Lochlan…his name whispered through her blood.

She had to find a way to meet with him secretly. Spending time with him was the only way she'd learn for sure if…. How had The MacCallan put it? Learn if it is only at his side that she could find peace. And then what? Her brow crinkled. She'd have to deal with that problem when she came to it. She needed to focus on small steps first, accomplish one thing before another.

Perhaps now that she was firmly installed in her own chamber it would be easier. She definitely had more privacy. Could she sneak out of the castle at night and find him?

Suddenly, stones under her hand warmed and the pinprick sensation in her fingers intensified. With a feeling of increasing wonder, Elphame stepped down into her bathing chamber. Purposefully, she turned to face the solid stone wall. She pressed both palms against the rough skin of the castle and tentatively repeated her last thought aloud.

"Is there some way I can sneak out of the castle and find him?"

As had happened the night before, Elphame watched in awe as a golden thread spooled within the stone beneath her hands. Like a flash of lightning it whipped, glowing through the wall, snaking around the room to come to rest in a thin disk of incandescent gold that shimmered in an area of the wall across the chamber from where she stood. Maintaining a connection with the stone through her fingertips, she walked the circumference of the room, following the pulsing thread.

The glowing disk was situated at the level of Elphame's eyes in the far corner of the bathing chamber. No torches illuminated that area and the sphere of brightness looked startlingly like an opened eye. Tracing the ends of the thread, she ran her fingers up and placed her palm against it. Her eyes narrowed as she studied the stone beneath her palm. Like the rest of the stones, it warmed under her touch, but other than its temperature, it felt decidedly different than the rest of the stone that fashioned the thick walls of the castle. Instead of being rough and many-textured, the palm-sized area was perfectly smooth. That close, she could see that it did not rest flush against the wall, but was raised slightly like a giant button made of stone. Testing, she slid her fingers around it. It hadn't been mounted on the wall. Instead it fitted into the wall itself. Not like a button, she decided, like a key.

And she blinked in surprise. A key?

Elphame pressed the disk. With the sound of an exhalation of breath, a door-sized portion of the wall swung away from her. Disbelieving, she peered into the dark recesses of a musty-smelling tunnel.

"Elphame!" Brenna's voice echoed down the staircase from the room above. "Are you down there?"

Frantically, Elphame tugged against the immovable slab of stone, trying to close it.

"Yes! I'll be right up!" she called over her shoulder.

Her hand found the smooth disk again, and this time when she pressed it she was relieved to see the hidden door slide silently back into place.

"Incredible..." she murmured before hurrying up the stairs to greet the Healer. Later, Elphame promised herself, later when she was alone and was sure of being uninterrupted she would explore her new discovery.

"Good morning!" Brenna said as Elphame emerged from the basement chamber.

Elphame noted that her bright tone contrasted distinctly with the dark circles shadowing her eyes.

"Good morning. You look tired. Didn't you sleep well last night?" Elphame asked.

The Healer began fussing with the tray she had just set on the table. "I'm fine," she said waving away her patient's question. "It's your sleep you should be concerned with anyway, especially after the busy day you had yesterday." Brenna motioned for Elphame to sit and she took her wrist, checking her pulse with one hand while she studied her eyes and carefully felt her head and shoulder with the other. "You look well this morning. Let me see that wound in your side."

Obediently, Elphame raised her nightdress. She watched her friend carefully as she nodded, obviously pleased by the wound's progress and gently rubbed a fragrant, soothing salve over the scab. Brenna looked tired—tired and sad. Elphame needed to find out what had happened to her.

"I hated to leave last night," she began, watching Brenna closely. "It was a wonderful celebration. Everyone seemed to be having a good time."

Brenna made an abstract sound of agreement. Elphame thought she detected a tightening around her friend's lips.

"Did anything special happen after I retired?" she prodded.

"No. Just music and dancing. I didn't stay long."

Elphame arched her brows in surprise. "Really? That surprises me. You seemed to be having a good time when I left."

"No. Yes. I mean I was having a good time. But it was late. I was tired. So I went to bed."

Elphame thought Brenna's nonchalance sounded forced. Her friend would not meet her eyes. Her face was unnaturally pale and her eyes looked haunted. For a moment the ridiculous thought crossed her mind that she wished Brenna was made of stone so that she could simply touch her and understand her thoughts. Elphame almost laughed aloud at the idea, but watching Brenna she suddenly realized that the little Healer did actually have a lot in common with the stone of the castle. Elphame considered what she had witnessed last night from the Chieftain's Tower. On the outside, Brenna looked placid, even stoic, but on the inside she must be filled with as many rich and varied emotions as was MacCallan Castle.

How could she get Brenna to confide in her?

Trust and love…one went hand in hand with the other. In order for there to be trust there must be truth. She should simply tell Brenna the truth and show her she could be trusted.

"I climbed up to the Chieftain's Tower last night," Elphame said softly.

Brenna looked up from ministering to her wound, a faint frown creasing her forehead.

"You shouldn't have done that. I know you're feeling markedly better, but you have to be careful not to overdo."

Elphame nodded impatiently. "I know, I know. I'll be careful."

"Well, at least you did no damage." Brenna smoothed down her nightdress. "I would not recommend a soak in your bathing pool this morning, though." She smiled lopsidedly at Elphame's scowl. "Tonight. You may bathe again tonight. Just be careful to reapply the ointment after you have dried the wound. Now," she said briskly, wiping her hands on her apron and turning back to the table. "I brought you a good, strong herbal tea and breakfast. It's important that you begin the day well fueled."

"I'll drink your wretched brew," Elphame said, pointing emphatically at the chair across the table from her. "If you sit and eat with me."

"Very well." Brenna looked pleasantly surprised. "I would be pleased to break my fast with you." Then she sent Elphame a teasing look. "And I think you'll find that my 'wretched brew' is more than palatable. This morning I added rosehips and honey to it."

"You're spoiling me," Elphame said, eyeing the teapot dubiously.

"Anything for The MacCallan." Brenna executed a cute little curtsey, grinning at her Chieftain.

Elphame felt her shoulders relax. Maybe it would be easier to get Brenna to talk to her than she thought. Their long hours together since her injury had cemented their friendship. Brenna inspected her body as if treating a woman who was part-human, part-centaur was completely normal. And she never hid her face from Elphame anymore. There was a sense of ease between the two of them that, until coming to Mac-Callan Castle, Elphame had only felt in the presence of her family.

And, Elphame reminded herself, there was definitely a relationship developing between Brenna and Cuchulainn, even if the two of them weren't completely aware of it yet. So she owed it to her brother, too, to find out who had hurt Brenna.

She waited until Brenna had poured tea for both of them and had begun to nibble at the cold rolls filled with meat and hard yellow cheese before she started speaking.

"The view from the Chieftain's Tower is incredible."

"Yes, I know," Brenna said through bites. "The stairs are too narrow for Brighid to navigate, so she insisted that I go up there and report every detail to her."

Elphame nodded, trying not to be impatient and blurt out what she wanted to say. "Did you notice how well you could see who comes and goes through the front of the castle from there?"

"Yes, that was probably the original intention of the builder—to give The MacCallan a way to keep watch without being easily noticed."

"I think so, too." Elphame cleared her throat. "Actually, that's exactly what I did last night."

"Really?" Brenna's expression was open and curious. "Did you see anything interesting?"

Elphame didn't answer. Instead she held Brenna's gaze with her own until she saw understanding, followed instantly by embarrassment, flash in her eyes.

"I saw you leave the castle," Elphame said gently. "You were very upset."

"I—I was just tired," Brenna stuttered.

"No. It was more than that. Someone had hurt you. Badly." Fighting against a lifetime of lessons that had taught her not to touch others, Elphame made herself reach out. She covered Brenna's hand with her own. "Can't you trust me enough to tell me what happened?"

Brenna's eyes were bright with a sheen of tears. "Of course I trust you, Elphame. You are my friend." She hesitated, and then she smiled a sad, crooked smile. "It's just that I feel like such a fool."

Elphame squeezed her hand. "At least you didn't fall down a ravine and break open your head."

Brenna sighed. "Actually, in a way I did fall—"

Her next words were interrupted when the door to Elphame's chamber burst open and Cuchulainn rushed into the room.

"Wake up, sister-mine! You can't spend all—"

Cu's words broke off as he caught sight of Brenna. Elphame watched her friend's expression change as her startled gaze shot to Cuchulainn. She pulled her hand from beneath Elphame's, before bowing her head and staring down at the table. There was no mistaking the flash of pain, raw and fierce, that contorted her face before she blanked all emotions from it and hid behind a veil of hair.

"I didn't know you were here, Brenna. If I had, I would not have come in unannounced. I don't mean to interrupt."

Elphame glanced over her shoulder at her brother. His expression, like his voice, was that of a contrite boy. He was staring pathetically at Brenna. El looked back at Brenna. The Healer was resolutely staring at the table, ignoring him.

It was Cu, Elphame realized with a jolt. Cu had somehow hurt Brenna last night. She was going to have a very serious talk with her little brother. What had The MacCallan called him? *Thickheaded.* She had to admit that the old spirit had a point.

"Cu, you should learn to knock. But now that you're here, have a seat. Brenna brought plenty of breakfast, and even though you have the manners of a barbarian, you're welcome to join us."

Brenna stood so fast that her chair tipped over.

"I must go. I haven't checked on the worker with the hand wound this morning. His dressing will need to be changed," she said as she hurried past Cuchulainn without looking at him.

"Wait, Brenna. Surely you have time for breakfast," Elphame said.

"No. I—I must go. No." She paused before leaving the room. "I will meet you here after the evening meal to inspect your wound again. See that you don't overdo today, Elphame." She rushed through the door as if she couldn't wait to escape.

Rooted in place Cuchulainn stared silently after her.

Elphame frowned and shook her head at him. "Well, why are you standing there like a silly statue? Go after her! You were too late last night, try to do better this morning."

Cu's body jerked in surprise.

"How did you know?"

"Later. Now just go."

He nodded once and smiled grimly. Before he jerked open the door he looked back at his sister and blew her a kiss. "Thanks, sister-mine."

"Just fix whatever you've done wrong," she muttered at the closing door.

2B

"BRENNA, WAIT!" Cuchulainn jogged down the hallway after her.

Brenna looked over her shoulder at him, and for an instant she thought about bolting away. She was almost to the end of the hallway; she could probably make it to the more public areas of the castle before he caught her if she hurried. And then what? Being in public would only make the confrontation worse. At least here there was no one to witness what passed between them. Brenna came slowly to a halt and turned to face Cuchulainn. She started to duck her head and hide her face when, unexpectedly, the anger she had felt so keenly the night before flared. No, she would meet his pity face-to-face.

"I owe you an apology for my behavior last night."

"You do not owe me an apology, Cuchulainn." Brenna held up her hand to stop him from speaking. To her amazement, he took her hand in his, and before she could protest, pressed it to his lips.

"Of course I do. I had entirely too much wine. I was rude and boorish. Please, forgive me." Still holding her hand his thumb traced lazy circles across the delicate skin he had just kissed.

Brenna felt frozen. To be kissed on the hand... It was such a simple thing. Men and women exchanged greetings thus every day. Yet until that moment no one had ever kissed her hand. Not in greeting, and not in desire. Brenna suddenly had to fight back the urge to weep.

"Please don't touch me like that."

"Why, Brenna?" Cuchulainn's voice was low and gentle.

What could she tell him? That he must not touch her because she wanted it so desperately, or that he must not touch her because he was an injury from which she did not think she was capable of recovering?

She could not say either of those things to him. If she did, she thought she might shatter into so many pieces that she would never find the way to make herself whole again. Instead, she searched for the thread of anger within her and found it when she remembered the sight of his body pressed against Wynne's as their sensuous dance movements mimicked lovemaking.

"Because Wynne would not like it, but more than that—I do not like it." With deliberate scorn she pulled her hand from his grasp. "I accept your apology. I know you did not mean to be intentionally cruel, but you do not need to play a pretty act with me today. It is degrading."

She turned to go, but he grasped her wrist.

"Wait, I—"

Brenna glared down at where his fingers circled her wrist and instantly he let loose of her.

"I won't touch you. Just don't go yet. Let me explain."

"Cuchulainn, there is nothing for you to explain."

"Yes!" The word exploded from his mouth and he ran his fingers though his hair, trying to get his frustration under control. Just talk to her! His mind screamed at him. "Yes, there is," he continued in a more civilized tone. "First, I want to explain to you that I am not interested in Wynne."

"That is no business of mine," Brenna said quickly.

"Brenna! Would you please allow me to continue?"

Brenna shrugged her shoulders, pretending a nonchalance she did not feel.

"Last night I was a drunken sot. My only defense, pathetic as it is, is to tell you that I usually have better judgment—at least where wine is concerned. I allowed the celebration of the evening to interfere with my better judgment." Cuchulainn took a deep breath and looked steadily into Brenna's dark eyes. "When the music began the only thought in my wine-addled brain was how very much I wanted to dance with you. When you refused me I was surprised as well as confused. I thought that you liked me, and as much as it pains me to admit it, the Huntress was right. I am not used to being told no by a woman who has captured my interest. I reacted like a spoiled youth." His expressive eyes sparkled with mischief. "When you said you did not know how to dance I should have sat beside you, whispered dance steps into your ear and told you how very much I would like to teach you to dance—privately."

Brenna reminded herself to breathe.

"I followed you. When I saw that you were gone I tried to find you. Brenna, I don't want Wynne. I want you."

Brenna felt her mismatched face flush with heat and her breath rushed out as her anger spiked. "How can you be so cruel?"

"Cruel? Why is it cruel to tell you that I desire you?"

"Because it's a lie, or a game, or sick, passing fancy."

"Now you insult me."

"*I* insult *you?*" She practically spat. "As always, you believe everything is about you. *You* drank too much—*you* thought only of what you wanted—*you* should have done this or that. Do you never consider the feelings of others?"

"Yes, I—"

"Listen to yourself!" She thought her heart might explode. "Yes, *I.* What about me? Did you ever consider that I might not want to be made a plaything for the great Cuchulainn? Did you ever consider that *I* might not desire *you?* Cuchulainn—" she spoke through gritted teeth "—you are my friend and Chieftain's brother and you are a warrior whose skill is much admired. I will treat you with the respect you deserve as such. And as with any other member of our clan if you are wounded I will stitch you up. If you become sick, I will try my best to heal you. But I will not be used as fodder for your personal amusement."

This time when she turned her back to him and hurried down the hall, he made no move to stop her.

"Cu," Elphame's voice carried easily down the hall. Her brother turned slowly and looked at her with an odd, blank expression on his face. "Come here, let's talk."

He nodded and walked back to her chamber. Elphame had never seen him move so woodenly. His usual swagger was gone. His broad shoulders slumped. It seemed as if he was dragging a terrible weight with him. As she watched him, The MacCallan's words echoed through her memory, *Wi' that thick head of his the lad is in for a verra hard fall.* The wily old spirit had certainly been right.

"Sit." She pointed at the chair Brenna had so recently overturned and closed the door behind him. Then she poured him some fresh tea. "Drink it. Brenna said it's good and strong."

Cuchulainn's bark of laughter was totally devoid of humor. He righted the chair and sat. "If she had known I was going to be drinking it, she would have made it good and strong and poisonous."

"Don't be ridiculous. She said she'd heal you if you were sick. If she'd have known you'd be drinking it, she would just have made it taste awful."

"She hates me, El."

"I don't think she does. Actually, I know she doesn't, but that's not the issue here." She cleared her throat. "Cuchulainn, as Brenna's Clan Chieftain it is my duty to inquire about your intentions."

"My intentions?" He blinked at his sister.

Elphame began to pace back and forth in front of the table. "Don't act so dense, Cu. You know very well that I'm asking about your intentions toward Brenna. You see, I think she had a point, at least about part of what she said. Of course I know you better, so I don't believe that you lied when you said you desire her, but I can't help wondering whether you might be chasing her as a game—after all, you aren't usually told no by women."

Cuchulainn's eyes slitted dangerously. "I am not playing a game with Brenna."

"I'm glad to hear it. Then do you want her because you can't resist giving the scarred girl a thrill? Or maybe you just have to get a peek at the rest of her so you can see just how far those scars really go?"

Her brother's fist slammed against the table with such force that the teacups jumped. "If you were not my sister I would knock those words back into your mouth!"

Elphame stopped pacing, planted her hands on her hips and grinned defiantly at her brother. "I knew it, you are in love with her."

Cuchulainn's head jerked back as if she had slapped him. "In love? No, I…"

"Is she too ugly for the great Cuchulainn to admit that he loves her?"

"Elphame." His voice lowered threateningly. "If you don't stop talking about her like that, I swear I'm going to—"

Her laughter interrupted him. "Then what you're saying is that you don't think she's ugly."

He glared at her. "Of course not. Brenna is beautiful."

"What about her scars?"

"What about them? They're just a part of her. By the Goddess! I can't believe you're saying these things. I thought she was your friend."

Elphame's taunting smile warmed. "She is, which is why I wanted to be sure of you, Cu. I didn't really think that you'd toy with her, but you had to say it aloud for both of us to believe it."

Cuchulainn looked around the room. "But no one's here except you and me, El."

"Exactly." She rolled her eyes skyward. "You were right. He is thickheaded."

Her brother scowled at her. "Have you been talking to that damned old ghost again?"

"Yes, but again, that's not the issue, either. Try to stay focused, brother-mine. You're in love with Brenna."

Cuchulainn hunched his shoulders, nodded his head, and stared at his cup of tea.

"And she's a little upset with you."

"Hrumph!" he said.

"Okay, perhaps 'a little upset' is an understatement," Elphame amended.

"I think she hates me, El."

"Nonsense, listen—" She pulled her chair close to him and sat down. "Last night I went up to the Chieftain's Tower."

"El, you shouldn't have done that. You know Brenna told you to be careful."

"Yes, yes, yes, she already chastised me," Elphame said impatiently. "Forget that and pay attention to what I saw from above. I watched Brenna leave the castle. She was crying, Cu, so hard that she had to lean against the wall of the castle."

"It was because of me. I embarrassed her. That doesn't mean she loves me, El. That just means I'm as self-centered and unfeeling as she thinks I am."

Elphame shook her head. "No, Cu, that's not what that means. Brenna leaned against the castle wall while I was resting my arm against the tower's balustrade. It's hard to explain, but somehow the spirit of the castle connected me to her and for a moment I actually felt what she felt—despair, pain, loneliness. Whatever had happened inside didn't just embarrass her or upset her, it broke her heart."

Cuchulainn put his face in his hands and moaned.

"Cu." Elphame squeezed his shoulder. "You can fix this. All you have to do is show her you love her and make her believe she can trust you."

Her brother looked at her through his fingers. "How do I do that?"

She grinned at him. "I have no idea."

24

ELPHAME STRETCHED GINGERLY and rolled her sore shoulder, careful not to let her expression reveal even the least little discomfort. She was seated on the newly dug ground between two rows of what would eventually be heartily growing mint plants—at least that's what Wynne had assured her. Elphame didn't know much about herbs or gardening, so the old garden that was situated behind the kitchen looked more like a confusing array of upended plants and haphazardly raised piles of soil to her than a plot of herbs meticulously being restored, but Wynne's militant assistant cooks seemed to know what they were doing as they selectively weeded and transplanted and chattered about this and that herb. Truthfully, Elphame would have rather been scrubbing the stone walls of the Great Hall, but Brenna had put an end to that before she'd even had time to settle into the work. Elphame scowled as she patted the dirt around the little mint plant. The Healer had refused to agree to allow El to do anything more strenuous than to sit comfortably and quietly and transplant baby mint plants.

Elphame sighed. She really shouldn't complain, at least she'd escaped the confinement of that awful chaise longue. The day was warm and clear, with just enough of a breeze to bring the scent of blooming flowers and the sea within the castle walls. The sun felt wonderful on her face and the busy sounds of her clan surrounded her with a feeling of peace. And, she admitted to herself, she was finding that she liked getting her hands in the rich MacCallan earth. She stretched again, and rolled her head, loosening the stiffness of her neck. Looking up, she watched the men who were hard at work repairing the ruin of the warriors' barracks, the entrance to which was located near the rear of the kitchen. Elphame thought the placement made perfect sense. Warriors, it seemed, were always hungry. At least Cuchulainn was always hungry.

A familiar kilted figure joined the workers, calling orders and checking the roofers' progress. El watched him closely. Cu's voice was definitely grumpier than usual. She stifled a smile. But Cuchulainn was no fool, and she knew how stubborn he could be when he truly desired something. Brenna had no idea the scope of the battle that was getting ready to be launched against her defenses. Elphame hoped fervently that Cu's campaign—whatever it was—would work. The two of them fit well together. She wondered briefly if she should bring her mother into the fray. Etain would make a formidable ally when she realized that her precious son's heart had been lost, and the glimmer of future grandchildren sparkled before her.

No, Elphame quickly decided against calling in her mother. Let Cuchulainn work at winning Brenna. The MacCallan hadn't been sure if the Healer could learn to trust enough to love, but Elphame had more faith in her friend—and in her brother's ability to woo and win a lover.

Absently, El chose another small plant and began to prepare a place for it next to the other sprig of mint. What about the question of her own lover? A little shiver of delight ran though Elphame as she remembered the way he had responded to her touch. His wings…

"You look flushed. Perhaps it's time you rested."

Elphame jumped guiltily. She looked up, shielding her eyes against the sun, silhouetting Brenna and Brighid.

"I'm not flushed. I feel fine." She stood with what she hoped was enough lithe grace to satisfy her Healer friend.

"She looks well-rested to me," Brighid said.

Elphame could have kissed the Huntress.

Brenna narrowed her eyes. "You're not—"

"No!" Elphame interrupted her friend. "I am not over-doing. I'm just planting these baby things."

"You're transplanting mint sprigs. They're not bairns," Wynne said cheerfully as she swung into the garden. The cook inspected the little row Elphame had completed. "And ye are doin' a fine job of it."

Elphame grinned. "See, I'm fine."

Brenna's face relaxed only a little. "Well, see that you go slowly. And if your shoulder begins to ache, do not push it." She smiled begrudgingly at her overactive patient. She would have to keep a close watch on Elphame. Her friend was healing well, but she pushed herself too hard. She was too used to depending upon the extraordinary abilities of her body. Elphame didn't seem to understand that even her strength had its limits.

Brenna snuck a quick look at Wynne as she discussed the castle's meals with Elphame and Brighid. The cook was voluptuous and beautiful. It was not possible that Cuchulainn did not desire Wynne. Just as it was not possible that the warrior truly desired Brenna. As the day had passed her anger at him had cooled to a simmer, and she had been left with a confused irritation. Why had he insisted that he wanted her? She chewed her lip, remembering her harsh words to him. She didn't really think that he was selfish and cruel—she'd just been completely unbalanced by his declaration. And his touch. And his nearness.

"Good afternoon, ladies." Cuchulainn's deep voice sounded forcefully cheerful. All day he'd been restless and irritable, and he'd known he was doing more harm than good as he snapped at the roofers. Impulsively, he'd decided to find his sister. She was a maiden. Surely she'd know something he could say to Brenna to repair the damage he had unwittingly done. One of the women had told him that Elphame was in the kitchen garden, and he'd hurried there with a single-minded sense of purpose that had blocked out everything else. Until he'd entered the little garden and caught sight of Brenna. He spoke offhandedly to the women, who waved warmly to him as he strode toward his sister—and Brenna. Cuchulainn set his shoulders. He wouldn't get a chance to talk to his sister alone and ask her advice first. He would just have to follow his heart—or his gut—or both.

Elphame grinned at him, pulling his attention from the silent Healer. "I'll bet you had no idea that I could garden, Cu."

He couldn't help smiling back at her, and he wiped a smudge of dirt from her cheek. "You can't."

"Ye may be in for a surprise, warrior," Wynne purred. "Our Chieftain has many hidden talents."

Cuchulainn hardly spared the beautiful cook a glance. Instead his eyes sought and found Brenna's. His smile was slow and seductive, and its warmth lit his face.

"You could be right, Wynne. There are many things about our Chieftain—and about others—that I have been surprised to learn. And I'm finding that I would like to learn more, too."

Brenna gaped at the warrior. He was looking at her like *that,* right there in front of all of them! Cuchulainn's message was clear. He was telling every one of them that he was interested. In her. She stood there, frozen, not sure if she wished she could disappear or if she wished he would keep on looking like that at her—and really mean it.

He kept on looking like that at her.

"Uh, Cu—is there something you needed?" Elphame said.

Cuchulainn's turquoise eyes never left Brenna's. "There is something I need, but I believe I have found it, sister-mine."

Brenna's breath left her body is a surprised rush and she felt the left side of her face flame.

"If you will excuse me, Elphame, there are things I must…I have to…" She wrenched her eyes from Cuchulainn's hot gaze and reordered her thoughts. "I have to go," she finished in a rush, curtsied to Elphame, and hurried from the garden.

"So that's how 'tis?" Wynne asked softly.

Still looking after Brenna, Cuchulainn nodded his head slowly. "That is how it is."

Wynne gave the warrior an appraising look, tossed back her red mane, and sauntered from the garden.

"That might not have been the smartest thing you could have done, Cu," Elphame said, wiping her hands on her thighs. "You know how shy Brenna is. I think you might have scared her more than seduced her."

"I want her to know I'm serious."

Brighid snorted.

"What do you have to say about it?" Cu rounded on her.

The Huntress shrugged her shapely shoulders. "Nothing except that you're like a bull in rutting season. Next thing you'll do is piss on the ground around her to mark your territory."

Elphame watched her brother begin to swell and she hastily

stepped between the two of them. "That's enough. Take it outside the castle walls."

The Huntress and the warrior blinked blankly at their Chieftain. She shook her head in disgust at them.

"Go hunting. Both of you. Brighid, try not to antagonize my brother every second. Cuchulainn, you need to work off some of your—" she gestured at the rigid set of his shoulders "—tension. It's certainly not helping you with Brenna."

The Huntress snorted again.

Elphame raised one eyebrow at her and crossed her arms.

Brighid sighed and glanced begrudgingly at Cuchulainn. "Come on, warrior. Let's see if you can bring down a stag."

Cuchulainn frowned at the Huntress. He had no intention of leaving the castle. He should go after Brenna right then and—

"Thank you, Brighid, that sounds like a lovely idea. I'm glad you thought of it." Elphame gave both of their shoulders a shove toward the garden's exit. "Wynne was just saying that she could never have enough venison. I'll see the two of you at dinner." She neatly ignored the dark look her brother sent her as he followed the Huntress from the courtyard.

With a sigh she resumed her seat in the middle of the mint plants, contemplating the benefits of bashing Cuchulainn over the head so that Brenna would be forced to treat him.

"He'd probably be a worse patient than me, and she'd end up poisoning his tea—not that anyone would blame her," she muttered.

Cuchulainn had to admit it; Elphame's idea had been a good one. He'd needed to get away from the castle and clear his head. His aim was certainly off—he'd be surprised if he could have hit the side of MacCallan's thick outer wall, but his muscles were warm and his tension had dissipated. He also had to admit that Brighid was a damned fine Huntress. He'd spent years at his father's side, so the grace and strength of a centaur was nothing new to him, but Brighid moved with a stealth that was almost preternatural.

"Through there." Her voice was hushed and he followed her gaze to the little stream that ran through the meadow. The stag was just dipping his head to drink.

Cu nodded and dropped silently from his gelding. Notching an arrow he crept forward to get a clear shot. A half-fallen tree was in the way, and he moved slowly around its splintered trunk. The breeze stirred and he froze, even though it was blowing away from the deer. An odor came to him then and Cuchulainn unconsciously curled his lip at the fetid smell. Death and rot—close by. He stepped over the edge of the downed limb, and with a sick, squinching sound he put his booted foot down squarely in the middle of the decomposing corpse.

Before he could stop himself, Cu jerked his body back. Nostrils flaring, the stag lunged away.

"Cuchulainn, what—" Brighid began, but her look of irritation changed to surprise as she joined him on the other side of the tree.

"Dead wolf," he said, wiping his boot on the mossy ground. "Sorry about scaring away the stag. It was just—" he grimaced at the corpse "—unexpected. Especially looking like that."

Brighid was studying the body thoughtfully. "Impaled," she said.

"Strange, isn't it? He must have run right into that splintered limb."

"She," Brighid corrected him.

He cocked a brow at her.

"The wolf is a female." The Huntress pointed to the underside of the bloating body. "And she had cubs. Look at her teats."

Cuchulainn was intrigued enough to ignore the smell and step closer to the dead wolf.

"I've seen this type of death only a few times, and always in lone females who have recently whelped. They're desperate for food. I can only imagine the frenzy that drives them to run after their prey with such blinding intensity that they lose all sense of everything else around them. She probably leaped over the log and at the speed she was traveling the limb shard was driven into her like a spear."

Cuchulainn crouched down. The wolf had impaled herself through her chest. He shook his head.

"But why was she hunting alone? Wolves live in packs."

"Most do, but look at her size. She's clearly a runt. She should have never been bred. My guess is that the alpha female drove her from the pack. She wouldn't have liked to share the alpha male, and the pack rarely lets substandard members breed." The Huntress peered down at the wolf, reading the history her corpse still told. "Look at her body, especially around her head and neck. She's badly scarred—probably was supposed to die. It's amazing she recovered and lived as long as she did."

Badly scarred...supposed to die...Cuchulainn's jaw tightened. Abruptly he stood and faced the Huntress.

"How long would you say she's been dead?"

Brighid shrugged. "Maybe two days."

"Not too long," he muttered as if thinking aloud.

"Too long for what?"

"Some of them might still be alive. Let's find them." Cuchulainn strode back to his gelding.

"Cuchulainn, what in the name of the Goddess are you talking about?"

He swung aboard the horse. "Prove to me you're as great a Huntress as I think you are."

Surprised, she raised her chin. "And how do you suggest I do that?"

He smiled grimly at her. "I want you to find her cubs."

25

THE EVENING MEAL had been delicious, and even though Elphame was beginning to wonder about the prolonged absence of her brother and the Huntress, she sipped her wine and chatted with Danann. She wasn't his nursemaid. Cuchulainn could take care of himself—as could Brighid.

And then there was Lochlan. When she'd told Brighid to take Cu hunting, she had only been thinking about Brenna and her brother. What if the Huntress had stumbled across more of those "unusual" tracks? Or worse, what if Cuchulainn had?

She tried to smile and pay polite attention as she nodded at something the old Stonemaster was saying, and then she turned to Brenna, trying once again to coax her into the conversation. The Healer wouldn't be coaxed. She was silent, resolutely staring at her plate, only glancing up fretfully at the sound of someone entering the chamber.

Maybe it hadn't been such a good idea to send Cu away.

Maybe she should have let him blunder after Brenna. Elphame sighed and was pouring herself more wine when the clatter of hooves announced Brighid's return. The Huntress entered the chamber with an odd, half smile on her lips. She caught Elphame's eye and winked before Cuchulainn rushed into the room.

"Brenna!" he barked. "I need you."

Elphame saw the Healer's body jerk, but when Brenna registered Cuchulainn's expression the shy maiden disappeared. Instantly, she was on her feet moving toward him.

"Where are you wounded?" she asked in the calm, clear voice of an experienced Healer.

Elphame's stomach rolled, Brighid's wink forgotten. Her brother was hurt? She pushed back from the table and hurried after Brenna. The room fell abruptly silent, causing the commands the Healer shot at Cu to seem amplified.

"Sit here." She ordered two workers from the nearest bench and pushed Cu's shoulder down so that he was forced to take their place. "I see no blood. Did you fall from your horse?" She shot a glance at Brighid. "What happened to him?"

"Brenna." He captured the hand that was trying to feel his wrist for a racing pulse. "It's not me. It's her." The warrior opened the front of his tunic and pulled out a small, disheveled bundle of gray fur.

Brenna tried to back a step away from him, but he tightened his grip on her hand and refused to allow her to retreat.

"What game do you play, Cuchulainn?" Her voice was cold and angry.

Elphame peered over her friend's shoulder at the dirty gray fluff. "Is it alive?"

"Just barely," he told his sister. Then he turned back to Brenna. "And I'm not playing any game. I need you to help me save the cub."

"Where is its mother?" Brenna shook her hand free of him,

but this time she didn't move away. She stepped closer and began examining the little cub.

"Dead in the forest. As are her four siblings."

"Did you kill her?" Brenna asked sharply.

Brighid snorted a laugh. "Cuchulainn was no threat to any beast today. The warrior missed everything he shot at." She ignored Cuchulainn's scowl. "We found the mother dead. He insisted that I track her trail back to her den."

Elphame moved to her brother's side and tentatively touched the little creature's matted fur. The wolf cub was young; she wasn't much bigger than Cu's hand. Her eyes were closed and matted with filth, as was the rest of her coat. The cub's nose was pale and dry. If she hadn't made a faint whimpering sound El wouldn't have believed she was alive.

"She is very weak and dehydrated—probably gone at least two days without any nourishment at all." Brenna put her finger in the cub's mouth and it suckled weakly. "It is a good sign that she's still interested in suckling, but she needs milk—lots of it, and often. And she may not live, no matter what you do."

"What I do?" Cu said quickly. "But I thought that you would—"

Brenna's narrowed eyes cut him off.

Elphame laughed at her brother's expression. "Looks like you have a puppy, brother-mine."

"Wolf cub," Cuchulainn grumbled. "She's not a puppy, she's a wolf cub."

"Bring your wolf cub back to the kitchen. Wynne will have cheesecloth. I can show you how to make a milk teat." All business, Brenna headed for the entrance to the kitchen. Cu smuggled the little cub back inside his tunic, and along with the chuckles that washed through the room, he followed her.

"A wolf cub, huh?" Elphame grinned at Brighid.

"In theory it was an excellent idea. Bring a baby creature

who needs healing to the Healer he's trying to woo. It would melt most maidens' hearts."

"Brenna is not most maidens."

"Exactly."

"She's taking it!"

Relief flooded Cuchulainn's voice. He was sitting on the chair that rested beside the little desk in the tent that was now his instead of his sister's. Part of his plan had definitely worked. Brenna was alone with him in his tent. Wynne had chased them from the kitchen saying that the only beasts she allowed there were dead and ready for the stewing pot. He'd wadded up a blanket and had the cub propped on his lap, makeshift teat filled with milk all ready to revive the creature. But she had refused to suckle. Whimpering and whining pitifully, the beast had seemed bent on dying.

"Carefully and steadily, she is not a battle to be won," Brenna had instructed him. "She has suffered much. You must make her feel that it is safe enough for her to suckle."

So Cuchulainn had cajoled and coaxed until, finally, the little cub had latched onto the milky cloth. He beamed at Brenna.

"This is good, isn't it! Look at how well she is drinking."

Brenna refused the smile that hovered just beneath the surface of her face. The virile young warrior had never looked as appealing as he did at that moment when he was tousled, milky and smelling of wolf dung.

"Do not get your hopes up. She is not out of danger."

Cuchulainn frowned and let one free finger rub through the cub's matted scruff, which caused the little creature to growl low in her throat and suckle harder.

"See," Cu's grin was fierce. "She has the heart of a warrior. She did not die with the others. She will not die now."

Brenna's lips tilted up just the slightest bit. "You could be right. Well," she said, all business again, "you have a long night before you. There's enough milk here, as well as fresh cheese-cloth. I think you should sleep with her tucked next to your skin. She'll stay warm that way, and she'll awaken you when she needs to feed again." She nodded at Cu, who was watching her with wide, incredulous eyes. "You'll be fine. I'll check on you in the morning."

"Wait—" He would have grabbed her and held her there, but he didn't have a free hand. "You can't just leave."

"Surely you did not think that I would be spending the night with you, did you Cuchulainn?" She would not duck her head and she would not hide, but her voice had grown soft and sounded much younger than her Healer's voice.

"Not with me," he assured her hastily. "With *us.*"

"Are you saying that I should treat this situation as if she is my human patient?" she asked, shifting instantly from maiden to Healer.

Cu nodded, looking relieved.

"Then my opinion as a Healer is that my patient is in the very capable hands of her…um…adopted parent, and does not need me until morning. Good night, Cuchulainn." Holding open the tent flap she hesitated. "Two last things. First, even though she smells like a nest of wild dog dung, do not bathe her tonight. It would be too much for her small system. You may bathe her tomorrow—if she lives. Second, do not forget that you must take a wet cloth and help her pass her liquids as well as her feces, just as her mother would." With those words she did smile, right before she turned and left the tent.

Cuchulainn closed his mouth.

The cub growled and butted against his hand, searching for more milk in the empty cheesecloth.

"All right, fearsome one. I'll do your bidding." He shifted

the cub around in his lap and prepared more milk. "But you saw her smile at us, didn't you? It's a good sign. It won't be much longer and she'll have to admit that she likes us." He kept up a one-sided conversation with the smelly little creature. Vocalizing determination was a positive step. Say it enough and it would be true. At least that was what Cuchulainn fervently hoped.

Elphame was finally alone, and, thanks to Cuchulainn's new acquisition, she was assured of her privacy—although at first he had been the reason that Brighid had insisted on accompanying her to her chamber and had even stayed during her Chieftain's bath, regaling El with her brother's misadventures that day. Elphame smiled in remembrance even as she wound the soft blue and green plaid around her body and secured it into place with the MacCallan brooch.

"Thank you, Mama," she whispered as her hand lingered on the fine fabric that had been one of the many gifts that had arrived the day before from Epona's temple. Honestly, she didn't care overmuch about the sumptuous linens and the other frivolities her mother thought necessities, but the gift of her clan's tartan—that was a jewel beyond price.

Dressed, she approached the arched entrance that led down to her bathing chamber, and to the secret passage beyond.

She let her fingertips caress the stones that were the body of her home as she moved resolutely down the stairs. Did she know what she was doing? Elphame drew a deep breath. Yes—yes she did.

Show me the door to the passage.

Instantly the familiar tingling tickled her fingers, followed by the warmth created by the golden string that glowed from her hand and around the wall, to end in a glowing sphere in the middle of the hidden door. She followed the thread as her heartbeat escalated. Taking a torch from its fitting on the wall of the bathing chamber, she pressed the smooth, raised spot. This time the door opened silently, as if it had been breathlessly waiting for her touch.

Elphame lifted the torch, and held it within the entrance as she peered into the dark tunnel. The walls were narrow and covered with a damp film of silvery cobweb. She shivered, thinking of skittering spiders. The ceiling was low and rough; the stale air smelled of damp rot. She pressed her hand against the wall of the tunnel. Through the cold, slick surface Elphame felt the pulse of the castle and the stone warmed under her touch. She breathed a long sigh of relief as she watched the golden string unravel and snake quickly along the wall. She couldn't see the end with her eyes, but she could sense it through the very blood that pulsed within her veins. She knew that somewhere at the end of the ancient tunnel, stone met forest and emptied into the night.

Before her determination could waver, Elphame entered the tunnel. It ran straight and level, and even though it was musty and cool the walls surrounded her with a sense of quiet strength. The echo of her hooves against the stone floor was a familiar, comfortable sound. As she made her way through the tunnel, Elphame's thoughts wandered to the MacCallans who had lived for generations in the castle. How many times had an ancestor trodden this path? How many rendezvous had the tunnel enabled? Rendezvous…her stomach pitched nervously.

"Epona, let me be doing the right thing." Her voice drifted eerily around her and she considered calling out for The MacCallan—his company would definitely be comforting. "Hrumph." El purposefully copied her brother's favorite expression. She was The MacCallan now; she needed to act like it. Her decisions were her own to make, and her own to act upon.

She broke off her thought as her torch's flickering light danced on the end of the tunnel. There were stone steps leading up to a tangled mass of roots and underbrush. She placed the torch in a holder conveniently located on the edge of the wall, freeing her hands to pull aside the jumble of plants and leaves that clogged the exit—and, with surprisingly little effort, she popped out of the tunnel like a cork coming to the surface.

Elphame picked leaves from her hair while her eyes accustomed themselves to the night's darkness. She was far enough within the forest that she couldn't detect any sign of lights from the castle, but she could clearly hear the pounding of the surf, so she knew she must be near the cliff's edge. She looked back at the entrance to the tunnel and shook her head in amazement. From the outside it looked like just another craggy hole in the forest where a little lip of land dipped and curved. It blended with the land so well that she'd have to be careful, or she'd have a hard time finding it when she was ready to return.

She looked around trying to see into the night-darkened forest. She should have waited longer, until the moon had climbed high enough to be of more help. Then what? Sure, she would have been able to see better, but how much help would that be if she didn't know where to look?

She had no idea where Lochlan was.

He had come when the boar attacked her. He had come when she was alone yesterday. But how had he known? She squinted her eyes, thinking. She hadn't even known that he existed the first time, but yesterday she had said his name aloud, and he had simply appeared.

"Call for me, my heart. I will never be far from you."

Her memory repeated his words in her mind. She shrugged her shoulders. There was really nothing else for her to do. She couldn't very well search through the entire forest for him. Feeling more than a little foolish, Elphame cleared her throat and tentatively spoke his name.

"Lochlan." It came out as little more than a whisper.

She frowned and chastised herself—as if he could hear that.

"Lochlan!" Elphame called his name. Her skin prickled with the power that suddenly surrounded her. The wind took the echo of the sound and blew it up through the piney boughs of the trees where it hovered, repeating *Lochlan… Lochlan…Lochlan…*over and over until it gently dissipated, like sun-kissed fog.

"Magic." Her lips formed the word, but no sound emerged. It hadn't been her imagination or the bump on her head; Lochlan's name was magic.

Elphame knew he was there before she could see him. She felt him. Like she felt the pulse of the castle through its stone, she could sense his presence through her blood.

"Lochlan." She repeated his name, delighted again at the magic it created as it flew on the wind and wrapped around her.

"I am here, my heart."

26

HE STEPPED FROM the shadows, wings folded neatly against his back. His skin and hair seemed to draw down the silver light of the rising moon, highlighting the ridges and planes of his body, silhouetting the velvet darkness of his wings. He moved to her with the soundless, gliding stride that was unique to his father's race. Elphame did not step back from him, but he was careful to halt just barely within an arm's length of her.

"I felt that you were near, but I would not let myself believe it."

"Then you heard me call your name?"

"Yes, it came to me on the night wind and I followed the sound of it to you."

Elphame felt flushed and nervous. She wished she had something to do with her hands.

"Would you like to go for a walk?" she blurted.

"It would be my honor." Lochlan held out his hand.

She hesitated. In the moonlight his hand looked ghostly and unreal.

"We have touched before, Elphame."

She looked from his hand to his eyes. Then, slowly, she laced her fingers through his. His skin was warm, and where their wrists brushed against one another she could feel the steady beat of his pulse.

"The cliffside is just through those trees." He pointed over her shoulder. "If we walk there the light will be better. It will be easier for you to see."

Elphame nodded numbly. Now that he was there, she felt completely unsure of herself. She couldn't even seem to make her legs move—she just stood, hand clasped with his, silently staring at him.

The white glint of his feral smile matched the teasing light in his eyes. "Or would you rather that we ran?"

His words broke the spell of awkwardness. Her lips twisted. "Not at night and not through this forest." Hand in hand, they began walking together. "I have definitely learned my lesson. Another fall and Cuchulainn would never let me out of his sight, which would be almost as inconvenient for him right now as it would be for me."

Lochlan picked up the thread of conversation. "I would imagine Cuchulainn is very busy with the rebuilding of the castle. It would be difficult for him if he felt that he needed to keep a constant watch over you."

"Not to mention he's in love."

Lochlan's eyes widened momentarily in surprise. When he spoke his thumb traced lazy circles on her hand. "I do understand how love can complicate things."

"Do you?" She felt childishly giddy.

They stepped from the forest. The moon played on the sleeping sea, turning it shades of silver and white. MacCallan

Castle stood in the distance, a dark chaperone, partially obscured by the tree line.

Lochlan turned to face her. "Yes, I do."

She was trapped in the intensity of his gaze. His eyes were filled with mystery and the seductive allure of the unknown. Suddenly, she was afraid that if she loved him she would be lost to herself, forever changed, and she wasn't sure she was ready to relinquish herself to any man—especially one who was so different from anything she had ever imagined. Elphame pulled her hand from his. With Lochlan following her, she walked restlessly to one of the many boulders that dotted the cliffside. She sat on it, trying to order her thoughts.

"Tell me." Instead of looking at him she stared out at the moonlit sea. "Explain to me how it is possible that you exist."

Lochlan knew what he said to her would set the course of their relationship. He kept his gaze on her strong, familiar profile and sent a silent prayer for aid to Epona.

"The question of my existence is a complex one. In truth, I do not know exactly why I exist. You know as much as I about the events that led to the Great War. More than one hundred years ago something cataclysmic happened within the Fomorian race. Their females began dying. I've often thought it must have been Epona's will that a race so demonic die out, but then if it was her will, why did she allow the war to take place at all?"

Without looking at him, Elphame answered with words that echoed those she had heard her mother speak many times. "Epona allows her people to make their own choices—she does not want us to be slaves, she wants strong, free-thinking subjects. With that freedom comes the possibility of mistakes—mistakes that sometimes lead to evil. If the warriors at Guardian Castle had not become lax about their duties, the Fomorians could not have entered Partholon and begun stealing women."

"But they did. My mother explained it as the way they set about repopulating their dying race." He shook his head and breathed out a sharp, frustrated breath. "You would think that mixing with human blood would weaken the demons, but it didn't. The race thrived, so much so that soon they were ready to invade Partholon." He paused, reordering his thoughts.

"Until my mother's time, no human woman had survived the birth of a child fathered by a Fomorian," he continued, choosing his words carefully. "She was young and strong, but she always insisted that her strength had little to do with it. She said that she survived because I am more human than Fomorian." He paused and drew a breath. "My mother was a part of what was, at first, just another of the large groups of women who had been captured, raped and impregnated by the Fomorians. They were being held captive until it was time for their demonic fetuses to be birthed. A human woman's impregnation by a Fomorian meant a death sentence for her; during the birthing process her body was always fatally torn." His voice took on a faraway tone as he repeated the story his mother had told him countless times. "The Fomorians saw human women as expendable, only a temporary encumbrance, a necessary means to attain their goal of the repopulation of their species. The hybrid females were especially prized in the hopes of rebuilding the race, but all the children were necessary.

"As Partholon united and the tide of war turned against them, the Fomorians attempted to escape into the Tier Mountains. Some did. They divided the women amongst them, planning to elude the army of Partholon while still keeping their means of procreation. But the Goddess had other plans. The demons grew ill with the same plague that had decimated the core of their army. Heavy with child, my mother led the women of her group in revolt. Then she and her sisters in arms searched within the mountain passes for the others, destroying the Fomorians as they weakened. She should have returned to Partholon and her home then, so that, surrounded by the comfort of their families, she and the other impregnated women could await their inevitable end. That was what she and the women intended. But then the unexpected happened. She survived my birth."

Elphame was unable to look away from him any longer. She turned her face to his. Lochlan's expression was fixed and tight with emotion.

"And then another mother lived through the birth of her mutant child, and another and another."

His words made her heart ache. "You are not a mutant."

"I am part-demon, part-human. What else does that make me?"

She answered his question with one of her own. "I am part-centaur, part-human. Does that make me a mutant?"

"It makes you a miracle."

She held his gaze. "Exactly."

He continued recounting the story of his life with the ghost of a smile on his lips. "Almost half of the women survived. My mother had no explanation for it except to say that Epona's hand was at work." His eyebrow cocked. "That was always my mother's explanation for any question she could not answer. But whatever the reason, there was suddenly a group of young women who had winged infants at their breasts." Lochlan's expression softened. "And they loved their children with a fierce protectiveness. They knew they couldn't return to Partholon with their babies, and leaving them was an option they refused to consider. So they made their way through the mountains and into the Wastelands beyond. Life was hard there, and our mothers longed for Partholon, but we survived, even thrived. And our mothers taught us to be civilized. To be human."

"Over a century ago…" Her words were a sigh. Even with him standing there beside her, winged, living and breathing, it was hard to accept.

"I admit it is a long time." He made an offhanded gesture, as if he didn't know what to make of his own longevity. "None of our mothers had much knowledge about the Fomorian race, but it was apparent early in our lives that we matured quickly and that our bodies were extraordinarily resilient. Aging appears to be just another thing our dark blood protects us against."

Elphame thought about what she had read in her mother's extensive library. "Fomorians had an aversion to daylight, but I've seen you in the light of day. It doesn't seem to harm you."

"It does not harm me, but I am stronger at night. My vision is better, my sense of hearing and smell are more acute."

Spreading his fingers, he held his arms away from his body. Elphame thought that he looked like the winged spirit of a shaman making ready to evoke the magic of a goddess.

"The night sky calls to me."

"Can you fly?"

He smiled, dropping his hands to his sides. "I do not think of it as flying; I think of it as riding the wind. Perhaps some day I will show you."

To glide through the air wrapped in his arms…the thought left her breathless.

"This doesn't seem real. You don't seem real," she said.

Lochlan moved closer to her. He lifted a thick strand of hair that hung over her shoulder and let it fall like water through his fingers.

"One night I had a dream. If I live an eternity, I will never forget it. In my dream I watched the birth of a child. She was born of a human female and a centaur male. When the centaur lifted her and proclaimed her a goddess, I knew that that wondrous child would somehow irrevocably alter my future. You have always been real to me, Elphame. It is the rest of my life that was only a dream. You are my destiny."

Elphame let out a long breath. "I don't know what to do about you."

"Can you not simply do as my mother did? Just allow yourself to love me?"

Everything within her—heart, soul and the blood that filled her veins—cried, *Yes! Yes she could!* But logic and years of enmity cautioned her to be reasonable.

"I cannot. I'm not just a young maiden. I have been named The MacCallan. My people swore an oath of loyalty to me. My first responsibility is no longer to myself, it is to my clan."

Lochlan's face broke into a joyous smile. "Ask me my mother's name."

"What is your mother's name?" she asked, surprised by the sudden question.

"She was called Morrigan, named by a doting father after the legendary Phantom Queen. She was living at the ancestral castle of her clan, where her eldest brother presided as Chieftain. She had just completed her education at the Temple of the Muse, and she was enjoying her sojourn by the sea while she awaited the date of her wedding—a wedding which never took place…"

"—Because MacCallan Castle was attacked and she was taken prisoner. Her brother was The MacCallan," Elphame finished for him, feeling a supernatural prickle along her skin.

With a rustle of wings, Lochlan dropped to his knees before her. He pulled his short sword from the scabbard strapped to his side and placed it at her feet.

"The blood of the Clan MacCallan runs thick in my veins. I invoke the right of that blood and I do hereby give you my oath and I swear fealty to you from this moment forth, even unto my death and, if Epona grants it, beyond."

Elphame stared down at him. The moon had climbed the sky and it sat over her shoulder, haloing Lochlan in its cool light. He was watching her with eyes that gleamed the bright reflection of what she suddenly accepted as her future.

He Felt right. She couldn't explain it rationally, but she had changed since she'd met him.

The old spirit had been right. She had found her peace at Lochlan's side. Elphame slid from her rocky perch so that she, too, was on her knees facing Lochlan. First, she took up his sword and offered it back to him.

"Keep this. You may need it to defend your Chieftain."

"Then you accept me?"

Reverently, she touched the side of his face. "I accept you, Lochlan, into the Clan MacCallan—as is your birthright."

The tension drained out of Lochlan's shoulders and he bowed his head.

"Thank you, Epona," he whispered.

When he spoke the Goddess's name, Elphame experienced a rush of preternatural foreknowledge. In a blinding flash she saw him on his knees, as he was then, but in the vision that was overlaid upon the fabric of reality, Lochlan was in chains, covered with blood…imprisoned…dying….

Her mind screamed, rejecting the vision. She would not let him be destroyed. The vision made her decision for her and she knew what she must do. If she accepted him, if she allowed herself to love him, it would alter his future—the death spell would be shattered. As his mother's love had conquered the darkness in his blood, her love would defeat a world's misplaced hatred.

"You say I am your destiny," she said.

It wasn't a question, but he nodded his head and spoke with a surety that closed the breach of time and blood.

"I love you, Elphame."

"Then handfast with me."

Lochlan's sharp intake of breath was the only outward sign of his shock. Handfasting was a marriage sworn to last exactly one year. At the end of one year, the couple could decide to continue the marriage, or, if either did not desire to remain together, the marriage was dissolved with no blame assigned to either party. But it was a binding contract—sealed by two people—witnessed by Epona. It was a sacred bond that could not be broken for the space of that year.

"Yes!" He grasped her hands. "Yes, I will!" *And may the bloody Prophecy and the world be damned,* he thought fiercely. Before second thoughts or hesitation could claim her, he began the timeless words of binding that had been taught to him by his mother, who had been taught them by her mother and her mother before her.

"I, Lochlan, son of Morrigan MacCallan, do take you Elphame, daughter of Etain, in handfast this day. I agree to protect you from fire even if the sun should fall, from water even if the sea should rage and from earth even if it should shake in tumult. And I will honor your name as if it were my own."

As she spoke the words, she knew she was choosing the right path—the path that she had glimpsed within Lochlan's eye—the path her own brother had foretold.

"I, Elphame, Chieftain of Clan MacCallan, do take you, Lochlan, in handfast this day. I agree that no fire or flame shall part us, no lake or seas shall drown us and no earthly mountains shall separate us. And I will honor your name as if it were my own."

"So has it been spoken," Lochlan said.

"So shall it be done." She completed the ritual.

They came together in a kiss that began as a tender consummation of their covenant. Elphame leaned into him and his arms went around her. His lips were soft—so much softer than the rest of his body. His scent enveloped her. Once again he was the living forest, wild and male. She drank him in. He was her oasis in a life that she had thought would always be barren of the love of a lifemate.

And now he belonged to her and she to him.

The purr of his wings flexing and filling was seductive music to her already aroused senses. She leaned away from him just enough so that she had a clear view of them.

"Your wings," Elphame breathed, "are like living velvet. I want to wrap myself in them and have you carry me away."

She reached up and touched the downy, butter-colored underside. Lochlan's breath exploded from him. He shuddered and closed his eyes. She pulled her hand back, and touched his face. Slowly, he opened his eyes.

"You have watched me for my entire life, so you must already know what I'm going to tell you. I am completely inexperienced in love. So, when you close yourself from me, I do not know why. You must tell me, guide me. When I touch your wings you act as if you are in pain, yet yesterday you begged me not to stop touching you. I don't understand, but I'd like to—I need to. Help me to understand, husband."

The endearment shook him to his soul. He was her husband. She was his wife. A sense of belonging settled over him. In gaining her, he had found his place in the world and no force would ever truly part them.

"My wings are an extension of my deepest emotions. They come to me from my father's blood, so they react with an elemental fierceness that is not always easy to control. When you touch them you touch what is most base about me."

"Do you think your desire for me is base?"

"No! Of course not. But sometimes the depth of it overwhelms me. When you awaken my need for you, the dark lust that pulses through the demon in my blood stirs, too. It can be raw and dangerous."

She thought of the bloodlust of the Fomorians and that Lochlan had admitted to her that the desire to drink her blood lurked within him. Elphame looked steadily into his haunted eyes; she saw no demon there, only the man who had been fashioned as her lifemate. "I believe your love for me is stronger than the demon within you."

He was wearing a simple, undyed cotton shirt. Her eyes stayed on his as she unlaced it and he pulled it roughly from his chest. The breath caught in her throat at his lithe beauty.

Slowly, she unpinned the chieftain's brooch that held her plaid in place and unwrapped the soft fabric from around her body. She pulled her fine linen blouse over her head. The cool spring night touched her naked skin, sending a delicious chill through her.

Except for his wings, Lochlan remained very still.

Pressing the tips of her breasts against the heat of his chest, Elphame reached over his shoulder to stroke his wing, letting her fingers caress the softness that made her think of velvet and cream. He shuddered, and took her into his arms. She molded herself against him, accepting his ferocious kiss. Her arms reached around him and she found the place where his wings met his body and let her fingers play a teasing game there, stroking and kneading and even allowing her fingernails to rake along his back.

With a sudden motion, Lochlan lifted her and then lay her back against the soft bed of grass and MacCallan plaid. He crouched beside her, wings unfurled, while he tried to regain control of his seething emotions. She reached for him, wanting to feel his body against hers.

He intercepted her hand, laughing breathlessly.

"Slowly, my heart. Let me explore you. I want to learn your marvelous body."

She moaned as his palm found her taut nipple.

"Yes—" his voice was thick with desire "—you are my Siren's call, and I would follow you even if it led to my death." As he spoke the word *death* his fingers traced the slash that puckered the soft skin of her waist. "But I will never allow anything to harm you. I make that pledge with my life and I will defend it with the last drop of my blood."

It won't come to that, Elphame thought fiercely. Not now. Both of them would be fine. Her clan had to accept him. Then all thoughts but the heat of his caresses scattered from her mind as his hand moved from the curve of her waist to meet the smooth coat that covered her lower body.

"You are an indescribable softness," he whispered huskily as he caressed her thigh, "merged with sleek strength. I have wondered all these years what it would feel like to touch you, and to be touched by you in turn, never really believing that I would get a chance to know." Lochlan stroked the inside of her auburn-coated thigh. "It was why I finally found my way to you. I could not bear the thought of being without you any longer."

He slid his hand up until he found the core of her wet heat. Elphame moaned and moved her hips restlessly. His wings pulsed with life and the dark blood of his father surged hot and hard through his body. For an instant he saw himself violently taking her, pounding her against the ground while he fed from her neck in time to her screams, which echoed into the night.

No! Lochlan's rational mind rebelled against the image and he wrenched himself away from her body. Breathing in ragged gulps, he sat beside her, trembling, with his head buried in his hands as pain cascaded through his mind.

This time it was she who knelt beside him. Elphame stroked his hair and murmured wordless sounds of comfort. When his wings began to close, she pulled his hands gently from his face.

"What is it you fear? Why do you pull yourself away from me?"

He looked into her clear, guileless eyes. What would she do if she knew that he had followed not just his heart to her, but that he had also followed a dark prophecy that demanded her blood? Would it matter to her that he had decided to betray his people and to refuse the Prophecy?

"Talk to me, Lochlan. Is it that you regret the handfast?"

"No!" he cried. "Never! It is you who should feel regret. I am a demon, barely able to control my impulses. I cannot make love to you without seeing violence and blood. And it fuels my lust, Elphame. Do you understand? Even as I love you and desire you above all things, my dark heritage yearns to tear and taste and ravage you."

Elphame carefully controlled the finger of fear his words caused. How she reacted now would set their future. She could not love him without trusting him. Lochlan was her choice. If he was not worthy of her, not worthy of her trust, would he be in such agony now? Elphame didn't think so. If he truly was a demon, there would be no struggle to retain his humanity—he would relinquish his soul to darkness. She believed in him; she had to.

"When you make love to me, you think dark, violent thoughts?" Elphame asked.

"Yes." His voice broke. "I cannot stop it."

Elphame rose to her feet and Lochlan knew with a drowning sense of grief that she was going to leave him.

"Then *I* will simply have to make love to *you*."

Instead of turning from him, she straddled his legs and with a fluid, sensuous grace sank down onto his lap. Elphame pulled him to her with infinite gentleness, and kissed his lips and caressed the underside of his wings while they pulsed, instantly beginning to fill once again with his desire.

"Elphame, you don't know—"

"Shhh," she pressed a finger against his lips, stilling his words as she worked the tie on his pants and pulled his erection free.

He stopped breathing as she explored his hardness, and when she lifted herself to place his throbbing tip against her wetness, he could only brace his hands against the grassy earth and fight the urge to sink his fingers into her soft waist and impale her.

"Open your eyes, husband. Look at me."

He opened his eyes to meet her luminous gaze as she sheathed his hardness within her. And all he saw was her, his wife, his heart—the visions of bloodlust abated as her soft heat enveloped him and she began to move up and down with ex-cruciating slowness.

She did have to stretch to accept him, but after the initial shock of feeling him enter her body, the desire that had been simmering in her dreams and fantasies ignited. She rocked against him, feeling the tension build. When Lochlan thrust up to meet her, Elphame threw back her head and increased her body's tempo. Over them, she saw that Lochlan's wings stretched fully erect. They blotted out the sky and the forest, making him her entire world. When he cried her name as his hot seed shot into her, Elphame rocked forward and held him close while her own body exploded in a spasm of release.

They were very quiet as they made their way back to the entrance of the tunnel. The sky was already beginning to lighten. Elphame could hardly believe that so much of the night had passed. It had seemed that she had only spent a brief moment in his arms. She tightened her grip on his hand. He smiled and lifted her palm to his lips.

"You're sure that I did not hurt you?" he asked again.

"Quite sure. Now stop asking me. I am not a delicate fainting maiden." Her lips twitched. "Actually, I'm not a maiden at all anymore."

"It is such a miracle to me. I did not think I could ever control…" He paused, clenching his jaw as he remembered the hunks of grass and dirt he had ripped from the earth during his orgasm. What if his hands had not been resting against the ground? What if they had been on the curve of her waist, or the swell of her breast, or the delicate indention of her neck?

"Lochlan." She spoke his name sharply, deliberately breaking through the self-loathing that was written on his face. "Nothing bad happened." She touched his cheek. "Can you not just enjoy the pleasure we shared?"

He pulled her into his arms, resting his forehead against hers. "Forgive me, my heart. It is just that the demons are within me, so it is difficult not to do constant battle with them. The truth is that you have brought me great happiness tonight, and I should not allow anything to taint that."

"You haven't tainted it. Nothing could taint tonight."

Lochlan bent to kiss her, hoping desperately that her words were true. They walked on into the forest until they came to the upturned lip of ground that disguised the entrance to the tunnel. The two lovers halted before it.

"Let me go with you," Lochlan said suddenly, cupping her face in his hand. "We are mated, and I have sworn my oath to you. Surely we can make them see that my love for you is stronger than the blood of my father."

Elphame covered his hands with hers. "And so I just thrust this marriage on my family as if they are so unimportant to me that I do not respect their right to know before strangers? Lochlan, it would wound me terribly if Cuchulainn suddenly announced that he had chosen a mate without first taking me into his confidence. Do you understand that I cannot do that?"

"You love your family very much. I understand that."

"It's not just about love. It's about trust and respect and loyalty. And it is nothing less than I have pledged to give you."

"I know that, my heart. It is just that I do not know how I will bear being parted from you."

"I'll send for my parents. When they arrive I will tell them and Cuchulainn together. Then we will all figure out how to explain us to the rest of Partholon." Elphame's voice sounded much more confident than she felt.

"How long?"

"I'll loose the carrier pigeon today. Once she gets the message, Mama will make certain that they waste no time in coming. She'll be thrilled that I asked them to come to Mac-Callan Castle—she's probably been brooding about not being involved in the decorating and she'll come bearing wagonloads of beautiful, shimmery things." Elphame's smile reflected the love she felt for her mother. "It will only be seven days, perhaps a little longer." She searched his eyes for understanding.

"I have waited years for you—a few days more is really a little thing to ask."

Elphame hugged him. "I'll try to come every night. You will be here, won't you?"

"Always, my heart," he said into her hair, "always."

Reluctantly, Elphame left his arms. She didn't look back as she climbed down into the tunnel, but she felt him behind her, watching as she left him. The torch sputtered and cast a feeble light that reflected her sadness. Wearily, she reentered her chamber and closed the secret door. As she curled into the thick comforter she could still smell her husband's scent where it lingered on her skin like a fleeting caress.

Before sleep enfolded her, Elphame sent a heartfelt prayer to her Goddess. *Please, Epona, help them to see the man and not the demon.*

27

BRENNA TOLD HERSELF sternly that it was perfectly natural that she would want to check on her unusual new patient so early. It didn't matter that the gray of predawn was just beginning to lighten, and that the night's mist still hung across the castle ground like a slate-colored curtain. The wolf cub was young and had been through a terrible ordeal. Actually, she should not have left the small creature alone with Cuchulainn. What did the warrior know about caring for something so fragile? That was why her sleep had been so troubled. She was worried about the cub. It was not because Cuchulainn haunted her mind.

His tent was silent, but she could see the flickering shadows thrown against the canvas sides by a lighted candle.

"Cuchulainn?" Brenna hesitated, her hand on the tent flap. No answer.

"Hello? Cuchulainn?" she said a little louder and thought

she heard a muffled sound in response. She pushed aside the flap and ducked into the tent.

Brenna wrinkled her noise. The lumpy form on the narrow bed moved, drawing Brenna's eyes. Cuchulainn lay on his back, sleeping soundly with a blanket thrown haphazardly across his lower body. His tunic gaped, so that the candlelight caught the deep auburn hair that gleamed on his chest. The sight of it intrigued Brenna, which she knew was ridiculous. She'd seen men's bare chests before—many times. Of course none of those men had been Cuchulainn, and not one of them had ever looked at her like he had, blatantly proclaiming that it was the scarred Healer he was interested in, and not the beautiful, willing cook. Brenna's stomach fluttered at the memory. Then a movement caught her eye. The cub made a mewing, puppyish noise. It was wrapped around the warrior's neck like a filthy scarf. One of Cuchulainn's hands dangled from the side of the bed, the other rested on the cub's body.

Brenna tried not to smile at the sight, and failed miserably.

She tiptoed over to the table, frowning at the mess. Cheese-cloth lay in scattered, milky heaps. She picked up a linen rag and sniffed it suspiciously, grimacing at its urine-soaked odor. She'd have to come back later with a scrub bucket. How could one man and one small wolf make such a mess? Brenna planted her hands on her hips, shook her head, and wondered if all the milk was gone because he'd gotten it inside the cub, or because he'd spilled it all over the tent. She glanced at his sleeping form. All over the tent *and* himself, she amended silently.

The cub stirred and Brenna sighed. She'd fetch more milk from the kitchen—and have a fresh pitcher of water brought to the tent with clean linens. The cub was bound to wake her surrogate parent soon, and, since she was obviously still very much alive, she would be hungry. Brenna smiled. The surro-

gate would, no doubt, be hungry, too. She gathered some of
the filthy rags. Bringing him something to eat would be no
different than bringing the cub milk. She was simply looking
after her responsibilities as the clan's Healer. It was only logical
that the health of her Chieftain's brother should be important
to her. As if they had a will of their own, her eyes slid to the
bed.

He was awake and watching her with a boyish half smile.

"Good morning," he whispered.

She wiped her hands nervously on her apron and marched
purposefully to him, ignoring his sleepy state of tousled
undress, ignoring the unique turquoise color of his eyes,
ignoring how his smile made her feel dizzy and off balance.

"Good. Now that you're awake I can examine the cub
and—"

Catching hold of her wrist he stopped her words.

"Let Fand sleep," he said softly.

Brenna lowered her voice to match his. "You named her
Fand?" As if answering for him, the cub nosed Cu's neck and
grunted before settling back into sleep.

"Yes, she was, after all, my legendary namesake's fairy wife."
His eyes sparkled. "After the intimate night she and I just
spent together, I thought it appropriate."

Brenna had to smile at him. His fingers slipped down her
wrist so that he was holding her hand.

"I was dreaming about you," Cuchulainn said.

"Stop—"

He kept talking as if she hadn't tried to speak.

"We were old. Your hair was all white and I was stooped
and lame." He grinned. "You will age better than I. But it is
of little matter. We were surrounded by our children and our
children's children. And playing in and amongst them all were
dozens of wolf cubs." He stifled his laughter when Fand

growled. "Fand is a jealous girl," he whispered, and winked at Brenna.

"Cuchulainn, please stop playing—"

This time when he interrupted her, his eyes flashed and all teasing humor had fled his expressive face.

"Do not say that I am playing games with you!"

He dropped her hand and gently scooped the sleeping cub from his chest, nesting her in the pillow that was still warm from his body. When he stood, he reclaimed Brenna's hand and pulled her out of the tent. The misty morning was dark and quiet, and Cuchulainn pitched his voice low, so that he would not wake those workers who still slept in the surrounding tents.

"What have I done to lead you to believe that I am the kind of man who has so little honor that he would use a maiden as a plaything?"

"Th-the other night. The dancing..." she stuttered.

"I apologized for that," he said through teeth clenched in frustration. "My behavior was stupid and insensitive, but it was *not* my typical behavior. I am a warrior whose reputation is known throughout Partholon. When has it been said that I am without honor?"

"It hasn't," she said quickly. "Your honor has never been in question."

"Hasn't it?" he exploded. Cuchulainn flung his hands up. "You say I'm playing with your feelings, using you, pretending to want you. How is that not questioning my honor?" With an effort he brought his voice under control. "I don't mean to shout at you. I don't want to drive you away from me. By the Goddess! Where you're concerned I seem to have lost the ability for rational conversation or thought." He put his hands on her shoulders and squeezed, effectively anchoring her in front of him. "Brenna, I would like to court you. Officially.

If you tell me how to contact your father, I will formally ask his permission to do so."

"My father is dead," Brenna said through numbed lips.

Cuchulainn's face softened. "Your mother then. I will ask her."

"She is dead, too. I have no family."

Cuchulainn bowed his head as a tide of feeling engulfed him. What terrible pain must fill her past. No more, he promised himself. He would never let anything hurt her again. When he raised his head, his eyes were bright with the depth of his emotions.

"Then your family is our Clan. The MacCallan and I have already discussed my intentions, and, though I don't believe she thinks I deserve you, I am sure she will grant me permission to court you."

"Elphame knows? You talked about me with her?"

"Of course. She's my sister."

"No! This can't be—this isn't possible." Brenna blinked rapidly, like she was having trouble focusing.

Cuchulainn could feel her body trembling under his hands, and suddenly he had a terrible, sick feeling in his gut. What if her reluctance wasn't about her scars or her shyness? What if she really didn't want him?

"Brenna, I would not force my love on you, not if you do not desire me in return. If you do not desire me, all you need do is to tell me, and I give you my word that though it will pain me, I will leave you in peace."

She stared at him. "Love? Look at me, Cuchulainn! I'm damaged. And it doesn't end at my face." She passed her hand from her scarred neck, over her breast, and down to her waist, clearly showing him the wide path of her scars.

Moving carefully, he lifted one hand from her shoulder. With a featherlike caress, he traced the path her hand had just traveled. Slowly, he touched the puckered scars that covered the right side of her face. When she made no move to stop him, he let his fingertips move over her neck, softly skim the material that covered her breast, and, finally, come to rest on the curve of her hip.

"How could you believe that you are undesirable? When I look at you I see the first woman to ever befriend my sister. I see the Healer, who has the heart of a warrior. And I see the delicate beauty of the maiden who fills my waking thoughts with desire for her, and my dreams with visions of our future."

"Cuchulainn, there has been so much loss in my life. I don't know if I can risk any more."

"That's all it is?" Relief flooded Cuchulainn. "It's not that you don't want me?"

"I want you."

Her voice was not that of a shy maiden. Once more, she was the Healer. Her words were strong and sure. Cu smiled and started to pull her into his arms, but her command stopped him short.

"No, I'm not finished. I admit that I want you, but I don't know if I'm willing to let you into my heart. If I do, and then lose you, I fear it would leave a wound from which I might never recover."

His mind raced around in panic. What could he say? What could he do to reassure her? Drawing a deep breath, he held open his hands.

"I can only pledge my word to you. If you do not trust it to be enough, then nothing I ever do or say would be enough to reassure you of my love. You must choose to believe in me, Brenna."

She studied the warrior. It was her choice—was she strong enough to make it? Her eyes widened. That really was her answer; the one thing she knew beyond doubt about herself was that she could trust her strength. She had been tested by fire and had triumphed.

"I choose to believe in you, Cuchulainn," she said slowly and distinctly. And then she smiled her lopsided smile at his stunned look.

Cuchulainn whooped and lifted her into his arms. "I am going to be sure that you never lose me."

He set her on her feet, but kept his arms around her. It felt so indescribably good just to stand there, holding her body against his. No woman had ever felt so right in his arms. He hadn't even kissed her yet, and Brenna had already given him more than any of the beautiful young women with whom he had frittered away so much of his time.

When he felt her shoulders shaking, he thought his heart would break. Didn't she believe him? Couldn't she see that he would never hurt her?

"What is it, love?" He leaned back just enough so that he could see her face, and was surprised to see her eyes sparkling with the laughter that was soundlessly shaking her body.

"Oh, Cu," she said through giggles. "You smell like puppy urine and old milk."

Cuchulainn scowled at her with pretended severity. "Fand is not a puppy. She's a wolf."

As if to second his words, there came from inside the tent a whimpering that almost instantly changed into a youthful version of the mournful howl of a wolf.

"Did I mention that you will have to share me with Fand?" Cuchulainn said.

The pitiful howl increased in volume.

"I'll get more milk." Brenna was already turning away, but Cuchulainn wasn't ready to relinquish his grip on her shoulders.

"You will return?"

She looked into the eyes that would eternally remind her of Epona's altar and the magic of second chances.

"Yes, Cuchulainn. I will return."

He dropped his hands from her shoulders so that she could hurry away, but she felt him watch her as she disappeared into the pre-morning mist.

"Soon!" he called after her, the urgency in his voice punctuated by the pitiful howls echoing from his tent.

The castle was quiet, but as Brenna rushed through the Great Hall and into the cook's entrance to the kitchen, she was quickly surrounded by the sounds and scents of an awakening castle. The kitchen was a hub of activity and smelled deliciously of freshly baked bread. Trying to stay out of the way, Brenna helped herself to a pitcher from the neatly arranged cupboard and dunked it in the barrel of fresh milk.

"Good morn to ye, Healer," Wynne called. Several of her assistants nodded friendly welcomes.

"Good—good morning," Brenna said a little breathlessly. She hadn't forgotten Wynne's beauty, but seeing her there, with her fiery hair pulled up into a mass of curls that spilled around her perfect face, Brenna's heart faltered.

How could Cu choose her over this vivacious young woman?

"Are ye gettin' milk for the warrior's beastie?"

"Yes." Brenna snapped the word. She hadn't meant to speak so sharply, but the memory of Wynne's body pressed against Cuchulainn's as they moved together to the beat of the drums suddenly had her feeling sick and uncertain. And, worse, she could feel the cook's sharp gaze studying her knowingly.

"There be fresh bread and a nice hunk of cheese if the two of ye have mind to break yer fast after feedin' the creature."

"Thank you, I'll add it to the tray," Brenna said quickly, wanting only to get out of the kitchen. Wynne's assistants, the same women who had been in the garden the day before, had paused in their work to watch the exchange between them.

"I'll aid ye," Wynne said, suddenly appearing at Brenna's side. With precise, industrious movements, the cook filled a basket with a loaf of still warm bread, a wedge of fragrant yellow cheese and several slices of cold meat. All of which she loaded onto Brenna's tray after rustling through a pantry and adding a wineskin to the meal.

Surprised, Brenna raised her head and looked directly at the beautiful young cook, who was studying her with large, emerald-colored eyes.

"I wish ye joy, Brenna. The warrior has chosen well."

Brenna flushed with unexpected pleasure. Foolishly, she couldn't do much more than smile and breathe, "Thank you."

Wynne winked at her. "Women must watch out for one another. The next time I get the ague, I'll be expectin' one of yer legendary horrid potions to put me back to sorts. Now, run along and be sure ye eat plenty, because Brenna, lass, ye may be needin' yer strength."

Smiling and blushing, Brenna carried her loaded tray from the kitchen, snagging some fresh linens from the basket near the door as the women laughed and called out bawdy encouragement.

Never in her life would she have thought it possible. They accepted her. They included her. And Cuchulainn desired her. The joy that moved in her chest was a small, newly fledged bird just beginning to spread its wings and soar from the secret place in her heart.

He gave her a haggard smile when she entered the tent.

"Fand's hungry," he said, grimacing as the cub suckled at his finger and growled in displeasure at receiving nothing for her efforts.

"If she feels well enough to be angry at you, I think I can safely say that she will live."

Brenna filled the teat while Cuchulainn grappled with the wriggling ball of cub. As the cub latched onto the milky ball of cloth, she suddenly wished for a wound she could tend or an arm she could set.

"Will you sit by me, Brenna?" Cuchulainn nodded at the spot beside him on the narrow bed.

Brenna sat, clutching her hands together to hide their trembling. For a little while the only sound in the tent was Fand, noisily sucking and making small, puppyish grunts. Brenna watched the cub, noting the gentle way Cuchulainn's hands held her. Every so often he would stroke the cub and mutter soft words of encouragement.

"It's just me, you know," Cu said, using the same soothing tone of voice with Brenna as he did with the small wolf.

"Just you?" she repeated, feeling incredibly stupid.

"Yes. It's the same me who you ordered around the night El was injured. It's the same me whose face you can read the instant anything goes wrong with any of our clan. The same me you've worked side by side with to bring our home alive again." He smiled and shifted his body so that their shoulders and the sides of their legs were touching. "I'll tell you a secret. For all of my rakish ways you, my sweet Healer, scare me almost speechless."

Disbelieving, Brenna shook her head. "That makes no sense."

"I've told you a secret—a rather embarrassing one at that. Now it's your turn."

She looked up at him. Her logical mind cried to protect herself—don't open to him—don't say anything. But his eyes rested on her, warm and expectant, and the hope that had fledged within her breast stirred again, beating away her fear.

"Your eyes are the same color as two gifts that were given to me by Epona." Her voice sounded soft and a little unsure, but she held his gaze and did not veil her face with her hair.

"Gifts from Epona? What are they?"

"A turquoise stone and the feather from a bird's wing." Saying it aloud suddenly made it sound trivial, and she could feel her face heating with embarrassment, but Cuchulainn didn't laugh or tease her.

"Will you show me someday?"

Brenna nodded. How could one simple question make her feel so amazingly happy?

The cub had finally slowed its ravenous suckling. Cu glanced at her.

"Please tell me that it is safe to wash this beast now."

She looked at Fand. She was curled against Cuchulainn, belly tightly distended, milk dribbling from the side of her mouth. Then her gaze shifted to Cuchulainn. His hair was a tangled mess and there was sleep in the corners of his eyes. The linen shirt that was unlaced and showed a broad expanse of his chest was stained and crusty with milk and waste from the cub, as was the kilt that was wrapped haphazardly around him. Warrior and cub desperately needed bathing.

"As your Healer I can say with great surety that you may bathe Fand." She wrinkled her nose at both of them.

Cuchulainn quirked an eyebrow up. "Though I sometimes appear to be a bumbling fool in your presence, even I can tell that my avowed intention to court you would have a much better chance of success if I didn't reek of wolf urine. Would you say that you agree?"

Brenna's stomach did a little flip-roll. "Yes."

"Good!" he said, standing so suddenly that Fand made a grumpy, *murrugh* sound. Cu hushed the cub by tucking her snugly within his shirt. "You brought food?" He eyed the basket and the wine. "Excellent." Then he turned and rifled through the chest that sat at the foot of the bed from which he quickly pulled out a clean kilt and shirt. Satisfied, he grabbed the basket of food and laid the fresh linens over it. Then he held out his free hand to the staring Brenna.

"Well, you must come with us," he said. "It's too early to be barging in on my sister. As much as I enjoy tormenting her, nothing puts El in as foul a mood as having her sleep interrupted. And I'll need her good humor later today when I formally ask her permission to court you—so using her bathing chamber is out. Fand and I could bathe in a basin." He peered down at the filthy cub nestled against his skin. "But in truth I do not think that would suffice." Absently, he scratched his head and muttered, "I hope the beast hasn't given me fleas." Then his face broke into a boyish grin. "So you will simply have to show me to the bathing pool that you and Brighid and El used."

Brenna stared at him, not sure what to say. For all of her avowed strength, she could still feel her fear of taking this amazing, surprising chance fighting with her longing for the warrior.

Cuchulainn closed the small space between them and took her hand, pulling her to her feet.

"Would you rather not spend time alone with me, Brenna?"

Brenna swallowed and heard herself speak the truth. "I'm afraid."

He lifted her hand to his face, and held it against his cheek while he gazed steadily into her eyes. "So am I, love."

The honesty of his answer made her decision infinitely easier. She let her breath out in a rush. "Then we'll be afraid together."

28

THE MIST WAS still thick and Brenna worried about not being able to find the pool, but when the road curved just so near the oddly shaped pine she knew instantly that that was the place she and her two friends had entered the forest. And, sure enough, after only a few paces she could hear the musical sound of water tripping down the three-tiered fall made of time-smoothed rocks.

The fog was thicker around the pool, and it seemed to Brenna as if Epona had conveniently veiled them from the prying eyes of the world.

"It looks cold," Cuchulainn said.

Fand had wriggled about until her head was sticking from the opening in the warrior's shirt, and she looked around with bright eyes, snuffling the air and making small, baby sounds.

"I remember it as being refreshing." Brenna smiled at him. Sometimes he sounded just like his sister.

"Hrumph," he said. Resolutely, he put the food-filled basket on a nearby rock and then lifted the cub from his shirt. "Well, the sooner I get this over with, the sooner I can eat." He handed Fand to the surprised Brenna, who held the squirming, growling cub a little uncertainly.

"Cuchulainn, I really think it'd be better if you bathed her. She's much more comfortable with you."

Cu nodded while he unwrapped his kilt. "Just hold her for me while I get undressed."

Undressed...the word echoed through Brenna's mind causing her thoughts to skitter around like darting birds. *Well, what did you think, Brenna,* said the rationally functioning part of her brain. *That he was going to bathe fully clothed?* Honestly, she hadn't thought about it until then. Until he unwrapped his kilt, kicked off his leather shoes, and...

...paused, before pulling off the shirt that covered him to the top of his thighs—the only thing left that covered him. He was watching her with a small, half smile teasing his lips.

"If my nakedness makes you uncomfortable, you can close your eyes. I'll take Fand and then tell you when I'm in the water so that it's safe for you to open them."

"It makes me uncomfortable," Brenna admitted. "But I don't want to close my eyes."

Cuchulainn's answering grin was filled with the rakish charm for which the warrior was so well known. He was still grinning when he pulled the shirt over his head and, naked, retrieved the cub and plunged with noisy splashing and cursing into the pool.

She just stood there and stared after him, thinking that the sight of his broad, naked back and his tight buttocks might forever be burned into her eyes.

"Brenna!" he called over the sound of Fand's whining protests at being submerged in the cold water. "Could you crush up some of that soapstone? Water alone—no matter how cold—cannot wash away all of this filth."

Brenna nodded and got busy finding a fist-sized rock which she could use to break up the soft stone that littered the edge of the pool. Of course she almost crushed several fingers along with the soapstone because she couldn't seem to keep her eyes from traveling to the pool.

"It's ready," she said, trying to sound nonchalant about crushing up soap for a naked warrior who had just declared his intention to woo her into being his lover.

He splashed toward her, exposing more and more of his body with each stride. Brenna scooped the soapstone into the cup her joined hands made and tried not to let her eyes wander down his emerging body—unsuccessfully. Grinning, he stood in front of her. The water covered him only to his knees. He cradled the sodden cub in his arms while he shivered and looked a little blue around the lips, but his smile was warm, mischievous, and heart-melting. He leaned toward her.

"My hands are full. Can you help me, love?" he asked, eyes sparkling.

Feeling very much as if she was moving through a delightfully naughty dream, Brenna sprinkled a liberal amount of soapstone on the complaining cub. Cu began working the powder into bubbles, but Brenna's eyes couldn't stay on the cub. They kept returning to the naked body of the warrior who stood so close to her. Before the logical part of her mind, which had dictated her very reasonable and responsible behavior for the past decade, could interfere, Brenna reached up and dribbled the soapstone over his chest and shoulders. With soft, hesitant strokes, she concentrated on rubbing the soap across his chest, reaching up and around the squirming cub. Cuchulainn didn't move, except to shift Fand in his arms so that she could have better access to his body.

Brenna finally looked up to meet his eyes.

"You could join me, love. It wouldn't be so very cold, with

the water covering us both and the warmth of your naked skin against mine."

She wanted to; she wanted to badly. But when she thought about baring her flawed body beside his—that expanse of muscle which was covered with perfect, golden skin—her heart skittered into her throat, leaving the taste of fear thick in her mouth.

"I can't," she whispered, praying that he wouldn't turn from her and reject her as a coward.

"Another time then, love. Another time. And we will have plenty of time," he said with gentle surety. "Until then you'd better soap my hair as well. Fleas make for uncomfortable courting partners." He sank to his knees so that Brenna could scoop more soapstone and work it into the thickness of his hair.

Brenna washed his hair while he scrubbed and admonished and coaxed the whimpering, squirming cub, railing about her lack of manners and gratitude. She laughed at their antics and tried to keep the gritty bubbles from Cu's eyes while attempting to stay semidry herself.

She couldn't remember ever feeling such happiness.

"Time to rinse, my girl," he told the cub, and, holding the growling wolf tightly against his naked chest, he stood, winked through soap bubbles at Brenna, and with a whoop dived into the center of the chilly pool.

Brenna shook her head at them as they submerged, splashing loudly, then got out and started drying. Everything the warrior did was bigger than life. An aura followed Cuchulainn—an aura that was filled with power and the promise of the ability to achieve the impossible. And Brenna was beginning to believe that it was so, that the impossible had happened. Her deepest, most hidden desire had been answered. Cuchulainn had chosen her.

"I'm starving," he said, laying one of the dry lengths of cloth on the forest floor. Grabbing the basket he motioned for Brenna to join him.

"You take your fairy wolf. I'll be in charge of the food." She handed the cub back to Cuchulainn, who grimaced, but tucked her—damp towel and all—inside his fresh tunic.

Brenna glanced slantwise at him, watching him try to position the cub comfortably as she unloaded their fare. In her best Healer's voice she said, "Now you know just a little about how a woman feels when she carries a child inside her body for all those long phases of the moon."

Cuchulainn flopped full-length on his side, finally getting the cub arranged so that she quit her restless squirming and settled sleepily against him. Then he turned his full attention to Brenna.

"A child, huh? You wish to speak of having children so soon?" He scratched his chin as if considering. "Mother will certainly be pleased."

Brenna stopped midmotion of passing him a piece of bread and a hunk of cheese. She felt her face flame with heat and she knew that the flush of the unharmed side of her face only called more attention to her ugly scars. Out of long habit, she ducked her head, letting her hair veil her shame.

"No, Brenna!" Cuchulainn leaned forward, put one finger under her chin and gently lifted her face. "Do not hide from me."

"That's not what I meant. I—I was just…" Her words trailed off as she met his steady gaze. She drew a deep breath, and again chose to tell him the truth. "I'm ugly when I blush. I didn't want you to see me."

And then Cuchulainn did something totally unexpected. He didn't offer platitudes to try and cover the awkwardness of the moment, or to disavow her feelings. He simply leaned closer to her and brushed his lips against hers. The kiss was gentle, but Cu slid his hand from her chin to the back of her neck and held her mouth against his so that he could slowly deepen the kiss. Brenna didn't think about the fact that his hand was resting on the scarred side of her neck; she didn't think about how

furiously she must be blushing; she didn't think about his desire
for her being impossible. She just closed her eyes and leaned
into him. When they finally parted, both of them were a little
breathless and Cuchulainn was gazing at her with lust-filled
eyes.

"I like your blush." His voice was husky. "It reminds me that
I'm not the only one of us who is nervous."

"You're not," she said, swallowing a small bubble of giddy
laughter.

"Would you promise me something, Brenna?"

She nodded, thinking that there was little she could deny
this man.

"Promise me that you will not turn from me or hide yourself
from me again. Promise me that you will trust me not to hurt
you."

Brenna looked deeply into his magical eyes. Her own eyes
widened with surprise as she understood what she glimpsed
there—vulnerability. *She* could hurt *him* with her answer. He
had never bared his heart to any woman before as he was
baring himself to her now.

"It won't be easy, but I promise you that I will not turn from
you or hide myself from you again."

"Thank you, Brenna, for the gift of your trust. I will not
misuse it." He kissed her scarred cheek while she held very
still. And then, as if kissing her was something he did every
day, he smiled and took the bread and cheese from her unresisting hand. "I should eat. I have to face my sister soon.
That's best done on a full stomach."

Brenna took sliced meat from the basket and layered it on
another piece of bread and cheese.

"Oh," he added a little sheepishly. "Just so you know. I'll be
calling for my parents so that they can meet you, too. We might
as well get it over with." He jerked his head over his shoulder

at the pool of cold water. "It won't be much worse than diving into that."

Brenna's heart thudded. "I've met your father. He is a great shaman."

"That he is," Cu said through healthy bites.

"But I've never met Epona's Beloved. I hear she is very beautiful."

"She is almost as beautiful as the young Healer I intend to wed."

"Ooh!" The air left Brenna's lungs and she felt a great, dizzying sense of delight mixed with a sickening tightening of her stomach.

Cuchulainn grinned. "Don't worry, love. My mother has been trying to see me happily wed for years. She will love you." Then, concerned at how pale she'd suddenly become he sobered and leaned forward to whisper against her lips, "And that is my promise to you."

The morning mist showed no sign of dissipating as Cuchulainn and Brenna followed the road back to the castle. They walked slowly, holding hands and letting their arms brush intimately against one another. Brenna thought the grayness of the day was magical. It seemed that the gate to the spirit realm had been left ajar for her and she had moved easily from one world to another, bringing Cuchulainn with her. Instead of finding it frightening, the idea that the spirit realm was embracing her was somehow comforting. She was so content that she didn't notice when Cuchulainn narrowed his eyes and began peering suspiciously into the fog-cloaked forest.

A vague, nameless Feeling of unease nagged at Cuchulainn's mind, and he loathed it. Could the damned otherworldly burden not leave him in peace? Elphame was safe back at the castle. Brenna walked happily by his side. The forest held nothing more evil than an occasional bad-tempered boar. Yet he suddenly had a skin-crawling Feeling of foreboding—and the Feeling was emanating from the forest, much like the premonition he'd had before Elphame's accident. Perhaps his sister was contemplating another run. If that was the case, he'd simply keep her from it. She could be reasoned with—occasionally—and it was too soon after her accident for her to engage in strenuous exercise.

A thought passed through his mind, so brief that his conscious barely acknowledged it. It whispered a reminder of what happened when humans rejected gifts given by the gods.

Brenna laughed as they rounded a curve in the road and startled a squirrel who jumped and then chattered at them noisily.

"Oh, silly thing! We won't harm you," Brenna said.

That's what he was being, Cuchulainn thought with disgust, a squirrel allowing senseless fears to rule him. He forced his shoulders to relax and refocused his attention on the lovely woman who walked so happily by his side. She was his future, not some nameless, faceless Feeling. He had chosen to live with his feet planted firmly in reality—he'd leave magic and the realm of the spirits to his sister.

29

ELPHAME CROSSED THE Main Courtyard, calling good mornings in response to the workers who greeted her. She stopped by the gaily tinkling fountain. She'd have to remember to commission Danann to carve a stone bench so that she could sit and enjoy the beauty right here, in the heart of her castle. The gray morning cast a reluctant light through the unfinished roof, but it could not dim the brightness that glowed within her. Her smile reflected her secret joy, and she did not notice that several men who were making their way to the Great Hall for breakfast lost the thread of their conversation to stare, openmouthed at her brilliant beauty. Elphame trailed her fingers through the fountain's water, thinking of how long she had had to soak in her bathing pool that morning to rid her body of the unfamiliar tenderness that lingered from the night's lovemaking.

Lochlan… She wanted to shout his name aloud and tell all of Partholon that she loved and was loved in kind. That it had really happened—Epona had fashioned a lifemate for her; she would not have to live her life as a solitary creature, filling her days with the reflection of other people's love.

Clan MacCallan had to accept him as her mate. And if they didn't? Would she be willing to forsake her position as Chieftain and return to the Wastelands with her lover? The thought sent a shiver through her blood. With a sigh, she sat on the lip of the fountain's basin and stared up at marble girl she so closely resembled.

"What would you do if you were torn between two worlds?" she whispered.

"Sister-mine!"

Cuchulainn's blaring voice startled El, but the frown she turned on him quickly changed to a bright smile when she saw that Brenna walked at his side, her hand within his. Cu's hair looked damp and there was a cub-sized lump within his tunic.

"Good morning, Elphame," Brenna said.

El could tell by the flush that darkened the unscarred side of the Healer's face that her emotions were running high—she could well imagine how nerve-racking it must be for her. Much like Elphame, Brenna had never expected to find love, and when she had, it had come from a most unusual place. It was—to say the least—a turn of events that took some getting used to.

"Good morning, Brenna," she said warmly. Then her eyes glinted with humor. "It is good to see you, even if you have taken to spending time with questionable individuals and wild animals."

"Be serious, El," Cuchulainn said. "She'll think you really mean it."

Elphame grinned at Brenna. "I do mean it."

Brenna smiled back at her, and her face lost some of its nervous color.

Cuchulainn cleared his throat and then, to his sister's

surprise, he dropped Brenna's hand and quickly covered the space between them to kneel on one knee in front of her. She quirked an eyebrow at him, but, noting his somber expression, she said nothing, waiting for his next move.

"Elphame, I come to formally ask your permission as Chieftain of Clan MacCallan to court your Healer, Brenna. You should know that I do so with the honorable intention of marriage."

Elphame wanted to shout with joy and throw her arms around her brother, but she would not dishonor the solemnity of his request, nor would she show disrespect to her friend who stood so silently waiting for the answer that would prove that she was either accepted or rejected, once and for all. Elphame's gaze met Brenna's.

"Have you no living mother or father to whom Cuchulainn could take his suit?"

"No. I was the only child of my parents. They have been dead for a decade."

"Then it is proper as The MacCallan that I stand in their stead. Brenna, do you willingly accept Cuchulainn's suit? And, before you answer know that I will support you, no matter your choice." She didn't need to glance at her brother to feel his scowl.

Brenna's doelike eyes shifted from her Chieftain to the warrior who knelt in front of her. He did not turn to look at her, but kept his gaze trained on his sister. She could see the tense set of his broad shoulders and she realized that that tension was because he truly was worried about her response. The knowledge that he did not take her for granted filled her heart and she had to blink rapidly to keep her tears from falling. Cuchulainn had chosen her above all women, and now he was waiting to hear whether she would accept him.

"Yes," she said in a strong, clear voice. "I do accept Cuchulainn's suit, with all my heart."

"Then, as her Chieftain, I give you, Cuchulainn, permission to court Brenna. And as your sister I want you to know how very happy your choice has made me." On impulse, Elphame raised her hands and tilted her face to the hazy morning light trickling in from above them. "I ask Epona's blessing on your union."

The moment Elphame evoked the Goddess's name, she felt the warmth of power tingle through her body, and the foggy morning sky suddenly blurred. For the length of time it took to draw a breath, time seemed to suspend. In that frozen moment Elphame felt a great rush of sadness and heard the sound of weeping.

She blinked and the illusion was gone, leaving only a sense of loss and a chill in her blood. Cuchulainn was watching her with a strange expression and Elphame hastily covered her discomfort by clapping her brother on his shoulder. "Arise, Cu, you've chosen well."

The clan members who had stopped to watch broke into spontaneous cheers. Soon the three of them were surrounded by a host of well-wishers and Elphame found it easy to shake off the eerie feeling the fleeting vision had left her.

"El, you know what this means?" Cu put one arm around Brenna and tucked the other through his sister's. "We may as well call Mother. If she hears by any other means, she will never leave us in peace."

Elphame smiled through the irony of her brother's words. "Yes, let's call Mama. I was just thinking that it was time she came for a visit."

Elphame stood alone in the Chieftain's Tower. This time she didn't gaze out from the balcony that overlooked the forest; instead she leaned against the casement of one of the long, narrow windows that faced the B'an Sea. The day hadn't cleared; it had only lightened enough to allow the sky to serve as a brilliant backdrop to illuminate the storm that was rolling in from the west. Huge, billowing clouds pregnant with rain were being blown ever closer to the coast. Elphame and Cuchulainn had ordered the clan to double-check the moorings of the tents and had even moved several of them within the castle walls. Restoration work paused while they readied themselves for the spring storm.

Lightning rippled across the sky and then down to slice the distant water. It reminded Elphame of another night that had been filled with rain and thunder and pain—as well as the miracle of her first meeting with Lochlan. She knew she should curse the storm for slowing her work on the castle, but she could not deny the excitement within her that seemed to build with each crash of thunder and flash of lightning. She would go to him, and she would only have to wait until the sky opened with cloaking rain to do so. It hadn't been hard to be assured of privacy, although she did feel a twinge of guilt at telling Brenna that her headache had returned. The Healer had assured her that it was the change in weather irritating her recently healed wound, and had kindly brewed her a tea to help her sleep deeply through the evening and night. Elphame had, of course, not touched the tea. Brenna would not check on her until morning, Cuchulainn's hot gaze and whispered words had made it clear that the two new lovers would be very busy throughout the night.

No more than seven days, she reminded herself. She only had to keep up her charade for just a few more days. Then she would reveal her secret and trust that her family would accept it, as they had accepted her all of her life.

"Do ye not think the tower is a good place fer thinking, lass?"

This time the start of surprise at the old spirit's appearance lasted only a moment, and she realized that she must have been hoping for his company.

"Yes, I do think so. Did you come here often?"

He nodded his head and quirked a semitransparent eyebrow at her. *"Aye, that I did. Especially when I had a problem that wouldna let me be."*

"Did you always want to be The MacCallan?"

Both brows raised as he studied her, considering the question. *"Aye, that I did."*

"Did you…" She paused, and turned from the view of the turbulent sea to look into his eyes. "Did you ever feel like you wanted to run away?"

"Aye, lassie." His smile was filled with understanding.

"But you didn't."

His eyes sparkled. *"And neither will you. To be The MacCallan is in yer blood. You canna deny your fate, any more that I could escape mine."* He crossed over to her and put a cool hand gently on her shoulder. *"It would do ye well to remember that lass. Fate can be a cruel mistress. She brings great sadness as well as great joy."*

The brief vision she had experienced earlier in the day suddenly surfaced in her memory and she felt the chill in her blood return.

"Today Cuchulainn declared his intention to court and marry Brenna, and she accepted him."

The old spirit nodded thoughtfully, but remained silent.

Elphame drew a deep breath, trying to decide if she truly wanted to know anything more. She was in love; Cuchulainn was in love. Wouldn't it be easier if she just drifted on the tide of their mutual happiness, at least for a few more days? She let out the breath she'd drawn. She already knew the answer to that question—it resonated through her blood. Elphame could not choose ignorance, even if it was deceptively blissful.

"I evoked Epona's blessing on their joining, and when I did I experienced an odd illusion."

"Odd?"

She swallowed. "Odd as in disturbing. I heard weeping and I was filled with a great sadness. Then it was gone as quickly as it came."

The spirit took his hand from her shoulder and shifted his gaze so that he was staring out at the B'an Sea.

"Did no others see the sign?"

Numbly, Elphame shook her head. "No one seemed to notice anything. The people around us cheered. Cu didn't say anything about it, and all Brenna did was glow with happiness."

The old ghost turned to face her.

"Epona sent the sign for me alone." She spoke her inner most terrifying thoughts aloud to the silent spirit. "It is a fore-telling of what is to come. The Goddess is preparing me."

"'Tis the responsibility of The MacCallan alone. And it will be yer strength that will be needed when the time comes." His echoing voice sounded sad and weary.

"I could stop them!" She felt cold and nauseous. "As The MacCallan I could forbid their joining."

"At what price, lass? You canna trick fate, but ye can cause much unhappiness in trying to do so. I do know yer pain. I had a sister, a bonny young lass who was as dear to me as was my own heart. Would that I could have saved Morrigan pain."

Elphame's heart pounded. His sister—Lochlan's mother. Did he know? What was he really trying to tell her?

The old spirit's gaze drifted back out to sea. *"Ready yourself for the storm, 'tis coming...."*

Before she could question him further, the spirit's form faded and drifted through the floor of the tower, leaving Elphame alone with her silent sadness. Thunder cracked and the sky finally opened, pelting the castle with rain. Elphame turned from the window and made her way slowly down the winding stairs. Her shoulders slumped; she was cold and empty.

She didn't feel strong and she didn't feel like the Clan Chieftain—she felt like a frightened sister.

And it will be yer strength that will be needed when the time comes.

The ghost's words whispered incessantly through her troubled mind. She wanted peace from them....

There was only one place she would be sure to find peace that night.

THE RAIN MADE a comforting, pattering sound against the tent as Brenna watched Cuchulainn wrap the milk-filled cub into the cozy bed she had made for the little creature. It felt so strange to have a man in her tent—not bad strange, just different…disconcerting…disturbingly intimate. Yet he was there by her invitation, in her tent as well as in her life. Fand whimpered and Cuchulainn stroked her behind the ears, whispering melodically what Brenna was surprised to recognize as a children's lullaby. She smiled. The warrior had such an incredible capacity for gentleness—that was one of the things that separated him from other men. He had a depth of emotion within him that didn't match the rugged exterior of a warrior. His ability to love the cub, and to love her, was evidence of the difference within him, and she breathed a silent prayer of thanks to Epona for fashioning him.

Cuchulainn stood slowly, and with exaggerated stealth

walked over to join Brenna where she sat primly on the edge
of her bed. He took her hand and raised it to his lips

"Thank you for making that bed for her. It was a messy thing
to have a wolf cub sleep all night on my chest." His voice was
just above a whisper. He looked around, taking in the tidiness
of the small tent. The bed was identical to his, only Brenna's
was neatly made and had a pillow stuffed with fragrant herbs
resting in the middle of it. She had two chests; one was at the
foot of her bed, the other had been placed near her desk. It
was open, and Cuchulainn could see that it was filled with jars
and bottles, strips of linen and a wicked-looking assortment
of small knives. He raised his brows. "Is that where your
legendary teas originate?"

"Yes, as well as poultices and salves and many other things
that heal."

"Do you have any dragon's blood or tongue of toads?"

"Probably, if I look closely enough. Would you like me to
check? I could brew you up something with them," she asked,
pretending innocence.

"No!" he said, then lowered his voice again when Fand
stirred. "But I would very much like to see the gifts Epona gave
you that remind you of my eyes."

Brenna's breath caught. She shouldn't be surprised that he remembered; she shouldn't be surprised at anything he said or did.
But his love was so unexpected that she couldn't help feeling
like she was living a dream, and that she would wake soon to
find that he had been nothing more than a beautiful illusion.

"Brenna? You do not have to, not if it makes you uncomfortable."

"It doesn't make me uncomfortable. I want to share them
with you." She stood and took his hand so that she could guide
him around the bed to the corner of the tent that was cloaked
in shadows. She knelt, motioning for Cuchulainn to kneel

beside her. Then she lit the four small candles, one for each of the four directions, and her altar blazed into life.

Brenna pointed to the first item.

"I carved this mare's head from the memory of a recurring dream I used to have when I was a child. In the dream there was always a beautiful woman riding the mare. She had golden-red hair with an unruly curl." Brenna smiled shyly. "I couldn't reproduce the beauty of the woman's face, so I focused on the mare."

"May I touch it?" he asked.

Brenna nodded.

He reverently picked up the wood carving, studying it carefully. "You did a good job of recreating the Chosen Mare. You even managed the arrogant arch of her neck."

"Epona's Chosen? But I didn't mean to carve the Chosen Mare."

Cu smiled at her and touched her face. "How could you not? You dreamed of her, as you dreamed of my mother."

"No—I—"

"Do you still remember the dream well?"

"Yes."

"Think about the woman's eyes."

Brenna concentrated on calling up the memory of the dream she had had so often during her painful childhood. It wasn't hard to do. It had always given her pleasure. The mare and the woman had been so beautiful, and they had always seemed so happy, so free from the horrors Brenna had been enduring. She thought about the woman, and pictured her clearly in her mind, focusing on her eyes…

And Brenna's own eyes widened in surprise. "She has your eyes!" They weren't exactly the same color, Etain's eyes were more green than blue, but their shape was definitely the same.

"Actually, as she will tell you, I have her eyes."

Brenna felt a little tremor run through her body. She had dreamed of Cuchulainn's mother, over and over again.

Cuchulainn carefully placed the mare's head back on the altar. First, he ran one finger over the turquoise stone, and then he gently touched the brilliant blue feather. "You were right, Brenna, these do carry the color of my eyes." Then his attention shifted to the single, perfect drop-shaped pearl, and the warrior began to chuckle.

"What is it?" Brenna asked.

"Oh, love! We are fated to be together." He touched her face. "You dreamed of my mother and you carry a carving of the Chosen Mare on your altar. You collect things that are the exact shade of my eyes, and now the pearl." He chuckled again. "My father will bring with him a ring I plan on presenting to you. It has been in his family for generations. It is a silver band, intricately carved with intertwining ivy leaves, and set in the middle of it is a single pearl in the shape of a perfect tear. The exact twin of the one you have here."

"I found it," she said, almost unable to talk through the joy that beat into her throat from her breast. "It was the year I became a woman. I was alone, and very unhappy. I was sitting beside a steam, and something caught my eye. I looked down and there it was."

Cuchulainn pulled her into his arms and held her against him.

"Never again. I promise you, Brenna, you will never be unhappy again."

Pressed tightly against him, sharing the strength of his body as well as his love, Brenna felt the last vestiges of the icy cage that had entrapped her heart thaw and break. She looked up at the man she had decided to trust and to love.

"Would you do something for me, Cuchulainn?"

"Anything, love."

She took a deep breath. "Make love to me."

Instead of answering her, he stood, lifting her with him. With her held securely within the circle of his arm, he led her to the small, neatly made bed.

"Blow out the candles," she whispered.

He raised her chin with his finger. "We will be spending the rest of our lives together. I will see you, Brenna, all of you—and often. I know this is difficult for you, but I would begin tonight with nothing but honesty between us."

The rain beat against the tent, isolating them in their own little world. Brenna pushed down her fear and met his steady gaze.

"Would you blow out some of them?"

He smiled and kissed her forehead before hurrying around the room to blow out all but a single candle held within a glass lamp. This he carried to the small table that sat beside the bed. For a few moments they stood together, face-to-face, just looking at each other.

"I'm nervous." Brenna smiled hesitantly and reached up to touch his face.

Cuchulainn took her hand and pressed it against his heart. She could feel its rapid beat.

"I'm nervous, too, love."

"Then maybe you should kiss me. It's better when we touch."

Cuchulainn bent to kiss her and Brenna stepped eagerly into his arms. She had meant what she said to him, when they were touching like this his closeness and the power that radiated from his body overcame her fear. As before, his lips made her forget that she was scarred. All she could think of was the taste and the touch of him—and how he made her body sing in response.

Somewhere in the haze of his kisses, she could feel his hands roaming restlessly over her clothing, molding a breast against the heat of his palm, cupping her bottom. She moaned as she pressed close against his growing hardness. Soon her own hands were exploring his body. They found the clasp that held his kilt to his shoulder, and loosened the plaid. Cuchulainn helped her unwind it from around his body, then he pulled the linen shirt from his chest, and almost without consciously understanding how, Brenna was pressed against his naked body, letting her hands travel the length of him to take delight in the controlled strength of his hard, muscular lines.

Abruptly Cu turned, so that he was sitting on the bed and she was standing between his legs. His hands rested over the lacing that held her dress closed at her throat.

"Let me see you, love." His voice was husky with passion. "Let me feel your naked body against mine."

Trying to still the trembling that his words had started within her, she bit her lip and nodded her head. Cuchulainn unlaced the prim bodice, helping her to shrug out of it before he unwound her skirt. She stood before him in her high-necked chemise. Slowly, Brenna lifted the soft fabric from her body and over her head, and let it drop to the floor beside her. Then she stood before him, very still, with her eyes tightly closed. When she felt the soft caress of his fingers following the edge of the thick scar tissue that went from her face, down her neck, and covered from her right breast all the way across the top of her arm and stretched almost to her waist, she could not contain the tremors that skittered through her body.

"Ah, love." His voice sounded raw. "I wish I could have been there. I would have found a way to prevent it, or comforted you afterwards and somehow tried to lessen your pain."

Tears leaked from her closed eyes as he leaned forward to kiss the path his fingers had traveled. When she finally opened her eyes to look down at him, she saw that his face, too, was wet with tears.

"You're here now," she said.

"And I will be here forevermore."

Brenna sank onto the bed with him, reveling in the sensation of having his naked skin pressed against her—all of her. He did not turn from her, nor did his desire for her wane.

For the rest of the night, Brenna kept her eyes open.

Lochlan raised his head in surprise. It was not yet dark, but he could feel her. Through the wind and the rain she had just called his name. The power of her summons tingled through his blood. His wings stirred and began unfurling even before he leaped from his hidden cave and began the ground-eating running glide that would take him to Elphame. His body welcomed the cool touch of the rain. He yearned to wrap her in his arms, to feel her stroke his wings and caress his body. This time he wanted to take her completely; he wanted to taste her blood. He shouldn't—he knew that. It was demonic, base, wrong. His breathing deepened. With an effort that caused the pain in his temples to spike familiarly, Lochlan stumbled to a halt. He had to get control of himself. He could not go to her wrapped in a haze of passion and bloodlust. He closed his eyes and bowed his head against the pain that denying what his blood demanded caused him.

He loved her! He forced his thoughts from the sleek heat of her body to her smile, and the trust that showed so clearly in her eyes. She was his wife, handfasted with him before Epona. His breathing steadied. They would talk. Perhaps tonight he would find a way to tell her of the Prophecy; together they could surely discover a way to save his people without the sacrifice he had already sworn he would not commit.

He began the gliding run again, this time with his dark needs repressed. She called to him, and he must answer her, but he would do so as a man, not as a monster.

She was standing beside the opening to the hidden passageway. Rain ran down her face and her body, and Lochlan thought she looked like she was covered in tears. When she saw him she smiled, but there was a great sadness within her that formed an almost palpable aura around her. Without speaking, he went to her and enfolded her within his arms. His wings rose over her, shielding her from the cold touch of the rain, but still her body shivered.

"Come back to my shelter with me. It is a simple cave, but it is dry and warm." He kissed the top of her head and held her closely against him.

She lifted her head, and he could see that she had been crying. Her tears had mixed with rain, blanketing her face in sadness.

"Would you return with me to my chamber, instead?" she asked in a voice heavy with emotion. "Tonight I need the walls of my castle around me, as well as your arms."

"Do you wish to tell Cuchulainn tonight, my heart?"

She shook her head in short, fast jerks. "No, I've sent for my parents. We'll still wait for them to arrive. Cu won't interrupt us tonight. He's with his new love."

"Is that why you are so sad? Has Cuchulainn chosen poorly?"

"He's chosen Brenna."

"The little Healer? I thought she was your friend."

"She is," Elphame said hastily. "I was unbelievably happy when they declared their love for each other today. But I've had a Feeling—a kind of premonition—of great sadness to come." She shivered again uncontrollably.

"Let's return you to your castle. You need the strength of its walls."

"I also need you, Lochlan. I need you badly tonight."

He held her tightly against him. "I am here for you, my heart."

LOCHLAN ENTERED THE Chieftain's bedchamber by El-phame's side. He held her hand tightly within his as a tide of emotions broke over him.

"My mother walked here." His voice was a raspy whisper. "Before she knew pain and self-imposed banishment, she knew love and happiness here."

"Don't do that to yourself. Do you think for one instant your mother regretted your birth?"

Lochlan blinked and focused on Elphame's face. He shook the self-hatred from his mind and answered her honestly. "No, from the moment of my birth, to the moment of her death, she loved me fiercely and completely."

Through their joined hands, Elphame could feel the tension within him relaxing. He looked around the spacious chamber while he continued speaking, his voice shifting back to the deep, rich tone she knew so well.

"I know it sounds strange, and your brother, as well as the rest of your clan, will probably never understand, but it feels right that I am here. It somehow completes things." He smiled at her and the sadness was gone from his eyes. "My mother would be very happy to know that I have returned."

She moved closer to him and leaned against his shoulder. His arm encircled her along with the tip of one dark wing. He bent to kiss her with a sweet tenderness that made her breath catch. She understood what his mother had felt—she, too, loved him fiercely and completely.

"Now, tell me about this Feeling that has so troubled you," he said, leading her over to the golden chaise that sat adjacent to her bed.

With a rustle, Lochlan's wings fitted themselves neatly against his back so that he reclined comfortably on the chaise. He bent his knees so that they formed a backrest for her and she curled up leaning against them, facing him.

"It happened when Cuchulainn came to me to ask my permission as Brenna's Chieftain to court her. Of course I gladly granted his request." Elphame's eyes stared over Lochlan's shoulders, as if she was trying to reconstruct the past. "Then, almost automatically, I evoked Epona's blessing. The moment I spoke the Goddess's name I was filled with a terrible sadness and I heard the sound of weeping."

"Perhaps your premonition had nothing to do with Cuchulainn and Brenna. Could Epona have been sending you a vision of what would come when you announced your own marriage? Could she have been trying to prepare you for the struggle ahead of us?"

Elphame shook her head. "I already considered that. No, this Feeling was definitely linked to Cu and Brenna." She drew a deep breath. "And then there's the spirit of The MacCallan. He agreed that it was a vision sent to prepare me to be strong."

Lochlan's brows shot up. "You've spoken with the shade of The MacCallan?"

"More than once. Actually, he has even appeared to Cu. That's how he knew to come after me the night of my accident. The MacCallan sent him."

"My uncle..." Lochlan shook his head, hardly able to believe it.

"And my great-grandfather." She hesitated before adding gently, "He mentioned your mother the last time we spoke. He loved her very much."

Sadness shadowed Lochlan's eyes again. "Do you think he would hate me?"

"I don't know," she said truthfully. "But I think that it's a good sign that he hasn't appeared to drive you from the castle. I have no doubt that the old spirit knows everything that happens within MacCallan's walls."

"Should I leave? I would not wish to trouble him."

Elphame took his hand. "Don't leave. I want you here. I need you here. Remember, you are of the Clan MacCallan, by oath as well as by blood."

"It's not the MacCallan blood that concerns me." He lifted her hand to his lips for a brief kiss. "What do you intend to do about your vision?"

Elphame sighed. "I don't think there's anything I can do. The MacCallan warned me to prepare for what is to come." She shrugged her shoulders, feeling the great weight of her responsibilities pressing down on them. "All I can do is to try to be strong, and wait."

"You are strong, my heart. And we will wait together for what will come."

His words comforted her, even as she realized that they shouldn't have. The vision did not pertain to him, but Lochlan was undoubtedly a part of the coming storm. She knew their relationship would be a bitter thing for her family and her clan to discover, but she could not turn from him All her life she had dreamed of, wished and prayed for a lifemate, never really believing she would be granted such a gift. And now that she had found him, she could not let him go.

She clasped his hand. "Yes, even great sadness will be easier to bear together."

"Did you ever think that Epona might be foretelling Brenna's rejection of your brother? If he truly loves her that would be a great sadness for him, but it is something from which he could recover."

"Brenna will not reject him. You should have seen them together today, Lochlan. It was as if they had discovered a wonderful secret. I recognized all too well their long looks and frequent touches. No, Brenna will not reject him."

"Then, if Epona grants it, let your brother likewise recognize our love when he discovers our secret."

Thunder boomed outside the castle and lightning cracked dangerously close. Elphame shivered as a sudden chill ran through her blood.

"The storm grows closer," she said, staring up at the window slits that glowed fitfully with lightning.

"It will pass, my heart."

Elphame's eyes turned back to her lifemate. He was watching her with a sure, steady gaze, which evoked confidence and made her suddenly want to believe his words. She thought that he must be a great leader among his people. Chagrined, she realized that, though he had mentioned other women who had survived the birth of their half-Fomorian children, and though she had understood that there had to be more beings like him, she had not asked him about the others he had left behind.

"Lochlan, tell me about your people."

All expression slid from his face, and he was silent for so long that Elphame didn't think he would answer her. When he began to speak, his words sounded strained.

"My people live in the Wastelands. Life is difficult, but, as you already know, we are long-lived, few of us die. And, though I wonder at the wisdom of it, many new children are born every year."

"Children?"

Lochlan's smile held no humor. "Yes, we can procreate. Whatever anomaly caused the Fomorian females of my father's time to become sterile has healed itself in us. We are strong and resilient. My people thrive almost as much as they suffer."

Elphame shook her head. "They suffer? I don't understand."

"Those of us who were born from living mothers all share certain similarities—our appearance is more human than demon, we have the ability to move about during the daylight hours without the sun causing us pain, we do not need to feed on living blood to sustain our own lives, and we all struggle to cling to our humanity as we fight against the pull of our dark heritage. You already understand more than you realize, Elphame. You have seen evidence of the struggle within me. What you don't know is that every time I fight against the demon within me, every time I choose humanity instead of the darker path, it causes me pain. The pain that my people and I experience as the price of our humanity is driving many of us into insanity." Lochlan's jaw tightened. "It is especially difficult for the children. They, too, are born more human than demon, but they have no human mothers to guide them, and our own mothers are long dead."

Elphame was overwhelmed at the thought of a young Lochlan struggling to be human without the aid of his mother's strength and belief.

"Then they must come here!" She squeezed his hands, suddenly not caring if she sounded young and idealistic. "We can help them. My family will accept you—they have to. When they see how good you are, that you struggle against darkness every day and defeat it, they will begin to trust you as I do, and through you, your people will earn their trust, too."

Lochlan could not look away from the bright belief in her eyes. Now was the time to tell her about the Prophecy. Now was the time to admit to her that his mission had been to seal her doom, but that he had forsaken his people and the Prophecy out of love for her. But he could not. She wrapped him in the sparkling web of her dream, and he did not wish to be awakened.

"If only it was that easy," he said.

"If it was easy, it wouldn't be worth doing." She smilingly echoed his mother's words.

"I do love you, my heart." He pulled her into his arms. "I will always love you."

Elphame leaned into him, returning his kiss. When she heard his wings begin to rustle with arousal, she whispered against his lips, "Take me to bed, husband."

With strength that was more than human, he rose swiftly to his feet, cradling Elphame in his arms. His feral, gliding steps covered the space to the bed in less than a single beat of her heart. Soon, their clothing, still damp from the rain, was pooled in a discarded heap around their feet. Naked, Elphame slid across the luxurious linens. Lochlan lay above her, his wings unfurling like a tremendous bird of prey. He held most of his weight on his elbows; his hands were balled tightly into the thick comforter. She could feel the tension that trembled through his body, and as she tried to deepen their kisses, he visibly held himself back, trying to steady his breathing and remain in control of his passion.

"Lochlan, you are my husband. You cannot be afraid to love me."

"I'm not afraid to love you!" His voice was thick with lust and frustration. "I'm afraid to harm you!" He drew a trembling breath and pressed his forehead against hers. "My hands become like claws. My pleasure becomes bloodlust. I cannot love you without fearing for you."

Something in the tone of his words stirred an instinct deep within her and she felt the ire of a goddess come alive with a slow, steady burn. Her skin tingled and her blood pulsed with a hot, sensuous rhythm.

"You insult me."

Lochlan lifted his head, surprise clearly reflected on his face. She pushed him back from her with a strength that widened his eyes.

Deliberately, she leaned forward and stroked the underside of his wing causing his breath to catch in a moan. "I do not shrink from your touch. Have you forgotten that I am more than human? I am faster—I am stronger." She stroked his wing again, and as he moaned she teasingly bit his shoulder, leaving a raised red mark like a brand. "Some even say I am a goddess. Do not treat me as if I am any less." She took his bottom lip between her teeth and tugged.

Lochlan's eyes flashed with a dark light that sparked an answering lust within her. She remembered the bloodlust that he had admitted to her. She didn't mean for it to be, but there was something erotically compelling about the thought of him pressing his teeth into her skin—a kind of sensual invasion, not unlike him entering her body. The aura of barely contained violence that surrounded him was palpable, but it did not frighten her—it drew her to him. As his mate she did not feel like an anomaly or a mutation, instead she felt that she had finally discovered her match.

"Love me, Lochlan," she purred. "I will not break and I will not turn from you."

His answering kiss crushed her against the bed. She met his passion with equal force, teasing and tempting with her hands and her mouth. When he entered her it was with none of the restraint he had shown the night before, and she arched beneath him, goading him on. He took her hands in his and pulled them over her head. His breath came in hot gasps as he bowed over her. She barely recognized the voice that whispered dark words into her ear.

"You do not realize what you ask."

"My trust is not something half-given." She raised her head and bit his shoulder again—hard—as she moved rhythmically against him.

Lochlan growled low in his throat. He pressed his daggerlike teeth against the softness of her neck. Elphame felt a brief burning and then a blade of erotic sensation slid from her throat down through her body. Waves of pleasure took her as he drank her blood at the same time he filled her with his seed.

Suddenly, with an agonized cry Lochlan hurled himself away from her body. Feeling disoriented, Elphame raised up on one elbow, blinking in confusion. He was standing beside her bed, staring wide-eyed at her. There was blood on his lips and a small trickle of crimson ran from the corner of his mouth down his chin. Elphame's hand went to her neck, and she felt two small, damp, puncture wounds. She smiled shakily at him.

"I'm fine, Lochlan. You didn't hurt me."

He wiped his mouth with the back of his hand, and stared in horror at the blood smeared there.

"No!" he cried in a broken voice. "It cannot be this way. I will not let it be this way."

He stumbled backwards, shaking his head from side to side.

Elphame sat all the way up, fighting a rush of dizziness. "Lochlan, what is it? Look at me—you did not hurt me."

"No!" he repeated. "I will not let it be this way!"

With the incredible speed of his father's race, he glided across the room and disappeared through the entrance that led to the bathing chamber and the hidden tunnel.

"Lochlan!" Elphame yelled as she lurched from the bed.

"Do not follow me. Stay away…" His voice drifted eerily from the stairwell.

Elphame fell to her knees and wept.

Lochlan burst from the tunnel and ran. He didn't care where he went; he only knew that he had to get away. The night was unrelentingly dark, but his vision was sharp, and he maneuvered between trees with little effort. The rain lashed his naked body, but he welcomed it. It was nothing compared to the shattered remnants of his heart. He shrieked his agony to the unhearing night. He could still taste her blood, and he still heard the whispering tale it had revealed.

He had been wrong. They had all been wrong.

The Prophecy was true—he and his people could be saved through a goddess's death. But it was not her blood that was needed as sacrifice, and it was not her physical death that was required. He knew that now. When he drank of her blood he had been filled with the infallible knowledge of a goddess. Elphame's blood would not save them. It was only by her accepting *his* blood that his people would find their salvation, and through him Elphame would absorb the darkness of their blood and take within her own body the madness of an entire race.

It would be worse than a physical death. If she drank his blood, she would be filled with evil. Elphame would live. Lochlan's thoughts screamed through his head in a cacophony of agony…. It wasn't a physical death the Prophecy foretold. She would live the long life of any being whose body held the blood of the demonic Fomorian race, but she would be driven completely mad. He knew too well what she would become, what the blood would twist her into being. He could not sentence her to centuries of agony. Not even to save his people.

He must stay away from her, and he must be certain than none of his people ever discovered the path through the rugged Tier Mountains that led to the lush pine forest of Partholon and MacCallan Castle. He must keep his clan's castle, his love's home, safe.

His arms pumped in time with his powerful legs. His heart thundered with the storm. Farther away…he had to get far enough away so that he could not hear the magical sound of her call or feel her presence so heartbreakingly near. The land rose steadily up and he welcomed the burning pain that quivered through his straining muscles. Lightning flashed and through the rain that pelted his face he thought he caught the outline of shadowy figures atop the next ridge. With a dreadful sense of foreboding, he slowed his ascent, waiting for the next flash of light to be sure. When it came, he stumbled to a halt. Standing on the ridge, silhouetted against the storm, were four winged figures.

32

ON STORM CLOUD–COLORED wings they glided down the ridge. Lochlan stood strong and naked, waiting for them to reach him. Though they could not literally read each others' minds, his people were intuitively linked through the heritage of their dark blood, and Lochlan knew that they must not detect the turbulence of his emotions. He pulled from within him the mantle of leadership that he wore so naturally, and cloaked his mind and his heart in silence. As they drew close, he could see their faces registering shock at his nakedness. Then they bowed their heads respectfully.

As was typical behavior for the headstrong half-Fomorian, Keir was the first to speak.

"What has happened to you, Lochlan?"

"You offer neither greeting, nor explanation as to why you are here, yet you believe you have the right to begin questioning me?" Lochlan ground the words through clenched teeth.

Keir's eyes flashed dangerously, but he could not hold Lochlan's gaze. He dipped his head.

"You are right to reprimand me," he said, but his voice held little apology. "Well met, Lochlan."

His three comrades bowed their heads and echoed his greeting.

"Not well met at all!" Lochlan snapped. "You should not be here."

Keir drew in a hissing breath, but before he could speak, the winged woman at his side stepped forward, curtseying deeply before Lochlan.

"You have been too long parted from us, Lochlan. We worried that some ill fate had befallen you."

Fallon's voice was sweet and for a moment the familiarity of it was a balm to his aching mind.

"Your instincts were not wrong, Fallon. Fate has not been kind."

"You did not find the hoofed goddess?" Keir said.

Lochlan's stare was ice. "I found her, but I have discovered that it is not of her that the Prophecy speaks."

The winged people moved restlessly, staring from Keir to Lochlan.

"How could you know that?"

"I know because she is not a goddess, she is simply a mutation of two races. She is no different than us!" Lochlan snarled.

"It cannot be," Fallon said brokenly.

"Hope is not gone. I have a new plan." Lochlan raised his voice against the storm.

Lightning split the night again, and the rain intensified.

"Must we stand here? Is there not some shelter you can offer us?" Fallon said.

He wanted to scream at them that he had no shelter and

force them to begin to retrace their path that very night, but he knew if he drove them away they would see the illogic of his actions—they would know he was hiding something from them. And they would not rest until they discovered his secret.

"Follow me, quickly and quietly. I will take you to my shelter." But as he turned, Fallon stayed him with a soft hand on his arm.

"Are you well, Lochlan? Why did we find you running naked with the storm?"

Lochlan looked from the gentle Fallon to her mate, and then to the other members of their party. They were watching him warily, as if they thought the time apart from them might have driven him into the madness that tugged at each of them. At that moment he didn't care what they thought—he only cared that the fabric of his world had been ripped asunder. The dream was over, and he did not think he could bear the light of day.

"Have none of you ever wanted to race the wildness of a storm?" he asked, showing his teeth to the group. Unfurling his wings he glided away from them, setting a pace that he knew they would have to struggle to match.

The cave he had been using as shelter was just large enough to accommodate all of them. Silently, Lochlan set about building a fire, something he rarely allowed himself the luxury of, but with the storm and the darkness of the night, there was little chance of his smoke leading anyone to discover their hiding place. He dressed and shared his meager provisions with his people, who were still eyeing him carefully. He should have known when they entered Partholon; he should have felt their presence. It was a testament to how distracted he had become with Elphame that he had not realized that they approached. Keir had chosen his companions well, Lochlan admitted to himself. Fallon, of course, would not have been parted from him. The twin brothers, Curran and Nevin, had always been completely loyal to one thing—the fulfillment of the Prophecy, at the expense of all else. Lochlan himself would have chosen them to accompany him on the quest Keir had planned.

And he knew beyond any doubt what it was that Keir had planned. Keir had come to be certain that Lochlan brought the hoofed goddess back to their people as a living sacrifice.

"Tell us about her, Lochlan," said Nevin.

"How can you be so certain that she is not the one?" As usual, Curran picked up the thread of his twin's thought and finished it.

Lochlan spoke carefully, cognizant of the fact that his words could either save or condemn Elphame.

"I have spent much time watching her. She is not a goddess. She is simply a young woman whose body, for whatever reason, carries the mark of her human mother, as well as her centaur father. She does not lead her people in the rites of Epona. She is only Clan Chieftain, not a goddess. She does not carry the power of the Goddess within her."

"You couldn't possibly know that." Keir kept his voice low, and nonconfrontational, but his eyes were narrow and slitted.

"I know it without any doubt. I read it in her blood."

"How?"

"Why?"

"What right had you?"

Lochlan raised his hand to still their shouting. Like a caged animal, he paced back and forth across the mouth of the narrow cave.

"I found her at the bottom of a ravine. She had fallen and was badly injured. A wild boar was attacking her. I killed the boar, and then I carried her to safety. Her blood ran freely that night, and in it I read the truth of her humanity. She is not a goddess—she is only an aberration, nothing more than a mutated human."

"You revealed yourself to her?" Fallen stared at him with stunned disbelief.

"She was unconscious and then delirious. She remembers me only as a dream that could not possibly be true." Lochlan almost choked on the bitter truth his words held.

"If she is not the one to fulfill the Prophecy, why have you dreamed of her for all the years of her life?" Keir's words sliced the air.

But Lochlan had readied himself for the question, and his answer came easily.

"The dreams were visions sent by my dark blood to taunt me, meant to drive me mad when I followed their trail and found that they were no more than a folly that I had chased for a quarter of a century."

"You said you had a plan. What must we do now?" Fallon asked.

Lochlan approached the beautiful winged woman who had been his playmate in their youth and his friend in their adulthood. Her white-blond hair had dried and it glistened in the firelight as it fell to her waist in a thick, straight curtain. Her features were delicate and fey. Her eyes were a blue that was so light that they seemed sometimes colorless. He hated to lie to her; he hated to lie to all of them. But he could not betray his wife.

"While I was watching the hoofed woman, I overheard many things. Often the humans spoke of the Temple of the Muse."

Curran and Nevin nodded. "Our mother was trained there."

"As was mine," Lochlan said. "As were many of our mothers. Remember what they taught us of it? The Temple of the Muse is a place of higher learning, where the teachers are all Incarnate Goddesses, each a living, earth-bound representative of one of the nine Muses."

"You believe one of them might be able to fulfill the Prophecy," Keir said slowly.

Lochlan stared into his eyes. "I believe any of them could fulfill the Prophecy. Think about it! The answer is simple. I would have realized it years ago if I hadn't been plagued with taunting dreams for so long, which is why my dark blood played such games with me—to keep my mind from recognizing the obvious. The Prophecy does not say that we will be saved by the blood of a *hoofed* dying goddess. It says the blood of a goddess will save us. Any goddess."

"So we will go to the Temple of the Muse," Nevin said.

"And capture a goddess," Curran completed for him.

Lochlan shook his head in disgust. "And how do you plan to do that? How can you possibly believe that all of us could make our way there without being discovered?"

"Perhaps it is time we were discovered!" Keir spat. "Perhaps it is past time!"

"You intend to attack Partholon?" Lochlan's voice was sharp and dangerous.

"Not attack! I want only to take our rightful place within Partholon."

"And you believe that rightful place," Lochlan sneered, "is at the head of an army of winged demons?"

"We are not demons!" Fallon cried.

"If we come into Partholon as an invading force and steal one of their goddesses for a blood sacrifice, what else could they possibly see us as?" Lochlan said. When none of them answered him, he shook his head in disgust. "If we think only with the anger of our fathers' blood, we will fare no better than they did, and, for all of our struggles against their dark legacy, we will be no more human than they were."

"What is it you suggest?" Keir asked bitterly.

"Go home. See to the welfare of our people. I will travel

alone to the Temple of the Muse, and when I return to the Wastelands it will be in the presence of a goddess. When her blood has washed the dark madness from our blood, we will peaceably enter Partholon. No Partholonian will ever know that the price of our salvation was the blood of one of their own."

"There is—" Curran began.

"—a certain logic to it," Nevin finished.

Lochlan turned his back on them and stared out into the rain. They seemed to accept his fabrications and half-truths, but he would not allow himself to feel relief until he knew that the four of them had returned to the Wastelands—until he was certain Elphame was safe.

Keir scowled and settled himself against the back wall of the cave. Fallon's eyes followed her mate before she joined Lochlan at the mouth of the cave.

"Do you still love her, my friend?" she asked him softly.

"No." Lochlan tasted the bilelike foulness of the lie. "I never loved her. It was all an illusion."

"It is better this way. Now you can finally choose a mate from your own people."

Lochlan managed a tight nod.

"You seem different, Lochlan." Fallon's eyes were clouded with concern.

"You were right. I have been too long away from my people." He forced himself to smile at her. "Now, you should rest. You must begin your return journey tomorrow. The castle is very near, and it is filled with human and centaur workers. It is not safe for any of you to remain here."

"As you say, Lochlan." Fallon inclined her head respectfully to him before drifting back to her mate.

Behind him, Lochlan could hear the four of them settling in for the night. His own weariness pulled at him, but he knew he would not sleep. If he slept, he would dream. He would dream of her. Tonight, he could not bear that. Silently, he slipped out of the cave. The thunder and the lightning had passed, but the rain still fell steadily. He climbed the ridge above the hidden cave and sat on the rocky mound of ground and gazed out at the land that he had begun to believe could be his home. The MacCallan land had called to him, but it was a call he could never again answer. No matter what his heart or his blood told him, no matter that Elphame would believe that he had betrayed and abandoned her, he must leave this place.

He would travel to the Temple of the Muse. He knew it was a futile trip. The idea that an Incarnate Goddess had the ability to fulfill the Prophecy was not a new one to him. He and his mother had discussed it often. It hadn't felt right to either of them. His mother had always been adamant that the key to the Prophecy would be revealed to him when Epona sent a woman touched by the Goddess to fulfill it. That his mother had been right was of little consolation to him now.

And what of the unsuspecting Incarnate Goddess of the Muse? Could he steal an innocent young woman and carry her away to her death? Wouldn't that just serve to feed the darkness within him and draw him farther from his grasp on humanity? He clenched his jaw. No matter. He would do it—if it meant saving Elphame, there was little he would not do. He could even leave her.

His shoulders slumped. But it would not save Elphame, not permanently. His people would discover that the Incarnate Goddess's death did not fulfill the Prophecy. For years they had believed that the hoofed goddess who haunted his dreams was the answer to their encroaching madness. Like a never-ending circle, they would inevitably revolve back to that belief.

Would he then have to battle his own people for her life?

Lochlan put his face in his hands and did something he had not done since the death of his mother. He wept.

Fallon nestled against Keir's body. He covered her with his wings, cocooning her in warmth. He pressed his lips against her ear.

"Your friend lies," he whispered.

She pulled back just enough to read his eyes. "What do you mean, Keir?"

"Even through the rain and his sweat I could smell her on him. He was rank with her blood as well as her sex," Keir hissed.

Fallon looked deeply into his eyes. She hadn't scented anything odd on Lochlan's body, but Keir's sense of smell was keener than her own; there had even been a few notable times when he had bested Lochlan's amazing ability to track through scent.

"All you need do is to think about what you have seen within his eyes, and you will know that I speak the truth. The hoofed goddess is The One, but Lochlan is choosing to keep her to himself."

Fallon closed her eyes and rested her head against her mate's chest. She thought about what she had seen reflected in Lochlan's eyes that night. The answer came too easily. She had seen agony and heartbreak—all the things the noble Lochlan would feel if he had chosen the lover of his dreams over the salvation of his people.

Keir was right. Fallon felt the anger within her stir.

SUNLIGHT PEERED THROUGH the high slit windows of the Chieftain's chamber, and Elphame blinked against the brightness of the early morning. She sat up too abruptly, and the room swam. Her head felt thick and her mouth was overly dry. It was like she had indulged in too much wine the night before, even though she had not touched the fruit of the vine. What was wrong with her? She rubbed at her neck, which itched vaguely, and her fingers found the scabs that clotted the two small wounds.

Lochlan…

The night came back to her in a rush.

He had left her. She breathed deeply and evenly. She would not cry again; she would think. Just go over what happened, she told herself, there must be a rational reason for Lochlan's behavior.

All had been well at first. He had comforted her fears about Cuchulainn's future sadness. He had promised that they would face whatever the future brought together. He had made love to her.

And he had tasted her blood. It was then that he had flung himself away from her. What was it he had said?

"It cannot be this way! I will not let it be this way!"

What had he meant? Yes, the bloodletting had made her feel strangely euphoric, and then had acted on her like a potent sleeping drug. She was still feeling its effects. But it had been nothing terrible. Her hand found the wounds at her neck again as she remembered the amazingly erotic sensations that had flowed through her body when he drank her blood.

She knew that he had spent his life rejecting his dark heritage, and last night he had even revealed to her that that struggle was driving his people mad. She shuddered as she remembered the sadness in his voice when he had spoken of the children. Maybe when he tasted her blood it had been, to him, a giving in—a kind of acceptance, a battle lost to that which he hated most about himself. Did that mean that in his mind she was now tied to that self-hatred?

No! She wouldn't believe it. Lochlan was her husband, sworn before Epona to love her. The night they had joined in handfast she had chosen to trust him. Their road together would not be smooth—the two of them already knew that. She would not falter at the first obstacle they faced.

He had told her not to follow him. So she would believe in him, and wait. Until he reappeared, she had to go on with the daily activities of restoring the castle and leading her clan. She didn't have the luxury of other young women. Her clan did not need a Chieftain who did nothing but moon around after her lost love.

Was he lost? The thought chilled her and she shook it from her mind.

Trying to regain some sense of normalcy, she went to the

pitcher and cup that sat on her vanity. She'd finished three full cups of water before her hands had ceased shaking.

Elphame looked back at the bed. Their clothes were still lying in crumpled heaps beside it. A tremor of fear skittered down her spine. He had rushed away from her, naked and alone. *Why?* her mind screamed. *Oh, Lochlan, what is wrong?*

Normalcy. She'd bathe, break her fast and then throw herself into the restoration of the castle. It had been too long since she had last demanded hard physical labor from her body. Today she would use that extrahuman strength of which she was so proud. She must do something physically tiring. Something that would force her body to stop aching for his caress.

In a fog that felt very much like she was moving through a fever-dream, she descended to her bathing chamber. The tunnel door was still ajar. Carefully keeping her mind blank, she closed it. Then quickly and impersonally, she bathed herself, washing away Lochlan's lingering scent.

Returning to her bedchamber she chose a simple linen blouse and then wrapped herself in her clan's plaid, securely fastening it with The MacCallan brooch. She turned back to face the bed. Its rumpled state and the discarded piles of clothing beside it made her stomach tighten.

Two knocks sounded against the wooden door. For a moment Elphame felt as if she had turned to stone, but when the knocks were repeated more insistently, she lurched forward, kicking the puddle of clothes out of sight under her bed.

The door opened slowly.

"Elphame?" Brenna's soft voice called hesitantly.

"Come in, Brenna," Elphame said, painting a welcoming smile on her stiff face. "Good morning to you."

The little Healer entered the room and it seemed to Elphame that all the brightness that had vanished from her own body had found new life within Brenna. Her hair, which she usually wore carefully pulled over her right shoulder so that she could easily duck her head forward and it would fall, curtainlike over her scars, spilled in messy disarray down her back, leaving her face open and glowing. Her step was light as she almost skipped into the room. Elphame even thought her dress looked different—then she realized that her clothing hadn't changed, it was simply no longer laced tightly beneath her chin.

"Love suits you, Brenna," Elphame said.

"It's Cuchulainn who suits me." Brenna's cheeks flushed, but she didn't look away from her friend's candid gaze.

"It's good to see that all of his past indiscretions have finally come to some use." As soon as she had spoken the words her hand flew to her mouth. What a ridiculously insensitive thing for her to say! Could she not think clearly enough to keep from wounding her friend? "Forgive me, Brenna! That was an awful thing for me to say."

Brenna's bright laughter filled the room. "It's not awful, it's true. I certainly did not believe Cuchulainn was an inexperienced virgin." She lowered her voice conspiratorially. "Last night it was a good thing one of us knew what to do." She giggled girlishly. "A very good thing. And anyway, I cannot change your brother's past. Why should I wish to? His life has fashioned him as he is, and I love him as he is." She grasped Elphame's hand and gushed. "Oh, I am so completely happy! I never allowed myself to dream of being loved by a man, any man, but to have won the love of a man such as Cuchulainn! If my heart stopped beating now, this very second, I would die happy and complete."

Elphame smiled fondly at her. Brenna's happiness was like balm to her wounded heart. It reminded her that love did happen—that happy endings were possible. "Your heart can't stop beating yet, not until you've given me at least a dozen nieces and nephews to spoil."

Brenna tapped her chin, considering. "A dozen in total, or a dozen of each?"

"I'll let my mother answer that question. And, speaking of the Incarnate Goddess of Epona, be prepared for her to insist upon conducting your wedding herself—and soon—even though she will probably weep during the entire service."

Some of the happy pink left Brenna's cheeks.

"Cu says she'll like me."

"Don't worry, Brenna, she'll love you. Where is that brother of mine? Still abed?"

"No, he went on to the Great Hall. I told him that I wanted to make sure you were feeling well this morning." She narrowed her eyes and studied Elphame, slipping easily from giddy young lover to Healer. "You look pale. Didn't you sleep soundly?"

"I slept fine. I'm probably pale because I've spent too much time inside and not enough time out under the open sky. Let's break our fast together and then I'll remedy that." She started for the door, but Brenna's next question brought her up short.

"What happened to your neck?"

Elphame ran her fingertips over the small marks and forced herself to shrug nonchalantly. "I must have scratched myself."

"They look more like bites."

"Could be a small spider. I suppose that proves that our new home isn't perfect." She took Brenna's hand and tugged her toward the door.

"I'll remind Meara to check the corners of your chamber for spiderwebs."

Elphame made a vague sound of agreement, and then quickly changed the subject.

"How is that cub of my brother's?"

Brenna rolled her eyes. "Did he tell you he named her Fand?"

Elphame felt real laughter bubble from her breast, and as she laughed with her friend the knot within her loosened. Chatting companionably they made their way through the beauty of the Main Courtyard and into the Great Hall, where her clan was congregating and an aromatic breakfast was being served. Elphame was greeted warmly, and it made her heart gladden to see her brother take Brenna into his arms and kiss her soundly.

She was Chieftain of this amazing clan. If Lochlan had abandoned their love, she would survive. No, she would do better than survive. She would live and prosper and spend her days surrounded by the love and respect of her people. And perhaps someday she would tell her nieces and nephews a tall tale about a winged creature, and the Goddess who had, for a brief time, loved him.

Elphame smiled at the cub that frolicked awkwardly around her brother's feet as they walked toward the group of workers who waited just inside the castle walls. She could hardly believe that the fat, energetic Fand was the same creature that Cu had dragged half-dead from her den just days ago.

"El, are you sure you're feeling well enough for this?"

"Don't start that, Cu. You heard Brenna. She said that I'm healed enough to go back to work. And this is exactly the kind of work I want to do today."

Cu cocked an eyebrow at her. "Why would you choose to help us chop down trees, and clear forest scrub instead of something—"

"Something easier?" Elphame interrupted him with a disgusted snort. "I've never been especially interested in *easier,* Cu. You tell me—what would you choose to do if you had been forced to be inactive for as long as I have been?"

"You were severely wounded, El," he reminded her.

"What would you choose?" she insisted.

His sigh turned into laughter. "I would choose to get my hands dirty and my muscles warm."

"As would I." She grinned back at him.

The workers greeted them, and were pleasantly surprised to hear that The MacCallan would be joining them in their work. They hefted their axes and blades and followed Cuchulainn and Elphame through the front walls.

"My thought is this," Cu said, pointing at the surrounding forest, "we have cleared the castle grounds, but I would still like the tree line itself to be moved back several paces. The roofers have called for more wood, so it will benefit us twofold." He was about to give them specific instructions when he felt a tingling against the left side of his body. He turned his head and his words stopped. His sister stood to his left, and waves of heat emanated from her. He felt a familiar trepidation, as he witnessed, once again, the power of the Goddess come alive within her.

Elphame stared above the trees. The sky was the startling blue that seemed only to happen on spring mornings that followed nighttime rains. The sun had just crested the sea of surrounding pines and it spilled waves of warmth and brilliance against the living walls of MacCallan Castle. Elphame's body absorbed the sun's rays like the touch of a long-absent parent, and she felt the power of the Goddess fill her.

"Epona has touched this day," Elphame's voice was reverent. "Let us thank the Goddess for Her presence and ask Her blessing upon our clan."

As Elphame lifted her face into the warmth of the morning sun, she felt the men kneel around her. She glanced to her side, and Cuchulainn, too, had dropped to his knees. She looked at her people. They knelt respectfully, but their heads were not bowed. Following her lead, they raised their faces to the sunlight. Elphame Felt the rightness of it, and when she lifted her arms to evoke Epona's name, the tingling power of the Goddess danced all along her skin.

"O, Great Goddess Epona, we feel Your mighty presence
today and ask that Your spirit flow through our clan.
We have set forth upon a new path here,
and with Your divine aid we will continue to
breathe life into MacCallan Castle, the ancestral
home of those whose blood You have always held dear.
We thank You, and ask Your blessing in
the soft and whispering winds from afar,
the warming and quickening light from afar,
the cool waters of the seas and streams,
and the far lands and wild places.
We are honored to have Your spirit among us.
Hail Epona!"

Those surrounding her took up the cry, and, to Elphame's delight, the words "Hail Epona!" echoed from the walls of her castle, filling the morning with a sense of love and magic that would linger between them for the remainder of the morning.

The winged creature watched from the safety of the forest's shadows. Lochlan had lied to them; here was the undeniable proof. The hoofed goddess stood before the walls of the castle, surrounded by her people who knelt in acknowledgment of her power. Epona filled her—she glowed with the Goddess's indwelling spirit. And she evoked the Goddess's blessing with simple words, as if it was her birthright—which it so obviously was. She was, indeed, a living, breathing goddess.

They must not leave Partholon without her. The fate of their people depended upon it. Dark thoughts surged through the creature's mind, and this time no attempt was made to repress them. The hoofed goddess needed to be drawn out into the forest, away from the protective walls of her castle. Lochlan would not do it, so they must find another way.

Within the darkness of the creature's mind, an idea formed, birthed in madness and bathed in blood.

34

THE SUN WAS high overhead and the ache in Elphame's muscles was a slow, satisfying burn when Brenna appeared, picnic basket in hand. She grimaced and laughed when Cuchulainn pulled her into his arms and gave her a sweaty kiss.

"Ugh! Both of you are dripping wet." Then her Healer's gaze sharpened as she studied Elphame.

"No, I'm not overdoing. Yes, I'm feeling fine," Elphame quickly assured her.

Fand, who had been napping in the shade of the closest pine, chose that moment to wake and she came galloping awkwardly up to Brenna, who knelt to scratch the cub behind her ears.

"Well, you do look better than you did this morning, for all your sweat and dirt, but it's past time you took a break." Her smile warmed and became private as her eyes locked with her lover's. "I brought the midday meal. Would you like to share it with me?"

Elphame watched as Brenna actually flirted with her

brother. It was as if the love that she had accepted from Cuchulainn had filled her so completely that she, like MacCallan Castle, had been born anew.

"Aye, lassie, that I would." Cu leered at her as she squealed and moved lithely out of his sweaty arms. Fand yapped at the two of them.

"Not just you, Cu," Brenna said laughingly. "Our Chieftain is invited, too."

"I would love to join both of you, but Wynne is a hard taskmistress. Remember when she pulled me aside this morning at breakfast?" Cu and Brenna nodded. "I promised that I would sit down with her and approve menu selections and talk about expanding the cook staff. I actually have to help her interview assistant cooks." Elphame gave a dramatic sigh. In truth, she was pleased that Wynne had asked for her advice in selecting her growing team of assistants. She was also pleased that it gave her a credible excuse to get out of tagging along with her brother and Brenna during one of their first lovers' trysts.

"So, that means it is just the two of us." Cuchulainn waggled his eyebrows at Brenna. Fand whined, and the warrior scooped the cup into his arms. "I mean the three of us," he amended.

Brenna frowned at him while he scratched Fand under her chin. "Cuchulainn, if you plan on touching anything except that beast, you had better wash yourself."

Cuchulainn leaned down and lowered his voice. "I'll meet you at our pool, Brenna." When she smiled at him, he thrust the wriggling cub into her arms. "You and Fand go ahead. El and I will finish with this tree and then I'll be right along." His voice changed to a staged whisper as his eyes slanted a teasing glance at his sister. "Don't tell our Chieftain, but I plan on taking some leisure time of my own this afternoon…."

"Oh, you're awful, Cu!" Elphame swatted at him.

"I agree," said Brenna happily, holding the cub against her

breast. "But I will wait for him anyway." And with a jaunty look over her shoulder, she flounced away down the road.

Cu watched her leave, grinning stupidly. Elphame shook her head at him.

"You don't deserve her."

Cuchulainn's voice sounded joyous. "Right you are, sister-mine! But she loves me well and truly. Now, let's get this tree cut so I can spend the rest of the afternoon in her arms."

They turned back to the trunk of the thick pine they were clearing. Elphame met her brother's eyes.

"I told you that she loved you."

Cu laughed heartily. "In this particular case, I could not be more pleased that you were right, sister-mine."

Laughingly, Elphame looked up at him. And her smile froze. Behind Cuchulainn's shoulder, a single dark cloud suddenly obscured the brightness of the sunlight. There was something about it—something cold and foreboding—that sent a finger of dread down her spine. Elphame shivered.

"What is it?" he asked.

She blinked, and the cloud vanished. Had it really been there at all? The bright warmth of the day blew back into her soul and the chill that had shaken her became nothing more than a trick of sunlight through trees.

"El?"

She shook her head and took a firmer grip on the tree. "It's nothing but my wandering mind. Let's hurry. You don't want to make Brenna wait, and I agree with her. You definitely need to bathe." She laughed and wrinkled her nose at her sweaty brother.

Brenna felt light and happy and very, very beautiful. She swung the basket that she had filled with fragrant cheeses, fresh baked bread, boiled quail eggs and slices of smoked pork. She had even managed a skin of Cu's mother's best wine. She stepped off the road and smiled at how green everything was becoming. Tiny purple flowers had sprung up overnight, and little lime-colored plants that looked like upside-down baskets formed pretty, oval clusters. The forest looked like it had dressed up just for her—and the silly, romantic thought made her smile widen.

Fand's whine let Brenna know the cub had fallen behind. She turned and peered through the trees. The cub had sat her rounding bottom down in the middle of the road, and she was staring piteously at Brenna.

"Come on," Brenna coaxed. "The big pine tree is there," she pointed above her, "which means we aren't far from the pool."

Fand didn't move.

Brenna clucked at the little cub. "Come on, sweeting. I brought some milk and a cheesecloth for you. I'll spread a blanket and you can sleep until *he* joins us." Of course she knew the cub couldn't really understand what she was saying, but her tone was soft and persuasive, and she patted her thigh and coaxed until the obstinate creature left the road and followed her into the forest. "Good, girl!" she gushed. "Cu will be so proud of you."

Brenna's attention was focused on the cub, so she didn't notice when the shadow detached from the nearest pine and began following her.

The musical sound of falling water was very near when Fand suddenly growled.

"Fand? What is it, baby?" Her initial reaction was to laugh. The scruff on the back of Fand's neck stood straight up as the cub showed her baby teeth and backed slowly toward Brenna. The small wolf looked adorably unimposing. She was just a round bit of gray fluff, making little pretend wolf sounds. Brenna thought she actually showed more resemblance to a hedgehog.

Darkness flashed, shadowlike across the edge of her vision. Fand's growls increased. Brenna turned her head and her breath gasped from her lungs in a rushing *uh!* sound.

The winged creature was very beautiful. Brenna noted the unique color of its eyes and the lithe strength of its body, almost as if she was cataloguing the symptoms of a newly discovered disease. Brenna did not panic, nor did she scream and struggle. With feral speed that was more than human, the creature closed on her. The clear light of the new day glinted dangerously from its fangs.

"I do this because he has forced me to. It is the only way." The winged being's voice was surprisingly soft and melodic.

Even though Brenna saw the surety of her death within the creature's eyes, she could not force her body to move. She was frozen, trapped within that doom-filled stare. Though her body would not respond, Brenna's mind remained very clear. Her first thought was how unlike the accident this was. That had been a day filled with fire and pain. This was, at first, a gentle invasion. The creature held her close and its head dipped to the unscarred side of her neck. Brenna felt the teeth press against the softness of her skin. When they broke through, she was filled with a rush of euphoria, and she could not hold back a moan. Then there was a hot, pulling sensation, and, as if from far away, Brenna heard the distinctive sound of tearing flesh.

She closed her eyes and thought of Cuchulainn. *Epona, help him not to mourn for too long.* It seemed time suspended while her mind formed her final prayer. *And thank you, Goddess, for allowing me to know love and acceptance before I knew death.* The pulling sensation at her neck increased and Brenna could hear her own breath coming in loud gasps. Her legs lost their strength. Still drinking from her neck, the creature held her in a crude parody of a lover's embrace. The world against Brenna's closed eyelids went from scarlet to black, but before pain, and death in its turn could claim her, she felt herself lifted up and out of her collapsing body and her soul was filled with the indescribable peace of Epona's welcoming arms.

"I think Kathryn would make the best addition to my staff," Wynne said, brushing an escaping curl from her face.

Elphame spoke through another bite of the excellent venison stew Wynne had concocted for the midday meal. "She admits to having little experience as a cook, but she is young and very willing. I agree with you, she will learn easily."

"Meara will be angry. She hates to lose one of her minions."

Elphame thought about the head housekeeper's pleasingly round figure. She smiled. "Cook Meara something special as a peace offering."

Wynne nodded thoughtfully. "Something sugary."

"A lot of something sugary."

A sudden sound interrupted Elphame's laughter, and she was just peering around Wynne to try and see what was causing the commotion when she heard the first shout.

"Elphame!"

She recognized Danann's gravely voice and she was already rushing from the Great Hall when the old centaur clattered into the courtyard. Her breath caught at the grimness of his expression.

"Your brother needs you."

The centaur spun around and rushed toward the entrance of the castle. Elphame beat him there. Just outside the castle walls was a sea of confusion. Men were frantically saddling horses. Centaurs were rushing up from the forest edge. Elphame could hear Brighid's name being shouted. And in the midst of the melee, Cuchulainn stood very still while his horse was being saddled. In his arms her white-faced brother clutched the wolf cub, who was splattered with blood. She sprinted to him.

"It's Brenna," Cuchulainn said.

"What's wrong? Where is she?" Elphame looked quickly at the cub. Fand had no wounds on her body. It wasn't the wolf's blood that spotted her fur.

"I found Fand in the forest near the pool. She was alone. I called and searched for Brenna. There were odd tracks. I did not understand them." Cu spoke quickly in short, clipped sentences, as if forming words was difficult. "I came back for Brighid and for this." His hand went to the claymore now securely strapped to his back.

The dreadful finger that had touched her spine earlier that day formed a cold fist which closed around Elphame's heart.

Brighid's hoofs pounded against the grassy ground as she galloped up to them.

"What has happened?"

"Something attacked Brenna." Cuchulainn handed the cub to the man who had finished saddling his horse. Then he leaped aboard the gelding. "Near the pool where the three of you bathed. I can't read the tracks."

"Show me," Brighid said.

Cuchulainn pointed the gelding down the road and, without another word, the group sprinted after him. Elphame ran by her brother's side. She tried not to think.

At the base of the huge pine Cuchulainn veered from the road. He dismounted quickly and continued for only a few more feet until he stopped beside the discarded picnic basket.

"Here." He pointed to a small section of the forest floor. The newly awakened wildflowers were smashed and scarlet drops darkened the delicate green foliage.

Brighid motioned for the group to stay back as she bent to study the ground. Elphame saw her face tighten, and for a moment the Huntress looked up and met her Chieftain's eyes before returning her searching gaze to the forest floor. When she spoke, she did so without glancing away from the story the tracks told.

"Stay behind me."

The group moved off in a silent column of twos, Elphame and Cuchulainn leading those behind Brighid. She moved quickly away from the pool back toward the road, following the tracks which ran eerily close to Brenna's original footprints. The Huntress crossed the road not far from where the group had left it, and plunged back into the forest. Soon she turned abruptly north.

Elphame jogged up beside her. "Is there any sign of Brenna?" she asked quietly.

"It carries her."

Feeling ill, Elphame dropped back to her brother's side. They shadowed the Huntress without speaking. At first Brighid moved with swift surety, but as the land began to form the familiar northern pattern of rocky ridges interspersed with streams and chasms, the Huntress's pace slowed noticeably, until she finally halted. When she turned to face Cuchulainn, her voice was sharp with frustration.

"I've lost it. It moves like nothing I've tracked before. Its strides are impossibly far apart—almost as if it can fly."

Cuchulainn dropped his horse's reins and covered the space between himself and the Huntress so that he was standing so close to her that his body almost touched hers.

"You can't have lost it. It has Brenna."

"I know that!" Brighid cried. "I would give anything if it were not so, but I cannot track a thing that moves through the air."

Cuchulainn took a step back, almost as if she had struck him. "If you cannot track her, then how do we find her?"

"We form a hunt line and we search." Elphame spoke

suddenly. She pointed to one of the men behind them. "Go to Loth Tor. Call out the village. Have them bring torches. Go, man, quickly!" she ordered when he stared stupidly at her. Then she turned back to the Huntress and her brother. "Spread out here. Begin searching. I'll return to the castle and call forth the clan. We will cover this forest like locusts. We will find Brenna." She hugged Cuchulainn fiercely and felt the tremor that passed through his rigid body as he softened enough to return her embrace.

With a nod to Brighid, she sprinted back through the woods. At first Elphame concentrated on her speed and on navigating the rough, rocky terrain, but as she drew nearer to the castle her thoughts burst through the wall of silent shock that had kept them at bay.

The tracks had been made by a creature of Fomorian descent. She'd have recognized them even without Brighid's telling look. It couldn't be Lochlan. She wouldn't believe it. It wasn't possible. Or was it?

Her arms pumped and her muscles burned in time with the tumult within her mind.

Her thoughts circled frantically, picking out words and images and forming them into a ghastly tableau of condemnation…her memory of sunlight glinting off Lochlan's fangs joined with his words, *I do have the blood of a race of demons within my body, and that is something that neither of us can ever forget.* The small scabs on her neck seemed to burn.

What if tasting her blood had driven him mad? Was that why he had run from her—had he forced himself to leave before he lost control? And now Brenna was paying the price for Elphame's silence and for her decision to place her trust in a creature who was part-demon.

No! Her heart shouted. He was her lifemate; his coming had been foretold by Cuchulainn himself. He could not be an insane monster. Yes, the tracks had been made by a Fomorian creature, but Lochlan had told her that there were others of his race who were battling against the mad pull of their demon blood. It could be that one of those creatures had followed him and had finally succumbed to his dark urges.

But she had to know. She had to be sure. There was only one way.

Elphame stumbled to a halt at the edge of the tree line that surrounded her beloved castle. Staying within the cover of the pines, she faced north—the direction from which Lochlan had entered Partholon. She raised her hands and spoke into the wind.

"Lochlan! Come to me…"

Her lover's name glistened in a magical haze before her, and then the wind swirled through and around it, picked it up, and scattered it out into the listening forest.

For a moment she bowed her head, feeling the weight of her decision pressing down through her soul. Then she stepped from the trees.

35

"STAY WITHIN TEN paces of each other. Until we are joined by the others we cannot afford to stretch our line too thin. The object is to find evidence of the creature's trail, so that we are certain in what direction we must search," Brighid explained, looking from Cuchulainn to the group of men and centaurs who surrounded her. "We'll move forward in a line together. Go slowly, match your pace with mine. The tracks are unusual, distinctive. Look for talonlike slashes in the earth. They are large, bigger than a centaur's hoof."

With little talking, the men spread out. Cuchulainn took his position near the Huntress.

"What is this creature?" His hushed voice carried easily to her in the unnaturally silent forest.

She stared out into the trees, remembering the glance she and her Chieftain had shared near the pool. Elphame had known the tracks were the same as those they had spoken of days earlier, yet she hadn't acknowledged it. What was Brighid to do now, tell Cuchulainn that they had knowledge of a taloned creature lurking in the woods, but they chose to ignore it? As if to wipe away her confusion Brighid rubbed the back of her hand across her brow and told the warrior a partial truth. "I do not know, Cuchulainn. I have never encountered a creature that could make such tracks."

"It's killed her, hasn't it?" His voice was devoid of expression, but his eyes pleaded with Brighid to argue with him, to tell him that he was wrong.

"It carried Brenna off, we know that, but I have found no further evidence of blood, and there was really very little blood at the site of her abduction. That tells us that she has not bled to death."

Unspoken between them was the understanding that there were countless ways to die without bleeding to death. Brighid looked away from Cuchulainn's tortured gaze to check the line of searchers that stretched from either side of them. She raised her arm so that their attention was focused on her and nodded grimly.

"Let us begin!" she shouted.

As one, they moved slowly forward. To Cuchulainn time seemed to bend in upon itself. His logical mind knew that time was passing normally—the forest shadows were lengthening, giving evidence of the waning day—but it felt like only the space of a few breaths had passed since he had held a laughing Brenna in his sweaty arms and then watched her skip off down the road to await their tryst. And nearer still in his mind was the Feeling that had crept over him as he and Brenna had returned from the pool the previous morning. It had been a warning; he had Felt Brenna's doom, and he had ignored it, as he had ignored knowledge that came to him from the spirit realm so many times in the past. What was happening now was his fault. If he had not rejected the spirit realm he would have been prepared. He would not have let Brenna leave his sight. Self-loathing roiled through his mind.

And then the echo of a distant sound brushed against his skin, causing the hair on his arms to lift. It swirled from behind him; it wasn't so much sound as touch or Feeling. It was living magic that traveled on the breath of the wind.

"Wait!" he cried.

Instantly, Brighid lifted her hand and called for the line to halt.

Concentrating on hearing with more than his ears, Cuchulainn stretched the underdeveloped preternatural senses that he usually rejected. The tangible sound *shushed* past him, up the rocky incline that angled before them, and then, just as suddenly as the Feeling had come, it was gone. He sighed at its loss and cursed his own incompetence. When trafficking with the spirit realm he was as a babe amidst elders. Defeated, he almost motioned for Brighid to call the line forward again when he felt an answering awareness spill down from the other side of the incline and tumble over and past him in a tumult of sensation.

Cuchulainn raised his head and pointed up the incline. "There—something is there."

Together, the warrior and the Huntress led the way. They topped the ridge, and were surprised to come upon a break in the unrelenting forest. The area was only a dozen or fewer paces across, a mini-oasis of grassy meadow ringed by what Cuchulainn recognized as ancient oaks, rather than the tall, imposing pines that proliferated the majority of the area surrounding MacCallan Castle. A movement within the darkness of the trees at the opposite side of the meadow caught Cuchulainn's attention just as the winged creature stepped from the shelter of the trees into the meadow. He carried within his arms the limp body of Brenna.

Fomorian! In a rush of recognition his mind registered what

the monster must be. Then time folded and changed again, speeding up so that movements and sounds became blurred and surreal. The creature halted and his eyes locked with Cuchulainn. The satisfying *twang* of Brighid's bow setting loose an arrow echoed the deadly sound of Cuchulainn's claymore being drawn from its sheath. The creature lunged to the side, and even as the arrow embedded itself to the quill in his shoulder, Cuchulainn noticed that the monster seemed to cradle Brenna's body carefully, as if in some sick corner of his mind he played at keeping her safe.

"Brenna!" The name tore from Cuchulainn's throat as he lunged across the clearing.

The creature stood silently and made no move to run or to protect himself. Only his wings moved. They rustled and opened, but the creature's storm-gray eyes never wavered. Cuchulainn could feel Brighid and the rest of their party behind him as he closed on the creature. He tried not to look at Brenna. He tried not to see how pale and still she was.

When he was an arm's length from the creature, it spoke.

"I was too late. She is dead."

His voice was deep and powerful and the obvious sadness in it hit Cuchulainn like a fist. The warrior pointed his claymore at the creature's neck.

"Put her down and meet your doom."

Slowly, the winged being knelt and with obvious gentleness lay Brenna's unmoving body on the grassy ground. When he stood, the searchers surged forward with one mind, but Cuchulainn's grim order halted them.

"No! He is mine to kill."

With blinding speed, Cuchulainn lunged at the unresisting creature. But the instant before his blade cut through the monster's neck he spoke again, and the one word he shouted caused Cuchulainn's arm to falter, so that the stroke tore the creature's wing and sliced through the same shoulder the arrow had penetrated instead of severing his neck.

"Elphame!"

The name seemed to become a living thing. It hovered in the air around them like a prayer before being swept up into the waiting sky.

Cuchulainn narrowed his eyes and held his claymore at ready, pointing the wicked blade at the creature's throat.

"How dare you speak my sister's name!" he spat.

Lochlan had fallen to one knee. His torn wing hung helpless and limp against the bloodied ground, and his hand tried to staunch the blood that flowed freely from his wounded shoulder, but the gray eyes that met Cuchulainn's were unwavering and his voice was strong and sure.

"I speak my Chieftain's name by right of blood and oath and I evoke the clan right to have her hear my petition. She alone may decide my fate."

"You are not of the Clan MacCallan!" Cuchulainn growled.

Lochlan struggled to his feet. Through teeth clenched against pain he made his proclamation in a voice that rang against the ancient oaks.

"My mother was Morrigan, youngest sister to The Mac-Callan who ruled these lands. Today I publicly claim my birthright. Only The MacCallan herself can call me false!"

"Take him to your sister." Brighid's flinty voice cut through the echoing silence. "She loved Brenna as well as you did. It will give her great pleasure to see this beast disemboweled."

Listening to Brighid's words, Cuchulainn stared at the creature. The wings, talons and teeth said undeniably that he was Fomorian, but even through Cuchulainn's rage and grief he could see the clear stamp of humanity on his features.

"Bind his hands and tie him to my saddle. If he cannot walk to The MacCallan, I will drag him to her."

While they bound the unresisting Lochlan, Cuchulainn knelt beside Brenna. She was so very pale. He touched her face. So cold—her skin was so cold. She looked peaceful, as if she was simply asleep. Except for her neck. The creature had torn a fist-sized piece of flesh from her soft skin. Cuchulainn felt the reality of her death settle down through the layers of his mind and into his heart and soul.

"Bring me a strip of cloth!" he called without taking his gaze from her sweet face.

The brightness of Brighid's coat registered at the edge of his vision as the Huntress handed him a silk strip of cloth torn from the inside of her vest. Cuchulainn wound it carefully around Brenna's neck, so that no one could gape at the obscenity of the terrible damage done to her. Then he bent and kissed her cold lips.

"I'll take you home, love," he murmured.

Brighid held his horse while he mounted, then gently she passed Brenna's body to him. Holding his lover securely in his arms, Cuchulainn kicked the gelding into a canter. It gave him grim satisfaction to hear the winged creature stumble, fall and be dragged several paces before he regained his feet. Let him suffer as Brenna had. He clutched her unresisting body, trying not to think of the reality of what her death meant—that she was forever lost to him—that he would never again know her gentle touch or see reflected in her smile the wonder with which she viewed the new world of love and belonging that had been unfolding around her. He could not think of it now. Now he would only think of two things. He would take Brenna home and he would see that her killer breathed no more.

The clan was silent, assembled and ready, waiting only for the last of the torches to be gathered and lit. Elphame stood a little apart from where they congregated in front of the castle walls. A chilling breeze brushed searchingly against her skin, bringing with it the almost soundless echo of the cry of her name. Elphame shivered. The sun was beginning to set, working its way down toward the sea in a blaze of scarlet and rust. Her mouth felt unnaturally dry. Even the sky was filled with blood.

"All is ready," Danann told her.

Elphame turned to look at her people, and a movement on the balcony of the Chieftain's Tower caught her eye. For an instant the setting sun illuminated the ethereal shape of the old spirit, and The MacCallan raised his hand to her in a silent salute. She blinked, and the ghost was gone. Her eyes settled downward on the somber group of humans and centaurs.

"It is still light enough for us to move quickly. Stay close. I left Cuchulainn and the group not far from here. When we come upon them, Brighid will reorder you."

Heads nodded. Satisfied, Elphame turned to begin moving the group across the northern side of the newly cleared castle grounds, but before she could kick into her ground-eating jog, light flashed within the darkening shadows of the forest edge directly across from her. Her heart caught and her steps faltered as first Brighid, then Cuchulainn broke from the pines.

No! Her mind cried the word but her lips formed only a silent, anguished scream. Cuchulainn carried Brenna's unmoving body in his arms. Elphame did not need to look farther than her brother's face to know that her friend was dead.

And then through the tide of grief, Elphame saw that Cuchulainn pulled something behind his gelding. It stumbled and fell as her brother kneed his horse into a gallop that quickly closed the distance between them. He reined his horse to the side and pulled him to a sliding stop so that the bloodied, torn creature rolled and then lay still mere paces from Elphame and the Clan MacCallan.

At first she saw only wings and long, scarlet-spattered limbs. For an instant she allowed her heart to believe that it might not be him. Then he struggled to his knees and lifted his face.

"Elphame, I did not reach her in time," Lochlan rasped. "Forgive me for not knowing what they would do until it was too late."

She heard gasps from behind her and startled exclamations. The word *Fomorian* whispered through the castle grounds like a curse too terrible to be spoken aloud. Elphame could feel her clan's shock and dismay, but she did not look away from Lochlan—not at her brother and her murdered friend, and not at the Huntress whose knowing gaze was almost a tangible pressure against her skin.

"Who killed her?"

He spoke into the sudden silence that Elphame's question evoked. "Four of my people followed me. I ordered them to return to the Wastelands and await me there. I thought they had left. They gave me their oaths that they would leave Partholon. Instead, they killed Brenna."

"You know this creature!" Cuchulainn roared.

Elphame looked away from Lochlan and into her brother's pain-filled eyes.

"I know him. He has sworn his oath to me." The murmuring grew louder and she raised her voice to be heard over the distress of her clan. "It was his right. His mother was Morrigan, The MacCallan's own sister, abducted during the Fomorian war, raped and left for dead in the Wastelands. She survived his birth—she and others like her."

Slowly, Cuchulainn slid from the saddle, careful to support Brenna's lifeless weight. He strode to his sister and faced her, his lover's body all that separated them.

"How can you say these things about the monster that killed Brenna?" His voice was raw.

"He is not a monster, Cuchulainn. I have handfasted with him. He is the lifemate you foretold that I would find here."

Cries of disbelief sounded from around them, but Elphame did not look away from her brother. Shaking his head wildly, Cuchulainn staggered back. When Elphame moved to him, her brother flinched from her touch. She pulled her hand back as if he had burned her.

"By the Goddess, this cannot be." Cuchulainn's voice seemed to come from a tomb.

"Cuchulainn!" Lochlan had struggled to his feet. His hands, bound and bleeding, pulled taut against the rope. "Go north of where you found me. There you will find those responsible for this atrocity. My people will not have traveled far."

Eyes blazing, the warrior's head whipped around. "And why would they still be there, creature? Could it be that you set a trap and that they wait there to spring it upon us?"

"They cannot fight you, they cannot run from you. I have torn their wings. They are at your mercy, as am I."

To Elphame's numbed mind, Lochlan's words were one shock layered upon another and another. Brenna murdered, Lochlan captured, their bond revealed, her brother looking at her with eyes that seemed not to see his sister, and now Lochlan said that he had torn the wings—those ultimately sensitive extensions of the soul—of his own people. The only thing that kept her from crying out in agony was the weight of The MacCallan brooch that held her plaid into place.

Then Cuchulainn's voice cut into her shock. "If you were at my mercy, creature, you would not draw another breath."

Elphame's reaction was born in her blood. The MacCallan raised her chin and drew back her shoulders. Unflinchingly she met her brother's blazing gaze.

"You are correct, Cuchulainn." Her voice was stone. "He is not at your mercy, he is at mine. Take a group of men and centaurs of your choice." She glanced at the Huntress. "Go with them. Track the hybrid Fomorians." Brighid bowed her head, acknowledging her Chieftain's order. Then Elphame's gaze returned to her brother. "Bring them back so that they can be judged." Steeling herself, she approached him again. This time he did not flinch away from her, but neither did his expression soften. She held open her arms. "I will take Brenna. She is home now."

Cuchulainn hesitated, and then a shudder rippled through his body. Reluctantly, he placed Brenna in his sister's arms.

Without taking his eyes from hers, Cuchulainn jerked his chin at Lochlan. "What will you do with him?" His voice sounded as dead as his heart.

"He is my captive and will remain so until justice is served."

He narrowed his eyes. "See that you keep him well guarded."

"See that you bring the others back alive," she retorted.

Stiffly, as if she were a stranger, Cuchulainn bowed to her before he began shouting orders. He unwrapped the rope to which Lochlan was tethered from around his saddle and tossed it to one of the men standing nearby.

"Guard him well," he said to the grim-faced man. Then, without another look at his sister, he and Brighid led the group of well-armed men and centaurs into the forest.

Elphame knew what she must do, and she gave the command without hesitation, but her heart felt like a leaden weight within her breast and she could not look at Lochlan. The legendary Mac-Callan Castle had no dank dungeons or iron-barred jailhouse. When a clan member committed a crime justice was swift and permanent—according to the will of the Chieftain, either the criminal's life was forfeited or he was banished. The clan whose battle cry was "Faith and Fidelity" tolerated no oath breakers.

"Take him within the walls of the castle and bind him to

one of the columns. While we await Cuchulainn's return he will be treated as my prisoner."

The man holding Lochlan's rope jerked it forward cruelly. Elphame's response was immediate—her voice a dagger.

"I have acknowledged his claim as a member of our clan and accepted his oath. You would be wise to remember to treat him as such."

The man looked hastily away. The fire in Elphame's eyes said that she was more than a Chieftain; she was touched by the Goddess. One did not evoke the wrath of a Goddess lightly.

As the group moved silently past her and into the castle, Danann approached Elphame.

"Let me help you with the little Healer, Goddess."

His eyes were filled with compassion and the anger within Elphame extinguished, leaving her feeling lost and exhausted.

"She's so light," Elphame said brokenly.

"Brenna's body did not define her. She was a great will housed in a small form," Danann said.

"Her heart was her strength," Wynne said, stepping into the space beside the centaur. Tracks of tears made smudged paths down her ivory cheeks.

"As was her kindness," said Meara as she joined them. Her voice trembled with emotion and she, too, wept openly. "We would be honored if you would allow us to assist you in anointing Brenna's body."

Elphame looked from the wise old centaur to the two young women. They did not shrink from her or accuse her of being the defender of a monster. They had not withdrawn their loyalty from her; she was still their Chieftain. Elphame struggled against her own tears. She was The MacCallan; her clan depended upon her strength. She would not cry.

"I accept your offer of aid. Come with me to Brenna's tent, we will prepare her there."

The four of them made a sad procession, weaving their way past the empty tents that littered the south side of the castle grounds to Brenna's temporary home. Sitting near the entrance of her tent was the little wolf cub. Elphame had forgotten about Fand, and she was surprised to see that someone had tied her to one of the tent posts. The cub bounced to her feet, wriggling a greeting, but as Elphame and her burden drew close, the young wolf's demeanor changed drastically. She dropped her ears and tail. Whimpering miserably, she slunk low to the ground. Elphame entered the tent and lay Brenna on the neatly made bed and they began anointing her body as the eerie sound of Fand's mournful howls echoed throughout the fading day.

36

ELPHAME STOOD CLOAKED within the shadows outside the Main Courtyard. The scene before her had a macabre, otherworldly feel. Torches burned brightly and the comforting sounds of people talking and finishing their evening meal drifted from the Great Hall mingling with the familiar splash of the fountain's ever-falling water. They were the noises of her castle at the end of a day. It would all be so normal if the scent of the oils she had used to anoint Brenna's body didn't still perfume her hands, and if guards were not positioned in the courtyard, standing vigilant watch over Lochlan.

Iron shackles attached to heavy chains cuffed Lochlan's wrists and ankles. The chains had been wrapped securely around the great central column of the castle. Lochlan sat at the column's base, leaning heavily against it. His eyes were closed. He was terribly bruised and battered. An arrow protruded from his left shoulder. Above the quill the muscle had been slashed and the laceration flapped open with an ugly heaviness. Blood coated the side of Lochlan's body. But the wound that drew Elphame's eyes and made her stomach tighten was the long tear that ran almost the length of his left wing. The undamaged wing was tucked snuggly against Lochlan's back, but the other one lay limp and partially opened, reminding Elphame of a dying bird.

Elphame drew several deep breaths, trying to ignore the overly sweet smell of the funeral oils. Her blood pounded fiercely in her temples. She wanted to rush to Lochlan and demand that they unchain him. If she had been anyone except The MacCallan she would have. She would rail at his guards that he had not killed Brenna—that he was not a demon. But she could not react as a distraught wife. She must deliver justice, not hysteria or tears. She could not save Lochlan. He must save himself. He must prove himself innocent of Brenna's death, or she would have to mete out punishment to him as she would to any other member of Clan MacCallan.

But as any other member of her clan, he was under her care and protection until his judgment was complete. As she had seen Brenna do so many times, she shifted the leather bag so that its strap rested comfortably over her shoulder and stepped into the flickering light of the torches. Her hooves clacked solidly against the smooth marble. The two armed guards bowed to her.

"Brendan, Duncan." She acknowledged them with a nod. Lochlan lifted his head.

"I'll need one of you to go to the kitchen. Wynne will have some broth ready soon. Bring it here to me, along with a skin of strong red wine."

Brendan bowed again before leaving to follow her orders. She met Duncan's eyes. "I would speak to Lochlan privately."

Duncan hesitated only a moment before he retreated reluctantly across the courtyard. Elphame noted that he remained far enough away so that their conversation could not be overheard, but close enough so that he could return to her side quickly if he thought she was in danger.

"How badly are you hurt?" she asked Lochlan.

He did not answer at first, he only stared at her while he shook his head slowly from side to side, and Elphame wondered again if madness might have begun to claim him.

"I did not kill Brenna." He enunciated the words slowly and distinctly.

Instead of speaking, she crouched next to him and opened Brenna's bag searching through it for the ointment that her friend had used to heal her wounds and linen strips to bind the wicked-looking cut in his shoulder.

The chains rattled as Lochlan grabbed her wrist. Drawing his claymore, Duncan took a step toward them, but Elphame motioned him off.

"I must know if you believe me," he said.

Elphame looked into his gray eyes and found that she could not answer him.

"The spirit of the stones can tell you, Goddess." Danann's disembodied voice carried from the entrance to the courtyard.

Elphame shook off Lochlan's hold and stood to face the centaur. He, too, smelled of the anointing oils. She had not known what oils to choose from Brenna's large selection; she had never before overseen the preparation of a body, and she knew that the care with which Danann had chosen the oils and led them in preparing Brenna was as indelibly imprinted into her memory as was the cool, slack feel of her friend's lifeless skin. The centaur's well-lined face reflected the strain of the past hours, but his eyes were still kind and wise. He approached her and studied Lochlan with a frank, open appraisal before returning his gaze to Elphame.

"Ask the spirit of the great column. Through it you will know the truth."

Elphame's eyes widened. The thought had not crossed her mind, but she realized that the Stonemaster was correct. She had within her the ability to tell infallibly whether Lochlan had any part in Brenna's death.

The chains clanked as Lochlan struggled to his feet. "What does the centaur mean?" he rasped painfully.

"He means that the spirit within the stone of this column and I are connected. Through it I can see within you and know whether you harmed Brenna or not."

Lochlan closed his eyes wearily, and for a moment Elphame thought that he might lose consciousness, but they blinked open. The sadness she saw within them washed over her with his words.

"You should not need the spirits of your castle to tell you that I could not commit such a crime."

"Should she not?" Danann broke in, speaking to Lochlan as if he were lecturing an errant schoolboy. "Perhaps your lifemate should be expected to trust you implicitly, but your lifemate is also The MacCallan. She must be more discerning. Do not ever underestimate the depth of responsibility she carries within her blood."

As he listened to Danann's words, a change came over Lochlan's face. The sadness lifted and only the weariness remained.

"You do well to chide me, Master Centaur," Lochlan said. "I knew what she was when I pledged myself to her. I should expect no less of her." He looked at his Chieftain and wife. "Ask the spirits so that The MacCallan's mind may be at rest."

Elphame approached him. He was still leaning heavily against the column. She touched the carved stone beside him. Her hand tingled with warmth as the spirit beneath her palm awakened and responded to her touch. She locked her gaze with his as she spoke.

"I need to know if Lochlan is guilty of Brenna's death."

She felt the surge of heat and the molten connection as her spirit merged with that of the great column. Like the exhaling of a long-held breath, part of her awareness flowed out through her hand, curled, and then poured from the stone into Lochlan.

He inhaled a breath sharply in surprise as he felt the warmth invade his battered body, but his eyes did not waver from Elphame.

"I did not kill Brenna." He repeated the words carefully.

And suddenly Elphame was shaken by bolts of emotion as she Felt the truth within Lochlan. *Shock…anger… despair!* She knew his devastation at discovering what had been done to Brenna. And then she Felt the remembrance of her own call engulfing him. *Resignation…sorrow…* He had answered her call even though he understood that in doing so he would probably be embracing his doom.

Her heart had been right; he was not guilty of Brenna's death. He was only guilty of finding her. She wanted to weep and cheer. The MacCallan could do neither, but with her power there was one thing she could do.

"Forgive me for doubting." She mouthed the silent words before she bowed her head and concentrated on sending healing warmth from her own body, through the heart of her castle, and into her lifemate's wounded body.

She heard him gasp as her strength poured into him and through their connection she Felt the echo of his thoughts, *There is nothing to forgive, my heart.*

A strong hand grasped her shoulder and her head jerked up.

"Enough, Goddess," Danann said. "You may have need of your own strength soon."

Reluctantly, Elphame pulled her palm from the living stone. Her head buzzed strangely and her arms felt unnaturally heavy.

"Bring your Chieftain some wine!" the centaur barked at

Duncan. "And warm water and linens so that we may care for Lochlan's wounds." When Duncan hesitated Danann spoke with gruff annoyance. "He can hardly move, man! I may be old, but I can certainly protect Elphame from someone who is half-dead."

"Go on," Elphame said faintly.

Frowning, Duncan hurried off toward the kitchen.

"Sit before you fall down," Danann told her.

Elphame did as she was told and sat on the marble floor not far from Lochlan. He smiled weakly at her and slid slowly down the column, joining her on the floor. He still looked terrible, but his breathing was easier and there was a hint of color in his cheeks.

"He did not kill Brenna," she said to the centaur, who was riffling through the Healer's bag.

He paused and glanced at her. "Of course he didn't," he said gruffly.

"You did not believe I killed her?" Lochlan blurted.

Danann raised one grizzled brow. "Our Elphame is not a fool to have chosen to handfast with a monster."

"Then why did you tell me to ask the spirit of the column?" Elphame said.

"You already know the answer to that, Goddess," Danann said.

But it was Lochlan who spoke before Elphame could. "For what is to come—she had to be certain, in more than her heart. She had to know the truth in her soul."

"You know the truth may not change things." The old centaur looked pointedly from Lochlan to Elphame.

The strength Lochlan had received from his lover seemed to drain from him and he slumped wearily against the column.

"I only know one thing for certain. I am sick to death of hiding, and come what may, Partholon will know we exist. What happens afterwards is in Epona's hands."

"Well, if you are to take on Partholon, I suggest we clean you up and care for your wounds."

Duncan returned first, with a skin of wine thrown over his arm and carrying a small basin, a pitcher of water, and some clean cloth. Danann took the pitcher and cloths, and motioned for Duncan to give Elphame the wine before the guard retreated back to his spot beside the fountain.

"Drink deeply," Danann advised her.

She was happy to comply; her mouth felt incredibly dry. She drank the reviving liquid and felt some of her weakness recede along with the faint buzzing in her head. Then she joined Danann beside Lochlan.

"Drink deeply." She echoed the old centaur's words as she helped Lochlan hold the wineskin to his mouth. He drank and Elphame tried to assess his wounds.

"The arrow must come out," Danann said, mirroring her thoughts. "The shoulder wound should probably have been sewn closed, but too much time has passed now and I think the pain it would cost him would not be worth the benefit."

Elphame nodded hastily. Her stomach quivered at the thought of sewing Lochlan's skin together.

"Get his shirt off and clean him up as best you can. After that arrow comes out the hole it leaves will need cauterizing. I'll go to Brenna's tent to find the iron she used, and then have it heated," Danann said grimly, and squeezed her shoulder before he left them alone.

Lochlan was holding the wineskin on his own, allowing Elphame's hands to be freed to pour the water from the pitcher into the basin. She felt his eyes on her as she wetted one of the cloths.

"This was not how we intended to make my introduction to the clan."

"No," she said softly, thinking of Brenna's lifeless body.

With fingers that felt clumsy, she began to unlace his blood-encrusted shirt. "Everything has gone so terribly wrong, Lochlan," she said as she worked the ties. His hand closed over hers and she raised her eyes to his.

"Not our love, my heart. Our love has not gone wrong. Remember that whatever happens I do not regret one instant of the time I have loved you."

"I've brought the broth, milady."

Brendan's voice broke between them and Elphame glanced up to see the man looking at their joined hands. Lochlan slowly took his hand from hers, though he stonily returned Brendan's stare.

"Give me your knife," Elphame said.

Though there was a clear question in his expression, Brendan complied and then watched as she cut the blood-covered shirt from Lochlan. She handed the knife back to the man, who was staring in obvious curiosity at Lochlan's powerful chest and the enormous wings that grew from his back.

"Do you want to drink the broth now, or wait until we're done…" Elphame gestured nervously at the arrow that must be pulled from his body.

"Now," he said, touching her cheek gently in a quick caress. "From what the centaur said I believe I will have need of its healing strength."

Without looking at Brendan, Elphame held out her hand and the man silently handed her the steaming mug. Lochlan drank it quickly, and then nodded at her. Steeling herself against the pain she knew she had to be causing him, Elphame set to work cleaning her lifemate's wounds. Lochlan closed his eyes and leaned against the stone column. Every so often he would raise the wineskin to his lips with a hand that shook only slightly.

Danann's hooves announced his approach. He held a wicked-looking pair of shears in his hand. With much cracking of ancient knees, the centaur settled himself beside Lochlan.

"This is what we must do," he explained to the winged man. "I will cut it off here, just below the quill." He pointed to the arrow. "I will count three and pull it out. Then will come the uncomfortable part." The centaur's gaze shifted to the man standing nearby. "Brendan, the cauterizing iron is in the kitchen hearth. When the arrow is out, fetch it quickly."

"That would be the uncomfortable part," Lochlan said wryly.

Danann smiled. "Not the fetching of it."

An unexpected chuckle shook Lochlan's shoulders and he winced at the pain. "Let's get on with it then, Master Centaur."

"Grasp the quill," Danann told Elphame.

Don't think of him as Lochlan, she ordered herself frantically as she took hold of the arrow's end. Think of him as a stranger you're trying to help. She clenched her teeth together, trying to forget that she had rested against that shoulder and tasted its sweat with her searching lips.

With a crack the shears snapped through the wooden shaft.

"Now lean forward," Danann ordered.

Elphame thought Lochlan fell rather than leaned forward. The torn wing lay across him, covering his back. Without looking at Danann, Elphame gently gathered the limp wing in her hands and lifted, then folded it so that the protruding end of the bloody arrowhead was exposed. The only sound Lochlan made was a pain-filled groan at the first touch of her hands on his wing.

One of the centaur's gnarled hands closed around the arrowhead, the other rested firmly against Lochlan's back.

"On three," he said. "One, two, three!"

The old Stonemaster's arm muscles bulged as he tore the arrow from Lochlan's body in one clean pull, then he pressed a cloth against the gaping hole, trying to stop the scarlet river that followed it.

"Quickly! Bring the iron," Elphame ordered Brendan, who was already turning toward the Great Hall.

Lochlan lay very still against the marble floor, his head hidden in the crook of his right arm.

Elphame stroked his hair, feeling the tremors that ran through his body. "It's almost over," she told him, trying to keep her voice from breaking.

In the space of just a few breaths, Brendan returned carrying a metal pole the length of a man's arm. The round end of it glowed with a sickening red light. Elphame barely noticed that he had been followed by several clan members, who stood watching in wary silence.

Danann motioned for Brendan to bring him the iron.

"Lochlan," the old centaur's voice was calm. "You must remain very still while I close the wound. Do you need to be held?" Danann asked him.

Lochlan turned his head so that he could look up at Elphame.

"Her touch will be enough."

He pulled his hand from under his body and offered it to her. Without hesitation Elphame clasped it within both of hers.

"Brace yourself," Danann said the instant before he plunged the glowing iron into Lochlan's bloody wound.

It was Elphame who cried aloud when Lochlan's body bowed in pain and the stench of burning flesh hovered like a toxic fog around them. Lochlan's eyes never left hers and he did not make a sound. When Danann finally took the burning iron away from his flesh and began salving the wound with balm, only then did Lochlan close his eyes and turn his head back into his arm. He did not release his hold on Elphame's hand.

"Elphame? I brought this for him."

Through vision blurred by tears she hadn't realized she had been shedding, Elphame looked up at Meara. The house-keeper was holding a neatly folded blanket, which she lay on the cold marble next to Lochlan.

"Thank you," Elphame said.

When Meara turned away, another woman took her place.

"Wynne sent more broth. The stew is for you, my Lady." Kathryn, the new addition to the kitchen staff, bobbed a quick curtsey before she placed the tray which held a mug of broth and a fragrant bowl of stew near Elphame.

Then another woman, who Elphame recognized as one of the weavers, broke from the watching group and approached her. She was carrying a small woolen wrap in her arms. With a shy smile she draped it around her Chieftain's shoulders.

"'Tis cool here at night, milady. Have a care for yer health." Her words rolled musically, placing her as one of the locals.

Unable to speak, Elphame smiled her thanks and her blurred gaze passed over her clan. Their expressions were somber, but she saw no anger or resentment amongst them, only the re-flection of the concern the three women had shown.

"Yes, have a care for your health, milady," called a man Elphame recognized as Angus.

His words broke the awkward silence of the clan. Several of the men approached Elphame, speaking softly to her and gazing with open curiosity at the winged man who needed only the touch of their Chieftain to endure such an agoniz-ing ordeal.

37

THE NIGHT PASSED slowly. Lochlan spoke very little as she and Danann finished tending his wounds. He drank the second mug of broth and then, wrapped in Meara's blanket, he settled back against the mighty column and appeared to sleep.

Elphame did not want to leave her lover, but she could feel her clan's need of her, and so while Lochlan rested she walked among them where they gathered in the Great Hall, stopping to talk here and there, but mostly being seen and letting them feel her presence. Her tears were gone and she had combed her hair and changed into a clean plaid, with the ancestral brooch of The MacCallan displayed clearly on her bodice. The clan's talk focused on the castle and the work yet ahead of them. No one mentioned the winged man chained in the next room, nor did they speak of Cuchulainn's mission, but there was a tangible sense of waiting, and many glances were cast surreptitiously toward the castle's entrance at the least sound of the wind brushing against the thick, expectant walls. No one left to sleep in the comfort of their tents, instead heads bobbed and then revived occasionally as the night aged, and Wynne and her cooks busied themselves keeping mugs filled with strong, black coffee and stomachs filled with thick stew.

The black of the night's sky was being replaced by the soft gray of predawn when Elphame crossed the Main Courtyard to check on Lochlan. Someone had brought chairs for Brendan and Duncan, who had refused to allow any of the other men to relieve them of their charge to guard the winged prisoner. Both men were sitting close to Lochlan and Elphame felt a jolt of surprise when she realized that the men were deep in conversation with him. Purposefully, she stepped lightly so that they would not notice her approach.

"One hundred and twenty-five years." Brendan shook his head. His expression was wary, but curiosity was thick in his voice. "I cannot imagine living so long. You don't even look as old as Danann."

Elphame's smile mirrored the one she heard in Lochlan's voice.

"I would not want to pit my wisdom against the centaur's. My years might outnumber his, but experience weights heavily in his favor. I would not want to cross wits with him."

Duncan snorted. "None of us would." He paused, as if carefully considering his next words. "I watched what happened when The MacCallan asked the spirit of the column to tell her the truth of you. If you had been guilty of the little Healer's death, our Lady would have known it then."

"I did not kill Brenna, but I tell you honestly that I will carry the guilt of her death to my grave. I should have found a way to prevent it," Lochlan said.

"Fate—she can be cruel," Brendan said.

Duncan grunted in agreement.

"Gentlemen, morning is near. Wynne has hot food and drink for you. I temporarily relieve you of your watch," Elphame said, stepping into the torchlight that illuminated the little group.

This time, instead of hesitating the two men rose to their feet, bowed to their Chieftain and walked silently from the courtyard. Alone with Lochlan, Elphame suddenly found that she didn't know what to say. She rearranged a pile of discarded bandages and placed the lid on a jar of balm.

"Sit here beside me for a little while, my heart."

Elphame's hands stilled and she looked into his eyes. His face was pale, and there were dark circles ringing his expressive eyes. The blanket that covered him had slipped from his wounded shoulder, and a pink tinge of blood seeped through to stain the white linen bandages. He was sitting more upright than he had been before when she had thought him sleeping, but he still leaned against the sturdy column, as if he, too, gained strength from its touch.

With a sigh, she sat on the cold marble near him.

"It's so hard to know what to do, Lochlan," she said miserably. "How do I balance who I am with what I feel?"

The chains rattled as he took her hand in his. "You are doing well. They are loyal to you, Elphame. You need not worry about losing your clan."

"And you? Should I not worry about losing you?"

"You cannot lose me, my heart."

"What if Cuchulainn doesn't find your people, or, worse yet, kills them and does not allow their story to be told? Or what will happen if he brings them here alive, and they lie— they say that you were in on the killing of Brenna? None of the clan can Feel the truth through the spirits of the stone. I can keep Cuchulainn from killing you, but I may have to banish you, Lochlan. Do you understand that?"

"I understand that you will do what you must do. But neither banishment nor death can destroy my love for you. And do not forget that Epona's hand is in this, Elphame. I have decided to trust the Goddess as my mother before me did."

Elphame shook her head. "I don't think I have your faith."

Lochlan smiled knowingly. "Don't you, my heart? You have been touched by the Goddess since before your birth. Perhaps you just need to trust yourself enough to listen for Her voice."

Elphame raised his hand so that she could press her cheek against the warmth of his palm. "Are you sure you're not as wise as Danann?"

"Quite sure."

He caressed the side of her face and she leaned forward to kiss him gently. Involuntarily, his wings stirred and he could not suppress a moan of pain. Elphame pulled away from him quickly, her face clouded with concern. She reached to touch his wounded wing, but stopped the gesture short, afraid to cause him more pain.

"The wing will heal," Lochlan said, trying to comfort her even though his voice sounded ragged. "I would not have survived in the Wastelands if I was fragile and easily broken."

"But it's your wing," she said.

"It will heal," he repeated. "Do not be afraid to touch me."

She was leaning carefully into him when the clatter of many hooves entering the castle caused her to jerk back. Heart pounding, she stood to face Cuchulainn and the dark news he brought with him.

When her brother rode into the courtyard she almost didn't recognize him. He was spattered with blood and filth, as was the golden Brighid who entered the room beside him. But it wasn't simply that Cuchulainn's visage had been changed by battle and exhaustion; his face had hardened into the mask of a stranger. Behind the warrior and the Huntress, men and centaurs crowded into the castle. Elphame recognized several of the men as having come from Loth Tor. Someone shouted from within the Great Hall, and the waiting clan surged into the courtyard.

Just within the torchlight, Cuchulainn reined his horse to a halt and dismounted stiffly. Then he unwound a thick length of rope from around the pommel of his saddle. Elphame held her breath as her brother's massive arm muscles bulged while he walked steadily toward her, pulling whatever was tethered to the rope with him. Elphame's sharp release of breath was lost in the collective gasp that filled the courtyard when the winged figures stumbled into the light. She heard Lochlan struggle to his feet behind her, but she could not take her eyes from her brother's captives.

There were four of them, three males and a female. Their hands were tied in front of them, and the rope that bound their wrists ran up to loop around each of their necks before it connected to the next prisoner, so that if one had fallen and been dragged by Cuchulainn's horse, he or she would have caused the others to be choked. They bled from multiple lacerations and were covered with dirt and blood, but their most terrible wounds were not on their bodies. The wounds that made Elphame's stomach wrench and her breath catch were the bloody shreds that their proud wings had become. Only the skeleton of their pinions remained. What used to be evidence of the strength gifted to them through their dark blood, were now only ribbons of mangled flesh.

They would not heal, Elphame realized with an understanding that sickened her.

"The creatures were where he said they would be," Cuchulainn said in the voice of a stranger. "They were not captured easily, but criminals seldom are." He gave another cruel tug on the rope and the male closest to him, who was obviously twin to the prisoner to whom he was bound, tripped and fell to his knees, causing the others to be wrenched together painfully.

Lochlan's chain clattered as he stepped forward to the end of his metal tether. "They are already defeated. There is no need for you to torture them."

Cuchulainn turned on him, eyes filled with fury. "They murdered Brenna!"

"*They* did not murder her, I did."

All eyes were drawn to the winged female. Her body showed the fewest signs of wounds; even her wings hadn't been as ravaged as the males. As she spoke she straightened her spine and attempted to hold her damaged wings tightly against her body. She tossed her silver hair back and her ice-colored eyes looked contemptuously around the gathering. Elphame thought she had a terrible beauty that burned from within her like a dangerous pale flame.

"Do not speak, Fallon," the tall blond male tied beside her hissed.

She ignored him and met Lochlan's eyes. "The time for silence is past, is it not, Lochlan?"

"Fallon, why—"

Elphame touched Lochlan's arm, breaking off his response, and Fallon's beautiful face twisted into an ugly sneer.

"That's right, Lochlan. Do not speak unless she allows it. As always, you are the hoofed goddess's puppet."

Elphame felt anger flare within her, and the ice in her voice matched the coldness in the female's eyes. "Take care how you address me. I am The MacCallan, Chieftain of Clan Mac-Callan, and your fate rests in my hands."

The winged woman's laughter was cruel and humorless, and Elphame knew without any doubt that she was looking into the eyes of madness.

"My long dead human mother would be pleased that I have

finally grasped the concept of irony. My fate does indeed rest in your hands, Goddess, except that until today it was you who were to have been sacrificed to fulfill that fate."

"Enough, Fallon!"

Lochlan had to roar over the sound of the clan's angry voices. No one came into MacCallan Castle and threatened its Chieftain without answering to the wrath of the clan.

Elphame raised her hand for silence. She walked toward Fallon and Cuchulainn moved so that he stood beside her. As they approached the winged female the male tied beside her stirred. Elphame ignored the jangle of Lochlan's chains as he strained against them, as well as the raw anger that radiated from her brother; her entire focus was on Fallon.

"Explain yourself," Elphame demanded.

Fallon lifted her chin. "Ask your lover the real reason he stole into Partholon alone and searched you out. It wasn't just that he had dreamed of you since your birth. It was more, much more." Her eyes turned sly. "But perhaps some part of you already knows that."

Elphame's clan murmured angrily and she had to lift her hand again for silence.

"By your own admission the blood of an innocent woman is on your hands, and now you stand within the heart of my castle and spew half-truths and riddles." Anger pulsed through Elphame's body, and as it filled her it shifted and changed into a righteous fury that tingled along her skin and make her thick hair swirl and crackle around her shoulders. In a voice magically magnified she repeated her command. *"Explain yourself!"*

Fallon's eyes widened at the clear evidence of the indwelling of a goddess's power, but instead of being humbled, it only seemed to fuel her madness. She turned her heated gaze on Lochlan.

"Look at how your lies find you out! There is no denying

that you recognized her as a goddess, yet in your obsession with her you thought to keep her to yourself. When you drained her blood and the curse was lifted from you, what then did you think to do with us? Or did you care so little for your own people that you did not think of us at all?"

"You have killed and embraced madness, Fallon. Your words are meaningless," Lochlan said.

But Elphame had been watching her lover carefully while Fallon had been speaking, and she had seen the guilt that flickered through his eyes before he schooled his expression.

"For once I will agree with the winged creature. These words are meaningless. The female killed Brenna, the female must die." Cuchulainn's voice was so devoid of emotion that it made Elphame's heart ache.

"No!" The male beside her growled through bloodied lips. "What she did, she did only to save our people. Lochlan abdicated the responsibility that was his as our leader. When he betrayed us and refused to sacrifice the hoofed goddess, Fallon believed she had no other choice."

Cuchulainn's angry roar was echoed by Clan MacCallan and several of the men drew their deadly claymores and moved forward as if they would strike the winged beings down.

"Silence!" Elphame's voice sizzled through the room, lifting the hair on forearms and causing prickles of power to move over skin. Silence fell like a snuffed torch.

Fallon's sarcastic laughter filled the power-thickened air with hatred. "I was wrong about you, Goddess. For all of your power, you really did not know. You had no idea that Lochlan sought you out to fulfill the Prophecy. You believed his cloyingly sweet words of love."

Lochlan's chains rattled as he pulled against them. "You know nothing of what you speak!"

"I know that it is your fault that the human female died!"

Fallon spewed her poison. "If you had fulfilled the Prophecy I would not have had to kill her to lure your lover from her stronghold." Again her maniacal laughter echoed throughout the courtyard. Then her crazed expression fell, like tallow melting from a candle, and her colorless eyes filled with tears. "But I was not prepared for your ultimate betrayal." Her long, slender hand touched the ragged edge of her torn wing, as if it did not truly belong to her. "Oh, Keir, look at what he did to us." She broke into sobs as the male beside her took her into his arms.

Elphame deliberately turned her back on Fallon. With a growing sense of numbness, she met Lochlan's gaze.

"Tell me about the Prophecy."

Lochlan drew a deep breath. Even though he was chained and wounded he stood tall and proud, looking more like a winged godling than a prisoner. When he spoke, his deep voice carried clearly throughout the castle, mesmerizing the gathered clan, but his eyes saw only Elphame.

"You already know that my mother was Morrigan, youngest sister to The MacCallan who was the last Chieftain of this clan. As many of the MacCallan women have been, my mother was touched by Epona. She passed on to me her deep faith, as well as a prophecy she swore Epona whispered to her in a dream. The Prophecy foretold that *through the blood of a dying goddess our people will be saved.*"

He paused. His words seemed to hover in the air around him, reminding Elphame suddenly of the way his name magically became tangible when she called to him. She shivered, feeling foreboding caress the length of her spine.

"My mother said that the Goddess promised her that it was me who was destined to fulfill the Prophecy. Even on her deathbed her faith never wavered. She died believing that I would someday find a way to make Epona's promise come true. When I began dreaming of an infant touched by the Goddess, born of a centaur and a human, I knew her prayer had been answered."

Lochlan's smile warmed his face, and for an instant it was as if the listening crowd faded away and the two of them were alone.

"I think I began loving you when you were a child, and then I fell in love with you as you matured into a beautiful young woman. But it was when I watched you speak to your people before the ruined gates of MacCallan Castle that I realized that there was nothing I wouldn't sacrifice to keep you safe—not even if I was dooming my people to banishment and madness."

"It was you," Brighid said suddenly. "You saved Elphame the night of her accident."

"Yes," Elphame said, her eyes never leaving Lochlan. "The boar would have killed me had Lochlan not killed it first."

"I don't understand." Brighid's voice broke into the gasps of surprise that came from the gathered clan. "What purpose does the Prophecy serve? If you aren't enemies bent on reliving the past of your fathers and rekindling the war, why did you not simply come into Partholon peaceably? Why did you think you needed the sacrifice of Elphame's life?"

"They're going mad," Elphame said with sudden understanding. "The darkness they carry in their blood calls to them. The more they fight it, the more painful it becomes for them." She gestured sadly at Fallon, who was still clinging to her mate. "Eventually the madness wins." Her eyes swept her people as she spoke calmly to them. "And there are children who carry the blood of their human ancestors—blood many of us share with them. It is worse for them. They have had no human mothers to nurture their humanity."

"So you believe that Epona wishes Elphame to be sacrificed so that her blood can somehow wash the madness from your people?" Cuchulainn sneered. "The Prophecy itself sounds mad."

"You may be partially right, Cuchulainn. I have discovered that all these decades we have misinterpreted the Prophecy," Lochlan said.

Fallon's torn wings rustled as she jerked painfully away from her mate. "You lie!" She spit the words.

"No," Lochlan said simply. "I have tasted her blood. I read the truth within it."

In the stunned silence that greeted his words, Elphame could not keep her hand from touching the two small scabs on her neck.

"What is he saying?" The words were low and angry and sounded as if someone had torn them from Cuchulainn.

Elphame did not turn away from her brother's rage. "Lochlan is my lifemate. He and I have handfasted and our marriage has been consummated. He tasted my blood as part of that mating ritual."

Cuchulainn stared at his sister as if he didn't recognize her. Elphame made herself look away from him before her veneer of courage cracked.

"What is it my blood told you?" she asked Lochlan, amazed that her voice betrayed none of the tumult that was taking place within her.

"The Prophecy says that it is through the blood of a dying goddess that we will be saved, but it wasn't speaking of a physical death, just as it wasn't literally your blood that must be sacrificed. What the Prophecy really meant was that you must take the dark blood of our fathers within your body, so that it would mingle with, and ultimately replace your own blood. When that happens—because you have been touched by the Goddess—you will take on the madness of our fathers. The battles my people fight daily to maintain their humanity will be transferred to you." He paused, the horror of what he was saying reflected on his face. "The madness would be washed from us, but for you it would be worse than your physical death. It would be the death of your humanity."

"That's impossible," Cuchulainn scoffed. Angry shouts of agreement erupted from Clan MacCallan.

Elphame's eyes remained locked with her lover's. In her mind she again saw his horrified expression as he fled from her bed after drinking her blood. With a surety that echoed throughout her soul, she knew her husband had spoken the truth. The veracity of it resonated within her as she finally understood, and then accepted, the choice she must make. She looked hastily away from Lochlan before he could read the decision within her eyes.

Her raised hand called for silence.

"My judgment is complete." At that moment she was neither a sister nor a wife; she was The MacCallan, and her words rang against the listening walls of her castle. "Cuchulainn, your loss as well as the clan's loss has been great. Reparation must be made." She turned from her brother to Fallon. "You took an innocent life. Your life is forfeit in return."

Cuchulainn moved toward the winged woman, his sword drawn and ready.

"No!" Keir shrieked.

"You cannot save her, but you can die with her." Death filled Cuchulainn's voice.

Fallon ignored her mate and stepped forward, as if she was eager to meet the warrior's sword.

"Then kill me and show your barbarism, *human*," she said haughtily. With a single motion, she ripped away the ragged clothing that covered her nakedness and exposed her pale body. One hand swept down to caress the bulge that was her abdomen. "But know that when you kill me, you also murder my unborn child."

Elphame did not have to command her brother to stop.

Cuchulainn's sword, which was raised for a killing stroke, faltered. Slowly, he lowered its tip to the marble floor. With pain-filled eyes, he looked at his sister.

"Brenna would call it vengeance and not justice if an innocent child was killed to atone for her death, though I would almost commit such an act if I thought her spirit would haunt me as a result."

"I agree, Cuchulainn. It would not be just to take the life of an innocent." Elphame's voice was steel. "But someone must pay the price of Brenna's murder."

"Fallon is my mate. The child is mine. I will pay the price," Keir said. Grimacing against the pain, he bent to retrieve Fallon's clothing, which he handed to her without looking at her. Fallon did not speak, but Elphame thought she saw a flicker of emotion within the winged woman's eyes that was not hatred or madness.

"Did you know Fallon planned to kill Brenna?" Elphame asked Keir.

"No, Goddess." He did not flinch from Elphame's gaze, but his voice was filled with bitterness. "We came only to see the Prophecy fulfilled, not to slaughter innocents. No matter what your people think of us, our ways are not our fathers'."

"Keir, it was through no fault of yours that Fallon fell into madness. You are not guilty of Brenna's death," she said.

Slowly and distinctly, Elphame turned to face Lochlan. The mutterings and whispered conversations ceased. In the silence that framed them, Lochlan's words were clear and strong.

"Keir is not guilty of Brenna's death, but I am. I am the leader of my people. I am also their betrayer."

"Your words are wise, husband." In the preternatural silence *husband* was a brittle echo, as if when she said it the word crystallized and then shattered.

Her hand was steady as she held it out, palm open, for

Cuchulainn's sword. Without speaking, her brother placed the pommel in her hand. Then with slow, methodical steps she walked toward Lochlan. He stood very still, watching her approach. Closer to him, but still beyond his chained reach, she stopped.

Lochlan ignored the watching crowd and spoke only for her. "When we handfasted I told you that I would follow you, even if it led to my death. I do not regret that pledge, just as I do not regret our love. When I answered your call and brought you Brenna's body, I knew what my end would be. I accepted it then, I accept it now." His smile held no bitterness and his voice reflected the depth of his love for her.

Instead of moving to strike him, she returned his smile. "Remember when you told me that I needed to trust myself enough to listen for Epona's voice? You were right, Lochlan. I have finally found that trust, and with it I have heard the voice of the Goddess. Now you must trust me as well."

"I trust you, my heart," he said, extending his hands open and away from his sides so that she could easily deliver a killing stroke.

"Good, I will soon have need of that trust." She glanced over her shoulder at her brother. "Forgive me, Cuchulainn," she said.

As she drew a deep cleansing breath, her brother's eyes widened and sudden understanding of what she intended flashed through him.

"Stop her!" he screamed, lunging forward.

His cry was echoed by Lochlan and the winged man tore wildly against the chain that held him, trying to reach his lover as Elphame quickly drew the razorlike edge of the sword along her own flesh from wrist to elbow in a long, deadly deep slice. Afraid Cuchulainn would reach her too soon, she tried to hurry and shift the sword to her other hand so that she could finish what she had begun, but strength was already leaving her body and she fumbled her grip on the claymore. Silently, her soul cried for more time—and the stone on which she stood heard her unspoken plea.

Through a scarlet haze, Elphame watched the spirit of The MacCallan materialize at her side.

"I am here, lassie."

He raised his glowing hand and the instant before her brother reached her she was enclosed in a translucent circle of power. Cuchulainn's body stopped as if he had run into an invisible wall.

"Nay, Cuchulainn." Like the knell of a death bell the spirit's eerie voice split the shouting that had erupted around them. *"Ye canna change the fate of The MacCallan. It is for her to choose, not you."*

"No, Elphame!" Cuchulainn cried, as he pounded his fists impotently against the invisible barrier of spiritual power.

Moving awkwardly, Elphame transferred the sword to her left hand and fought against a tide of dizziness to maintain her hold on it. Blood poured from the long slash in her arm in a jutting scarlet river. Setting her teeth she ignored the pain and pressed the blade against the unbroken skin of her right wrist, following the path of her vein down to her elbow. Only then did she let the sword clatter to the marble floor. She felt the warmth of the liquid that rushed from her body bathing her arms and legs. As if she was moving in a dream, she looked through the circle of power the spirit of her ancestor had invoked, to Lochlan. Tears coursed down his face as he strained against his chains to reach her.

Through the blood pounding in her head, she could barely hear the sound of her own voice. "Save me, and in return I will save you." The effort it took to form the words was too much, and the world began to gray at the edges as she fell in slow motion to her knees.

"Ye know what you must do, nephew."

At The MacCallan's words, the circle of power dissipated along with the spirit, and with an anguished cry, Cuchulainn pulled Elphame into his arms.

"Bring her to me before she loses consciousness!" Lochlan shouted.

Cuchulainn's frenzied eyes searched the winged man's face.

"Trust me," Lochlan said.

The warrior did not hesitate an instant longer, but began dragging his sister to Lochlan. He was joined by other strong hands, as the clan tracked through the ever-widening trail of blood to reach their Chieftain.

Lochlan dropped to his knees as his arms closed around Elphame's unresisting body.

"The sword! Give me the sword!" he roared. The reddened handle was thrust into his hand. With a blindingly swift motion, Lochlan slashed the tip of the blade into the bare skin above his heart. Then he threw the sword from him as if it was a loathsome insect. He cradled Elphame's head in his hands and pressed her cold lips to his wound.

"Drink, my heart," he pleaded.

Her eyes were closed and she did not respond.

"Drink, Elphame," he cried, his voice breaking. "I have done as you asked—the only chance at life you have now is to fulfill the Prophecy. Drink!"

Slowly, her lips moved against his skin, and with a choking sound she swallowed. Her eyes snapped opened and red-tinged tears spilled from them as her mouth tightened against his chest and the blood of demons rushed into her body. At first she knew nothing and felt nothing except the metallic taste of Lochlan's blood. Then the heat began. She was drinking from a volcanic river, but she could not pull away, and soon she no longer wished to. The heat seduced her. It filled her body and caressed her soul with the hypnotic power of darkness as the madness of an entire race flowed into her. The bleeding wounds on her arms dried and then sealed themselves. Alien thoughts began to coil within her mind.

Blood...she could never get enough...she would drink him dry...she would drink them all dry...she could begin her own army...part-demon, part-goddess...first she must kill Lochlan...kill the betrayer...

Kill Lochlan? Kill her lifemate?

Her own consciousness broke through the mist of demon whisperings and with a gasp she pulled her mouth from Lochlan's chest. On hands and knees she skittered away from him, feeling the panic within her rise as she realized that the crimson pool that covered the floor and coated her body was her own blood. No, that wasn't right her mind frantically corrected her. The blood that covered her was no longer hers because hers was now mixed irrevocably with that of demons.

Now she was a demon...her only choice was to accept and embrace it.

"Don't listen to the dark whisperings," Lochlan panted. He slumped against the floor looking pale and ill. "Fight it, Elphame!"

The phantom sound of Fallon's mad laughter danced around her.

"Elphame?" Cuchulainn approached her slowly, hands extended. "Come to me." When she didn't respond to him, his voice broke. "You can't leave me too, sister-mine. I cannot bear it."

Still on her hands and knees, she shuddered at the familiar endearment. The darkness that she had accepted was responsible for Cuchulainn's loss. And now she was a part of it. *Yes...* She felt the voices stir and writhe within her as if thousands of dark insects fluttered under her skin. *Yes...feel us...hear us...we are you now.*

"I'm not your sister anymore. You can't help me."

She didn't recognize the alien sound of her own voice. She didn't recognize the staring faces of the people who surrounded her. Her thoughts and memories fragmented—everything she was began slipping away, drowning in the dark tide that pulsed within her. Feeling trapped, she whirled around on the floor and was confronted by the ancient centaur who loomed above her.

"Call upon the spirit of the stones—they will aid you," he said.

She shook her head wildly. No, the spirits would no longer answer her call. She was alone, lost to the voice of madness in her blood that was silencing her world.

Be at peace, Beloved. I will never abandon you.

The cool words washed through her body. And Elphame clung to them as a dying soul to the breath of life.

"Epona!" Elphame sobbed. As she spoke the Goddess's name she felt a quivering within her body, and a thought, less substantial than mist floated through her battered mind; she clung to it with all of the humanity left in her soul.

She must trust herself.

Struggling against fear and darkness, Elphame lurched to her feet. She stumbled forward and the crowd of stunned people and centaurs parted until she stood before the fountain in the middle of the great courtyard. She gazed into the face of the marble girl who was her ancestor, and the first shaft of morning light touched her. With a clean, caressing hand, the ray found the brooch of The MacCallan and it flashed with a brilliant light. Within that light, Elphame sought and found her heritage—a heritage of faith and fidelity and the strength of love triumphant that could not be usurped by the dark lure cast by evil. The new day broke over her like a beacon of hope, and Elphame remembered who she was, and with that knowing the alien darkness that had thought to steal from her the strength of a goddess's love, writhed and shrieked, but was forced to retreat from the blinding light of trust and courage. With a sound like the scurrying of spiders' feet, the evil whisperings retreated until they were no more than the memory of echoes.

As if she was awakening from a long sleep, she languidly held her blood-drenched arms under the stream of clean water and watched as the cool liquid washed the stain from her, swirling it around the basin, diluting and weakening it before draining it away. When her arms were free of stain, she threw back her head and bathed her face in the pure light of Epona's morning. A cry swelled within her like a burgeoning child and then burst from her to echo from the walls where it was taken up by the joyous voices, first of her brother, then of her husband and then her clan.

"FAITH AND FIDELITY!"

"FAITH AND FIDELITY!"

"FAITH AND FIDELITY!"

Smiling triumphantly, Elphame collapsed to the marble floor and welcomed the peace of unconsciousness.

LIKE THE SWEET fragrance of honeysuckle on a spring breeze, her mother's voice drifted into Elphame's dream.

"I wish it could have been easier for her."

"I know, Beloved." This time Elphame instantly recognized Epona's voice. *"I, too, wish she could have been saved the agony of it, but your daughter's path has never been an easy one. You see now how well the difficulties of her past readied her to face her destiny."*

"She did well, didn't she?"

"Very well. She has made me proud."

Elphame's soul quickened with happiness at their praise.

"Her way will still be difficult," the Goddess continued. *"Most of Clan MacCallan will accept Lochlan and his people out of love for her, but the rest of Partholon will not be so easily won."*

Her mother sighed. *"Now will you allow me to go to her? At least I can formalize her handfast with him."* Then her mother's voice saddened. *"And Cuchulainn has need of a mother's touch."*

"*Go to them,*" the Goddess said. "*But do not be surprised if Cuchulainn's pain is greater than a mother's touch can soothe....*"

Her mother's response faded away as Elphame drifted up through the layers of sleep. As her waking senses came slowly alive her body told her that it rested comfortably upon down and fine linens. Light flickered delicately against her closed lids. Her eyes fluttered, and then opened.

Her first waking thought was that it must be night because the only light in the room came from the large, iron candelabrum and the fire cheerily burning in the hearth, and she wondered how long she had slept. Hadn't it just been morning? Then a shape took form out of the corner of her eye, and she turned her head to see Lochlan. He was sitting in a chair beside her bed. His head had dropped forward and he was asleep. Her eyes drank him in. He still looked battered and bruised, but his skin had lost the porcelain tint of shock it had had the last time she'd seen him, when he had been slumped weakly against the floor and covered with her blood....

And her memory flooded back. For a moment panic fisted her stomach as she listened within, waiting for the mad voice of darkness to begin its lethal whispering through her tainted blood. But the voice did not come. There was only a vague stirring of something buried deep within her, like a half-remembered dream. With intuition born of the Goddess's touch, Elphame knew that though she carried inside her the madness of a race of people, love and trust and faith had been victorious against its evil legacy.

You must remain vigilant against the darkness for as long as there is breath in your body, Beloved. The voice of Epona washed through her mind. *But remember that I will always be with you. You have been touched by the Goddess....*

She must have made some involuntary sound in response, because Lochlan's eyes suddenly snapped open. When he realized she had awakened he reached for her hand.

"Cuchulainn!" he shouted.

Almost instantly her brother joined Lochlan at her bedside.

Dark circles framed Cu's eyes and the stubbly beginnings of a beard covered his usually smooth-shaven chin. Elphame thought her brother appeared to have aged a lifetime.

"You look terrible," Elphame croaked.

Cuchulainn's haggard face broke into a smile and Lochlan's relieved laughter sounded more like a sob. She looked from her husband to her brother.

She cleared her throat before trying to speak again. "Well, neither of you are in chains, and I don't see any wounds that look new. May I assume that the two of you are learning to get along with each other?" she rasped.

"She isn't mad." Lochlan pressed her hand against his lips and she was shocked to see that silent tears wet his face.

"I told you she wouldn't be," Cuchulainn said. His eyes, too, were suspiciously bright.

"*She* can hear both of you," Elphame said, exasperated.

"Welcome back, sister-mine," Cu said.

"How long have I been asleep?"

"It is the night of the fifth day," Lochlan said.

She blinked in surprise. "No wonder I'm so hungry."

Cuchulainn's smile looked out of place on his deeply lined face. "Wynne will be very pleased to hear that." He started to hurry toward the door.

"Cu, wait."

Reading the expression on her face, Lochlan kissed her hand softly before releasing it and then stepped aside so that Cuchulainn could take his place beside her.

Elphame sat up and held out her hand to her brother.

"I wanted to tell you about Lochlan—"

Looking incredibly tired, Cuchulainn shook his head. "You don't have to explain, El."

"Yes, I do. I wanted to tell you about Lochlan from the moment I met him. I just didn't know how, but I didn't want you to find out on your own and think that I didn't love you enough or trust you enough to confide in you. That wasn't it—it wasn't you I doubted, it was me. I couldn't find the words, and then you were so in love with Brenna."

Cuchulainn clenched his jaw and looked away from her.

"I don't blame you or Lochlan for Brenna's death." He paused and drew a deep, shaky breath. "I don't even blame Fallon. The madness wasn't her fault."

"Cu, look at me," Elphame said. When her brother met her eyes she looked into the depths of his grief and understood that he was telling her the truth. He didn't blame them for Brenna's death—he blamed himself.

"Cu," she began, but he dropped her hand and stood so abruptly that the chair almost toppled over.

"I can't talk about it, El," he said. Without looking at her he turned and moved hastily to the door. Over his shoulder he said, "I'll get you something to eat," before closing the door on his pain.

"He refused to allow her to be burned on a funeral pyre," Lochlan said. Instead of taking the chair, he sat beside her on the bed, facing her. He took her hand in both of his. "He said that fire had caused her too much pain already."

"Oh, Cu," Elphame gasped, staring at the closed door.

"So the Master Centaur made a tomb for her and carved her effigy to seal it. This morning Cuchulainn finally laid her to rest within it."

"Where?" Elphame whispered, wiping tears from her cheeks.

"In the spot in which her tent stood." He shook his head sadly. "I think the warrior entombed his heart along with Brenna."

"I should have been there with him. He needed me."

"You had much to recover from. Do not blame yourself. Your brother spoke truly. He does not blame you, nor does he blame my people or me. He has acted nobly in your stead these past days."

"Fallon and Keir and the other two—what has happened to them?" she asked.

"Cuchulainn ordered that Fallon be imprisoned at Guardian Castle, where she will await the birth of her child, as well as your decision as to what penalty she must pay for the crime she committed. Keir chose to go with her. Curran and Nevin remain here, healing from their wounds."

Elphame studied his face. "The madness, is it truly gone?"

"It is." The wonder of it still lingered in his voice. "It has left me, as it has left the others. You have fulfilled the Prophecy and saved my people." He stroked her cheek gently. "And within you, my heart? Do you feel the burden of its weight?"

Elphame's gaze turned introspective. Like breath blown over a still pool she felt the dark ripple deep within her. "It is there, within me. I can feel its presence. The madness has been beaten, but I think not totally silenced. I have the word of Epona that I have won a battle against it, but the Goddess has warned me that I must be ever-vigilant if I am to remain victorious." She shivered.

"There is no other possibility than victory," Lochlan said fiercely. "Together we will not let it conquer you."

The bright strength of his love filled her and she felt the waiting darkness within her retreat again.

She drew a deep, satisfied breath. "We must send for your people. They must bring the children here."

Lochlan pulled her into his arms and his healing wings wrapped around her, filling her with his warmth.

"We shall, my heart, we shall," he said.

★ ★ ★

Elphame stood before the marble tomb as the morning sky sent out hesitant tendrils of mauve and violet. The effigy was very beautiful; it almost looked as if Brenna had fallen asleep and turned to stone. Except that Danann had carved her image free of any scars.

"I didn't ask him to leave off her scars. It didn't even occur to me." Cuchulainn's haunted voice came from beside his sister. He stepped forward, bent and placed an armful of turquoise-colored wildflowers in the stone girl's arms.

"When I asked Danann about why he had not shown her scars, he said that he had simply carved her the way he remembered her," Brighid said. The Huntress touched the effigy's right cheek, which was now as clear and smooth as the left side of her face.

"Brenna would be pleased to be remembered thus," Elphame said. She turned to her brother and took his hand. "Please don't leave, Cu."

"I must." He looked over her shoulder at the castle that was beginning to awaken. "Everything here reminds me of her— every scent and every sound seems to speak her name." His grief-filled eyes met his sister's troubled gaze. "It is not that I wish to be rid of her, I only wish to learn to bear her loss. I cannot do that here." He squeezed her hand before releasing it.

Elphame's mind understood what he was saying, but her heart ached at the thought of her brother's absence.

"I will miss you, Cuchulainn," Brighid spoke quietly as she reached forward to clasp his arm in a warrior's salute.

Her skin was warm against his strong grip. "I was wrong about you, Brighid Dhianna. You have been a faithful friend."

"Perhaps someday we will go hunting together again." She smiled sadly at him.

A muffled *woof* drew their attention downward and Fand jumped from a tuft of tall grass to growl and snap at Brighid's hooves. The Huntress frowned.

"I amend my offer. I will hunt with you again, only if you promise not to bring anything back that is alive."

Cuchulainn patted his thigh and the cub gamboled over to him to wriggle around his legs. "The next time you see Fand, she will have better manners."

"That is what all parents say," muttered Brighid as she started back to the castle.

Brother and sister stood silently looking at one another. Then Elphame was in his arms, hugging him hard and burying her head in his familiar shoulder.

"Can't you wait for Mama?" she asked through her tears. "You know the runner said she was only a day's ride away."

Cuchulainn patted her back. "She'll understand."

"No she won't. She'll be mad."

Elphame heard his brief chuckle. It sounded gravelly and painful and so completely unlike the lighthearted brother she knew so well that her heart contracted with a rush of sadness.

"You're right, but she'll be so busy clucking around you and Lochlan that she won't have time to dwell on it." Gently, he pulled away from her and kissed both of her cheeks. "This is something that I must do," he said. Then he turned and tossed the gelding's reins over his neck and mounted him in one smooth movement.

As if on cue, Fand launched into a series of pitiful whines and Elphame quickly scooped her up and handed the plump cub to her brother.

"I love you, sister-mine," he said, and then he pointed his horse to the north and kneed him into a trot.

Elphame watched as he joined the two winged figures who waited patiently before the castle's main entrance. Their wounds were not completely healed and their wings were still painfully tattered, but Curran and Nevin had insisted on accompanying Cuchulainn when he announced that he would be journeying to the Wastelands to guide the displaced children of Partholon home.

Elphame kept watching until they faded into the trees. She felt like her past had disappeared with Cuchulainn, and with his absence the happiest part of her youth had also departed. What would happen to her beloved brother? Would he always be a broken shell of himself, or was there some way he could be healed? Elphame knew the bittersweet irony of her thoughts. Cuchulainn needed to find a way to mend what was broken within him without a Healer. She had felt so helpless over the past days as she had watched a horrible emptiness permeate his soul. Could he find happiness without Brenna? She didn't know. She had believed she would lose Lochlan, so she knew something of what her brother was feeling. She could have gone on without her lifemate, as had Cuchulainn, but could she have truly found happiness again? That she didn't know.

Please, Epona. She sent a silent, fervent prayer to her Goddess. *Watch over him and bring him safely home. And help him to find happiness again.*

Elphame's heart ached and already she missed Cuchulainn's familiar presence. Her shoulders shook with sobs and her steps were leaden as she began retracing her path back to the castle.

As if it were a physical caress, she felt his gaze touch her and she looked up. Epona's morning light haloed the winged shape of Lochlan standing on the balcony of the Chieftain's Tower. She could not read his face, but as she watched, she saw him touch the place over his heart, then his lips, and then he held his hand out to her.

Cuchulainn held her past, but her future was with Lochlan

and Clan MacCallan. They would have to face a land filled with people who mistrusted and judged them harshly. Partholon would not be easily won, but with Epona's blessing, they would meet the future together. The Chieftain of Clan MacCallan wiped her face and straightened her shoulders. Elphame's steps were strong and sure as she hurried to join her lifemate, and the beginning of a new day.